To mark her vow, she rose on tiptoe and kissed him.

Kissing stone was just like she'd expected: hard, gritty, and entirely one-sided. Her lips covered his, forming to them for one brief moment, her eyes closed against the bright room and ridiculous actions that made sense only in her heart.

For some reason, her left hand suddenly *needed* to curl around the back of his neck and her right *needed* to guard his heart. She needed to rise to her toes and press her lips to his and hold him, promising anything to take away his pain.

What was she doing? Kissing a statue in the basement of a church, expecting some sort of response from him—she was going crazy.

She started back, releasing the dream—but something changed. His lips blazed against her lips, scorching hotter than the flames of a bonfire. Hard granite gave way to satin, pliant and seductive. Dry resistance gave way to wet, hot welcome and she sank into it.

Until this moment, Kalyss had not realized a kiss could be this passionate, this full of desire—this swollen with longing. . . .

Betrayed

JAMIE LEIGH HANSEN

tor paranormal romance

A TOM DOHERTY ASSOCIATES BOOK
NEW YORK

This is a work of fiction. All of the characters, organizations, and events portrayed in this novel are either products of the author's imagination or are used fictitiously.

BETRAYED

Copyright © 2007 by Jamie Leigh Hansen

A Tor Book
Published by Tom Doherty Associates, LLC
175 Fifth Avenue
New York, NY 10010

www.tor.com

Tor® is a registered trademark of Tom Doherty Associates, LLC.

ISBN-13: 978-0-7653-5720-5
ISBN-10: 0-7653-5720-8

First Edition: January 2008

Printed in the United States of America

0 9 8 7 6 5 4 3 2 1

For Craig, always. Without you, nothing would ever be complete.

For my girls, the most supportive and encouraging I could wish for.

For my family and their belief in me.

For my friends, especially those who never thought they'd own a romance novel.

I love you all.

Acknowledgments

There are so many people to thank for all they've done to help me write and finish this book. It would be impossible to list them all, but there are a few that must be named because their support was so invaluable.

Desireé, for reading every draft and loving each one.

Joyce, for all the trips to the post office and your patience as I recounted each and every page. Along with all the other reasons, great and small.

Debbie, for falling in love with *Betrayed* and lending a hand wherever needed.

IECRWA, for endless learning opportunities and equally endless support. I couldn't wish for a better group of writers and I am so thankful to be a part of yours.

Natasha, for seeing something special in my writing and in me, and choosing both.

Most of all, I thank Jolene for our writing dates and long talks during the most difficult of times and after. Without you, my career would be dead and buried.

Betrayed

A love through time
Their fates are set
Living through death
In a stone of regret

The betrayer must prove
Until his dying wish
That fate is forever
And love doesn't perish

Loyalty be brave
Woman be strong
Conquer death
And right the wrong

PROLOGUE

October 6, 1900—England

"I WILL DIE TONIGHT." Caylus stared through the window of the small cottage into the darkness. Her death was coming again, but even after all these centuries, she still feared it.

Geoffrey's hand rested on her shoulder, the comfort cold but welcome. He was her guardian, her protector. He risked everything to reunite her with the one man whose touch she yearned for. "Then we will try again."

And again. And again. Her inescapable destiny.

"Do you ever tire of burying me?" Her heart pounded with the endless roll of the thunder. The storm was coming, as it always did. Wind blew through the open window, cold and crisp. Ominous—yet inviting. There were rewards for braving storms.

"It will be different this time. I will make it so." He stood tall beside her, his strength her temporary shelter. "I owe your husband a debt that will be repaid."

"No promises, Geoffrey. The disappointment is worse than this never-ending cycle." She turned to him and grasped his hands, her voice now hoarse. His eyes softened. "The pain, not just death, but remembering him, yearning for him. Almost saving him, yet never close enough, never hearing his voice . . ." Her throat closed and she couldn't speak.

"You must have hope, Caylus."

"Hope hurts. A little dies with me every time." He'd taught her hope, her husband. Dreux's deep whispers in her ear had promised a lifetime together. He'd taught her to dream during their one beautiful night. The future had seemed so certain. They only had to wake with the dawn for it to begin. Now it seemed that she fought in vain for a love that was never meant to be.

Geoffrey's blue eyes iced over in a pitiless gaze. His voice came harsh and unforgiving. "You are weak, woman. If you retreat so easily, you don't deserve him."

She froze for a stunned moment; then her fury burned between them. "Easily? Easily, Geoffrey? It's been eight hundred years! God clearly does not want us together!"

"God believes in love, Caylus. Why else would we be given so many chances to change fate? It's for honor and duty and love. God believes in those for us. Be strong. Earn it."

"What if he's in a better place? At rest? At peace? What if we're being selfish and taking more from him than ever?" Desperate fear and doubt warred with righteous certainty. She needed to save her husband, but what if failure *was* her destiny?

"Do you really believe such a thing?"

She closed her eyes. No. He was right. There was no better place for Dreux de Vernon to be than in her arms. Geoffrey fought longer and harder and suffered every bit as much as she. How could she give up after so many centuries? She had to be strong. She would win; neither despair nor Kai de Lyre would defeat her.

She would free her husband from any lethal trap Kai set. His unpredictability was his strongest asset, but she would have to find a way around it. Her voice trembled, fear holding tight, but she firmed her lips and lifted her chin. "Then may God make me strong, Geoffrey."

Slowly, he nodded, then looked outside. "It is time."

With a deep breath, she followed him from the stone cottage into the dark surrounding their island of Sanctuary, the glow of the moon their only guide. But they knew the way well. The path to the water was rough, rocks and grass showing through the tracks. After eight hundred years of use, harsh winds, wild rains, and merciless erosion that spoke well for the survival instincts of those straight, thin, green blades.

They passed eight unmarked mounds of rich dark earth covered with thick grass. The first was flat, almost indistinct. It belonged to Kynedrithe of Clifhaefen, the source of Caylus Graye. Each grave grew more noticeable until the last, the most recent, sloped softly over the ground. It was only a hundred years old.

Caylus smelled death. Tomorrow there might be nine. Her lives always seemed to bring her to this final resting spot.

She shuddered as thunder rumbled above her, through her. Her heart beat faster and her skin tingled with the rise of the wind, making her feel more alive. The despair she suffered was real, but the energy in the air dared her to shake off her fears and believe. They'd paddle the boat across the sea to the shore of her ancient home. They would enter the tower and this time, they would reach the top.

Finally, she would feel Dreux's arms around her, his warmth enfolding her. He'd hold her safe, his broad chest protection and comfort at once. Her husband. Her love. He waited for her. How could she possibly give up?

Geoffrey led her to the small dock, where nothing blocked their view of the sky over the water. The moon shined bright, like a brilliant beam of light amidst black velvet clouds, its beauty enhanced by the jagged streaks of lightning that crossed the sky. It would rain soon; the air was heavy with the approaching storm's perfume.

Geoffrey turned to her and held out his hand. She gathered her midnight skirts and black cloak in one fist and took his hand with her other. She settled in and he moved, silently untying the boat and tugging it from the dock before pushing off. The water swished and they were afloat, gliding through the dark silk, hearing the soft lap of water against the sides. The paddle dipped into the water and a low swoosh carried them farther from shore, closer to danger and destiny.

They took the small river-way through the cluster of islands that hid Sanctuary. The hidden opening between the cliffs had protected them from spies her assassin sent, but now it was time to leave and face him. Either Kai would kill her, or she would free Dreux. Tonight would tell.

Geoffrey rowed. The paddles slapped the water and quietly slid beneath the surface, steadily moving them forward. Small swells from the rising wind rocked and rolled the tiny boat. She gripped the sides tensely and kept her eyes moving, looking into shadows for unexpected shapes. She needed to reach Dreux this time. She ached to see him.

They passed through the opening in the cliffs, a gliding charge through the black night. She could see the tower now, standing tall in the distance. Parts had crumbled to ruin over time, but the main tower had been kept in decent repair. Lights shone bright around the base. The guards were ready, monitoring movement around the base of the tower. Kai's men were always ready.

"Are you sure this will work?" Caylus whispered softly, unable to stop her question.

Geoffrey's eyes met hers, his lips thin. His expression reproached her for asking such a question. There were no guarantees. Failure was always a possibility.

Her heart beat faster the closer they came to the area Geoffrey had chosen. Guards patrolled along the shore a small distance away. Moisture gathered on her palms as the boat flowed toward the edge of the threatening torchlight. Surely they could make it. Her blood thundered through her veins with more force than the storm.

The boat grounded with a grinding crunch and she froze, not daring to breathe. She waited, her heart beating hard, as if blood was forcing itself in a thick rush through too-thin veins. She watched a small snail, its iridescent shell a beacon in the darkness, crawl up the sloping cliff. Its pace was so slow and the water lapped so high, so swift. How could the snail get away safely? How could it go far enough, fast enough, from the danger that trailed behind so deep and dark?

A hand grasped her shoulder and startled Caylus, stealing her breath and ending her intense focus on the tiny shell. Just another living being facing destruction for the promise of a true life. Some risks were inescapable.

"Breathe."

The pressure nearly killed her. She gasped in air, starving for the precious necessity.

Geoffrey's hand squeezed lightly. His voice was dry. "Breathe quietly."

She must've been close to suffocation, she felt so dizzy. The boat rocked and he slipped into the water with barely a sound. How did he do that? He lifted her and lowered her into the water beside him. The cold depths dragged at her skirts, nearly pulling her under. She grabbed his shirt, his height and bulk, his strength and balance reassuring. He held her securely, one hand at her waist and the other free to grab his dagger, his sword being too bulky in the water.

"Now, quietly, glide with me." His silver eyes reflected the forked lightning above them.

She closed her eyes and swallowed her pulse. Her husband, brave and handsome, waited for her. Both of them waited for her. Her champion and her killer.

And only one could guide and protect her. Her guardian, Geoffrey. A triad of men who shaped her destiny with every movement, every thought, every emotion. Was she strong enough to face any of them?

They glided, moving ever closer to a dark shadowy entrance in the depths of the cliff. It was the one entrance Kai didn't know existed, hidden as it was. When they were there, she couldn't see it, but she could feel a crevice wide enough to admit them. They moved into the cliffs, the opening almost too small for her to fit. How Geoffrey managed, she couldn't tell.

Step by step, they slid deeper into the crevice, the water receding. The tunnel widened until the walls were at her back. He didn't light a candle, but strode confidently into the blackness. She held his hand and pressed close, unable to see, trusting him to guide her.

The walls shifted, became smoother and softer, the floor more etched and even. A spark struck and she smelled sulfur as Geoffrey set flame to a candle.

"Finally." She blew out her breath in relief.

"I couldn't risk the light leaking out." The tunnel was just wide enough and tall enough for him to walk.

"Where are we?" She knew it was an entrance, but not much more.

"In the escape tunnels. I spent centuries looking for the out-side entrance and only found it by accident when I floated into the cavern."

"Why were you floating?" She looked at his grim face and away again, wincing at her thoughtless question. While she rested until she was reborn, Geoffrey schemed new ways past Kai's defenses—a sometimes fatal quest resulting in a painful resurrection.

They came to a fork in the tunnel. The right led up, to the tower, he'd told her. The left led elsewhere. They turned right and climbed the carved, crumbling steps of small stones and hard-packed dirt. Up and up, until her legs ached from the strain and her arms hurt from holding up her sodden skirts. And still they climbed.

Then, at last, they came to a small door. An escape door, built low and easily hidden, but large enough for a grown man to crawl through.

Geoffrey stooped and etched around the wooden square with his finger, dislodging dirt that had settled there, sealing the edges. He opened the door, easing it into the tunnel with the slightest of whispers. A waft of cool air made her shiver.

Solid wood blocked the way. She leaned against the side of the tunnel and waited. Her breath came in great gasps, punc-tuating Geoffrey's silence.

She heard a click. Caylus leaned forward and looked over his shoulder as the wood shifted and a dark opening appeared. Geoffrey slid inside, silent as a shadow. Apparently, the open-ing grew larger since he fit easily.

She moved up behind him. He motioned to the candle, nearly gone now, and she inhaled to blow it out. He scowled. Of course, smoke could warn anyone with a keen nose. Cay-lus licked her fingers and pinched the wick.

Geoffrey pressed against the other side of the space and lis-tened. After a bit, he pushed and she could see through the dark space to low light bathing a room in gray. He exited and she followed. She looked behind her at the nearly invisible hole they'd crawled from, then forward again. At the window, the large shadow of a man blocked the moon's light, making her gasp.

"Be easy. No harm will come from him."

Caylus held one hand to the pulse in her throat. In the darkness, she'd mistaken the shadow for her killer, for danger. But it wasn't her killer. The shadow was her husband, trapped in stone for eight hundred years, and only she could free him.

Her hand shook as she released her throat and held it out, daring to reach through the darkness for him. Her ears strained to hear even the smallest of movements, but all was still and quiet, except the waves crashing on the cliffs below. Then a small click behind her made her jump and turn nervously.

Geoffrey sealed the hidden tunnel entrance and gently covered it. He faced her and read her questions in a single glance. Regret flashed across his face before he whispered, "In case we need this entrance again."

She jerked her head in a shaky nod and watched him pull his sword and look around the room before facing the door, her only protection in this life. She didn't even know if they'd have another chance to use the entrance. No one had given them the rules to their strange cycle. They could only struggle along. But one thing she did know without a doubt: she needed to free the man who waited for her.

This was it. Blood began to thunder through her ears in a deafening roar. Time to free her husband. They were so close. At last. Finally. So close. Her fingers tingled. She would touch him, see him, hold him for the first time in over eight hundred years.

She turned to the shadow and walked forward. He stood facing a window, built unusually low and wide. Nothing blocked the view or the elements that must've torn at him these centuries. Her teeth gripped her bottom lip.

He was larger than in her memories, his broad back growing the closer she came to him. So tall, her warrior. His battle scars marked him, even in stone—thick ridges that crossed his shoulder, down one side, and below the back of his neck.

Dreux had survived so much before coming to her. Now it was her turn to survive, to free him. But, how? What was the key to unlocking him?

She reached for him, touched the cold stone. He didn't feel too different from when he'd been alive. Strong, a little rough, a little smooth. But he'd been warm then, had teemed with life and limitless energy.

Her hand trailed to his arm, outstretched as if his wrist were being restrained, and she braced for what she'd see on Dreux's face. She'd only asked Geoffrey once and his silence had told her she'd hate what she'd see. For, frozen on her husband's strong face would be all he'd felt as he'd watched her first death. Her heart pounded with dread and relief both. So close.

Slowly, she stepped to his side, feeling again the wonder as he towered over her. This strong man had made such gentle love to her lifetimes ago. She wanted more. She wanted forever. She'd dreamed for so long, memories of him. His smile, his frown, his caress. How could she make it real? A look? A touch? A kiss?

The pounding waves beat each passing moment with urgent crashes. Time was sand falling through her fingers. She gazed past the sword propped by the window, gleaming as it did in her dreams, ready to be used once more. Her hand brushed over the muscular stone arm of her husband, tracing the smooth scars there, her mind searching for the key. *Time to wake, my love.*

Sudden movement sounded behind her, but before she could turn, the cold bite of sharp steel pressed against her throat. She froze, ice trickling down her spine. No, not yet. Please, God, don't let it be over yet.

"Not so fast, princess." Kai's husky voice sounded in her ear and she heard Geoffrey struggling behind her. "The game's not over."

Even as she heard Geoffrey's yell, the blade sliced across her throat, biting deep and true. Her blood flowed down, warm and sticky. Again. Her face twisted in a silent scream of denial.

She was shoved forward, to the window, and she turned, hands holding her throat, blood coursing over her fingers. Ropes hung from a ledge built into the darkened ceiling, down which Kai and his men had dropped directly between Caylus and her guardian.

Geoffrey fought wildly, locked in battle with two of Kai's men. A battle-trained and hardened warrior far beyond the experience of the men he fought, Geoffrey dispatched them both, but they'd slowed him down enough that it was still too late.

Caylus was weakening, her heart quickly pumping blood

out of her body, her hands unable to cease the flow. She was so close. Would she ever be this close again?

Staring up, her husband's stone face wavered then focused above her. Endless grief was engraved in his eyes, his lips. She cried out and reached for him, tears pouring from her eyes, mixing with her blood. Her handprint marred his chest. Then Geoffrey was there. He pulled her close, stepped on the windowsill, and jumped to the crashing waves below.

"You will live again," he half-vowed, half-commanded, holding her tight as they fell.

What if she didn't live again? What if this was her last chance? Over Geoffrey's shoulder, Caylus stared at her husband, her gaze trapped by his face, his frozen pain tormenting her. Her husband stood, waiting eternities for her to free him.

Eternities she failed.

The sunrise broke over the horizon, a golden glow against ice-blue water. Geoffrey's determined eyes, for once not cold but full of the pain of centuries, commanded her attention.

"I won't fail again."

She tried to nod, wasn't sure if she did. Wherever she was born next, whoever she became, Caylus could only pray: *may God make me strong, Geoffrey.*

Her eyes closed as she and Geoffrey crashed over the rocks and into the waiting sea. Cold and dark, death claimed her.

Chapter 1

October 6, 2004 — Spokane, WA

The moon hung half-gone, casting a glow throughout the sky and trees. The world was a beautiful black and grey contrast where even the most vibrant colors barely registered. Wind billowed around Silas, gently ruffling his robes, his long brown hair, and the soft white feathers of the wings that rose to an arch above his head and trailed gracefully to the rooftop where he knelt, an elbow on one upraised knee.

Tension filled the air, a harbinger of the storm that was to come. Or, perhaps, it was an echo of the tension that gripped him with steel jaws snapped tight. His kind could afford to make few mistakes and he and Draven had made the biggest of all.

Even in trying to do good, harm can be the result. Never interfere.

That instruction had been drummed into him from the moment of his birth, two thousand years before. But just once, nine hundred and twenty-nine years ago, he'd been convinced one moment of interference wouldn't hurt anyone. It would simply save one tragically suffering man, Dreux de Vernon, and his cruelly warped half-brother, Kai de Lyre, from the damning sin of fratricide—a second, even worse, curse upon them both.

But, oh, how they'd been wrong. Draven by his side, the unlikeliest of allies, they'd dispersed the first curse, temporarily saving the two brothers, trapping one safely in unbreakable stone with the other unable to reach him. But, in the process, they'd drawn two innocent souls into a nightmare.

Kynedrithe, in this century Kalyss, who'd been caught in a cycle of death and rebirth, her soul unable to move on, doomed to remember the love promised her and search for ways to free him.

And Geoffrey—what could he say about Geoffrey?

Silas gripped the small ledge in front of him with one hand, clenching the other into a helpless fist. The limit of the curse was up. Tonight was the last chance. The four cursed souls could free themselves—or they could die without a chance to have ever really lived.

Silas and Draven would pay for their interference no matter the outcome of tonight, but how much worse would it be to know their sacrifice was for nothing? That they hadn't healed the damage they'd caused?

The air stirred beside him, darker and more oppressive than the light breeze that brushed him. Draven had arrived. Wrapped in a cowled black cloak that hid all distinguishing features, Silas knew no more about Draven than he had centuries ago when Draven had come to him, requesting his aid in saving the brothers.

"You're late," he said, his expression, his tone, grim.

"You're a master at deducing the obvious," Draven's husky voice whispered with its typical sarcasm from inside the voluminous black cowl. "At least I didn't miss the rerun."

Silas held in an irritated sigh. Frustration and disappointment built with each failure. Draven always took it especially hard, chafing more each time at the limits Silas had imposed on them both. Limits like no more interference. Though Draven's society ignored it, that rule had been ingrained in Silas from birth and the consequences of breaking it once had been tragic.

"Actually, it's the series finale."

He heard a quick indrawn breath, a hiss of sound.

"Then you weren't able to extend the length of the curse?" Over the centuries, Draven's desire for redemption had suffocated under endless failures, casting the dark figure into ever more intense periods of anger, sarcasm, hopelessness, and finally despair. Now every bit of hope seemed dashed.

"I have examined the curse, searching for a way to lengthen the time it grants. It can't be done." There was only one set course that would correct their mistake—for the four to find their own way through it—and it left Draven and him helpless. Silas paused, glancing between them.

Black smoke steamed from Draven's enveloping cloak, but once it reached the light that glowed from within Silas, the light that pierced darkness, the smoke recoiled. It gathered again, amassing its strength like a ghostly battalion to send volleys of darkness against his shields of light. The light absorbed the blow and struck back in a single stabbing shock.

"We still have time before the thousand years of the curse ends," Draven insisted.

"This is Kynedrithe's tenth life. If they fail, if Kalyss dies, it is finished. We will not have atoned for what we did to her— to all four of them." Silas crossed his arms and nodded to the building across the street. "But much has changed in this century. There is some hope."

Draven's head turned toward the words painted on the window below them.

AK MARTIAL ARTS.

"*She* has changed, then." There was an energized speculation in Draven's voice.

"Yes, but don't get too excited. This is still their last chance." Silas stood, grasped one wrist with his opposite hand and widened his stance.

Draven's voice was sober, more focused this time. Black-gloved hands clenched the sleeves of the cloak. "Who's the *A*?"

"Another unknowing descendent. But powerful."

Before Draven could speak, a door shut firmly on a black vehicle parked a few yards from the building across the street. Silas looked to the street below.

Geoffrey had arrived. As if sensing the rise in tension, the wind rose, billowing fallen leaves around the man's feet. Geoffrey stood in front of his black SUV, staring at it, then at the keys in his hand. Fixing them in his memory, Silas would guess.

To their right, a dark shadow approached the back of the building. Kai.

It was show time.

"OSCAR ONLY WANTS a date with you." Alex blocked Kalyss's jab with his left arm and turned to the side to avoid her kick. Sometimes he wished he wore pads for this.

"Then Oscar can waste away from his unfulfilled cravings. I'm not interested." She followed through with a quick jab-punch series that had him backing away. Quickly.

"Why? That's what I don't understand." Kalyss was a gorgeous woman—clear blue eyes, golden blonde hair, and a curvy, muscular body. And she seemed depressingly determined to be alone forever.

He regained his balance and struck back. Sparring like this always energized him. She was quick, clever, and dangerous.

"Oh, please, you know what I've been through. You're the only man I trust."

"So? Don't trust him. Use him and leave him. Just open the door—unless you want to spend the rest of forever alone." A woman had to move past her abusive ex eventually, didn't she?

"Back off," she snapped.

He laughed at her threatening tone. "Think you can intimidate me? Please, Minnie Mouse, don't hurt me."

Her jab to the stomach caught him off guard. He doubled over, struggling to breathe.

"You know I'm not interested in a relationship with anyone." Her ponytail held tight, no tendrils falling free to block him from her piercing gaze.

"Not interested or scared to try?" he gasped.

"*Ugh*." Her hands punctuated the air and she turned away from him. "Why are you pushing this? I didn't even think you liked him."

"I don't." He straightened behind her. "He's slick, too slick. Selling himself, almost."

She faced him again, hurt plainly visible on her face. "And you want me to go out with him? Gee, thanks."

He walked toward her and framed her face with both hands. Sometimes he felt so tall next to her. Other times, he felt dwarfed by her sheer personality. "Which is why I say use him and dump him. The point is, move on."

"When I'm ready. Not before." Her eyes beseeched him to understand.

The difficult thing was, he *did*. "I doubt you'll live until the next millennium."

She flashed a grin at his humor. "It won't take that long. Just a little longer."

"I worry about you. Just think like a guy for a while. Be in it for the moment, the date, the thrill. Worry about commitment later."

She laughed, her face close to his. Her eyes softened. "We could do this the easy way. You. Me. No danger."

For a moment, he thought about it. He and Kalyss. His childhood friend. His confidante. His partner. It would be easy—but not good enough. He would always have the never-quite-forgotten memory of sunshine hair and blazing blue eyes standing between them. *Beth Ann Raines.* Kalyss may look enough like her for them to be sisters, but it still wouldn't be the same. Some things weren't meant to be easy and being in love was one of them.

He grinned crookedly. "Where's the fun in that? Besides, we deserve more."

"Then go get what you deserve and leave me in peace." She grinned, her knowing gaze proving he had no secrets from her.

The front door of the dojo jingled. "Saved by the bell," he grumbled.

"It's always been fairly reliable." She smirked, but her eyes had darkened with sadness.

He sighed and walked away. He reached the door and looked back. She didn't see it: what she could have, what she could miss. She was too busy fighting a nightmare that needed to be forgotten.

KALYSS HELD HER hands behind her head and stretched back. Why didn't he understand? Alex was her best friend. He'd driven her away from that hospital, that life, barely alive and not at all thankful for it. There were just certain things she couldn't have; she'd learned that lesson.

She bent forward, touching her toes and stretching her back. She'd spent too many years of fear, self-loathing, and weakness with Sam. The memories wouldn't just fade away. They'd be with her forever. But now that she knew how to fight, how to defend herself, it wouldn't happen again. She knew that with every cell in her body. She'd never repeat her mistakes. Distancing from Alex, isolating herself, cowering before a threat. Knowing that, maybe he was right. A date. Here and there. No pressure. No commitment. Easy does it.

God, she wanted to vomit.

She could still feel Sam's warm, threatening presence against her back. His grip in her hair. Bruises forming along her arms. No, dating could wait. She wasn't ready yet. Maybe in a month or more—when she'd had more time to think about it. For now, she was a strong businesswoman who'd built her life and her body from death and pain. That's all she needed to know—she was in control.

Again she felt a presence at her back, but the breath on the nape of her neck, in her ear, wasn't Sam's. It wasn't a memory. Her heart stopped. Sweat broke out. It was real.

Kalyss ducked and rolled, then landed on her feet and faced where she'd stood. A red-haired man lifted a brow over one glittering emerald-colored eye.

"Well, that was new." He smiled, apparently delighted with her.

Normally, she would've returned the smile,—he seemed that charming—but the knife in his hand killed the impulse. Kalyss crouched, her eyebrows twisting.

"Who are you? What are you doing? Where's Alex?" Ice trickled down her spine as questions crowded her mind. He was big, not just tall, but solid, imposing—and between her and the door.

"You only get one question, Kalyss. We don't have much time." He was *laughing* at her. Her eyes narrowed.

"What the hell are you doing?" If this was some joke . . .

"Killing you, of course." He struck, his deadly knife slicing straight for her.

Killing her? She knocked aside the blow and pivoted, her

left foot kicking his knee. He stumbled and laughed. Chills trickled down her spine. "Why?"

"It's the game, love." He jabbed. She blocked and kicked, but he deflected skillfully.

"What the hell are you talking about?"

He shrugged. "Don't tell me you weren't expecting *something.*"

A dark looming danger. Rain-filled clouds and gray-black skies. Tension and fear choking her screams. Kalyss whispered, "No, I definitely wasn't expecting you."

He struck again and the battle was on. She defended and struck back when she could, but he fought hard, stronger than she was, much more skilled than she was. He really was going to kill her and she didn't even know why. At least with Sam it had been about control. This guy . . . who knew? She'd never even seen him before.

"We don't really have time for this, fun as it is. Your precious guardian will be along any moment."

"What does Alex have to do with this?" She dared a quick glance to the doorway.

Surprise flashed through his eyes. "Alex?"

"Who are you?" How did he seem to know her, not just with his words, but with his eyes, and not know Alex? Apparently this guy hadn't come through the front door.

"Where is he?" His tone changed, became dangerously serious.

"Who? Alex? The nuthouse must be worried about you. Why don't you call and check in?" If he didn't know where Alex was, she was *so* not going to tell him.

He laughed. "Funny. You know, I've never had the time to get to know you before. It's kind of nice."

"Huh?" She tried to edge to the door, but he blocked her.

He took pity on her ignorance. "I'm talking about a game without end. I kill you, you come back. I kill you again. It's usually quite fast and painless."

"You're insane," she whispered.

His grin cracked. "If only."

She tried to scream, but he struck out and it was all she could do to focus on holding him back. He maneuvered again, striking out as he had at first. Only this time he anticipated her kick and grabbed her ankle. She twisted her upper body until her hands braced on the wood floor as she kicked with her right leg. She was free.

When she came up, he was behind her somehow. He pulled her back against him.

"Where is the statue, Kalyss?" His knife rested against her throat, the sharp edge cautioning her to remain motionless, but he was likely about to kill her anyway.

"The what?" She grabbed his arm, kicked back, and connected with his knee.

He stumbled, pulling her with him. They grappled, fighting for control. Kalyss barely avoided the knife. They twisted. He punched. She blocked and kicked. This was familiar territory. She didn't know the who or the why, but everything else was the same. She was on her own against a man determined to hurt her. Kill her.

Kalyss was agile and fast, but she'd also had a long day and adrenaline was all she had left. Adrenaline and fear. Her attacker, though, was taller, weighed more, and seemed more experienced.

A door slammed in the front of the building. Alex. Where had he been? One moment's distraction was all the stranger needed. He grabbed her, twisting her back against him, and held the sharp edge of his dagger to her throat.

"Alas, no more time to play. This was getting fun." He sounded winded. And surprised. At least she wasn't alone in that.

Her heart pounded so hard, she was sure he could feel it with the hand that clasped her just under her right breast. She tried to breathe, but the effort was shaky and scraped her throat against the blade.

She searched the room with a panicked gaze. Alex? Still at the front door. Her friend. Her protector. She'd be dead before a sound left her mouth and he'd come in the room to find his worst nightmare. Her dead body. Why wasn't there a weapon in here? Swords, poles? Anything?

"It's a shame. These moments together are so fleeting. I wish we had more time together."

What? Doesn't matter. Keep him talking. Oh, God, what to say? Was he enjoying this? "Then don't make it quick. Let's just . . ." She inhaled shaky and shallow. "Let's just calm down and talk awhile."

He laughed again, his voice oddly pleasant. Terrifyingly attractive. Oh, God, a mass murderer. "Nice try, but your protector is too close. With no statue, the game ends here."

What statue? She felt him shift. Looking toward the door? Yes. She slammed one elbow back, grabbing his weapon wrist at the same time. He grunted and the towering body behind her slumped forward just enough. She took advantage and flipped him forward. The tip of the blade scraped her throat, shallow but painful.

He landed and rolled in front of her, easily regaining his feet. He tucked the blade in his belt sheath and they squared off. He laughed again and she shivered. Her throat burned and breathing was difficult. When he rushed her, she moved too slowly to stop him. He slammed her back against the wall, his hand against her throat, lifting her to the tips of her toes and pinning her. Her head snapped back, nearly exploding with pain.

Her breath was gone. Her head pounded dizzily. She mustered what remained of her strength and struck out at him, but he only grinned and secured her hands on either side of her head, against the wall. He leaned forward, his face an inch from hers. His green eyes shined bright as he looked deep into hers and smiled again. Who was he?

"Look at you, fighting so hard. Do you remember yet, what you're fighting for? Have you dreamt of him, when you're lying in your bed alone and lonely? What do you miss most? His embrace? His kiss?"

Her brow twisted and she demanded hoarsely, "What are you talking about?"

"You'll remember soon enough. If I give you time." He stopped suddenly, and stared at her, his brows twisting and his head tilting, his expression puzzled. Then he seemed to shake it off, and after he checked the doorway, he smiled at her, handsome and horrible. "Why not? Let's make this interesting. Bring me the statue, Kalyss."

He kissed her, hard and fast, deep and promising, lips and teeth. A kiss of death. Then he was gone.

She trembled. Her head spun until she leaned against the wall. The trembles became bone-deep shakes.

The kiss hadn't been gentle or seductive. Nor had it been controlling, bruising, or sexual. It was a challenge.

She watched the doorway as another strange man appeared in it. She couldn't speak out, warning him. Her legs melted beneath her and she slowly slid down the wall.

He rushed to her, speaking words she couldn't hear above the fast pump of blood past her ears. The room darkened. She understood nothing. Felt only fear. She'd been here before, felt this, but this game was new and she didn't know the rules.

October 6, 1075—England

HER WEDDING DAY. Her wedding night. Kynedrithe of Clifhaefen stared out the small window to the wild sea below, measuring, weighing. The wind howled and she could almost feel the stone tower sway before its fury. Dark clouds roiled across the sky and distant booms of thunder prickled her flesh.

The ceremony and feast had passed too quickly and soon, her husband would come and claim her with all the brutality his people had shown hers during these nightmarish years.

She would bleed and her people would cheer. Her blood, her vows, all for the safety of her people. It was what she'd been born to do—but not with the thought of a bloodthirsty Norman as her new husband. William the Bastard's baron, sent to quell the rebellions of her people.

The castle had run red with the dead and dying. Wounds gaped open, displaying to the world parts of a man never meant to be seen. The violence, the smell of sweat and blood, the clash of swords and shields, the whisper of arrows freshly released from their bows. The shrieks of pain, harshly yelled orders, the panicked prayers, and the heartbreaking last words of brave men she'd dined beside. He'd brought that here. They'd all brought that here. The rebels, the lords, and the Normans.

She'd lived here the entire eighteen years of her life. Had worked and slept and cared with people now gone forever. Land planted and harvested, now razed. The sick she'd visited, now dead in huts burned to the ground.

The older ones shrugged, heads down, backs bent. All the horror around her was just a taste of what one group of men could do to another for land and power. It wasn't new to them, but she felt she'd never get used to it. She'd hoped for a bit of peace, of restoration, until the Normans had come further north to quell the rebellions.

Tension stiffened every muscle until she wondered if the next wild gust of wind would break her. The next wild gust, or the stranger she'd been forced to marry?

Her hands gripped the casement until her fingers were bloodless. After witnessing him in battle, the calm with which he brought death, the firm stance, his confidence and strength, she feared him for good reason.

And that was just in the bailey. She could only imagine him in the midst of battle. He would be the eye of the storm, the only hut not torn to the ground. Instead, he'd fell all those around him, all who opposed him.

Chaos reigned around him until he brought order. Such had been his actions for the fortnight he'd been lord. The keep cleaned, the land cleared, any provisions they'd saved carefully counted and stored. The defenses rebuilt. Who could stand against him? What could stop him? He decided he wanted something and he got it, through battle or control, through sheer strength and determination.

But there were still the rumors of women he'd killed, women who'd died violent, bloody deaths in their beds with only twisted sheets to cover parts of them. Would that be her fate come the morning? Or would his wife's fate be different, left alive until she provided an heir?

She couldn't do this. She wouldn't survive. What if he killed her? What if he hurt her? She would live based only upon his good will. She was too weak to even try. The shaking in her limbs told her that, even if the pounding of her heart didn't.

Glancing down and twisting to the left, she could see the torch-lit ground, far from where she stood at the top of the tower, the top of the new castle. These Normans with their stone homes and their forbidding presences, they overtook everything.

Then she saw him, her husband, by the stables. He dismounted and stalked toward the keep. He was coming. For her. For her blood to consecrate their vows and seal the fate of Clifhaefen's village. She was the sacrifice and he was the cleansing fire. The flames moved closer to the tower and her knees weakened. Her heart nearly beat through her chest.

His boots pounded on the hard-packed dirt even above the thunder. No, they were the thunder. Her stomach twisted in knots; she was thankful it was empty.

After the dinner, which she couldn't eat, she'd been brought here to bathe and wait as the sun had set into the sea below her window. If she jumped from this point, would she hit the cliffs or fall away from the tower to crash into the sea? Some said what would happen tonight was worse than death. Bedded by a Norman.

She twisted to the side again. She couldn't see him. Did she want to see him? No. Most assuredly not. Except, she did. She needed to know. Was that last bit of thunder him? Was he pounding up the stairs even now?

Kynedrithe ran to the second window. Not far from the first, but with a view of the ground and the stables, and most importantly, the entrance to the hall. He stood with his back to her, torches casting a demonic glow about him, and faced his best knight—the one with the blue eyes. His had been the only smiling face at the wedding, as though he was trying to reassure her that all would be well. Geoffrey. Geoffrey was young and naïve. Nothing could be well when you married a murderer. Only vows, blood, and death.

Her husband turned and strode toward the door to the keep. She remembered his warm, amber eyes with their coal-black rims. They were deep, mysterious, and she could see nothing beneath that smoldering gaze. It terrified her. The thunder boomed again. Then she heard another boom, this one from below and behind her, climbing higher and higher. She ran to the cliff window again and stared at the sea. Dared she? Did she have the courage?

Nightmare images flashed through her mind. To be at his mercy, in his power, his blood-covered hands on *her* body.

She swung up on the window ledge, rested her bottom on the frame, and dangled her legs inside the round room. She drew on her courage to swing them over as she stared down at the waves crashing against the jagged rocks below.

She imagined falling down, down to the jagged rocks. They'd pound and slice her body until she reached the freezing depths of the sea. Would she die right away? Or feel the pain of each gouge as her body crashed along?

The sky spun and her stomach heaved again. She couldn't do it. Kynedrithe quickly pulled herself inside and crawled to a large chest, where she knelt, shaking and gasping. The steps behind the closed wooden door pounded closer. She would have to face him. She could survive anything for one night, couldn't she?

The booted steps paused outside the door and she held her breath.

Chapter 2

H IS IMAGE WAVERED, blinking in and out before steadying. Apparently it was Kalyss's night to deal with strange new men. One wanted to date her, one tried to kill her, and this one stared at her, his light blue eyes an empty sea. Then he hunkered down and efficiently felt the sore spot at the back of her head.

"Who are you? Did Alex call you? Are you a doctor?" she asked, wincing at his rough touch and nearly choking with the effort to speak. He tilted her head back and examined the shallow scrape at her throat.

"Geoffrey. No, but I've had extensive experience with various injuries over the years." He felt along the bump until she winced again, then parted her hair at the back and examined the injury. "How are you feeling? Do you know who attacked you?"

Geoffrey's image wavered again. She closed her eyes. She needed Alex. He could heal her. "Dizzy. Nauseous. No. Where's Alex?"

Each word was a scrape against her throat. She pulled away from him and slid fully to the floor, laying her cheek against the cool faux-wood linoleum. All the world revolved around the burning bile prickling the back of her throat. The room tilted and swirled behind her closed eyes.

"He's on the phone. I don't think he heard anything. You'll be fine in a few minutes. It was a good knock, but the skin isn't broken or badly bruised." Could the stranger sound less upset? Sure, he didn't know her, but he treated this like a scraped knee.

On second thought, that was fine. She wasn't a victim and she didn't need to be treated like one. She'd come through worse and she'd be in kick-ass shape in no time. Bad news for the redhead.

"I doubt you have a concussion."

Been there, done that. It didn't worry her, but she'd kept the hard times of her marriage a secret from Alex. He'd only witnessed the aftermath of the worst of it. He'd freak when he saw her, but hopefully she'd be able to calm him down. If he ever showed up. On the phone with who?

Just breathe. In. Deep. Out. Slow. She concentrated on her chilled face as she felt the seconds tick. Geoffrey was right. She'd be fine. Sam had slammed her head harder more than once. She could deal with this. Just hold still and hope it didn't leave her with too bad of a headache.

A whisper of movement made her open her eyes and face Geoffrey's light blue gaze. Who was he? A new customer? From the look in his eyes, she doubted it. He wasn't new to battle.

"Who attacked you?"

That same old question. Again. Only, this time . . . "I don't know."

"Did he look familiar?"

Bile rose again. She closed her eyes and gritted her teeth. When she opened them, his unwavering gaze bored into her.

"What did he look like?" His calm, robotic voice annoyed her. Her head hurt. Her stomach twisted and knotted. And he kept asking questions she didn't have answers for.

"Look, I'm sorry if my pain interferes with your—"

"We don't have time for this, Kalyss. Think."

At the sound of her name on his lips, a chill broke over her entire body, colder than the floor beneath her. She pushed herself up. Two men who knew her. Two strangers. One tried to kill her. And this one? Besides a description, what did he want from her?

"What did he look like, Kalyss?"

His voice. Something was there. Something intangible and deep, buried beneath layers in her mind. Answering him was almost automatic this time.

"Tall. Built tough. Red hair. Green eyes."

His expression didn't change, but her chest vibrated with a sudden deep thud of her heart. The warning prickled her flesh, up her arms to the nape of her neck. The nausea died under this new rush of adrenaline. Suddenly, she doubted Alex was on the phone.

"We need to go." He reached for her.

She pulled back and rose to her feet in one swift motion. "Where's Alex?"

"We need to go. Now." He rushed her to the doorway then stepped in front. He turned left down the hall toward her office. He was too big for her to pass, so she tried looking around him, under his arm, anything, but she could see nothing.

"What is it? Where's Alex?" He kept ignoring her demand for an answer and it terrified her. Had he done something to Alex?

Geoffrey peered in the office doorway for a moment. She felt him tense, then he turned and herded her back.

"What's going on? Is Alex in there?" He pushed her along in front of him, too large and heavy for her to avoid. They passed the door to the sparring room and headed toward the back storage room. She dug in her heels and braced against the wall. "Stop it! Where is he?"

With hands around her waist, he picked her up and kept going, his pace quickening. "He's dead. Kai came back."

"What?" She hadn't heard him right. Or he was a lunatic. There was no way Alex was dead. She looked around at the rushing walls of the narrow hallway. As they passed through the door to the dark storage room, she reached out, guided by memory, and grabbed one of the spray cans from the shelf. Black for touching up the wrought-iron railing, which they'd done themselves, together. She and Alex. Best friends forever.

There was no way he was dead. Maybe hurt, maybe the redhead had come back and hurt him, but not dead. Alex could heal anything but death. She'd just have to outwit the blond Neanderthal and save him. Her head throbbed. The cool metal can pressed into her hand, a promise of liberty waiting for its moment.

"You're lying," she accused.

Geoffrey didn't pause or fumble. He simply charged though a dark room he shouldn't have known well enough to navigate. If warning bells were real, they'd be breaking her eardrums.

"Doubt me if you will, but you'll remember the truth of it all soon enough."

She'd heard almost those same words from her attacker. "Screw you both and your talk of memories. You're both nuts."

He released her waist and she dodged to the side. Kalyss darted away but one arm clamped around her before she could get far.

"Truth exists beyond sanity."

He wrenched open the back door. Rain slashed down in the blue darkness beyond, each grey drop a pellet shot to the black asphalt. He pulled her behind him and in seconds she was soaked.

Kalyss turned back toward the door, but he yanked her along behind him. Turn. Just once, please. Her finger tightened against the spray nozzle and she swung her right arm as she twisted her wrist out of his hand, grabbed his sleeve, and pulled him back with her left hand.

She almost fell into him. It shouldn't have been so easy, but he'd swung around swiftly. She stared up into his eyes and time nearly stopped, moving in the barest of increments. Her arm was still raised with her finger poised, slowly advancing forward. Silence descended with a heavy, oppressive weight. Only her harsh breath sounded in her ears.

Geoffrey's eyes widened and her gaze fell to his shoulder. His shirt tented to a tiny point. Then the shirt split and silver glinted against the dark fabric. A blade. It grew and grew, longer, sharper. All the way through his shoulder. A knife. A sword. Impaling him from behind.

Her left hand loosened from his arm, where she'd pulled him. He grabbed it, filling her hand with something small, something sharp. Cold metal bit her palm and he roughly closed her fingers in a fist around it and held tight. She couldn't

look away from his pierced and bleeding shoulder long enough
to see what he'd given her.

Suddenly the world spun around her, altering, changing.
The wet blade in a shadowed alley became a black SUV on a
dark, tree-lined street and her mind filled with a torrent of
visions.

A rush of street lights lit the cloudy night. Buildings, signs,
lights, and cars flashed past at blinding speeds. Engines
roared. Horns blared. Ambulance sirens shrieked behind her.
To the side. In front. The road rolled like a snapping tape measure, then was gone.

The rush of pictures froze. A tall tower, stained glass and
stone, loomed over her, guarding from the hilltop. She knew
this place. A key slid silently into a lock. A door swung open,
revealing a split-second glimpse of stone and grief.

Then the vision was gone and the blade slid through Geoffrey toward her. He started to slump and her attacker's green
eyes glinted dangerously from behind Geoffrey's shoulder.

The rushing sound in her ears shriveled to a pinpoint of silence. Instant and total, vast as space. Like a gunshot in the
still night, Geoffrey whispered one word.

"Run."

Sound burst to normal, the pelting rain loud after the silence. Everything moved faster, less time to think. No. God,
no. The familiar claws of panic bit into her lungs, slicing
deep. But she'd moved beyond helpless, frozen terror. Her
right arm was still in motion. She refocused her aim and followed through. The can completed its arc and she sprayed the
glittering green eyes of her attacker as Geoffrey fell at her
feet.

Then she was off. Full run for her life mode. Her hand
gripped hard around the keys Geoffrey had given her. Where to
go? Did it matter? She spun around the corner of the building,
one hand slapping against the wet brick. No sound followed her,
no footsteps, no brush of fabric. Would she hear him? Or would
he appear as suddenly as he had in the sparring room? No
sound, no warning, just a blind attack?

Faster. Speed is there, just reach for it. Don't look back, just
run. Don't slow, don't stop. Don't listen for him. Just run.

Down the semi-lit street, under the trees. Vehicles lined the curb. She saw the black SUV and stopped, used the keys to unlock it, and climbed inside. Quickly she locked the door again and fired the engine.

No fumbling. Plan the move and execute it. She pulled away from the curb and gunned the engine of Geoffrey's SUV. Geoffrey's keys. Geoffrey's full name. How did she suddenly know any of this? Was it his driver's license she'd seen in the vision?

She'd watched him die. She'd watched the sword pierce his shirt, knowing it was already through his heart. Blood, dark blood, coating the blade, coating him, his eyes as all light winked from them. His last word, his last deed, had ensured her safety.

She held the wheel tight as the SUV lurched around the corner and across the four lane street. She pressed the gas harder. Don't look in the mirror. If he was close behind, she didn't want to know.

Dear God. Geoffrey. Right in front of her. She didn't know him and his death shouldn't cause sorrow or grief. Yet it did. But mainly, it caused fear. Could she still doubt that Alex was dead? Had Geoffrey seen Alex in his office? Is that why he'd rushed her away? Had he truly tried to protect her the entire time, not just at his moment of death? If so, then by fighting him, she'd killed him.

KAI FELL BACK against the side of the building, wasting precious moments as Kalyss sped off. He'd closed his eyes in time to avoid the worst of the spray, but paint still coated his face. Kai scrubbed until he could open his eyes to the darkness, then stared at his hands. Rain washed away the thick black paint, letting it stream through his fingers like blood at night.

How ironic. *He* wasn't the monster, yet it always seemed to be *his* hands covered in a woman's blood. Only, this time, it wasn't blood and Kalyss was gone. She'd run, her feet pounding the wet pavement then not. Running in grass? There was a lot of that around here. And the rain wouldn't help locate her. The skies poured as loudly as a firefighter's hose.

He rubbed cleaner hands over his face and head again, then

knelt by the body at his feet. Geoffrey lay sprawled on his side on the black asphalt, Kai's sword impaling his shoulder through the top of his heart. But the game wasn't over. If it were that easy to win or lose, they'd never have come this far—but some people refused to stay dead, no matter how often he killed them. Kai braced one hand on Geoffrey's shoulder and slid the sharp steel free.

Kalyss was gone. That had never happened before, nor had she ever fought him so well. The realization had begun to hit him slowly as he'd held her against the wall and now was a fully confirmed thought. Thinking he might use her to find the location of the statue, he'd released her and planned to follow her after she'd talked with Geoffrey and learned where it was. But this time, Kalyss had escaped fully on her own. Using her wit and her skill.

With this night's work, Kalyss had upgraded herself from victim to adversary and that deserved his respect. Perhaps she even deserved a different kind of hunt. Kai raised his brows. It was something for him to consider.

Hefting Geoffrey's body over his shoulder, Kai strode back inside the dojo. He'd watched her over the last few years, as Geoffrey had, but it was still a guess as to where her erratic woman's mind would take her or if Geoffrey had taken the time to tell her anything. In the end, though, it wouldn't matter. She would return, with the statue or without. Then Kai would either fight the monster she released or he would help her realize the error of her ways, through logic—or death.

Kai strode directly to the shelf that hid the door to the basement, moved it aside, and took Geoffrey down the stairs. In the light of one dim bulb, he tied a rope around the dead man's hands, threw it over a thick, sturdy beam that crossed the ceiling, and tugged until Geoffrey hung, his toes barely brushing the floor.

Now to erase any evidence of tonight's struggles. It wouldn't do for someone to find them while he waited for Kalyss. Kai shut the basement door, tugged the shelf back into place, and headed through the darkened storage room. A low groan echoed through the silent building, reversing Kai's direction from the back door so he headed toward the offices. In the front one, Kai stopped and eyed the man on the floor. Blood

welled from the swelling knot at the back of Alex's head, but
he was groaning and beginning to stir.

"You should be dead, too." Kai bent and pulled Alex over
his shoulder. He'd have to come back for the puddle of blood
after securing his second hostage. Kai headed for the basement. "Guess I didn't hit you hard enough. Don't worry,
though. You'll regret it soon."

KALYSS DROVE QUICKLY, pushing the speed limit. She could
look in the rearview mirror now. He wouldn't appear there
when she was driving forty-five miles an hour, she was pretty
sure. The doors were locked. Her foot pressed the gas harder.

The sound of police sirens pierced the night from not too
far away. She forced herself to slow. If she was pulled over,
she'd have to stop driving and she didn't think she could do
that yet. Soon, she'd have to. Just not yet, not while her heart
pounded and her breath stuttered as if unsure whether it
should go in or out. Not while her hands shook, even while
gripped, white and tight, around the steering wheel. Not when
she couldn't speak, only gasp.

Her life had changed irrevocably tonight, and she couldn't
even begin understanding all the ways how. Not even the obvious ways. Someone had tried to kill her. Someone who'd
killed Alex and Geoffrey, a man whose name she shouldn't
know, whose life she shouldn't care about. But strangely, she
did. With his death, she felt lost. Vulnerable.

It didn't matter how many times she repeated herself, she
still couldn't grasp it. Where was the sense? The logic? Absent tonight, apparently.

Division became Browne and she took the winding road
until it turned into Grand. This headlong rush had to stop. She
was away. She was safe, even if she didn't feel it. It was time
to stop and think.

She turned left on a tree-shrouded street and pulled to the
side, behind an empty vehicle. She turned the lights and engine off and tried to let the silence settle her. Darkness surrounded her. Trees danced in the shadows. She pushed the
automatic locks again, just in case.

What came next? She pulled the keys free of the ignition and stared at them. Two small keys and a box to hold them together. A car alarm. Or a remote door lock. Or a remote engine starter. Which one? She pressed the small button on the box and the locks sprang free. Urgently, she pressed it again and the car locked. She held her breath a moment, as if that would make everything slow down: her pulse, her breathing, her thoughts. Her head swam and she forced air into her lungs again.

She looked at the keys rattling in her hand. One large, black-cased one with a Dodge symbol. The Durango key. The one other key was smaller, silver. A generic key that could belong to any lock on the planet. Talk about mysterious needles and large haystacks.

She looked around the inside. Nothing on the carpets or the seats. Nothing in the back. No pop in the drink carrier. No change in the holders. No ornament hanging from the mirror. On impulse, she opened the glove box and dove inside, ready to shove aside the usual bits of uselessness and search the good stuff. Nothing. No insurance with a name and address. No extra napkins or straws. Nothing any vehicle owned by any other human on the planet would have. The emptiness surrounding her seemed to describe Geoffrey more than containers and papers could have.

There was nothing here for her. Just a strange key and a full tank of gas. Kalyss leaned forward, careful not to press the horn, rested her arms on the wheel and her forehead on her arms. She closed her eyes and waited. There was only one thing she could do—she needed to call the police. But to do that, she'd have to unlock the doors.

She breathed in deep, let it out slow. She pressed her right temple against her knuckles, trying to focus and steady her heart. But when she opened her eyes, all peace was ruined. Right in front of her, looming in the darkness was the building from her "vision".

St. John's. The church on the hill that could be seen from most anywhere in Spokane. She'd never had visions so detailed. Or had it been Geoffrey? His thoughts and memories were so fine-tuned—like a movie in fast-forward, she had seen the drive straight to this place.

Stained glass arched high while the stone walls rippled like gothic armor. Why had she driven here of all places? Yet, its very vigilance promised sanctuary.

The shadows around it promised no such thing, however. The leaves whispered words she didn't understand. The shadows hovered, offering protection to those who wanted to be hidden, but not discriminating in who that might be.

Her mirrors promised black emptiness behind and to the side of her. Untrustworthy promises. If only she could learn the language of trees and know the secrets they whispered. But that was for Elven fantasies and this just wasn't the night for fantasies of any kind.

The keys bit into the palm of her hand. With one more look around, she took a deep breath and unlocked only her door. It released with a sharp thunk that made her jump.

She looked around again. Nothing moved. Instead, the night waited, a pulsating presence that promised doom with every heartbeat.

Good God, could she get any more dramatic? She simply needed to get out of the car, walk to the door, and knock. Three seconds, tops. She could crawl that distance in three seconds. But then, how long had he stood behind her, his dagger poised to slice, without her knowing?

For someone who'd been here and done this, she wasn't very on the ball anymore. Four years without an abusive man hovering over her had apparently relaxed her too much. She swallowed back the self-loathing. This wasn't her fault. She couldn't have predicted or prevented it. She could only move through it. Wasn't that what the self-help books said?

The opening door creaked slightly, but it sounded like a shriek in the still air. She jumped out, locked the door again, slammed it, and ran. There was no sneaking at this point, just the rush for safety. Her tennis shoes whistled on the pavement with every quick step.

She raised her hand to knock, but the door was open. Just slightly. As if someone had known she'd be here and left it waiting for her slight push. As if whatever needed protection inside was already doomed if the enemy had reached this far. With one last glance behind her, she entered the church.

Her steps echoed on the stone entrance. Bouncing off the high ceiling and stained glass back down to the floor again. To the right the choir pews poised for song. Straight ahead, the pulpit angled toward the dark, silent pews to her left. She could see only one direction left to go, through the center of those pews to the wooden doors at the back. Hopefully there would be an unlocked office with a working telephone, if it wasn't just an entranceway.

And then what? Wait here for the police to arrive? Go back to the dojo? Keep running until her attacker was caught? Or go back and wait for him to attack again? Refuse to cower and run. Believe that forewarned is forearmed and trust in her skills to protect her should the need arise. Kalyss walked between the pews to the double doors behind them.

Pride said take a stand and never bow before any man again. Fear said *Are you nuts?* And logic, the true weapon of common sense, reminded her of how close she had come to dying.

Instead of banging her head on the wall, he could have drawn his knife across her throat and ended it there, as he'd threatened. Undeniable proof that no matter how good she thought herself to be, she wasn't anywhere near his level.

That left either running—though how far and for how long remained in question since she didn't know why he was after her in the first place—or hiding behind someone else to keep her safe.

Both options repelled her. She'd have to stay put until she could think of options to replace them. She paused at the double doors and faced the back of the church.

Thunk. Thunk. Thunk. The deep tenor of measured steps thrust through the silence behind the door, approaching closer and closer. No deviation. No pause. The Terminator from the first movie came to mind. The constant, indestructible plodding of heavy male steps . . . The unflagging pursuit . . .

She grabbed her stomach, confirming it was above her waist and not a puddle at her feet. Security guards paused. Ministers stopped to pray or continued on with decisive purpose. Only serial killers stalked.

She ran back through the pews, toward the door she'd entered through. The double doors behind her rattled. Kalyss saw a door to her right, one she'd missed the first time through. Opening it, she stared into a black pit where dark stairs led to the basement. Oh, hell no.

Chapter 3

She turned toward the doors leading out when the steps abruptly stopped on the other side of the double doors. She'd never escape in time. With no choice left, she slipped through the basement door and ran down the stairs.

There was darkness, cloying and black, ominous and still. She put her hand on the wall and rushed away from the stairs. The stone was cold and slightly damp. Or was it her hand that was damp? Clenching her other fist, she discovered it was her. She was drenched all over, but had barely noticed.

The door at the top of the stairs opened. She rushed faster, one hand following the wall and the other held out in front of her to guide her around any furniture that might be leaning against it. Each step on the stairs behind her kicked her heart to a faster pace.

A doorway passed under her fingertips. If he flipped on a light, she was doomed. There was no way he could miss her. The handle bit into her hand without turning. Locked. Out of the only place she could hide before he reached the bottom of the steps.

She felt them, then. The tears of defeat. Of overwhelming struggle. Her forehead rested against the door, her shoulders slumping. She could just wait here. Listen to the unflagging steps measuring the distance between life and death.

Geoffrey would have known what to do now. She wasn't sure how, but she knew it with a spiritual certainty. A faith that went beyond tactile experience. She'd only met him tonight, yet he'd shown her what she needed.

To run, to escape the assassin and flee. To his car, operated with the key he'd given her. So she could drive to this church and enter the open door upstairs . . . No. His car, operated with one of the *two* keys he'd given her.

She felt in her pocket for the small silver key, the other hand searching for the slit to fit it in. There. It slid in. The stalker's foot hit the last step. The key turned and the door slid open. Something scraped along the wall. His hand searching for the light switch?

She slipped inside, freeing the key as she went. Rays of light pierced through the door crack just before it clicked closed, sealing her in darkness. She paused, then felt for the small protrusion of the lock and turned it, thankful there was no sound.

She held the door closed, both hands bridging the gap as the footsteps began again. Closer. There was a dead bolt under her hand. Closer. She turned it slowly, slowly. Closer. It clicked. The steps stopped.

She closed her eyes, held her breath, and pressed against the door, adding her strength to the dead bolt. He stopped on the other side of the door, his breath whispering low and harsh. Chills claimed her body. The handle turned, then stopped, held by the lock. A weight pressed against the door. It didn't move. Not even a shudder.

She swallowed tears, her body tense with fear. It was one thing to know your attacker, to know you'd married him and that sometimes, if you were really good, if life was really good for that day, that moment, all would be well. Those moments braced you for the ones when it all fell apart.

But not knowing who was behind her . . . feeling full of fear with nothing, no one to brace her, to protect her . . . was even more terrifying. The steps backed away. Preparing to charge? She left the questionable safety of the door. Back.

Back. Something touched her shoulder. Breath left her, then rushed in with a silent scream.

The footsteps left. Away. Away. Gone. She felt behind herself, felt cloth over something hard—a statue. She released her breath and fell at the base, sobs no longer containable. Long, but quiet, she cried out her confusion and pain and fear. Too much air, then not enough. No strength. No courage. She huddled in the dark, embracing her terror, for only that was familiar.

When her sobs dried to sniffles and sighs and her body shut down with overload, she settled back against stone feet. She still needed to call the police, but exhaustion weighed down her limbs. Her eyes fought to lift, but were too heavy. She could only hope she'd be safe until morning. Kalyss sighed and ceased her fighting. Warmth settled around her as the sheet pulled fully from the statue to surround her.

SILAS TWISTED THE knob once more before pulling away. He heard Kalyss's sobs through the door, felt her fear like a dark fog brushing his skin. Draven's kind found that soft caress an aphrodisiac. But to those like him, it was sickening. He didn't enjoy inspiring fear in someone, even when it was necessary.

He brought forth his inner light, like a shield, to cloak his entire body with a radiant glow and hold back the blackness of the fear that slithered like snaky tendrils beneath the door.

Draven's loud steps pounded up the stairs to his right, for Kalyss to think her pursuer had left, then all was silent and the black cloaked figure appeared at the edge of his glow, the smoky tendrils of sin wafting from it. Theirs was such an unlikely alliance, but necessary. And this time, finally, it might be worth it.

"Did you lock the outside door?"

"Of course," Draven's low voice rasped from beneath the deep cowl, and Silas was reminded of the first time he'd heard it.

October 5, 1075 AD

"YOU'RE THE ONLY one who can help. The only one powerful enough." The husky voice issued from beneath a heavy black cowl. In fact, every inch was covered in black, from cloak to leather gloves and boots. Even the slight tendrils of smoke that rose like steam from every fold of Draven's cloak were black.

"Why would I choose to help one of your kind?" Silas's own innate glow battled with Draven's darkness, tangling and fighting to lighten it. The mere thought of an alliance between them would break the laws of nature.

"Because what I propose doesn't defile your principles. In fact, my plan obeys them well." There was a straightforward, factual tone to Draven's words, but still . . .

"I'm to trust your word on that?" Silas examined the pacing figure in front of him. Draven wasn't tall or short, fat or thin. There was nothing distinguishing to determine an identity. Only a husky, neutral voice that whispered so he couldn't surmise a gender.

"Without even the willingness to trust, we will accomplish nothing." Draven stopped before a table of candles and scrolls then turned toward him. "I will not lie to you, Silas."

He couldn't help but be skeptical. "How do I know that? I don't know you. Show yourself, instead of hiding like a threat."

Draven walked to him, stopping only a few feet away. Draven wasn't short, but Silas was still taller. Larger. "There is no threat from me, Silas. Not for you. But I cannot show myself."

Silas narrowed his eyes. When the angels had fallen, some of their forms had altered, changed. Deformed. Many had passed this curse on to the children they'd sired, either with other demons or with humans. Either fallen angel or Nephilim, perhaps Draven was ashamed of the form beneath the cloak.

If Draven refused to show Silas this form, there was likely a prideful reason. Silas kept his own soft, white, feathery wings folded neatly behind him. They arched over his head to flow in clean lines to his ankles. Eternally part of him. Eternally marking him. He felt neither pride for having them, nor disgust when others did not. It just was and he accepted that.

Just as he would accept the mystery of Draven, though reluctantly. His mouth grim, Silas nodded, then crossed his arms over his white robed chest. "There are laws against interference, Draven."

"Maeve's one of the evil ones. She enjoys manipulation, be it through lust, jealousy, temptation, or vengeance. She doesn't obey your rules, isn't interested in returning to heaven. But the ones she plans to curse . . ." Draven paused. "She wants to invoke the Cain/Abel curse."

Silas inhaled sharply. There was no curse more damning to a soul than for one brother to kill the other. Just imagining the repercussions was terrifying.

But interference with humans was not allowed, not even if someone else interfered first. The law of Free Will was a primary one. Fallen angels and their descendents could influence, suggest, even manipulate humans for good or ill, as long as they didn't interfere with the humans' right to choose their own path.

There were some who took those allowances too far, those who lived in Draven's part of the world. But in Silas's world, this was strictly limited. Even in trying to do good, like trying to save the two Draven wanted his help with, harm could be the result.

No, interference was not allowed. Silas waved a hand and opened the portal for Draven to return to wherever Draven had come from, an unspoken dismissal.

Draven waved a hand to close the portal, refusing to leave just yet. "You don't see the larger picture."

"What more do I need to see? They are human. We do not meddle in their affairs lightly lest we become more like your kind, bent only on destruction and our own selfish will."

"If this is selfish, why am I here?" Draven demanded.

"My question exactly. Why are you here?"

Draven was silent a long moment before responding. "This is good work."

"Works do not save."

"Are you so sure that means we should do nothing?" Draven's voice was low and intense. " 'Show me your faith without your works, and I will show you my faith by my works.' "

Silas crossed his arms. "Great, another demon quoting the Bible."

"Don't mock me, Silas." Draven pointed a gloved finger at him. " 'Even the demons believe—and tremble!' "

Silas closed his eyes, seeking the truth. Was Draven manipulating him? Is that why he was hearing sensible words from the black depths of a sin-soaked, cloaked figure? Or was it that at this time, that figure spoke the truth? "Demons also betray."

" 'He who turns a sinner from the error of his way will save a soul from death and cover a multitude of sins.' " Draven's voice held not one tremble as the mysterious figure vowed, "I will not betray. Not you. Not them."

Silas opened his eyes, considering Draven's promise. Considering the work proposed. A demonic curse was interference in humanity's right to free will. Blocking or altering such a curse was technically within the laws. But doing so without making things worse would be tricky.

Draven moved back to the table and opened one of Silas's blank scrolls. Dipping a quill into a small pot of ink, Draven wrote. "This is the curse Maeve embedded in her emerald before she died to the world. It calls to her son, demanding vengeance against his half-brother for her death. But Dreux is innocent, and his death at Kai's hands will invoke the Cain/Abel curse."

Curious despite himself, Silas leaned over Draven's shoulder and stared at the parchment.

I curse you, lowly by-blow. You are a blight before my eyes.
I curse you a thousand years, a thousand lives, and more.
May those you love turn from you and die, trapping you
alone and cold, as I am, tormented and cursed, unable to
walk away from your pain.

Silas straightened, frowning. By the rules of their people, once having "died" in front of humans, one of their kind would rest deep in the tunnels of the Forgotten Ones until all who had known them as human were dead, thus shielding humans from this alternate realm that existed alongside theirs. Maeve would sleep until those who saw her alive were dead.

He and Draven could alter her curse, if they weren't strong enough to break it altogether, and she'd never know they'd interfered. She would awaken in a century or so, see the brothers had escaped her wrath, but were dead by normal human means and beyond her reach. With no choice, Maeve would move on—and probably find another evil interest to pursue.

Draven tensed beside him, carefully still and waiting. Could Silas trust someone so mysterious? What ulterior motive did Draven have for undermining Maeve's curse? Either way, Draven was right. It was good work. And who alive couldn't use the redemptive powers of a little good work?

"There may be something we can do. It will take both of us, though."

OH, HOW FAR they'd come in the centuries since that first meeting. Their motives had been pure, their intentions sincere, but as he'd feared, harm had been the result. Now a frightened woman lay on the other side of the door, finally alone and relatively safe, able to free her husband. Once she remembered him, anyway.

Silas eyed the locked door, then he and his companion stepped through it, their bodies as insubstantial as spirits one moment, then solid the next. Kalyss huddled at the feet of the statue, her breath ragged in the still, dark room.

She wouldn't be able to see or hear them. A barrier stretched between their realms so they lived on the same planet, at the same time, but those of the human realm would never know the other existed until someone from that realm was powerful enough to cross the barrier with more than thoughts and suggestions. Only together were even he and Draven that powerful.

"I'd begun to doubt we'd make it here. Safe inside a locked room with only the two of them." Draven paused, the blacker face of the cowl facing him. "Which raises the question—how did we make it here?" Draven pointed a gloved finger at the statue in front of them. "How did *he* make it here?"

"It's easier to believe if you see it." Silas knew the request was coming and prepared to alter the image of the room, so they'd see what they needed superimposed on the things around them. It was the best way without leaving Dreux and Kalyss unprotected, which would certainly be a mistake at this crucial junction.

"Then show me," Draven said.

Silas motioned Draven back against the door and waved his hand, revealing the images he'd saved for this exact purpose just that morning.

93 Zoo FM played the latest combination of hip-hop and rock. The volume was low, but the sound clear. A 52" flat widescreen TV with high definition and an LCD screen honored one wall. Muted, it was tuned in to the local news, with captions scrolling at the bottom of the screen. Below it, a flat desk held a laptop with a black screen.

To the right, one wall was a window, transparent from the inside, a dark shield from the outside so nature in all its glory was clearly seen from the depths of the room. Scattered through an area were the parts of the latest techno-victim of a grown man's search for knowledge. On each wall there were mirrors to show all angles of the room, which was more like a one-room university.

In the center of it all, silent and motionless on a wooden pedestal, perfectly positioned to observe everything around him, stood Dreux. Still frozen in stone, but no longer trapped in the tower room.

Draven inhaled sharply, still sounding surprised. "How? When?"

"Just after Kalyss's last death. Geoffrey hired ex-Marines." Silas spoke quietly, not wishing to disrupt the atmosphere.

"They had Marines back then?"

Silas raised a disbelieving brow. "They've had Marines since 1775."

At that moment, a door opened to their left, next to an open bar with a direct view of the bright white kitchen. With a steady and determined stride, Geoffrey flipped off the radio and TV. He shut the laptop and closed the curtains, then strode to the center of the room. Another flip, this time of a switch at Dreux's feet, and the statue swiveled until Dreux's anguished expression faced them. An eternity of torment, that's what he suffered inside his shell.

A soft cone of light descended from a small fixture recessed in the ceiling to a circle around the base of the statue.

Geoffrey knelt in the base of that circle, a black backpack sliding from his shoulder, and stared up at Dreux.

"My lord," he began.

Draven jerked in surprise as he spoke in a modern dialect. Silas smiled to himself.

"It is time." Geoffrey turned to stare at them. No, behind them. He couldn't see them. They were invisible to his eyes.

Silas pulled Draven away from the wall behind them. Every inch of the wall was Kalyss, in all her lives, with all her names. Ancient paintings in oil, drawings on yellowed parchment, glossy posters in full color. From childhood to adulthood, playing with puppies or wielding a sword, the wall was her.

"The plan I've set stands. She will be alone and unprepared for the changes this night will bring." Geoffrey eyed the most recent photograph. "And yet, she'll be the most prepared ever. Each lifetime has seen her change in small, indefinite ways, but this time . . ." Geoffrey paused as his voice roughened, then continued in an even tone. "This time she is stronger, tougher, in ways I was never cruel enough to teach."

He faced Dreux again. "You must remember, *she will not know you.*"

Geoffrey bowed his head, one knee on the floor, one hand clenched on his raised knee as he appeared to silently pray. A few moments passed, then he rose and grabbed a long board propped against a wall.

"What makes him think Dreux can see and hear?" Draven's voice was suspicious.

Geoffrey latched the board, one wall of the moving crate, to the top of the pedestal. The board stretched from Dreux's feet to a foot over his head.

Silas shrugged innocently. "Suggestion. Influence. Only what's allowed."

Geoffrey attached another board behind Dreux, casting shadows on the gray granite from the two walls. The silent room was nearly deafening. So much depended on tonight.

This time, Draven's voice was dry. "A TV and radio? Showing him how to operate all the trappings of the twenty-first century? Sounds like more than a suggestion."

A third wall went up on Dreux's side. Only his front could be seen, bright gray.

"Perhaps he'd already considered it, to carry my suggestion so far." And Silas had only suggested. Perhaps strongly, but nothing more. Humans weren't puppets to bend to his will. God had made them in such a way so they wouldn't be anyone's puppets. Even His.

A square board was placed over Dreux's head, leaving his front open as long as possible. Allowing his anguished eyes to face Kalyss's pictures for just a few more seconds.

"Right. You only suggested." Draven still sounded doubtful, but less so.

Silas had built a reputation of integrity. He never lied, though he could understand Draven's doubt. Geoffrey had taken his suggestions quite far. The fourth wall slowly slid into place, hiding Dreux from view. Now there was only a large, solid crate on a wooden pedestal.

"Of course." Silas raised his left hand, palm up. "Ready?"

Draven slowly held one hand, palm down above his. "There's more?"

"Oh, yes."

The room wavered, folded in on itself and disappeared. Now they stood in a clearing with the morning sun rising through the trees at their backs. In the center, Kai held a spread-legged stance and slowly moved his arms and hands in smooth motions, focusing and centering himself. At his throat, an emerald cabochon glinted in the light, all he had left of his mother, and yet, it was Maeve's power and influence embedded in the emerald that drove Kai's need for vengeance over her death. A death he didn't realize was a false one. Since Silas and Draven had altered the curse that would have fulfilled his need, Kai was caught as the villain as surely as Kalyss was the victim.

Silas considered the determined man before them. Without Kai's thirst for retribution, Kalyss could live long enough to free Dreux, the one man who could end this cycle. "Kai's mother's hold on his mind and heart is strong. Possibly unbreakable."

"Unwavering and determined in his vengeance. Maeve will be proud of him."

Silas frowned at the hint of approval in Draven's voice. "Unfortunately. But he'll hate her when he discovers the truth of her lies."

"And the truth of *her*, no doubt. Learning his mother is an evil fallen angel bent on manipulating and destroying human lives for her own amusement will drive him to even more desperate levels of fury."

Silas nodded in agreement and waved his hand again. The clearing wavered, folded in on itself, and disappeared. They were once again in the stomach of the church with a concrete floor beneath them and stone walls with stained-glass windows around them.

Silas took a thankful breath, enjoying the moment. Safe behind a locked door, so close to awakening Dreux. It was only the beginning to breaking Maeve's curse and preventing the even worse one that awaited, but it was still a moment to savor. After failing nine times, hope seemed a luxury, but it was a necessary one to afford.

"This is about the only way to keep Kalyss alive long enough to awaken Dreux. Geoffrey planned well. The vision, the keys, a sanctuary." The cloaked figure glided toward Kalyss, then knelt beside her. "But don't get complacent. They could still fail."

Silas nodded, reminded of his earlier warning to Draven, and walked to each of the windows, making sure they were locked and protected. "She fought well. Kai won't reach her again tonight."

"Or underestimate her." Satisfaction filled Draven's voice. The helpless hare had become a panther, full of strength and cunning. Draven passed a gloved hand over Kalyss's bent head, close but not touching. "She's dreaming now, but we still need time. Too many things need to happen before Maeve is awakened."

Though he and Draven failed to break the curse altogether, they had altered it, believing the curse could then be broken easily and Maeve would never know of their interference. But it hadn't worked that way. Instead, it had lasted nearly a thousand years and sealed the fate of everyone touched by it.

Over nine hundred years had passed with Maeve trapped in a deep sleep. When she awakened, she would be furious over losing so much time. She wouldn't stop searching until she discovered who had interfered. And when Maeve found them, her powerful fury and thirst for vengeance would destroy them both.

Their only hope now was to complete their good work and earn redemption for their mistake before Maeve awakened and killed them.

Silas glanced down at the sleeping Kalyss. Her eyes were puffy from crying, her brow wrinkled from worry. Even deep in her dreams, her lips trembled with a heart-wrenching vulnerability.

Vulnerability wasn't usually seen with powerful Descendents, but for those raised as human, as Kalyss, Dreux, Geoffrey, Kai, and Alex had been, different rules applied. All children of angels were marked *different*, but few raised as humans knew it.

No matter how far back in the family tree the angel appeared, angelic genes survived. Due to the variables of genetic inheritance, each child or descendent differed in how much they were affected. Yet each of them held in their minds the key to amazing abilities. They only needed to learn to unlock them.

Kalyss and Dreux needed to unlock theirs.

Draven leaned over Kalyss, whispering in her ear. "Remember and use your memories. Your gift will only obey the limits you place on it. Reach further. Test yourself. Believe in yourself. You've come so far, accomplished so much. You can achieve your dreams."

Silas stood behind Dreux and placed a hand on his shoulder. "She's so very close. Closer than ever. Be patient and you will have her again. You will have more than you ever imagined."

There was no telling how a human would take suggestion. Sometimes they listened to a small degree or, like Geoffrey, to a much larger degree. Sometimes they rebelled and went exactly the opposite way suggested. And some sad times, they did nothing and nothing moved them.

Despite being a statue, Dreux was a mover. And Kalyss had proven herself one many times over. They weren't content to sit and dream. They made dreams come true.

Silas positioned himself between the windows and the back of the statue. Draven assumed position between Kalyss and the door. They held their hands out, bracing an invisible shield around the room. None could enter. None could interfere. Not this time. It was their last chance.

Chapter 4

October 6, 1075 — England

THE WOODEN DOOR scraped against the stone floor until it stood open. Her new husband paused in the threshold, his eyes searching the seemingly empty room before he walked in. Stalked in, more like, his boots heavy and thunderous on the stone floor, mimicking the weather outside. His strange eyes searched the room until he found her hiding by the tall chest, shivering and trembling like a veritable coward. His gaze narrowed and she huddled deeper. He would despise her for this weakness, this fear.

He turned from her and walked to the fire, holding out his hands to a warmth she couldn't feel. His back was to her. Did he trust her or simply not fear her? If she'd had a dagger, she could've ended this night.

For a moment, as she listened to the snap of the fire and wished the warmth could reach to her little corner, she imagined how easy it would be to strike down the demon before her.

But not even she could be enough of a coward to plunge a blade into a man's back, be he innocent or evil, without immediate cause. Without some further action from him. Strangely, the blood of her people that covered him, the blood only she could see, was not just cause.

Tears gathered in her eyes. She couldn't end it here. She couldn't end her life, or his. They were trapped in this room for the night. Together. He would need her blood and she would have to sacrifice it.

More of the red liquid to cover his hands. His face. Dripping down his back and legs, yet never puddling on the floor beneath him. She had the Sight, yet it was never a sight of the future, only of the past. And something in this man's past covered his soul in blood.

Tears threatened to fall, burning her eyelids. She blinked them back and swallowed the tears choking her. She must have made a sound for he swung around and faced her, his gaze burning into her.

Like a sorcerer's, his stare was hypnotic. The strength and sheer will in those eyes sent her head spinning. He wanted something from her. Her brow furrowed with fearful imaginings until, in a heart-stopping moment of breathlessness, she knew. Not just blood, but her soul. Dear God, she had married a demon and he wanted her soul.

He frowned and pulled his hands from his gauntlets. He set them on a chest by the fire and faced her again.

Disgust. It was visible in his eyes. Her cowardice disgusted him. He was the conquering warrior, here to hold the lands for William, away from the rightful Saxon owners. He'd fought them well until his blade ran with blood and his soul bathed in it while she could only cower. Kynedrithe looked down at her drawn up legs. Her teary eyes blurred them, but she could see herself clearly through his eyes.

To be so strong and invincible and married to such a weakling. He couldn't have truly meant this marriage to her—one cut, one more soul trapped in his blade, and he'd have it all without ties to a witch such as she. One last dramatic act to discourage rebellion.

He was the one covered with blood, but she was the disgusting one. Crying and shivering because she could see what others could not. Did that give her the advantage or them? Was living in ignorance safer?

No. She knew that. She'd learned that lesson when her closest friend, Maredudd, had been courted by the blacksmith's son, Dunnagaul. She'd seen him for the fiend he was, but Maredudd hadn't and it had landed her in the midst of a creek, cleaning virgin blood from her thighs.

For a moment, the memory bloomed in front of Kynedrithe, between her gaze and her husband's. Real and vivid, tangible and terrifying. Maredudd floated, face to the side, her gown billowing around her in that same creek just inches above the cold stone floor. Her white dress wavered and moved with a gentle beckoning. Her arms were outstretched on either side of her head. Maredudd's open eyes stared straight at Kynedrithe, as if death held no fear for her as living had.

Kynedrithe blinked, dispelling the memory and its too real visual. When Maredudd's pregnancy had been discovered, she'd been ordered to marry Dunnagaul, but by that time Maredudd feared him so much she'd sought a more desperate reprieve. It was the one time they both had wished Kynedrithe truly were the witch many claimed. They couldn't bear the thought of harming an innocent babe. However, if they could have rid the world of Dunnagaul, Maredudd would have been spared. But Kynedrithe was no witch. She held no harm in her, just a gift to see inside someone's past.

She reined in her Sight and focused on the danger of her husband's eyes. Dreux de Vernon, the priest had named him. He stood tall and large, and so incredibly intimidating in his heavy armor. Would he be a lord who cared for the pain and anguish of his people? Would he have spared Maredudd from marriage to Dunnagaul, from an eternity of sleeping with the man who'd raped her?

Or would Dreux be the cold-eyed conqueror, uncaring for the people of this keep, merely seeking to scavenge what riches he could from this land? That is what they wondered, in the village, what they feared. And when they sought her knowledge, she had no comfort for them. The blood on his soul left no room for promises of peace.

Her people had hoped marriage to their lady would tie him to this land and its people, inspiring him to treat them with kindness despite the rebellions, but if it didn't work that way, they only lost someone they feared. Someone with the Sight, beloved by no one now that all of her family was dead.

So a few of the maids had trussed her up in as fine a gown as could be found, a forest green of thick wool, and brightly encouraged her to please him well. But Kynedrithe knew beneath their false smiles, their real concern had been for themselves. For as long as he was pleased, they believed they were safe.

Then they'd delivered her to the church door and stood watch as she'd exchanged promises with the man who held her hand so tight she feared his soul would stain hers. And when it was finished, the villagers had left, wordless but with their fears in their eyes. Everything depended on her.

Some savior of her people was she. Had she no pride? A dark corner of her heart said no. But it wasn't true. She did have pride. Certainly enough that to continue hiding in her corner, cowering before him, was untenable. This night was here whether she'd willed it or not, and it would end whether she cried through it or not. Eventually, everyone ran out of tears, even she.

She cleared her throat of the tears that still choked her, the sound suddenly loud in the silent room, drowning even the pop and sizzle coming from the hearth, then dabbed at her eyes until they were dry. She edged up the wall until she was standing—shaking, quivering, nauseous, but standing. He didn't move, but she could feel his eyes following her every movement, as she had followed his. Waiting, judging.

She tried to put some steel in her spine, starting with the very bottom. Bone by bone, she pictured each segment locking into place until she could raise her head. Even the small act of standing seemed bold and brave to her—at the very least it was an improvement over cowering in the corner. Warmer, too. She forced her chin up and her gaze to meet his.

His eyes blazed, and the smoky dark ring outside the amber contrasted more sharply. Her small act of bravery mocked her now, and she wanted to shrink back into herself, but that would accomplish nothing. Nothing could save her. Theirs had been deemed a worthy match. A witch bride for a demon conqueror.

She took a step from her tempting bolt-hole and then another. She stopped just a few paces from him and kept her eyes on his face. Dreux was handsome, well put together if she could look past his stained soul. As hard as she tried, she couldn't. It threatened her, warned her not to forget he was covered in the life force of others. How could she be a bride to him, seeing him as she did?

There was a strange sparkle in the dark depths of his gaze, as if he were laughing. But then she looked at his grim mouth, hard jaw, and the arrogant tilt of his head. As if laughing were beneath him. As if the light of humor had never touched him. What must it feel like to never laugh? Never feel cause to? No, he definitely wasn't laughing at her.

"Are you no longer afraid of me, then?" He raised an eyebrow. His fluent French was almost too fast for her, but she'd learned the language well in the last few years.

"I surmise you could kill me whether I were standing or sitting." Her fear was palpable, so why should she lie? Her trembling, halting voice would have betrayed her regardless.

"Then it's just a matter of how you want to die. A coward or a warrior." He stepped closer, his expression inscrutable. Did that mean he planned to kill her? She swallowed thickly, her stomach roiling and twisting. Her shaking hands tangled in her skirts, seeking even their flimsy support. His hand rose and, for an all too brief moment, was suspended between them.

She couldn't help it, or stop it, though she tried. She flinched and her gaze fell to the floor, waiting eternities for death or absolution. But he continued toward her as if nothing had changed. He grasped a strand of her hair from her face and pulled it away.

Lightly, he tucked it behind her ear. She trembled. His touch was warm and gentle. But he was Norman. Some became rough after a moment of gentleness. She'd seen them. And only a few had even bothered with that single moment.

He towered over her, stealing her breath with his sheer size. She could feel his presence encompass her, his strength hold her, an almost physical presence demanding to be noticed.

But his gentleness wasn't finished yet. His hand fitted to her cheek. And he stood there, waiting. For what, she couldn't guess. She could feel herself sway, but it was as if his hand were an anchor, holding her in place. She raised her gaze and met his again. What did he want?

His finger trailed ever so slightly over her skin, then further, down her neck. She'd never known it was so sensitive. She shivered, her flesh prickling beneath the wool. His hypnotic eyes held hers, daring her to continue her courage. What game did he play?

Raising his hand to her cheek again, he brushed his thumb along the curve, much rougher and harder than her own touch and all the more gentle for the difference. Her chest rose and fell, too full then too empty as she held her breath, then gasped for air. His thumb followed her cheekbone to the corner of her lips, barely touching her. Her lip trembled against the feather-light caress. He traced over it slowly before trailing all his fingers over her chin and down her neck, stopping for one forever-heartbeat on her pulse, then moving on.

Over the curve of her shoulder, down her trembling arm, even through the sleeve she felt his heat without absorbing any of it and she shook more. His fingers curved around her hand, barely touching, but constricting nonetheless. He pulled his palm away so only the tips of his fingers touched hers. He entwined their fingertips lightly and pulled away, bringing her hand with his.

Her heart beat hard and her mouth dried. Uncertainty clawed at her until she didn't know if she should hold very still or run.

He pulled until her arm was outstretched and then he stepped back. When he tugged, she was forced to step with him. He took another, and another, until they stood before the fire. He knelt before her, his knees bending, his armor chinking. He'd been so tall. Now, she looked down on him, taller, more in control.

Except, she wasn't. Not really. He controlled her. With his eyes, with the very tips of his fingers. He continued to pull until she almost fell over him. The silvery-grey chain of the hauberk pressed through her skirts, against her skin, hard and cold with just an edge of violence.

He unbuckled the leather straps that held the lamellar in place and lifted the heavy chain mail shirt as high around his broad chest as he could, then he waited, staring at her. Hesitantly, she reached for his armor and pulled it over his head, struggling under the weight. The strength it took to walk wearing this armor, let alone ride into battle with it, was fearsome. She laid it carefully in the corner, amazed he could wear such a heavy garment as simply as she wore her shift.

When she returned to him, he sat on the one chair before the fire, his long legs stretching before him. For an instant, she had the impression fatigue weighed down his entire body, calling her to nurture him, care for him, protect him at sunset as he protected them while the sun traversed the sky. The fire snapped beside her, heating her chilled flesh as she knelt before him and removed his boots.

When she finished, she looked up, into his intense gaze. Oh how gullible she was, to imagine, even for an instant, that this man needed care and protection. He was not the defender, he was the conqueror. Pursing her lips, she placed the boots beside the pile of his armor and waited, back turned, as he removed the rest of his armor himself.

He placed the metal leggings on the pile at her side before hooking a finger to hers and pulling her to the hearth. "Are you so helpless you cannot seek the fire even when you sorely need its warmth?"

She translated his husky words. French words that sounded so beautiful until she understood what he said. Her eyes fell from his, looking at the red and gold flames. Everything seemed marked by him, by his presence, but, even in his absence she hadn't sat before the fire. For some reason, she had felt restricted.

"None of this is mine." She raised her eyes as far as his clenched jaw, shrugging awkwardly. He wouldn't understand her inadequate answer. She barely did.

His hand rose again and she strained not to flinch as his hand curved around her arm, pulling her closer to him.

"The fire is yours," he said gruffly. His other arm came around her, but tentatively, as if he were unused to this intimacy. She raised one hand to his heart, curving slightly against him, yet maintaining a slight distance.

His chest was broad, muscular. His heart beat against her palm. She could barely breathe through the heat that suddenly surrounded her, between the fire's blaze and the slow burn of his arms. His arms encircled her waist, pulling her closer and eliminating any distance between them. Toasty warmth soaked through her chilled skin until she barely remembered what being cold felt like. She raised her gaze, confusion likely painted on her face, it was so strong. He looked into her eyes and she again wondered if he was laughing at her.

"I remember, when I was young, my father held my mother like this."

Her eyes widened. He looked away, into the fire. Her glance traced his hard jaw where a small muscle flexed. He breathed deep and regular. After a moment, her neck hurt and her position was too awkward. She tentatively laid her head against his chest, staring into the red and yellow blaze instead.

She couldn't quite relax. She'd never lain against a person before. But he was so big. And warm. Like when she woke up, snuggled in blankets in the middle of the bed on a cold winter morning. He was warm like that. And his hardness wasn't too hard. It supported her. He supported her.

The fire crackled and spit. The flames flickered, twitching the shadows above them. The blood faded more, only a slight red haze coating him. But she could still see it, still remember when it was bright and thick. She still knew the condition of his soul and she could not relax.

"You have parents?" She hadn't meant to ask. Not out loud, anyway. He raised his hand and she wished more than ever that she hadn't said a word. Would he hit her for such an audacious question that sounded like an insult?

"Had." He brushed her hair from her shoulders, loosening its fall against her back. She exhaled a shaky breath, fighting empathy.

"Me too," she whispered against him.

His hand rose and covered hers against his heart.

The darkness outside was total, now. Isolating them in the tower, away from the battles, away from the villagers, away from his men. Just the two of them, standing before a fire at the end of a very long, very fraught day. Trusting him, relaxing with him was a temptation she fought. She couldn't entirely eliminate her vision of blood on him, or her fear of him because of her vision and the rumors it seemed to prove true. She had to keep them fresh in her mind as the warning they were.

In deep thought, she started to relax against him, letting his weight support hers. Almost immediately, she realized what she was doing and stiffened, pulling away a little.

"Am I not ridding you of your fear after all?" he whispered, his voice deep and rumbling. She could feel it echo through his chest.

"Are you going to hurt me?" Her voice cracked. She had to know.

"Yes." No apology. No explanation. That simple affirmative scared her more than any vision ever had.

Softer, more tentative, she looked up at him, "Are you going to kill me?"

He smiled.

His was a dangerous sort of smile. The kind that didn't ease her fears or invite her to share the humor. Kynedrithe waited, hoping there was more of an answer coming. But all was silent. Her hands nervously twisted the material of his tunic. Her eyes widened. The moment stretched until small shudders rippled through her. What did his smile mean? That he would kill her? That he wouldn't have to, others would for him?

What did it mean? Her mind screeched. Her heart sped and her hands clenched. When she could stand it no longer, she pulled away from him entirely. He watched her with his strange dark gaze, similar to when he'd first entered the room. Judging, calculating.

No pity. No compassion. Instead he leaned back, relaxed, his gaze fixed on her like a curious predator waiting to see which way the prey would run.

It was a challenge. Like when she'd hidden beside the chest. He hadn't commanded her to come out, but had stood there until she'd chosen to either continue to cower or face him. And he'd approved when she'd faced him. And he'd commented, "Then it just depends how you choose to die. A coward or a warrior."

Was he was right? What would come would come. Did it just depend on how she chose to handle it? A coward or a warrior? She'd always wanted to be a warrior.

She raised her chin, holding it firm against her trembling. "Have you no answer for me?"

His grin crooked at the side. "How could I wish to kill someone so beautiful and brave?"

She narrowed her eyes. A spark of anger gave her strength. "Do not mock me, my lord. We both know I'm neither. I just wish to know the answer to my question. And that was no answer."

His grin flattened, but not into a frown. He simply met her gaze with all the seriousness the situation called for. "What do you think?"

"I think I will die tonight." She widened her eyes against the fear, praying she was wrong.

He nodded. "Then you will die."

Chapter 5

Her entire body stopped working for one ice-cold instant, then she ran across the room to the door, wishing she could escape the tower altogether. But there were servants somewhere on the other side of that door and they would stop her, if her husband didn't reach her before she'd even opened the door. She looked around the room, darting her eyes from the darkened window to the sword by the fireplace. She'd reach neither before he could stop her. She braced with the solid wood at her back.

Warrior. She wanted to die a warrior. She firmed her jaw and met his gaze again. "So you will kill me. It's true, then. Do you have your ritual planned?"

He chuckled. Her firm jaw became more like clenched teeth. Did warriors have shaky knees? She locked them in place before they betrayed her more completely than her quavering voice had.

"There is only one ritual planned for this night. But I think you'll find the altar more comfortable than the one you're envisioning." He glanced to the bed.

She followed his gaze. The curtains were pulled back, displaying piles of furs and pillows. The altar where she would sacrifice her virginity. Maredudd had told her what it would be like. How painful and shaming it was. How could she face it?

When she looked toward him again, he was less than an arm's length away. She shrieked, spun, and fumbled with the door.

He placed an arm against the door and stepped closer until he was pressed along her back. His sheer size now terrified, instead of comforting, her. She disappeared against him. He heated her from back to front as he held her to the door with his body. She pressed her left cheek to the rough wood and closed her eyes breathing deep, struggling to hold the panic at bay.

He didn't move. Merely stood behind her and prevented her escape, imprisoning her securely against the door. Her heart fluttered at the trap. He planned to take her, make her his. If she couldn't bear it for one night, there was no way she could bear it for a lifetime. His heat blazed through her, until her trembling lessened.

They were married. Her vision told her what kind of man he was. But what kind of husband would he be? Could she live with a warrior bathed in blood if he continued to be gentle with her? But like all women, she didn't really have options. She'd been given to him and her only choice now was to make the best of it.

Coward or warrior. The never-ending decision. She wouldn't know if she could bear what would come until she calmed herself enough to face the night. Face her husband. Possibly face her death. Did she want to die against a door? No. That was not the action of a warrior.

Of course, a warrior fought physically. There was no way she could do that with him. He'd hurt her if she did. Neither did she want blood on her hands, but to have a warrior's strength, a warrior's bravery, that she wanted. As her heart slowed to a normal pace, her shivering abated.

He moved as if he'd waited for this moment. His hands encircled her waist, firm and unyielding, but not painful. The outline of each finger burned through her tunic. His embrace was possessive, challenging. She was captured, held as surely as any prey.

Instead of devouring her like a coarse, hungry beast as she

half-expected, his hands slid up, bracing her back with rough fingers she was well aware were unused to gentility. Prickles sprang over her spine at the intimate touch. His fingers pressed into the muscles, grasping and holding until they relaxed, slowly moving to the base of her spine, then massaging up, his touch soothing her until she was no longer cold. No longer shivering and weak, but hot and strong, the challenge breathing hope and defiance into her heart. *Anything,* his touch said, *but this sniveling fear.*

She didn't want to feel anything at his touch. She wanted to be calm, a cold-eyed warrior, strong and brave. Instead, his touch felt like dark magic that made blood rush through her in an entirely different way. Backwards, it seemed. Draining her, but without weakening her as her fear had done.

She trembled as his hands moved to her shoulders, then down, trailing over her arms. He pressed her fingers to the wood of the door, covering them until they disappeared beneath his larger hands. He was swallowing her until there would be nothing left of her. But then his left hand, the one she couldn't see, began to move again. Firm pressure from her hand, to her elbow, up to her shoulder, under her hair. His hand gripped her head, roughly massaging, his fingers threading through her hair.

She was losing her breath again. She felt his size, his strength, his control over her. When his hot breath brushed against her ear, she shivered.

He whispered, "This truly will not be so horrible," and his left hand gentled in her hair. His right thumb stroked over her hand. "Where's my warrior?"

She closed her eyes again, willing away the trembles his deep voice in her ear caused. Pressure built inside her. Was it tears or screams? She wasn't quite sure. There might even be laughter in the mix.

"Do you really need the words?" He sighed, his breath brushing her ear harder. His chest rose and fell against her back until she almost swore his heartbeat had become hers. "Will you believe them?"

She stayed silent, but a small stream of tears escaped her closed eyes.

He rested his cheek next to hers, the wetness covering them

both. His whiskers, just beginning to push through his skin and especially rough, scraped her chin. Although the abrasion was an unintentional harm, it emphasized his presence and the hundreds of small ways he could hurt her. No words escaped her lips.

He tugged through her hair, gently easing his hand against her head, caressing as if to soothe her. He sighed again and she could feel the vibration of it against her lips. "No harm will ever come to you by my hands. No harm at all, from anyone, if there is strength in me to prevent it."

She dredged her voice from deep inside and managed a whisper. "But you said I would die tonight."

"Any warrior facing battle with the thought that he will die—will."

Slowly, his words penetrated through her mind. What he'd said. What he'd meant. It lessened her fear slightly. Enough to breathe. Enough to open her eyes.

"Will you face me, little warrior?"

"I'm afraid."

"So much terror. I can feel it trembling through you. Your body is shaking against mine. Is there no way it can end?" His voice was a plea, a seduction.

She closed her eyes, gulping in air. Everything confused her—the things he said, what her vision meant. But he'd been gentle with her, gentler than she'd thought he could be. Blood graced his sword and the hands that now held hers. Which was truth? Both, probably, in the strange, contradictory way only men knew.

Shhhrriip. Metal slid against leather, a deadly glide. The sound reached her and she stiffened, waiting. What did he intend now? His hand eased between her and the door, pulling her firmly against him. A solid weight pressed against her breast and she looked down. His dagger rested between her breasts, the material beginning to split at the slight pressure. She whimpered and leaned away from the blade, further into him and his unyielding strength.

His right hand still held hers against the door. Her left gripped the door with no urging. He'd promised! She'd scream if she could breathe, but then his right hand curled, grasping hers and lowering it to curl her fingers around the blade's hilt, one by one. Then his hands left the dagger dangerously in her care.

She gulped in air and blinked away tears. Here it was again. Her chance to be brave. A warrior. Her hand fluttered against his and pulled free with no resistance from him. Slowly, she turned. His fingers slid from hers and his hands came to her waist. She leaned against the door and met his gaze.

Concern, tenderness, and a certain resolve swirled in his gaze.

"I'd never want to end the life of someone so beautiful." He didn't smile. He lifted one hand and brushed her hair from her face.

"But you said you were going to hurt me."

"It can't be helped. It is what happens the first time a man and woman are together."

"Then I'll bleed." Would she be left in a puddle of tears, trying to wash the blood away?

"You'll bleed," he agreed. "But we will try to keep it from being too terrible."

She looked deep into his eyes, then laid her head back on the door and stared into the fire. What about the rest? The vision? The rumors? Did he kill for pleasure? Her gaze caught on the sword again. She could see the grooves where the blood of his victims would have run in tiny streams down the blade.

Blood covering him, staining him. He'd been free to rape and pillage her from the moment he'd married her; before, even. Instead, he'd been gentle, patient with her terrors.

His fingers delved beneath her hair at the nape of her neck. Light, barely touching.

"Why do you look at me as if I'm a demon, here for your soul? What do you see when your eyes are upon me?" His lips curved, as if he were attempting humor, but his eyes were serious, watchful.

Kynedrithe looked down, at his throat, at his chest, anywhere but his eyes. How could he not already know? The villagers, but no, they'd not risk their own lives by telling their lord he had a witch bride. Yet lying had never been a skill for her, she had to tell him.

"What do you see?" His voice was still soft, yet a demanding edge had crept in. It commanded the truth, compelled her to answer.

She raised her eyes to his, watchful of his reaction. "Blood."

He inhaled sharply, his eyes widening. Disbelief filled his voice. "You see blood when you look at me?"

He almost seemed pained at the thought, as though nothing she could have said would have hurt him more. Her hand clenched the dagger to her chest, protection that didn't protect. He raised her chin. She opened her eyes and met his gaze again.

He held his hand before her, drawing her attention to the appendage. "Do you see blood?"

She swallowed, tense with uncertainty. "It's fading, now. But at first . . ." Her eyes met his again. "At first it was vivid."

He stilled, his eyes searching hers. Secrets surrounded him, like shadows, gathering and concealing. When he spoke, his words were slow, cautious.

"I do not enjoy taking a life." He took her left hand and held it against his chest. He caressed the tops of her fingers and seemed to study the small veins running along her hand. "That is simply the cost of battle."

Her throat closed and she swallowed several times. "Am I in danger, then?"

"Never from me." His voice was whisper soft.

She stared into his eyes and trembled. Dare she believe him? Was the blood paler now because she was beginning to see past it or because she was choosing to ignore her vision?

"I will not hurt you."

"Because I am your wife?" What to believe? What to feel? Indecision twisted her stomach.

"And for many other reasons. You can trust me. I will not lie to you." He lowered his head closer to hers, hesitated, looking into her eyes, then continued until his lips softly brushed hers.

Her hand tightened around the dagger—flimsy and useless against him, but the sharp blade gave her a small bit of comfort. She held it against his chest, point up. He continued as if the blade meant less than nothing, his lips curving into hers, pressing, coaxing.

She fell into his caress, closing her eyes and willing fear to

drift away and allow her some measure of peace. His kiss was
gentle and light. She could learn to enjoy this, with him.
Slowly, he pulled away, and her eyes opened and focused on
his watchful gaze.

"Do you still see the blood?"

A haze, light and insubstantial. But it was still there. "I do,"
she whispered reluctantly.

His face hardened into grim lines. This was the man she'd
married, gentle and seductive but a warrior, a knight, a conqueror. Like many of the men she'd known all her life, but still
different. Another country, another language, the killer of
those same men she'd known forever. The murderer of those
women she'd never met.

Her heart pounded and her breath choked her, the fear that
had never quite left roared to life again. He gazed into her soul
with his dark, piercing eyes, neither promising nor beseeching. Instead, another dare, another challenge.

"The evidence is quite damning." The chill in his tone, the
bleak acceptance in his eyes tore her heart.

She nodded shakily.

"I accept what I am. The things I've done. The lives I've
taken." His voice was ruthless, a blunt-edged weapon that
pummeled and brutalized.

The trembling began again in her arms and her shoulders.

"The question is, can you?" His lips pressed tight, waiting
for her answer, her absolution.

Could she? Could she really hold him to a different stan-
dard than every other man she knew? If only she couldn't see
the blood.

"Are you worried I will stain you with it?" His accusation
was spoken low and harsh. She had angered him, finally. He
leaned closer again, his lips a breath from hers. "I have killed,
Kynedrithe. And I will kill again."

The clearest truth, with no doubt in his mind or heart.

She jerked, the dagger slicing through his shirt. Blood welled
immediately, running down the blade, dripping on her hand.

He hissed, backing away slightly.

Harming him had never been her intention. She wanted to
apologize, but the words would not come. She whimpered.
He'd surely kill her now. She shoved past him and sought an

easier death. Kynedrithe ran, rushing for the window and the velvety dark sky beyond it. She wasn't a warrior. She wasn't even a witch. Just a powerless woman afraid of everything around her, of everything others could see—and especially of the things they could not.

He moved, faster than she could have imagined, grasping her waist and spinning her behind him until he was standing between her and the window, blocking her escape. She wavered, grasping for balance and brought the blade up. He blocked the window, and escape, as surely as any wall. She could run for the door, but it would be futile.

So instead, she faced him, the blade raised, her breath thundering through her chest. Warm and wet, his blood dripped from the blade to her hand. Dear God, had she truly cut him so deep? The dangerous blade did nothing for her. It didn't protect, it only hurt. She tightened her grip on it anyway and waited, trembling, certain he wouldn't kill her since he'd saved her, but all too aware of the present danger.

Fury visibly welled in him—the words didn't even need to be spoken aloud. No matter what happened between them, she would live. He would not allow her to seek the escape of death. He towered over her, forcing her to tilt her head back to stare into his eyes. Accept his will.

They could fight. She could defend herself, even with a weapon. But she would not be allowed to run from him. She would not be allowed to end her life. Kynedrithe lowered her gaze, submissive. What would happen would happen and she had no fight left.

Chapter 6

At her apparent acceptance of the situation, Dreux nodded and eased back on his heels. Fury tied his throat as it never had—the combination of terror and anger choked him. She'd come so close to reaching the window before him, choosing death over trusting him. He was disappointed. He shouldn't be. It was natural and expected, yet it hurt.

She was nothing to him, just a woman he'd married to please his king—but the memory of his parents holding each other before a warm fire emerged in his mind as it often did. A love like theirs was all he'd ever wanted from a marriage.

He'd thought she was calming. He'd been wrong. Her white face, wide eyes, and shaking hands gave testament to her fear. His chest stung where she'd cut him.

His first instinct was to wrestle the dirk back from her and force her compliance. But he halted himself—he didn't want to fight her, or frighten her more than she already was. And he could not deny the beauty that shone in her through her fear.

The midnight of her eyes, blazing against her pale skin, her gold hair curling wildly around her shoulders, and her hand, small and delicate, clenching the dagger, all of it was beautiful to him.

But it wasn't only her physical form that entranced him. It was also the courage that emanated from each trembling inch of her, the bravery that tightened her grip on the dirk even as she must have heard her mind scream that she was about to die. Only warriors could hear that scream and stand firm against all odds. He knew from experience.

No longer a weak, shivering mass hiding in the corner, she stood as tall as she could, taller than her size, in the center of the room, prepared to defend herself.

Yes, he could enjoy marriage to such a woman.

He stared into her eyes, waiting for her movement. She seemed even more terrified than she had when he'd entered the room. The blade shook as if she weren't certain what to do now that she held him. But he could see that she did not want to die, which she must know would happen if she killed him. His men would see to it.

In addition to the will to live, he now saw the *passion* to live, her passion to defend herself. Her passion to feel—love, hate, loyalty, anger, fear, and desire all were there in the blue of her eyes. He could see it and he wanted it. He wanted all of her—but the only way to get it was for her to give him herself.

So he waited, searching her eyes. She might try to kill him, but he was willing to wager she wouldn't. Wager for the promise of passion. She glanced away, then jerked her gaze to his, as if remembering she shouldn't let him out of her sight. Heartbeats passed the time, their breaths the only sound in the room.

"I've told you, I won't hurt you."

"Words. Words! They're all words. Why should yours be the ones I trust? You've the least proof of all." Her voice quavered in the darkening room. She glanced around, at him, at the bed, at the fire and the shadows it created, then back to him, gripping the dagger even tighter.

"Why did you agree to marry me?" he demanded.

KYNEDRITHE BACKED AWAY, her chest rising and falling rapidly. Tears prickled her eyes. Why ask that most damning question above all others? Nothing good could come from her answer.

"Believing what you do, why would you marry such a man without even trying to fight it?" His eyes narrowed on her face. His lips thinned. "Of course. You were the sacrifice."

She'd been born to her position, but God had chosen wrong. She shouldn't have been the one in this room. She couldn't even pacify him for one night, let alone a lifetime. She wasn't brave. She wasn't strong. She wasn't the bride, the lady, he or the village needed.

"And a poor one I am."

"No. Never that." His eyes darkened. Sadness? His lips quirked, as if only half his mouth could overcome his disappointment long enough to respond to the command to smile.

But then, suddenly he stood straighter, shoulders back. His face hardened, his eyes bare of expression. His hands rose to his tunic, lifting it over his head. Her eyes widened, tears drying as she stared in horrified fascination.

No more words. This was it. His arms moved and his tunic rose, up, up, over his head, off his arms. He tossed it to the side and stood straight before her. Broad shoulders with bulging ropes of muscle for arms. The strength there intimidated; the skill with a sword, etched into each vein and sinew, terrified. He seemed larger with each patch of skin exposed.

Sun-darkened skin covered with curling black hairs filled her vision until her gaze met his once more. This was it. The moment she'd dreaded since he'd announced their wedding. Since she'd been brought alone to this room, to wait. She needed more time. *Not yet, please, not yet.* She shook her head, a slight moan slipping past her throat.

"Hush. You will be fine," he whispered.

His broad chest narrowed into firm, muscled hips that surely had to be strong just to support his upper torso. Above the ridges of his ribs, hidden in the depths of dark, curling hair, were two flat, copper nipples. She swallowed, her throat dry. Were they as sensitive as hers? She couldn't help but wonder, astonished that anything so potentially sensitive could inhabit a body so incredibly tough.

Then his hands moved to the ties at his waist. Her breath hitched and her startled gaze flew to his eyes. His head tilted again, and he stilled, waiting, watching her watch him. His chest rose with a deep breath. For a moment she was distracted by his body, but she forced her attention back to his eyes. What was he doing? Drawing this out? Trying to terrify her more? Wasn't she scared enough?

No. She needed to be honest with herself. She wasn't terrified for her life anymore. There was actually very little fear left. Maybe apprehension. Worry. Dread. But there was also . . . anticipation. Curiosity. She licked her lips, trying to gather her thoughts. Then she read the look in his eyes. Challenge. Did she have the courage to face what this night would bring?

No. She didn't have the courage. She couldn't face this. Didn't deserve this.

Her mind froze at the thought. She didn't deserve to marry a murderer, or to live in terror, but if he wasn't really the enemy—if he was, in fact, the gentle husband of the past few hours—did she deserve him then?

Not if she was a coward. Not if she was too afraid to be a woman. That was what he proposed. Making her a woman, as fully as any married woman she'd ever met. She couldn't continue to hide behind fear. She needed to earn the tender husband.

He was gentle. He hadn't forced her. Instead, her demon spouse had seduced her soul. She shivered, swallowed, her throat thick, and watched as small drops of blood eased from the shallow wound on his chest and slid, down to his small, dark navel. Then farther.

His fingers tangled in the ties of his braies, then began to tug them down his hips. Her gaze jerked to his. To her embarrassment, the heat spreading through her had little to do with terror. And he knew. She could see it, behind the flames in his eyes. His lips quirked again—amused by her. Irritation welled inside her.

He leaned against the window frame as he lowered and rid himself of his braies. Her gaze remained fixed firmly to his eyes. She refused to look down. Her face burned and she knew her cheeks were as red as a ripe apple. Then he started forward and she backed away, startled and skittish. The bed behind her stopped her flight. She arched away from it, refusing to give in so easily.

He strode forward, each step silent and more terrifying for

it. But instead of coming toward her, he moved to the side, just slightly, but ready to block her if she went for the window again. She watched him untie the cord that held the bed drapes to the post. The ends dangled threateningly from his hand. She glanced nervously to the window and he was suddenly beside her, so quick, so silent. She jerked back but he only reached for the next post and untied the cord there as well.

He moved, directing her without touching her. At the third post he collected the cord, and walked forward. She backed away until she was pressed to the wall at the head of the bed, with him firmly blocking any escape. He gathered the cord from the fourth post and loomed over her. When he spoke, his voice was low and rumbling.

"For no one else would I do this."

Her eyes widened as he backed away, leaving the bed between her and the window. He stopped by the door and lowered a large wooden beam across it, barricading them inside the room. Preventing anyone from entering—and her from leaving. Her mouth was too dry to swallow.

She stared from the ropes to his face. He stepped forward and she paled, but tightened her grip on the dagger. Then he stepped to the side and away. She sagged against the wall.

Dreux stood before his chair and lowered himself, one heartbeat at a time, watching her watch him. He widened his legs, displaying himself fully. Then he bent over and tied one length of rope around the leg of the chair, and around his ankle, binding them together. Slowly, he did the same to the other foot. Then he leaned back and began tying his left arm to the arm of the chair. It was awkward at first, but when he used his teeth, he managed.

Then he took the fourth length of rope in his right hand and rested it on the right arm of his chair. She was still on guard. She stared with wide, open eyes. At the rope, then the dagger, then into his eyes.

The power was more fully in her hands than it ever would be again. It left him entirely too vulnerable. A man of war such as him hated any action that left him open to attack. Why was he doing this?

Dreux's dark eyes held hers, tension building. Her stomach churned, her back straightened, her arms tensed, her legs flexed. She could run away. What could he do to her? He was naked and tied to a chair. Except for one hand. That one hand could free him and nothing would be any different than when she'd first run to the window.

"Come, my warrior. Show me your bravery."

"I have none, my lord." She believed it to the bottom of her soul.

"That I do not believe. Come."

She held the dagger still, and his sword was by the fireplace. He was completely at her mercy. Had he no fear? She met his gaze again. It was challenging, waiting. Her gaze fell to the cord in his hand.

"You will have control," he whispered in temptation.

She shook her head. "It is a deception."

"Are you going to run?" His head tilted to the side, arrogant and challenging. His quirky lips dared her to make a dash for the window, or the door. He could still stop her and they both knew it. "Or . . ." He drew out the one word, teasing, inspiring. "Will you finish and tie my arm? Will you come closer and make an attempt at trusting me as I'm willing to trust you?"

She eyed the distance between them. Only a step or two, then she would tie his last free hand and, for a time at least, have no reason to fear. Could she do this? No—no more would she question herself. It was time to move. Go to him, run from him, or—she glanced at the window—run from life.

Kynedrithe stepped toward him, slow, but not hesitant. She tied his hand. This night was hers now.

"What do I do?" she asked, her voice barely a whisper.

"Kiss me."

October 7, 2004—Spokane, WA

LIGHT PIERCED HER eyelids, awakening Kalyss to more than just one ache. Her eyes were gritty and swollen. Her side ached from the hard concrete beneath her and she was chilled to her bones from the floor and thin sheet. But, she was *alive*.

"Alex," she sighed, her eyes filling with tears.

Kalyss struggled upright, pulling the sheet around her and

leaning back against something hard. The statue, she remembered, and blinked the tears back.

She stared blankly around the dusty storage room, vaguely taking in the piles of wooden furniture and a small black bag, likely forgotten by some student who worked here.

Kalyss leaned her head back and stared at the play of light on the ceiling. There was movement above her head, but it seemed normal sounds. The footsteps last night must have been a guard, since the redhead hadn't burst in with his knife while she slept. Now she just had to figure out what to do. Kalyss sighed. There were stories of people who woke up the morning after a tragic event and felt fine until the memories came rushing back, but she didn't have that dubious mercy because hers had never left.

She hadn't been blessed with a deep, dreamless sleep, either. Instead, her mind had tortured her with nameless fears. So terrified and for what? A dream that wasn't true.

She couldn't hide from her troubles, even in fiction.

Strangely, she could remember every moment, from hiding, huddled in terror, to a tied man's challenge: "Kiss me."

Kalyss's dreams weren't usually quite so vivid and detailed—they were usually a jumble of thoughts and feelings that passed quickly, similar to last night's vision: rushed, blurred, a race from beginning to end without obvious logic. But even last night's vision had held more detail than usual. She'd never pulled a name from one before, let alone an entire map. Yet, this dream beat them all in detail. It had felt as if she'd lived it, despite her different name. It was as real and tangible as waking up in the storage room of a church, wrapped in a sheet.

Damn, was that dream prophetic or what? Right down to the nitty gritty of her situation. What were her options? Hide, run, or face her fears, just like in her dream.

She could hide forever in this storeroom, until she starved or froze to death—but that would mean sleeping on this floor again. Kalyss sighed and shifted, stretching her back.

She could run. With no clue of how far or how long, and no knowledge of the man she ran from or what he'd do to find her.

Maybe he was Melanie's husband. Maybe he'd learned about the self-defense lessons she'd secretly taken from Kalyss in preparation for leaving him. Kalyss had taken one look at the woman's black eye and bruised wrist and taken Melanie under her wing. How could she not? Her husband's involvement would explain the attack on Alex, especially if it had been done in one of his rages.

But Melanie had said he had black hair and black eyes and a dark temper that could scare the devil. This guy was more of a tall, handsome leprechaun with an evil, mischievous nature. Kalyss doubted he'd been hired to hurt her by Melanie's husband.

Sam had always done his own work or she'd suspect him. He was still in jail for assault and battery with intent to kill, and he'd likely come for her himself once he was out.

Who was her attacker, then? Why kill Alex and Geoffrey? Why attempt to kill her? She'd dismissed his nonsensical words, focusing on his threatening actions, so all she remembered was he'd made no sense. And she'd had to run.

How had she found the right car? The key to this room? Why did she know Geoffrey's full name?

She'd "read" memories from a few people before, but last night was the first time she'd pulled a name from one. Maybe because in the past she'd always known the players in her visions. Like when Sam came home after screwing his secretary. She'd only seen a hazy gloss over lust-flushed skin and ripping clothes and heard the grunting, moaning, and smacking atop the mahogany finish of his desk. It had seemed a pretty clear vision at the time, but it had been downright vague compared to last night.

She'd "read" Geoffrey's name on his driver's license. Seen his wild rush from her place to St. John's Cathedral. Watched how he'd used his keys . . . His memory had been so informative she couldn't have planned a better one.

For one second, Kalyss froze. How could Geoffrey know about her visions, let alone plan one for her? Only Alex knew about her visions. Sam had always thought she smelled his secretary's perfume on him.

Yet, even the murderer said she'd soon remember him.

For a fleeting instant, she could imagine Alex planning this elaborate hoax, and she grinned. That would mean he still lived.

No. Her smile died. There was no way to fake the empty darkness in Geoffrey's eyes as he'd slumped to the ground. The hoax theory was just wishful thinking.

Her eyes burned and she closed them. Her mind spun with thoughts, impressions, memories, snippets of conversations, visions, and dreams. She couldn't make sense of it. Couldn't find the logic. She was almost dizzy with information, but none of it fit.

She only knew she couldn't hide and she couldn't run. Not only could it make things worse, but the truth was that she didn't want to. She owed it to Alex and herself. Even to Geoffrey.

She'd fought too long, too hard, with Alex right beside her, to become a stronger, braver person—and Geoffrey had died trying to save that new Kalyss. Running and hiding now would be a slap to their sacrifice.

Which was not to say she should go right back to the madman and try to take him on. He'd almost kicked her ass. She'd barely held him off. Indeed, in the end, he'd held her to the wall, pinned and at his mercy.

So, no hiding. No running. And no rushing back. Too bad her apartment was an extension over the dojo. Too bad she had reason to regret what had previously been a convenience. She pushed to her feet, groaning, and dusted off her pants. No more concrete floors, either.

Call the cops? What if they suspected her? She had disappeared from the scene of the crime. She'd run. Hidden. Trespassed. Obviously for no reason, because there was no way a simple door would've stopped the evil leprechaun man. Should she explain that she'd run, locked herself in a church, and cried herself to sleep? Or maybe just call anonymously.

What she wanted was a change of clothes and a shower. And definitely more sleep. She needed her mind working at its best. She'd wait for the police to find Alex so his parents could be informed and his funeral planned. Her breath hitched.

She closed her eyes, took a deep breath, and readied to face the day. Grabbing the sheet from the floor, she rose and turned to throw it back over the statue. The first thing to do was definitely get out of this church before she got arrested for trespassing and vagrancy.

Kalyss froze, awestruck, staring at the statue she'd leaned against the entire night. She released the sheet and reached for him with one shaking hand, letting the rough stone graze her fingertips.

Chapter 7

The graded granite, its texture barely smooth and seemingly lit with tiny diamonds, rippled with shadows and secrets. The carving of each line and curve was so realistic, it almost seemed he'd move any moment, like a man in statue paint. Rays of sunlight beamed through the basement windows, straight at the statue's eyes, making them sparkle with a mysteriously familiar glint. One ray cruelly exposed a small furrow under his eye, highlighting bits of crystal so they shone like a trail of tears. As if his pain were so great it dug into him, marking him irrevocably.

Why was he in a church? His arms were held out shoulder high, but his fists were clenched, his muscles bunched and straining, fighting his fate with defiant determination. This was not the usual sorrowing figure choosing to make a sacrifice for mankind that Kalyss had seen on many crosses. In fact, there was no cross, no crown of thorns, no holes in his hands and feet—the only thing on his naked form was something obviously not carved.

Over his heart, like a child's art, was one dark-red handprint. The sheet fell from her hand, blanketing her feet, as she placed her other hand over the dark, dry mark. Her lungs seized up, painfully halting her breath. She wanted to cry for him, for his pain—not just cry, but scream and howl, as if his pain were her own.

But then, it probably was her own pain she felt, pounding inside her like a wild storm demanding freedom. Her own loss that shook her hands and weakened her with a grief that could cripple her, though she refused to allow it free, but this man— her left hand palmed his cheek—this handsome statue with his lips forever twisted in rage and horror . . . she could cry for him.

"What artist could bear to make your torment eternal?" She stepped closer, holding his heart with her hand perfectly arranged over the handprint. Tracing his lips with her left thumb, familiarity beat at her mind, refusing to be ignored.

Recognition was like an electric shock, unbalancing her so that she fell into him.

"You're the man of my dreams."

Literally—he was the man she'd dreamed of all night. The man who'd worked so hard to coax his wife's acceptance of him. She searched his stone eyes as though they held all her answers. It had seemed so dark last night, but had she some-how seen him? As a dream, could she have "read" a memory of an artist through his work? Had he forged his fury and agony in every line and groove he'd created? Had she put her-self in the place of his wife in her dream?

Kalyss searched for an artist's signature, but there wasn't one.

Tears burned her eyes. She hadn't cried so much in years. Three years, eleven months and twenty-eight days, to be ex-act. In the hospital, fighting for her life, and alone the few days it took for her to be conscious enough to reach Alex.

Yes, this statue grieved. The artist had created a man caught in the very moment of the most horrific injustice of his life, vowing a revenge that lasted as long as the stone he was made of. Someone had hurt him.

"The worst thing is when the bad guy gets away, huh?" There had to have been a bad guy, considering the betrayal in the stone gaze, and he must have gotten away for the statue to vow vengeance.

The stain beneath her hand was a woman's handprint, just her size, full of yearning, hope, and blackest despair. A desperate plea of anguish and self-sacrifice.

"Well, he won't get away this time. I don't know how I'll fight him, but I will." If not his nemesis, then her own.

She searched his face, foolishly looking for acknowledgement in his stone eyes. Some softening in the stone mouth. Maybe for his lips to settle in peace and his voice, the one in her dream, to whisper again that she was a warrior.

"I will, you know. I am a warrior now and I'll show you." Feeling stupid in the face of his silence, she nevertheless pushed forward and promised, "I won't run."

To mark her vow, she rose on tiptoe and kissed him.

Kissing stone was just like she'd expected: hard, gritty, and entirely one-sided. Her lips covered his, conforming to them for one brief moment, her eyes closed against the bright room and ridiculous actions that made sense only in her heart.

For some reason, her left hand suddenly *needed* to curl around the back of his neck and her right *needed* to guard his heart. She needed to rise to her toes and form her lips to his and hold him, promising anything to take away his pain.

What was she doing? Kissing a statue in the basement of a church, expecting some sort of response from him—she was going crazy.

She started back, releasing the dream—but something changed. His lips blazed against her lips, scorching hotter than the flames of a bonfire. Hard granite gave way to satin, pliant and seductive. Dry resistance gave way to wet, hot welcome and she sank into it.

Until this moment, Kalyss had not realized a kiss could be this passionate, this full of desire—this swollen with longing. Demanding, full of a desperate need, the kiss branded every inch of her. After everything she'd suffered, if this was insanity, she'd take it.

Strength surrounded her, trapping her against a hard body that felt only slightly softer than the stone. She couldn't bear the thought of opening her eyes and finding that this passion was all in her imagination, that she'd finally found the feeling she'd dreamed of for so long only for it to exist solely in her own mind. But she had to.

She opened her eyes. Sparkling bright stone inexplicably turned a dark tan, the diamonds or crystals, or whatever they were that shone inside the stone, slowly absorbed into his skin, until it looked real and vibrant. Ready to blink away the illusion, she closed her eyes and forgot to open them as she fell into another impossible kiss that might actually be real.

He devoured her, and she let him. Encouraged him. He clenched his fists in her hair until she was trapped against him, until she ached to meet his every demand. He thirsted, he hungered, and she'd never been needed this way—it was addicting, a salve to every doubt she'd ever had about herself.

An eternity of lips and tongue, licking and rubbing had passed and she couldn't breathe. Once again, she was the woman in her dream, standing before an intimidating, naked man, fully clothed and facing a challenge.

"I missed you." His voice was husky, unused. Yet it sent chills through her.

Her heart stopped painfully, for one long second. She'd sensed it coming, but seeing him alive, staring back at her, a man instead of a statue, shocked her. She stepped back with slow deliberation. His arms tightened, resisting her retreat, before reluctantly releasing her.

DREUX ALLOWED HER retreat, allowed the silk of her hair to slide through his fingers. He needed to feel her, craved her touch so much he trembled from it. Trembled from everything he could feel now. The sun's touch on his skin—even air nearly overloaded his senses. But neither the sun, nor the air could affect him as her lips on his did.

A violent, dark energy swirled in him, demanding release. Captive for so long, now he was free and she stood before him. Alive. Breathing and moving. She'd spoken to him, slept at his feet the long night before. And now nothing held him from claiming her.

Her skin, her smell. Her warm body and soft heart. All his. His vision swirled, colors running together until he blinked for the first time in centuries. He reached for her, swift and determined, nearly grabbing her arms and pulling her to him again.

But she stepped out of reach with a slight, agile movement,

equally determined not to be caught. Her tears from the night still echoed in his ears, still stained her cheeks with red and swollen streaks.

He fought the need churning his gut and clouding his mind. He'd won her from fear once before; he'd do it again. How could he not? She was his survival.

She will not know you. Geoffrey's voice echoed in his ears. *She will not understand any of this at first.* Dreux knew this. Had prepared for this moment, if only in his mind.

Desperate as he'd ever been, he closed his fists and pulled away from the dusty cellar, the clouded glass windows, and the woman he loved but could not hold. Away from the black insanity that terrified him. Back to that deeper calm he'd learned to manifest inside himself.

He loved this woman. He had to show her.

I MISSED YOU.

"How could you miss me when you don't know me?" That seemed the most obvious question to Kalyss. Sometimes obvious and simple was best when the world made no sense, when down was up and fainting wouldn't conveniently rescue her from the moment. No, she felt very clear-headed. She wouldn't be passing out any time soon.

He smiled gently, his warm eyes loving. From frightening desperation to an equally intense love, his eyes had run the gamut in moments. Darkening, then lightening, now a rich, seductive chocolate. "I know you, Kalyss. Better than you imagine."

He knew her name! She glanced around for the hidden cameras and special effects equipment. This couldn't be real. But she'd felt the heat as he'd come to life in her arms, had seen his skin turn from cold gray to warm tan. Could that be faked? She checked her hands for makeup, but found only dust. She rubbed them against her pants.

He stepped forward again. She braced to flee, but he merely traced along her cheek with one finger. "I've waited for you. Centuries upon centuries, grieving my loss of you."

Her lips stretched in a tremulous smile before falling straight. "I'm not that old."

He stepped closer, all muscled height and naked strength. Callused hands framed her cheeks. She shivered at the slight strokes of his thumbs.

"Old? No. You are still as fresh and vibrant as the moment I first saw you. All your travails could never touch your beautiful spirit."

The sheer adoration in his eyes was humbling. The print above his heart, the dark red stain, now glistened—becoming brighter, wetter, the unmistakable color of fresh blood. She couldn't tear her gaze from the handprint, feeling it draw her in, closer, until she raised her hand and covered it, fitting it perfectly.

Instantly, she was swamped with anguish, falling into a vision faster than ever.

THE STATUE STOOD in front of her, stone and diamonds. Her own hand, covered in blood, reached for him. It was night and the sea roared behind her. Someone screamed, the horrific wail of a woman who's lost, who has suffered.

Kalyss recognized that sound. It was hers.

"I'm sorry," her voice said. "I've tried and tried and failed every time. I'm so sorry."

She flew backward and away from the statue. Farther and farther into darkness.

THE VOICE IN her mind, Kalyss's own voice, echoed in her ears as the man in front of her came back into focus.

"What the hell?" She jerked back. She was insane. A dream man, then a statue, then very real. Certifiable, Grade A lunatic. That's what she was.

She backed away several steps and averted her eyes from the hard, muscled body before her. A lump behind her nearly caused her to trip. Her hands flew out for balance, her back arching and her legs splayed. He reached for her again, but she caught herself before he could touch her. Her trembling body couldn't handle another one of his touches.

"Just stay back." Her hands braced in the air, palms out. Keep the sexy naked man away. Her lips still tingled from his kiss and her body shivered, missing his heat.

"Kalyss—" He stopped when she glared at him. He tilted his head, seeming fascinated by her every move.

She looked down at the black bag she'd noticed earlier, then grabbed it and unzipped the various compartments, frowning as she pawed through bottles and a bathroom kit to yank out underwear, jeans, socks, and a shirt. Thank you, God. She threw the modern garments at him. Another piece in a puzzle that didn't fit.

"Get dressed." She turned to give him privacy, staring through the dusty windows to the sunshine outside. The confusion roiling and bubbling through her was frustrating. Grief mixed with wonder, lust with anger, fear with the indefinable feeling that she held something precious and fragile, true and enduring, and that with one wrong move she could destroy it all.

"Whatever game this is, I . . ." She shook her head.

"It's no game, Kalyss." His clothing rustled, like sheets on a freshly made bed.

"That's not what the red-haired man said." Before he nearly slit her throat. She touched the scrape at the base of her neck. The atmosphere changed so suddenly it chilled her. Hard and cold behind her back. Fury and violence. She swung around, arms angled for defense.

He'd halted, half-dressed, his socks on, his jeans unzipped, and his shirt draping unbuttoned over a powerfully muscled chest. She blinked away her reaction.

"You've seen him?" Intense dark eyes demanded an answer.

"He attacked last night. Killed Alex. Killed Geoffrey. Nearly killed me."

"But you escaped this time." His eyes lit from the inside, awe in his voice. He reacted as if he'd only taken what he wanted from what she'd said.

"Did you hear me?" she snarled. "He killed Alex."

His broad, muscled shoulders bunched with a slight movement. God, Sam was nothing. If this man ever hit her, she'd die. "I don't know Alex, Kalyss, but I *am* sorry for your pain."

He sounded completely sincere. Kalyss straightened, looking around, anywhere but at him. Of course he didn't know Alex. How could he? *This time.* What did that mean? Nothing made sense. *Think,* damnit. "How long were you a statue, anyway?"

He fumbled a bit with the small buttons on his black shirt, nearly misaligning them. Reluctantly, she stretched forward and straightened the sides for him, buttoned a button, and stepped back, leaving him to it. It was better if she didn't touch him. Her head would swirl with visions or he'd take it for a chance to kiss her. Either way, she couldn't handle much more.

Grabbing the bag again, she rifled through the smaller bits inside. More keys, a manila envelope, a wallet. Triumphantly, she whisked it open and stared at the driver's license. "Dreux Williams." She turned, holding it up before her. "Nice picture."

He merely blinked, as if her discovery meant nothing to him.

"Born . . ." She glanced at the ID again. "October 7, 1975. Happy Birthday." She stared at him in challenge.

"No, Kalyss, not born." His voice thickened. "That was the day you died. And I became a statue, nine hundred years before that date."

"Oh, please." She rolled her eyes. "You're some thirty-year-old bodybuilder hired to do this for some reason only an idiot would find funny. And I've had enough."

She threw everything on the floor and stalked to the door, furious, confused. Statues did not come to life with full ID and credit cards. If Alex was behind it, she'd kill him for real. Maybe he thought she needed to find a relationship, but this was not the way. And this definitely was not the man.

She froze and closed her eyes. Alex didn't do this. He was dead. Grief tried to overwhelm her but she fought it back and opened her eyes to the bright glare of day. She had to call the cops. Alex's parents. Plan his funeral. Get her business, and her life, back. She didn't have time for this weird drama.

She grasped the handle and yanked, but the door was locked. Huffing at her own forgetfulness, Kalyss reached for the lock but Dreux's hand covered it. His body pressed against hers, trapping her against the door just like in her dream. She doubted he'd hand her a knife this time.

"What?" Anger tightened every muscle, clenched her jaw. She nearly shook with it. "What do you want from me? I have a screwed-up life to deal with and you're not a part of it."

"Don't you remember me? At all?" He lowered his head to

her shoulder. "Geoffrey warned me you'd forgotten, but I'd hoped you'd remembered at least a little."

"I don't know you. I've never met you. And I've never died." She'd come close, but that was different. This story was insane. Nine hundred years ago?

"Touch me, Kalyss," he whispered. "Read me."

His hands caught hers against the door and all she could remember was the dream. The dream that had kept her warm the entire night as she rested at his feet. Heated by all the tense passion she'd felt in that dream for the man behind her.

His hands traced her arms, hand to shoulder. A tactile reminder of the same touch her dream man had given her. She shivered. How did he know what had happened in that dream?

"It wasn't real. We never married."

He tensed.

"I never tried to jump." She forced certainty into her voice.

His hands clenched around hers. "You terrified me the night you did. The night Geoffrey took you over the edge."

Her throat clogged and she couldn't clear it. She spoke around it. "That is not my handprint on your chest."

He turned her to him, framing her face with his hands and huskily whispered, "Remember me, my love."

Her eyes widened, staring at him, but with the first touch of his lips on hers, they fell closed. Gentle, entreating, he caressed her lips with his, making love to her mouth. Honesty was in his touch. Truth in his embrace.

She did. She remembered him. Dear God, help her, but she couldn't deny it. She didn't understand, couldn't make sense, but she remembered. She melted against him, her hands curling around the lapels of his shirt, and kissed him back. Illogical. Crazy. Mental. They all described her situation, but, strange as it was, being in his arms seemed right.

The sound of footsteps on the floor above separated them, but he still retained hold of her waist. She gasped for calming breaths. "We need to leave."

His chest pumped with the effort to draw in air. His eyes burned with his desire to pull her back to him and ignore the rest of the world. She could actually see the savage need inside him, to claim her. Possess her. Here, now, before they could be separated again. She almost hoped he would. Then questioned her sanity for hoping such a thing. Had she just landed in her own version of Oz?

He stilled. Completely and truly, not a breath moved him. Not a tremor shook him. He could be a statue again if it weren't for the colors of skin. The war that swirled in his dark amber gaze. The leather and white of his clenched fists. The absolute control of himself that he exerted to keep the battle inside him instead of releasing it outward, awed her.

Slowly, he blinked. Then nodded. Releasing her fully, he stepped back. She shook and her knees wobbled as she made her way to the bag. She pushed the envelope inside it and grabbed both sets of keys, his and the ones she held to the SUV.

They moved quietly, silent, not knowing who was above them. Whoever it was might not be friendly, but if they were, then Dreux's and her presence would be way too hard to explain here in the bottom of the church, behind a locked door.

He donned Nikes from the bottom of the bag. Kalyss absently folded the sheet and made sure nothing that might belong to them was left behind. Finally, she placed the white cotton on the table and pulled the key to the room from her key chain. She laid it in the middle of the squared material, praying she hadn't gone truly insane.

SILAS FOLLOWED, QUIET and unseen, as Kalyss and Dreux left the room. Draven was upstairs, stomping again to get the two to leave before someone came into the main sanctuary. It was a miracle they'd come this far. Dreux was awake. The cycle was irrevocably changed now, and no one knew what that meant.

Kalyss was tense, her movements jerky. Silas placed a hand she couldn't feel on her shoulder and whispered to her unconscious mind. "The answers will come. Wait for them."

She would probably ignore his suggestion. He could feel her trying to control her life's path. She felt the road should be straight, and she kept trying to keep her life driving straight with it, but Silas knew the road was supposed to wind the way it was. She needed to stop fighting it and turn the wheel a little.

The two passed Draven, oblivious to the cloaked form, and left the church. Silas followed, afraid to allow them out of his sight. It had taken too much time and energy to accomplish this. Draven stopped him, whispering, "We need to know what Kai is doing."

"We can't leave them, yet. They will need help." Silas watched after them, his brow furrowed, his entire body tense. "He's awake, but there's more they must do within themselves before the curse can be broken."

"No. They need no interference in this. This part is their path to travel alone."

Silas looked at the cowled head, wishing he could see Draven's expression. But it didn't matter. Truth was truth and perhaps watching the threat to Dreux and Kalyss's future would be more effective than trying to ease their already treacherous path to love.

Chapter 8

Luck was finally on Kalyss's side. She and Dreux made it to the truck without encountering anyone. They'd avoided the offices with open doors and bright lights. The cool October air chilled her and cleared her mind, but confusion still gripped her. She wanted to panic, but wouldn't allow herself to be that weak.

Dreux sat quietly as Kalyss drove to the nearest Starbucks. The car was silent without the radio, but the noise would get on her nerves if she turned it on. Instead, they filled the vehicle with a quietly vibrating tension. Each time she glanced at him out of the corner of her eye, she almost couldn't believe he was alive and breathing.

He'd been a *statue*. Her visions were coming more often, more vividly, and more powerfully. Geoffrey had been killed right in front of her, just after telling her Alex was dead, and some guy had attacked her for no reason.

"Why is this guy trying to kill me?" She stopped the SUV, feeling the slight sway as she put it in park and turned it off.

"He wanted to keep you from awakening me." Dreux faced her, almost too big to fit sideways comfortably.

"Why is that important? Are you a serial killer or something? A danger to society?"

He raised his hands toward her, palms up, studying her expression. "The only blood on my hands is from honest battle."

She looked at him blankly before remembering her dream. The Kalyss in her dreams had had visions of him covered in blood, but she didn't see it anymore. Was that because she trusted him or because she wasn't as powerful as she supposedly used to be? She licked her lips, her whole mouth dry from nervousness. "Then what does he have against you?"

Dreux lowered his hands to his lap and his eyes narrowed on hers. "He was raised to hate me. To hurt me any way he can. You're the way he's chosen."

"Will he leave me alone now that you've already awakened?" She gripped the wheel tight. Would she be able to return to the dojo ever again or was that no longer a safe haven?

Dreux spoke softly, his voice filled with regret. "No."

Kalyss nodded, felt her head jerk too erratically and stopped. She stared at the front door to the coffee shop, her mouth feeling drier and drier. She definitely needed coffee to deal with this. Coffee, food, answers. She pulled the keys from the ignition and unbuckled her seatbelt.

She paused, watching him undo his buckle without hesitation or confusion. Was that because he'd just watched her do it? His seatbelt slid across his broad chest. The deep blue of his shirt perfectly offset his skin, leaving it tanned and healthy looking. Seeing him outside, in bright daylight didn't lessen his attraction even a little.

She jerked her gaze away. "You can come in, too. I doubt the redhead has an eye on all the coffee shops in Spokane. Probably not possible, there's so many."

"I have no intention of allowing you to brave the public alone." His deep voice was utterly sincere.

DREUX BIT BACK a grin as Kalyss arched a blond eyebrow at him. He wasn't completely ignorant of this century, just the practical application of its workings. So while he knew women didn't appreciate heavy-handed men, he didn't know how to speak around it and still get his way. He'd just have to be himself then, as barbaric as she might consider him.

She harrumphed, grabbed the black backpack, and exited

the car. Dreux opened his door with a minimum of fumbling and followed her to the tiny building. He was about to experience twenty-first-century coffee at its finest, or so Geoffrey had said. Kalyss seemed to look forward to it. Her forehead was creased with a desperation that worried him.

Dreux glanced around at the scattered tables and chairs. Some of the chairs looked fragile and insubstantial. But a few toward the back looked big and well-stuffed. They were filled with people of varying ages, wearing various styles. They all found a way to be different, be it with clothes, hair, or makeup.

Some of them typed on laptops. He couldn't wait to play with one of those. And surf the Net. There were so many things Geoffrey had shown him how to do with computers, miraculous things. Dreux couldn't wait to do them all. Now.

The smell hit him next. Sweet and creamy. His mouth watered, but his stomach ached and twisted at the thought of food. Fasting for so long made breaking it nearly as difficult as beginning it. The first days of hunger, missing the smell and taste of food, had combined with his grief and enforced inactivity. It was a miracle he hadn't gone insane centuries before.

Kai had much to pay for.

The lady who served them whatever Kalyss had ordered wore a ring in her nose, her brow, and several in her ear. As she backed away from the counter, he saw, for the first time in a public place, in real life, that part of a woman only a husband should see, her belly button, winking with a small sapphire dolphin, just like the ones off the coast of Normandy. It wasn't just rumor, those rings really were sexy.

Kalyss yanked at his arm. "You can quit staring and hand me your wallet any time now."

He reached into his back pocket, where she'd told him to store it. Kalyss's eyes were narrowed, her lips pursed. Jealousy hadn't changed its face in a thousand years. It was as loud and clear as ever. He bit back a grin, and handed her the wallet.

She pulled a card from it and held it out to the girl, then leaned close and whispered tensely, "Maybe when you sign it, you can take your eyes away from her."

"I was just thinking you'd look great with a ring like that. And I can't sign."

She shuddered, a darkness entering her eyes. "I don't show

my stomach. It would be a waste to decorate it. Why can't you sign?"

"I never learned to write."

Her bright blue eyes widened, then even further as the girl slid a small slip of paper and a pen over the counter. "I just need your signature, Mrs. Williams."

For a moment, Kalyss seemed to stop breathing. Her face was as white as her knuckles. She choked out, "Don't you need ID?"

The girl smiled. "No, not with your picture on the card."

Kalyss stared down at the card then picked up the pen as if she were in a daze. Geoffrey had a way with pictures, whether drawing, painting, or snapping them. It was a skill Dreux had become very thankful for. Kalyss didn't look so thankful.

"It's a great picture, too," the girl continued. "I never get mine to turn out so perfect. Usually there's something wrong with my hair or my smile."

Kalyss gave a weak grin. "Usually mine suck, too. I have no idea how I got so lucky."

There was no way Dreux could miss the irony in her voice, or the pallor of her features as she put his wallet back together and handed it to him. When she picked up their drinks with a shaky grip, she didn't even notice the appreciative once-over the girl gave him.

He gave the girl a grin, which she returned, before smoothing his hand over the base of Kalyss's back and following her to a small seating area at the back of the store. He was grateful to find the chairs were as comfortable as they'd appeared.

Kalyss set his coffee on the small table between them, flipped her ponytail over her shoulder and leaned over, holding her own cup between her knees. She eyed the black bag at her feet. Carefully, quietly, she asked, "Mrs. Williams?"

"You are my wife." Determination hardened his voice, though he tried to smooth it out. She stiffened anyway.

"I am no man's wife." She was just as determined, though she avoided looking at him.

"Did you think you were a woman's wife?" He'd hoped to relax her tension with humor.

She glared at him, obviously not relaxed. "We aren't married."

"October 6, 1075. Yesterday was our nine-hundred-and-twenty-ninth anniversary. It's understandable you'd forget, under the circumstances." It'd been a long, long time since he'd even thought of humor. She didn't appreciate it now, but he'd keep trying. It might be the only way to make it through this without her becoming overwhelmed and running from him. And making it through, surviving, was the only option.

Kalyss pursed her lips, ignoring his humorous, yet serious tone "How come you haven't?"

"Forgotten?" Too much information too soon would only overwhelm her further, but she needed answers. At her nod, he carefully answered, "I was a statue, not asleep."

"You mean you . . ." Kalyss eyed him critically.

"Saw. Thought. Remembered." His voice dropped, nearly stolen as he remembered nightmares. "Heard."

She looked away, nearly whispering, "So, you heard. Last night. Me, I mean."

He stared into her eyes, steady, serious. "Every tear that fell."

KALYSS SIPPED AT her coffee, taking that in. He sounded like he cared. Only Alex had before. But she couldn't easily trust that. Feelings could be so deceptive. "I don't remember a marriage because, according to you, I died. Doesn't that negate the marriage?"

"You're here, alive. Doesn't that reinstate it?"

Don't sink. Swim. Fight the current, no matter how much it overwhelms you. "Do marriages get reinstated?"

He shrugged.

His calm annoyed her, but she used her annoyance to weld herself together. She sipped. "I was supposedly reincarnated. Not resurrected. Technically, I'm someone different."

"Who do you know that has studied supernatural law and can debate the case in court?"

Kalyss opened her mouth, ready for rebuttal, but no words came to mind. She closed her mouth and swallowed. Then sipped her coffee again, careful not to burn herself.

He wasn't arrogant or smug. She'd have walked out if he had been. She watched him test his coffee. It was still hot if hers was any judge. Did she believe him? Had she married him over nine hundred years ago? This whole situation was insane, but . . .

Did she believe someone had killed Alex and attacked her last night? Had Geoffrey died right in front of her? Had a statue truly come to life in her arms, from her kiss? She gulped her coffee and burned her throat.

Nope, not dreaming.

Supernatural law. In natural courts. If warriors could become statues and back again, who knew what other natural laws were broken? According to Dreux, reincarnation was real. Was everyone walking around, trying over and over to fulfill some destiny they didn't remember? What would happen once they had?

Would Alex come back, in this lifetime or any other? As a snake? A frog? A defenseless baby? Who held the controls? If there was a destiny, someone preordained it. Nature of the beast, right? So, God.

Or was there some paranormal council watching everything? If so, what were their plans? At least God had laid everything out in the Bible. Kalyss frowned. Or was there another answer, another organization she couldn't figure out? Either way, the question of their marriage seemed the jurisdiction of someone else. Didn't it? Or . . .

"So many *questions*," she murmured.

"There are no answers, Kalyss. You can go crazy wondering."

She looked up. "I guess you've already tried to figure this out."

His mouth quirked. "I've spent some time thinking on it."

"What did you decide?" She tilted her head to face him better.

"That until someone stood in front of me and gave me answers, I'd never really know. I'd just be guessing."

"And you're okay with that?"

He smiled. "I went in circles long enough. The answer for now is: what do I have faith in? As long as I put my trust in that, I won't go insane with questions I can't answer."

She couldn't understand letting go so easily. She needed an answer. She'd always loved puzzles, crosswords, anagrams, Tetris. Anything where she had to make the pieces fit. Her visions of other people's memories were confusing and she had to work to understand them. The first rule of putting together a puzzle was to examine all the pieces. It helped to have a finished picture on the cover of the box, but she wouldn't have that advantage this time. But she could put away all the pieces she couldn't place and examine the rest, trying to find a framework.

The first pieces to examine were likely in the black bag. She grabbed it by one strap and unzipped it. The envelope from the bag was plain manila. No addresses, stamps, or labels of any kind decorated it. There was a heavy lump at the end of the thick envelope. Whatever was inside, there was lots of it. It wasn't glued in back. Just a small brad held it together.

"I'm almost nervous to open it," she said.

Dreux leaned forward and reached for it. Everything else in the bag had been his. Kalyss released it into his hands, but leaned over curiously.

DREUX HID A smile at her curiosity. She was bouncing back, admirably resilient. He flipped the small metal piece up and opened the envelope. Upending it on the small table between them, he watched bits of his new life slide out.

Identification papers bearing his new name, Dreux Baron Williams. Dreux's lips twisted. It was fitting. At the end, he'd been King William's baron.

"Social Security card, bank statements . . . Lord, look at that balance." Kalyss stared at the numbers on the paper she held.

"Want to marry a millionaire?" He chuckled at her glare.

"Billionaire. And no. I'm not that way." She looked at his papers again, her brows raised. "I've just never seen a statement like this. Maybe Mel Gibson has."

"Geoffrey said he'd been investing for me."

"Boy, did he." She moved the papers to the side and stared at him. "He talked to you?"

"Incessantly. He had a lot of information to fit in. In case I could hear, he wanted to make sure he prepared me for this life as much as possible."

"Wow. He didn't seem like much of a talker." She set the papers aside and picked up the cell phone. She turned it on and laid the contents of the envelope in a neat row on the table.

"You did see him, then?" The hesitation on her face had him sitting forward.

"I saw him," she said reluctantly. "He pulled me out of the dojo before the redhead came back."

"Kai." Soon, Dreux would have his moment to speak with Geoffrey. To tell him his efforts hadn't been in vain, that he'd heard every word and to thank him.

"He didn't make it, Dreux." Kalyss met his gaze, hers serious and uneasy.

No, that couldn't be. There was a plan here. *Wait for the call, Dreux. It will come.* Whatever situation he was in, Geoffrey wasn't dead. When the time was right, Geoffrey would lead Dreux to Kai, so Dreux could end the cycle.

Dreux looked at the cell phone. "I wouldn't mourn for him quite yet, Kalyss."

Kalyss blinked. She picked up the phone, her fingers clenching around it. Her lips pursed. "Are you saying Geoffrey isn't dead? After I watched it happen?"

Dreux watched her, almost as if he were afraid of her reaction. "It's his gift. He resurrects."

"So everyone lives again but Alex? Did he just forget to stand in line the day they were handing out multiple chances in heaven?" Kalyss dropped the phone onto the table and grabbed a few more papers. She flipped through the pages, each movement more irritated than the last.

"I thought you'd be glad to hear at least Geoffrey survived."

Kalyss ignored his words. "*Geoffrey* left you paperwork to check into the Hampton Inn. I know where that is."

"Kalyss . . ."

She quickly stuffed everything back into the envelope. "I can drop you off there and you can wait for your call."

"I? And where will you be?"

"I have a funeral to prepare. Family to notify." Her voice was cold.

His fingers encircled her wrist, halting her as she tried to stand. He was losing her. No, if she could be a little more patient, she'd have answers. "Kalyss, you can't go back."

"Don't tell me what I can't do. I already know what I can't do. I can't bring my best friend, who actually dies only once, back to life. I can't believe in all this BS. Life is complicated enough." She yanked her wrist from his hold and rose.

He tried to express his sorrow as best he knew how. "I'm sorry he died."

"How can you be? You didn't know him." Tears filled her eyes. "I did. He was wonderful. And he died because you freaks won't leave me alone."

"You're a freak, too, Kalyss."

"I only have your word that I'm reincarnated."

"No, that isn't your only gift, is it?" He stared straight into her eyes, daring her to admit to her gift. Her secret gift. She'd hidden it before. He bet she still did.

She froze. Her eyes wide and a little scared. "I don't know what you're talking about."

"These things are more acceptable now than they were in our time. Why are you afraid?"

"Because I'm talking to a crazy loon." She turned to leave, but he rose and grabbed her wrist again.

"It's not as strong as it once was, but it's there. It will become stronger with time." He wouldn't let her deny anything, not their situation and certainly not a part of herself.

She looked away, then down to her trembling hands. He'd clearly shaken her. But then her beautiful spirit, briefly hidden, flared to life. She raised her gaze and her stubborn chin.

Quiet but firm, she said, "I don't want it to be stronger. I don't want any of this. I'll drop you off at the hotel, go home, with a police escort if necessary, find Alex, and bury him. Then I'll live my life. Good luck with yours."

She broke his hold and stalked to the door.

Sighing, Dreux grabbed their coffees, the black bag, and the envelope and followed her to the car. She'd lasted longer than he'd thought she would before trying to bolt. That hadn't changed completely in nine lifetimes. What amazed him, though, was her new lack of fear in expressing herself. That was something to be proud of her for.

Once inside the car, he leaned over her, caging her between the steering wheel, the door, the seat, and himself. He hadn't let her leave him their first night together and he wouldn't allow it now. Looking firmly in her eyes, he reminded her, "You promised you wouldn't run, Kalyss."

Her eyes widened, desperate and defensive. "I didn't know what all this was about."

He hardened his voice, his hands squeezing the seat and steering wheel. "You knew you didn't have all the answers when you made the promise. You said you wouldn't let the bad guy get away."

"All of you are the bad guy." Her brow was twisted, her eyes wild and furious.

Dear Lord, she really believed her words. Dreux pushed the painful knowledge away. "No. Just Kai. And he's Alex's bad guy, too, Kalyss. Should he get away?"

Tense, they stared at one another for a long moment. He wanted nothing more than to gather her in his arms and take all her confusion and pain away. Protect her from this life they led, the cycle they were trapped in. But she had to be strong a little longer. He needed her.

Finally, she slumped against the seat, momentarily defeated. He waited a heartbeat then subsided on his own side of the vehicle. He buckled his seatbelt in the roaring silence.

Just when he worried he'd pushed her too far, that maybe she'd open the door and flee, she put the truck in gear and backed out of the parking spot. It was just as well. She wouldn't have run far before he caught her. The possessive streak inside him stated unequivocally that, selfish or not, he could never let her go.

THE HAMPTON INN was a large building on the outskirts of downtown Spokane. Surrounded by tall trees and lush greenery, it was an oasis of natural beauty only ten minutes from downtown, easily reached by Interstate 90. Check-in went smoothly as Dreux simply showed his ID and Kalyss signed for everything.

They were shown to a large suite. With no bags to put anywhere, their guide left. Kalyss crossed to the small desk with a phone on it and opened the phone book.

"What are you doing?"

Kalyss flipped the pages. It was probably too late to call 911. She needed a direct number to the police station. "Calling the cops."

"What are you going to tell them?" Dreux leaned against a wall and crossed his arms.

Kalyss paused with her hand on the phone. "The truth."

"You've already died nine times and your personal serial killer attacked you again last night?" Dreux kept his voice carefully blank. His words would irritate her enough.

Kalyss huffed and stared at the ceiling.

"He killed your friend and another man, who's probably resurrected already, and you escaped to break into a church and crash for the night?"

She rubbed at her temples.

"You woke to a statue, kissed him, and are now waiting with him in a hotel for them to make sense of everything you can't? That truth?"

Kalyss glared at him. "I was thinking more like, 'I've been attacked, my best friend killed, and I can't return to my business for fear the killer will return.'"

Dreux smiled regretfully. "And you waited how many hours to report this?"

She snapped, "What are you, a cop?"

Dreux shrugged, his worried expression belying his casual attitude. "Just trying to help."

"Go back to being a statue." Kalyss snatched up the phone and dialed, but she knew he was right. She wouldn't be able to think of anything to say that wouldn't point to her as Alex's killer. In the end, Dreux listened while Kalyss gave an anonymous tip. For her sake, he hoped they didn't consider her a crank.

Chapter 9

Kalyss sat on the small settee and clenched her hands in her hair because that was all she could do. She was overwhelmed with the need to scream, cry, and explode in anger, but couldn't even focus on one emotion long enough to give in to it.

She could only sit and breathe, hold still and empty her mind. Think nothing. Feel . . . a warm body settle beside her, an arm cradle her head, along the small back of the love seat. He didn't speak. Didn't move. She rose to her feet. Didn't he understand? She didn't want or need him to hold her or protect her.

Dreux pulled her back down beside him, holding her still. Kalyss wanted to struggle, but he didn't move and she lost the will to fight his comfort. Slowly, she relaxed back against his arm, against his side. Her mind finally emptied. No thoughts, no analysis of the future, no worries about the business and home she'd just abandoned or the family she needed to inform of their son's death. No, she wouldn't think about it.

She would just *feel* the warmth, security, and strength of the man beside her, bracing her but not trapping her. It was safer than the maelstrom inside her.

Dreux's hand settled over hers. She looked at it curiously. It wasn't heavy or gripping. It made no demands, only offering comfort. Then his thumb stroked along hers, to her wrist and back to the knuckle. Light, feathery touches that focused all of her attention on one usually ignored but suddenly sensitized area of her skin.

"What do you want from me?" She didn't wail the words, but the desire was there. A desire to cry, to beg for some relief from her confusion.

"Have you ever allowed yourself to live so completely in one moment, no thoughts of yesterday or tomorrow or even five minutes away—just right then?" His voice was low, hypnotic.

"Like emptying your mind of everything? I've tried, but—"

"No. Like feeling everything about one moment, tasting it, smelling it, all of it, just your body. Without your mind."

"I don't know. Is that what you do?"

"I have. In battle, thinking beyond a moment can kill you, but living that moment slows it down. It gave me time to plan, to notice every detail around me. Sounds, voices, where that axe was headed, when to duck, when to strike—I lived it all."

"I'm not sure I've ever wanted to live a moment like that."

His thumb stopped and he held his hand perfectly still. "How about this one?"

She looked around, then at him, questioning.

"Close your eyes."

She did and held still, bracing herself. With no images to distract her, though, her mind drowned in chaos again.

"Feel my hand."

She tensed, waiting. "It's not doing anything."

"And it won't."

Her brow crinkled. That made no sense. What did he want her to do?

Gradually, impressions seeped into her mind. Heat surrounded her. She hadn't known she was chilled until her flesh prickled from the change in temperature.

He breathed slow and deep beside her. Steady, calming. Soothing. She'd never just listened to someone breathe before. Had never known it could evoke a sense of safety, as if the world really would wait. Nothing was so urgent she couldn't take these moments for herself.

His thumb stroked again, a callus abrading the top of her hand ever so softly. And it wasn't a callus made from a pen, but a rough and deep scarring of his skin. He could avoid labor for the rest of his life and his skin would never heal.

His calluses spoke to her of tenacity. Determination. An iron will to persevere no matter the cost. They not only made promises, they promised to fulfill them. She'd never known a man to have that kind of tough, weathered strength in his hand.

"Your hand is softer than silk. Warm and gentle. But better."

She angled her head, looking in front of him but not at him.

"Silk snags. It clings, needy and desperate." His thumb stroked again. "Until it's destroyed. Threads pull out and it unravels."

She raised wide eyes to his dark chocolate ones. She'd been needy and desperate. Nearly destroyed.

"But silk is also strong. Protective." He spoke slow, gentle. His voice smooth and rich. Deep and sweet. "A man can wear it over his heart in battle and find it deflects many blows, many arrows. With the right silk, the right circumstances, it can save a man's life."

His thumb moved slowly over her skin. "You are like silk. But better."

Oh, he could make her melt, this one. She raised one cool brow but it fooled neither of them.

"I wished, as I waited these years, that I'd lived every moment with you like I had in battle. Making love to you. Holding you. Talking to you."

Moments. Fleeting, but they held all the meaning of life, didn't they?

"Now I want to spend a century holding your hand."

She looked away, leaving her hand in his. For now.

KAI SEALED THE end of duct tape that secured Alex's hands to the pipe behind him. A fresh gash swelled over the man's right eye, blood dripping down in a steady trickle. It would hurt like hell, but it would be a handsome scar, ensuring Alex a woman in his arms every night for the rest of his life.

"You should probably thank me for this." Kai grinned into

the hazel eyes of his prisoner. His finger pressed roughly to the wound, gauging the damage and making Alex wince.

"Somehow I think I'll manage to refrain." Alex probably would've spit in Kai's face if he'd had the saliva. Good thing Kai hadn't given him water.

"Don't try to escape and I won't have to hit you. I'm really quite reasonable that way." Not that Alex would have a chance. He'd just have to piss himself. He wouldn't be the first man ever to do so. "Or you could end your hassle and tell me where she would've ran. Where is her haven?"

"In your insane dreams, sure."

Kai rested on one knee before the bound man. A shifting movement sounded behind him. Geoffrey was awakening finally. Kai shook his head sadly. "You simply don't understand what you're driving me to do." He slapped Alex once, hard, on the knee, then rose. "Don't worry, though. You will."

He turned and walked toward Geoffrey, who was awakening from that nightmarish sleep both Geoffrey and Kai suffered when they died. His silver eyes were wide with the horrors he'd witnessed. Each death was a glimpse at hell: feeling the heat, tasting the fear, hearing the screams. Die enough times and you'd begin to fear you'd never leave.

"Hello, my friend." And they were. Friends, of a sort. Trading death blows, sharing nightmares, seeing each other in the black pit a time or two—it could bond two men beyond understanding.

Geoffrey gazed back at him, the nightmare fading from his eyes to leave them as empty and cold as ever. His expression quickly eased into that familiar look that silently said Kai wouldn't make him talk until he was ready. Unfortunately for them both, it was a promise Geoffrey knew how to keep.

"It's been a while. A hundred years. I was beginning to worry about you, disappearing like that." Kai's eyes narrowed and his anger leaked out. "And with the statue, no less."

Again, no response. They'd played this game often during their attempts to defeat each other over the years. Fights to the death, torture, imprisonment. Neither could break the other. Neither could hold the other for long. It was a pain in the ass, really.

"You were gone several hours this time. Kinda scary, huh?"

Geoffrey remained passive. Watchful and alert, but otherwise indifferent. He knew his role well.

"Sometimes a short death. Sometimes a long one. And we never know which is the last." Kai shook his head and held out his arms in an expansive gesture. He had his own nightmares. That's where they held common ground. "Some bastard is having a lot of fun with us, don't you think?"

No answer, but he'd known there wouldn't be. "That's okay. This time, we'll make our own fun."

Slowly, Kai turned to look over his shoulder at Alex. He turned back in time to see just a ripple of a shadow in Geoffrey's frosted lake eyes. He smiled and cocked a brow. "What do you think he'll tell us?"

Alex likely wouldn't know where the statue was, but he would know where Kalyss would run for safety. He would understand how her mind worked and the things she would likely do. The longer it took for her to return to the dojo, the more Kai knew she'd gone *somewhere,* would plan *something.* Kai needed to plan for any eventuality, but for now, he'd wait, give her time and see what she would do.

A sudden thump outside the small basement window snagged Kai's attention. He'd left it open to let in the slight breezes of cool, fresh air, but that would have to change, judging by the voices coming from outside the building. The gleam of intelligence in Geoffrey's eyes said he heard them, too.

Kai slapped a hand over Geoffrey's mouth, his face grim. "This is inconvenient, isn't it? If they'd just leave us alone, we'd be fine."

He sighed and drew his knife. "Sorry, old friend."

With an angle of his body and a swipe of his free hand, his knife plunged into Geoffrey's kidney. Retaining his hold on Geoffrey's mouth, Kai released the hilt of his dagger. It didn't take long for Geoffrey to bleed out. Kai had learned the hard way how to do that without leaving blood all over himself.

Dead silence lay behind him, but it wouldn't last long. Alex would holler as soon as the shock wore off. Kai pulled a handkerchief from his pocket and wiped a few small traces of Geoffrey's blood from his hands as he strolled to Alex. The voices outside grew louder.

When Alex opened his mouth to yell for help, Kai drove the

handkerchief deep into his throat. If he didn't choke, he'd be lucky not to suffocate. Kai smiled mockingly. "I wonder who that could be. Your new student, Melanie, maybe?"

He cocked his head as Alex's eyes widened in surprise that he knew the name. "Have you seen those bruises? I might have to pay that man of hers a visit. There's no reason to hurt a woman. Killing them is sometimes necessary, but I've never hurt Kalyss doing it."

Alex's brows twisted in disbelief, too stunned to react to the knock on the front door.

Kai frowned. He could practically hear that "insane" label through Alex's gag. Why were his motives always misconstrued for insanity? "Or it might be Oscar looking for a date. Have you seen the way he looks at Kalyss? I wouldn't trust that guy. He's just like Sam."

Alex choked on the gag again, trying to breathe, eyes wide. Kai relented and gave it a small tug to loosen but not dislodge it. With a wicked arch of his brow, Kai decided to let Alex stew, wondering what else Kai knew. "Gotta go."

The person outside knocked again, harder. Kai untied the black belt from Alex's waist, used it to reinforce the gag, and rose. "Wait right here."

Kai paused, examined the bound man, and grinned at him. "Sorry, that was in bad taste."

He walked to the stack of boxes in the corner, grabbed a long one, and carried it over to Alex. Setting the heavy box on his legs, Kai leaned on it, ignoring Alex's groans, and whispered mockingly, "In case you find a way to escape, I'll just make sure you're slow."

Kai's grin widened and he whistled his way upstairs.

ALEX CLOSED HIS eyes and leaned his head back against the pipes. Some defense expert he was. Bound and gagged in his own basement with a dead man hanging several feet in front of him. At least, he assumed it was dead this time. He'd assumed that during the past several hours locked in the basement with it and had been very wrong.

Alex squeezed his eyes shut tighter, wishing he could do the same for his ears and nose. As unnerving as seeing the body was, the steady drip from the hem of its jeans and the coppery stench of fresh blood nauseated him most.

If only he could go back a few hours. Change a few things. Never turn his back on a stranger, no matter how seemingly friendly they were. Never assume the guy was a customer, there for harmless reasons. Never let the needle get close.

It hadn't taken effect immediately, whatever drug the Dead Guy had used. Enough time for Alex to break into a cold sweat, knowing Kalyss was alone and unprepared for whatever Dead Guy had in mind. Alex had fought, grabbing him and holding him back when he headed for the training room. But Dead Guy had pushed Alex away and the weakness had taken over.

I need to protect her, Dead Guy had said.

Then Alex had heard it. The scuffle of shoes, the thump of a body being thrown. Punches. Voices. *Kalyss.*

Dead Guy's eyes had widened. *He's here.*

Then Dead Guy had run. Alex could barely move, but he'd crawled and half-dragged himself to his office, his body fighting the drug inside him. He couldn't help, but hopefully the police could. That had been his last thought before he'd passed out before even reaching the desk. He'd only roused again at the sound of footsteps behind him, but a sharp blow to the back of his head had knocked him out again.

Alex was a healer. Had been since he was six. He could heal any damage to himself faster than most people, but whatever drug was in him slowed that down. Apparently it wasn't through his system yet since the gash over his eye still hurt.

No, there probably wasn't much he could have done differently beyond being more on guard from the get-go. But that didn't make him feel better. Where was Kalyss? Was she hurt? Alex stared at the body and the dark puddle underneath it, thoroughly, deeply afraid.

Who would protect Kalyss when the crazy man decided Alex was next?

"KAI IS HAVING way too much fun." Silas clenched his fist and stared with disgust at Geoffrey's drained body. He'd never developed an appreciation for wanton carnage.

"You can't say he hates his job," Draven said, shrugging. Violence was a fact of life and Draven had learned long ago it was no use to respond to it. It happened or it didn't.

Silas scowled at the blackness where Draven's face should have been. "He needs to be stopped."

"We can only observe, remember?" Draven hissed mockingly. It was about time Silas felt restrained by the limits he insisted on keeping. They made things harder. If they could interfere with human lives as wantonly as Maeve had, then Kalyss would have awakened Dreux long ago. But their purpose was to be forgiven the evil they were born with, not to become it.

Silas paced around Geoffrey to stand in front of Alex. He wasn't happy with doing nothing in the face of carnage and it was vastly humorous to watch. Not the carnage, just Silas's reaction. Draven grinned beneath the cowl.

Silas sighed. "I remember."

"How interesting that you've preached caution all these centuries and now that they're finally winning, you're impatient with your restraints."

"They might win this time, true, but if there's even the slightest mistake, they fail and it's all over." Silas's eyes were hard and grim. "Maeve will awaken and kill them. Then kill us. Then move on to world domination and destruction. You know her nature."

"I never realized you were so full of drama." Draven was amused. Maeve was the big, bad wolf, yes, but they still had to build their house the best they could to try to hold the wolf back. Pacing and fretting were no good at all.

"Are you going to spend all day taking shots at me?" he snapped.

"Well, there's nothing better to do. Unless . . ." Draven dragged out the word temptingly.

"We're only here to observe," he stated, in a flat don't-argue-with-me tone.

"Then quit your bitching," Draven returned, fed up.

"Sorry." Silas stopped beside Draven, crossed his arms, and watched Alex. "But we've seen how Kai gets when his curiosity is aroused. What do you think he'll do when he finds out Alex can heal himself?"

"Right now, Alex believes the drug is preventing him from healing his injuries. As long as he believes that, he won't heal. He'll be safe."

"So let him deal with his gift on his own. A suggestion could do more harm than good." Silas pursed his lips, reining in his impatience. His words were obviously more to remind himself than explain to Draven and they seemed to help him regain control. He took a deep breath and let it out slow. "We'll have to wait and see how it plays out on its own."

"No interference," Draven agreed with an exaggerated nod of obedience.

Silas scowled.

Draven grinned, unseen beneath the hood.

KALYSS TURNED FROM the window. He was staring at her again, possessive, determined. Dreux sat on the end of the bed, his elbows propped on his knees.

"Why do you keep staring at me?"

"I'm happy to see you alive and well."

Her gaze skittered away. She crossed her arms, hugging them around her. Alive and well. Alex had been alive and well. Joking with her. Laughing with her. And now she wasn't even with him, by his side, making arrangements for him to be comfortable in his eternal peace. She bit her lip and held her breath.

Dreux rose and stood in front of her. His hands grasped her elbows, the closest to a hug she would allow. "Don't. You'll overwhelm yourself with guilt and grief. They become a haze covering your mind, taking centuries to lift."

His eyes, gentle and understanding, warmed her. It didn't make sense. *He* didn't make sense. But his words did. Whether she really believed his story or not, he did. With all the will in him, he believed. He knew the pain Kalyss felt.

Her pain reflected in his eyes, his face. He was so close, looming over her, almost surrounding her with a field of comfort. His broad chest hovered in front of her gaze, tempting her, seducing her. She could lay her head down, lean against him. She could close her eyes and let him carry her burden for a while. Let his arms wrap around her, hold her, and protect her.

She actually felt herself tilt before she straightened and jerked away. She spun around, her back to him. The curtains gaped, sunlight still pulsing through them. This time the pain of the glare was welcome. She reached for the string and pulled them open wider. Then she stood there, fiddling with the string and staring blankly ahead.

"How did it feel? Being a statue?" She could imagine depression, the ever-present black cloud, finally descending completely. A long, deep, sad sleep.

She felt, or maybe imagined, his deep breath at the nape of her neck. He warmed her back, but she still felt cold in the sunlight. A light pressure at her elbows told her he touched her. But so lightly, so tenderly, it didn't threaten her.

"I stood at a window when it happened. Much like this one. Big, wide, low. It was a foolish, vain design. Tall, jagged cliffs ripped from the sea at the base of our tower and I'd taken a false sense of comfort from that. But I'd made a mistake."

He breathed deeply before continuing in his low, rumbling voice. She could hear his pain. "At that window, held by two men, I watched Kai pull you onto his ship. He jerked you to the front, directly where I couldn't miss watching and seeing everything. He stared at me the entire time, enjoying the moment. My pain, your fear, what he was taking from us both."

His voice dropped lower. "Then he killed you."

She shivered. Trees swayed in front of her window, but she could see the sea. Smell the salt and fear. Feel the brisk wind and rising warmth of the sun. She could imagine being his wife, staring from the ship, up and up, her head tilted back, her gaze latching on to his. The sharp metal at her throat. The darkness at the edges of her vision. His skin, shining oddly in the sunlight just before . . . nothing.

"You were so quiet," Dreux whispered. "Not crying or screaming. Just watching me, waiting for me to save you. We'd made many promises to each other that night and you waited patiently for me to fulfill them."

Guilt. Regret. Did he want forgiveness? Was that something that should come from her? She didn't even remember what he described. It would mean nothing. But still, she knew the guilt of promises. Both those made and those not made.

Alex had wanted one promise from her. For her to live

again. To quit hiding. To prevent fear from overwhelming her. She hadn't given it to him. And now she couldn't. He'd been taken from her by that same shiny-eyed bastard Dreux described.

"Then you slid to the deck, slow, graceful. It was obscene. Seeing your blood. Knowing the violence of death. I've been in battle before, Kalyss. I've seen men die with the horror of it upon their face. But you were peaceful."

He nuzzled the side of her neck, his hands at her waist in a quick, hard hug. "It took many, many years before that brought me comfort."

He grasped her wrists and raised her arms up and out, bent at the elbow. His foot nudged her feet apart a few inches, in the exact position he'd been frozen in. Then he backed away.

How had it felt to be a statue? She stared through the window, seeing through the trees to the death of his wife. Imagining the death of Alex, picturing it happening in front of her. Her death. Alex's death. Geoffrey's death.

Her arms strained a bit as a night sleeping on the stone floor of a church with nothing but a thin sheet and a statue to lean upon caught up with her.

Kai. The grinning, emerald-eyed assassin that had attacked her from nowhere. She could see him kill that helpless woman, yanked from her bed, from her husband's arms as dawn broke on the morning after their wedding. Tears pricked her eyes. Burning.

That woman had lost so much. Alex had lost just as much. A home, a family, children. He'd always wanted children. Now he was dead. All thanks to that damn bastard who thought he could waltz into people's lives and destroy them.

Her arms wavered. The muscles pulled and strained. Weak. She'd always been weak. She'd allowed her ex to beat her. Allowed him, loved him, lied for him. She'd stayed for more, never escaping until he'd nearly killed her. And if the statue man's story was true—and who couldn't believe a statue that came to life right in front of them—she'd been weak even before.

How many lifetimes had she cowered her way to death

while some man took from her the life she dreamed of? The husband, the friends, the children?

That bastard. That dirty, rotten, murderous, insane bastard. Her muscles clenched in her arms and her legs. Her tears dried. She'd go. Her fighting back clearly had surprised him last night, but this time she'd show him what she could do. The damage she could cause him. She'd do more than surprise him. She'd kill him.

She hadn't trained all these years, made herself stronger, survived all she had just so he could take it from her. Whether she was the Kalyss of centuries ago or not, she *was* the Kalyss of *now*. Her adrenaline built. Her muscles were strained, but ready.

Kalyss realized she was still standing in the position of the statue. And she knew, felt it deeply. This anger, this rage, had infused the man behind her. This determination to kill, maim, and destroy the assassin, to hunt him down and cut him to shreds, to hear his pain and be glad of it. To act. To *do*.

And Dreux hadn't been able to move. Her arms were shrieking now. The strain pulling and stretching her triceps all the way down the sides of her back and into her thighs and calves. Her biceps bunched and knotted. She shook with the strain.

The pain overwhelmed her body. Fatigue, depression, and anger warred in her mind and heart. There was no rest, no respite. It was torture in the cruelest way possible. She gasped, struggling with the pain.

"Enough." He pushed her arms down to rest at her sides. She shook from head to toe. She let him pull her close, his chest curving against her back, and hold her, supporting her weight. Her knees buckled and she pulled them back in line.

That was how he'd felt, what he'd thought and seen for over nine hundred years.

"In this last century, Geoffrey focused me. He took me from the tower, taught and trained me for this time. I could hear him. See what was in front of me. I listened. And I knew the plan. To rescue you and keep you safe. To awaken me. To give us the life that was taken. All we had to do was find you."

And that was what Alex had died for. His last wish for her

to open her heart and not be alone. To dream and have a future with more life in it than her present life had. And that future, which came from the past, had killed him.

"What took so long?"

"We moved, constantly. Kai was ever on our heels. We didn't want to lead him to you. But, in the end, that didn't matter. You had married Sam and we didn't find you until the night he nearly killed you."

It could have been avoided? Her years with Sam could've been prevented?

"That night, Geoffrey and Kai made a pact. To leave you alone. To let you heal."

"How generous." Slowly, she stood and pulled away and faced him. Faced his eyes. His gentle, understanding eyes. "Why would Kai do that?"

Dreux brushed hair from her eyes. "He often has many reasons for the things he does and Geoffrey's come to understand him a bit over the centuries, but even still we can only make guesses. Kai doesn't hurt women. He kills you, only you, and he does it as quickly and painlessly as he can."

"I feel so special," she said sarcastically.

Dreux grinned at her tone and facial expression, then his laughter died. "Maybe what happened to you so reminded him of his mother's death that he couldn't finish it, not that night. You'd fought a battle and like any survivor, you deserved your chance to beat the odds, heal from your injuries and pull yourself together. Or you'd die on your own and he'd have one less of your lives on his conscience. Besides, it wasn't like you were about to hop out of your hospital bed and come awaken me."

"He was giving me a chance to make a different choice, a different life."

Dreux nodded. "All this time, he only wanted me—dead or in stone, it didn't matter which. He'd have left you and Geoffrey alone if you hadn't kept trying to free me. If I could have spoken, I'd have told you to stay away. My sacrifice would have been worth it."

She was in danger again, when they could have let her be. Kai, Geoffrey, and Dreux. All three could have left her alone.

She saw that fact in his eyes. The guilt. The need. The torture. Would she have rather left him like that? A statue frozen with crippling grief?

She hugged her arms around herself and headed away from him. "I need a moment."

Chapter 10

It just wasn't his century. No matter where Kai had searched, all the hidden places of the world—Africa, Japan, Rome, Brazil—he'd even had to check each space shuttle and satellite once that option had opened—he hadn't seen grey nor grain of the statue. He'd seen Geoffrey many times, tiny glimpses, but never long enough to follow him to the statue. Geoffrey was too fast, even the night they'd made their pact over the injured Kalyss.

Kai turned the dojo sign to CLOSED as soon as the colored lights disappeared around the corner. Policemen. Wherever Kalyss was, she was thinking clearly. She could fight. She could improvise weapons. She could focus, even after watching a man die. And she was fast. All grown up with powers of her own. She'd be harder to kill this time, and, paradoxically, he was glad of it. He preferred honest battle with a warrior to attacking a victim who was, well . . . a victim. Kai flipped the lights off and started toward the back of the building.

Light from outside struck the glass of the frames along the wall to his right. He moved closer, examining pictures of the new Kalyss. Her black belt. Her arm around Alex. The awards named him Alexander Michael Foster. Considering how close they were, how inseparable, Alex could only be Kalyss's lover.

Love and trust for Alex shined from Kalyss's eyes in every picture. Oh, Geoffrey had to hate that. For once, he hadn't imprisoned her from childhood to death, hadn't isolated her from life, love, and children, overprotected her, and kept her pure.

It would burn when he pointed out to Dreux's servant how much better she'd lived without his interference . . . until she'd met Sam, anyway.

Kai chose a particularly friendly picture, where she and Alex hugged and kissed over an award, and strode with a jaunty step into the back room where he moved the shelf that had hidden the door to the basement from the cops and slipped into the darkness beyond.

One flick and the low-watt bulb that hung from ceiling wires blinked to life, tossing a dull yellow glow through the black. It was time to get answers about this new Kalyss. See how long she'd wait before coming back, what kind of actions she would take, how serious of a threat he would need to consider her in this new lifetime. Yes, she was more capable of fighting him, but would she also be capable of telling Geoffrey no? To move on and let her be? Before Kai searched her apartment above the dojo again, he'd try asking the man who knew her best—Alex.

He walked past Geoffrey, casually pulling the knife from his side as he went. The man would never give answers, until he was ready. Which Kai needed him conscious for.

Kai grabbed a metal chair from the wall and slung it around, its back to Alex. He straddled it and crossed his arms, over the back, staring at the slumped man. Alex's hands were taped behind him and his belt held the gag secure, leaving his gee to gape open down his unprotected chest. His dark hair hung slightly over his forehead with blood trailing down his temple.

Well built, solid, and lean. If Kai hadn't caught him unawares and drugged last night, the fight would have been interesting. Alex stared back, his jaw clenched and his eyes hard with defiance. Kai grinned and waited, watching impatience drive through the man. Some cruelties were easy. Simple. And a little fun.

Sure beat the ones that tore at your soul with their necessity. Finally, he untied the belt and pulled the gag free, ignoring

Alex's attempts to swallow and moisten his overly dry mouth. If Alex wanted water, he'd have to give something for it. "Your girlfriend is in danger. Believe it or not, I'm the only one who can save her from it."

"By attacking her? I doubt it." Alex's hoarse voice was almost unintelligible.

"That was necessary. I don't want to do it again."

"But you will," Alex accused.

"If it comes to that. Yes." Kai opened the handkerchief and started cleaning his blade.

"Who decides that? Just you?" Alex ignored the silent threat of Kai's blade.

Oh, that wouldn't do. Not at all. "Some destinies are inescapable. Mine is to prevent her from awakening a monster."

"Awakening a monster? Is Godzilla around somewhere?"

Kai chuckled. "No. Someone much worse. Dreux's penchant for violence is not an instinctual act of survival but a true nightmare. Sam is a wimp next to this man."

"And why would she awaken him?"

He nodded toward Geoffrey. "Because he convinces her she loves Dreux. She is in danger and we must stop her."

"By killing her?"

"By any means necessary. But we can try knowing her, stopping her that way. And if she is diverted in time, I will leave her alone with you."

Alex glared at him and Kai waited. Alex would work with him, eventually. Kai may be the man who'd hurt Kalyss, who'd knocked Alex out and tied him up and who'd dragged a dead body into the room then tortured it when it came to life, but Kai was also Alex's only ticket out of the basement. And if the basement wasn't a comfortable place to be, well, how long he suffered in it was up to Alex. "Now, let's talk."

"Not tonight, dear, I have a headache."

Kai laughed and inspected the shine on his blade. "I think you'll find I can be quite persistent."

KALYSS EXITED THE bathroom in a rush, refusing to hide any longer. Dreux was sitting on the edge of the bed. Watching her, again. She was temporarily trapped in a hotel room with a very large, battle-trained man who should still be a statue. Or dead. She grimaced.

Either way, she'd only stay here until the police inspected the dojo, found the bodies, or at least blood, and declared it safe. Then she could call Alex's parents, plan the funeral, and return to work. Too bad she couldn't draw worth a damn or she could give the police a picture of Kai.

Trying to ignore Dreux's stare, she found some fast-paced alternative rock on the radio and began clearing a wide space on the floor. Growing up, she'd hated the never-ending chore of exercise, but through Alex's influence and the necessity of physical therapy, she'd come to love the peace it gave, the way it emptied her mind and allowed her to block out everything.

Except a certain dark-eyed stare.

HER MOVEMENTS WERE brisk and confident, her black pants whispered with each purposeful stride, but Kalyss was a ball of nervous energy. She clearly didn't know what to think or do now. Not that Dreux did, either. He'd had a much longer time to think about it, too. Still, he floundered.

She'd cried again, judging by her red eyes, but she'd washed her face of any other traces. She was amazing. Strong, resilient. She might fear something or someone, but it never overwhelmed her for long. Just like on their wedding night, when she'd fought her fear and won. Now she fought her grief, her uncertainty, and her fear.

She was his dream—everything he'd needed and wanted, whittled down to one small woman. All roads branched from her. He was no longer a knight with armies at his command. Nor did he have the support and ear of a king. His only friend was a man who'd once betrayed him and his only family wanted to kill him. Or, barring that, everyone important to him.

No home. No career. No social life. Few twenty-first-century skills. He was a bum. A rich bum, though. His lips twisted. What a catch. No wonder she didn't want him.

To have once been so great. To have ruled his world and everyone in it, deciding the courses of battles and, therefore, wars, an instrument of history. And now . . .

Now he was nothing but the greatest thing of all: the last defense of a tiny, indomitable woman battered through lifetimes by a cruel, capricious destiny.

The will of God. It was an awesome, fearsome thing. How had she held up so well for so long? Surviving . . . striving . . . strengthening. Now, destiny, God's will, would be fulfilled. They had come full circle with Dreux's awakening.

DREUX WAS GRIM. Deep in thought. His hands were clenched, the menace around him clearly focused inward. Yet, Kalyss was afraid.

Sam had been a slight man, slim and of medium height. He'd looked good in suits, impressive and powerful in a way that was all personality. Alex had more of a basketball player's defined musculature—tall and athletic, but appearing deceptively average. Only training with him gave her a good idea of what he was capable of.

Sam had destroyed her. Body, mind—and nearly soul. Alex had made her feel safe, supported. He'd helped rebuild her.

She didn't get either feeling from Dreux, but, rather, a mixture of both. He was so wide and imposing, true strength in his every movement, she knew. If he ever turned on her, she wouldn't recover. His size was terrifying, but his words and actions said he would never hurt her. She wasn't safe, but she wasn't in danger and the tense nervousness inside her was less fear and more excitement. It was very confusing.

She refused to face him or put her back to him. She turned sideways, keeping him on her left. Her heart pounding with the beat, she began her routine.

HOW MUCH TIME was left? Dreux would face Kai, end all threats to Kalyss, and possibly die in the process. Death held no fear for him, but what of Kalyss when he was gone? It was the first time he'd considered that—it was hard to think of the future beyond the fight with Kai.

Kalyss didn't want a husband. From the report Geoffrey had given him when Dreux was still a statue, she had good reason for her feelings. But that left him only two options:

Forcibly take everything his body and heart demanded, whether she was ready or not, or convince her to open to him, to love him, need him. But then, if destiny demanded his death, she would be left alone.

He knew that man did not decide his own fate or death, no matter how he might convince himself he did. Control on a battlefield did not equate to control over anything else. But as he'd told Kalyss one autumn night nearly a millennium ago, if a warrior entered a battle expecting to die, he would.

And he had entirely too much to live for to defeat himself that way. He wanted his fantasy—to live with her every day and love her every night. He wanted a little girl with his curly brown hair and brown eyes on Kalyss's face, with Kalyss's spirit and his own will. A perfect mixture of them both.

That's what he would believe in. What he would fight for.

DREUX'S FOCUS SLAMMED into Kalyss so intensely, that she felt it physically and nearly lost her balance. Gooseflesh prickled every patch of bare skin and her ponytail felt like she could be Pippi Longstocking, with braids sticking straight out from her head.

She forced her breath out evenly and her hands to steady.

If the man's eyes were hands, there wasn't a single bit of her skin that escaped his notice. She could feel the touch of his gaze where her breasts pushed above her black tank top and her waist burned as if his hot hands gripped it.

His eyes, when she gathered her nerves enough for a quick glance at them, were hot, appreciative. Not lewd, but still not acceptable—her life was screwed up enough right now. She didn't need, or want, to mix in a relationship. Even though the man had a bottom lip she could nibble on for hours. Even though her own lips tickled with the need to see if his kisses were always as good as the one that woke him. Even though her body reminded her what it felt like when he held her against his—the comfort, and the desire to sink inside him and never separate.

For a brief moment, Kalyss closed her eyes and gathered herself together. Then, with a disapproving purse of her lips, she focused away from him and back onto her kata.

* * *

KALYSS WAS NOT immune to him. That was good. Dreux had drifted eternities with the mere memory of *her* in his arms. His immunity to her was nonexistent. He clenched his hands, bracing his arms against his thighs to refrain from grabbing her.

She required finesse. Seduction. She no longer hid in corners, but he sensed she still needed to feel safe. He could appreciate that, work with it, even if it killed him.

Running his eyes over her body, he allowed his imagination free reign. He'd seen skimpier shirts than Kalyss's black tank top—some had mere strings to hold them up—but the inch more of black fabric over her shoulders protected her from nothing. Not the sensual kiss of the sun through the window. Not the chill in the hotel air. Definitely not from his gaze.

The slope of her breasts over the neckline looked soft, inviting slow caresses from his hands. His tongue prickled with the desire to lick each plump curve, through the shadowy valley visible when she bent forward to touch her toes.

He wanted to slide his tongue underneath the black fabric to sensitive coral nipples and tease them until they tightened in his mouth, as they had one chill night, too far from the fire for proper warmth. But oh, how golden and soft she had looked in the firelight.

A thousand years was too long for a man to wait to make love to his wife.

Kalyss stood straight and reached toward the ceiling and her shirt stretched taught against a firm, slim waist. Much as he wished it would ride up, allowing him to imagine licking along her stomach and waistband, it remained stubbornly tucked into her pants.

She'd mentioned never baring her stomach. Why was that? He'd seen commercials. Victoria's only secret was that she didn't have one. Women's fashion had changed to a point where they could do anything in any color or size, yet Kalyss was shy with her body.

The slim, supple softness he'd once taken such pleasure in now held a hard core of strength, both physical and mental. She wouldn't care what others thought of her body. Therefore, she had to be hiding. But from what? A memory? An imperfection only she could see? Or one others could see that would make her too vulnerable if they did?

He watched each tensile tendon stretch under the thin skin of her hands and neck. He loved the healthy flush that pinkened her cheeks and chest as her blood rushed only where it should: inside her body. The skin over his heart itched.

STILL DREUX STARED. Kalyss couldn't concentrate, let alone clear her mind. She was trying to loosen her muscles, but they only grew tenser. She executed a sideways lunge, holding her arms steady and stretching her right leg out. She looked straight at him. "You aren't a statue anymore." At his inquiring look, she added, "Remember?"

He grinned and rose to his feet, big and broad and all muscles. She gulped.

"I guess I forgot," he said, his voice slightly rough.

Yeah, likely story. She let it pass without comment. "You're probably pretty stiff. You should stretch out."

He grinned. She played back her words and realized the invitation that could be gleaned from them.

"I mean, I don't know if Geoffrey told you about different exercises. I teach a few classes on aerobics and Pilates in addition to karate. They really help loosen muscles."

His voice was deep and warm. "I could definitely use a good stretch."

"Right." Then she blushed. Her cheeks felt so fiery hot there was no way he couldn't see, but he didn't comment, thankfully.

They faced off and he mirrored each of her movements. Reaching up high, touching toes, reaching to the sides. Kalyss finally realized that having him work out didn't ease the tension one bit. If anything, he watched her more intimately, from even closer.

Instead of trying to ignore him, she forced herself to look straight at him and analyze his ability to move. She'd stood completely still at the window for only minutes and she'd nearly fallen at his feet. Yet his muscles hadn't given out once. Not when he first awakened or now. He moved with an amazing fluid ease considering what he'd gone through.

The devil's advocate inside her never quite silent, she tried to fit this new piece of the puzzle in at a different angle, reviewing the events of the day. But if he truly had been pretending, just the time she'd stared at the statue would have been enough time to wear down a normal human. He hadn't moved, blinked, or flinched, though.

So fitting the piece into his story, why would he have felt the pain of standing all this time and not be stiff now? Unless all his pain had been mental? As a statue, he could hear, see, and smell. He could think. But could he taste and feel? Was his body asleep, protected in stone, while only his mind was alive, thinking he could still feel his limbs, as amputees often did? Was that why he hadn't aged? Had he felt her blood when she'd left the handprint?

She huffed a quick, deep breath. "Okay, time to lie down."

He raised his eyebrows. "Really?"

Kalyss ignored the boyish sparkle in his eyes. She couldn't face him one moment more. Really she couldn't. She turned her back to him and said, "Lie on your side, like this, and raise your top leg, arching your foot then pulling it into a ninety-degree angle."

She demonstrated as she did in all her classes, launching effortlessly into her instructional spiel. "This is called the Up and Down and is most effective if you visualize squeezing a bellows between your thighs."

Her eyes popped open. Thank God he was behind her. That had never sounded like *that* in class. No one needed images of her squeezing *anything* between her thighs.

"This does interesting stretches to these muscles. How does it help?"

Thankful for his matter-of-fact tone, she replied, "It works your hips, thighs, butt, and inner thighs, giving more flexibility to your movements while stretching your ankle."

They quieted for a moment while she counted the beats to the Up and Down, the Small Leg Circles and the Leg Beats. Her embarrassment began to fade.

Why only now, after two years of giving these classes, was she realizing how suggestive they were? Had she secretly amused every guy in her class for the past few years?

They turned to stretch their right legs and his back was to

her giving her the opportunity to observe him without his dis-
concerting stare. He was well put together. She'd seen a lot of
good-looking, handsome men before, but there was something different with Dreux. He didn't only look good to her,
he was also attractive—as in attracting her, drawing her to
him. She couldn't walk through the room without knowing he
was in it even if she wanted to.

Lost in thought, she automatically finished counting the
beats and rolled to her back. "Now lie on your back for the
Teaser."

She closed her eyes, listening to his hasty, choking cough
and silently gave in to her own laughter. It was time to cut her
losses and just give up. Shaking her head at herself, Kalyss
rose to her feet.

"I think I'll just go order some food." She started away,
adding, "And put something in my mouth besides my foot."

Dead silence.

She paused a moment, slumped her shoulders, and dropped
her chin to her chest. Her cheeks were now so hot, they
brought tears to her eyes, and she shook with the effort to not
giggle aloud at herself. Before a heartbeat passed, she
marched to the door where the menu lay on a small table.

Dreux straightened behind her. "I'll go take a shower. Cool
down and all that."

She didn't even look at him. "Next time, we'll just spar."

Gently, he brushed her hair over her back and turned her to
him. She stiffened, but let him move her. One small measure
of trust—one small triumph over fear. "Kalyss?"

"What?" she snapped.

He grinned, then softly kissed her cheek. Pulling back and
looking into her eyes, he said, "I like you."

Kalyss watched him disappear into the bathroom. She
knew he loved her, or he thought he did, but love was a dangerous, threatening emotion—it lacked logic and safety.

But liking . . . liking was different. Liking was special.

She smiled and went to order food.

Chapter 11

They passed each other as he exited the bathroom, clean-shaven and smelling of fresh rain-scented shaving cream. Kalyss accepted their food from the waiter, trying to ignore Dreux's scent. Light and there, but gone too quickly. The kind of scent that made her want to curl into his neck and breathe it deep. After tipping the waiter five bucks from Dreux's wallet, she grabbed the food tray and followed Dreux into the main area.

Once more, he sat on the end of the bed. This time, he held the remote to the TV and channel surfed with the expertise of a pro.

"You're surprisingly comfortable with that for an eleventh-century knight. Is it truly a guy thing?" Kalyss arched her right brow. It was little things like this that made her wonder about him, about his story, even now.

He grinned charmingly, his eyes sparkling. "TVs still fascinate me."

"Still?" she challenged.

He shrugged."What else is a statue to do? Eight hundred years of the bird poop Olympics got old."

Her lips quivered. "I'm afraid to ask."

He pursed his lips and looked at his feet as if embarrassed. He shrugged again. "How many times a day can a windowsill get pooped on?"

She couldn't hold it in. A laugh burst from her and he smiled reluctantly. "And?"

"I think the winner was forty-seven."

"Do you remember the date, too?"

He'd been embarrassed, but having fun with her. Now he sobered, holding himself statue still again. Kalyss refrained from going to him and trying to offer any comfort that might promise more than she could give.

"I had no calendar, no way to mark the days. I lost entire seasons, entire years at a time." His voice was low with memory.

She frowned, taking in what he didn't say. Eight hundred years, every muscle straining, the same view, nothing to do, no way to do it. Only time to think. To grieve. To go surely, irrevocably insane. It was amazing that he wasn't.

He met her gaze. "A hundred years ago, I watched you die again. Closer this time, smelling your blood. I saw anguish in your face, felt it in your hand on my chest." He unbuttoned the top three buttons of his shirt and pulled it to the side. Like a new tattoo, her bloody handprint still marked him.

"I thought it was another nightmare."

She absorbed that, biting her lip and trying to keep a distance between them. A distance that became harder and harder to maintain with each conversation they shared. She shifted and the tray in her hands rattled, reminding her it was there.

Tentatively, she eased onto the bed beside him and settled the tray. She couldn't move more than that, couldn't eat, couldn't think of a single thing to say. She was alive and well now. But that didn't negate the centuries he'd mourned her.

His hand reached toward her and he tucked a few stray strands of her hair behind her ear. Then, with his hand on her chin, he raised her eyes to his. For a long moment, he simply stared at her, as if looking past the face of his wife to the woman she'd become. His thumb lightly caressed across her lips before he released her.

Casual now, he opened the covers of the plates, revealing

soup and sandwiches, a slice of pizza and a hamburger. He raised his left eyebrow and quirked a grin. "I hope you're hungry. I think my stomach shrank."

She shrugged with an awkward shift of her shoulders. "I wasn't sure what you'd like."

"Thank you."

She nodded. The silence between them stretched a moment before he picked up the pizza and took a bite. She took half a turkey sandwich and watched him tasting the mixture of tomato sauce, cheese, and pepperoni.

"I've always wondered what pizza tasted like, if the commercials lied or not."

"Did you watch a lot of TV?"

He looked at her and smiled. "What do you think?"

She grinned back. "Lots."

"And lots." He chewed another bite, then spoke again. "Geoffrey liberated me from the tower a hundred years ago and hid me from Kai's constant searching. The first few decades he read to me, talked to me, tried to teach me everything he knew, getting me ready for you."

"He really didn't seem the type to talk so much." She grinned.

He grinned back, his dark hair framing a squared, rough face. His lips were the only soft part of him—at least when they tilted, full of charm, as they did now. "I don't think he was used to it. His conversations were awkward for a while. But he'd decided he had two options. Live his time with me as if I could hear and see, or as if I was dead inside the stone. And to live as if I were dead inside, then find he'd wasted a hundred years he could have used to adjust me to the new world . . . well, that just went against everything he fought for."

"He did so much for you." She raised her brows. "That's very loyal."

He faced her soberly. "He felt he owed me. Us. He wanted to atone."

"Atone for what?"

"Leading Kai to us the first time."

She looked down at the food before them. "Oh."

"His actions killed you and froze me. He's refused to rest until he's fixed it."

"And?" She met his gaze again. "Has he?"

"It's not over yet." He took a bite and swallowed, looking at his pizza. "But there's not much left he could do to prove himself."

Dreux stuffed the rest of the pizza into his mouth and grabbed the remote. He turned the sound up and a woman's voice over a distant connection spoke urgently: "*Apparently, the man entered through the back door, surprising the female owner of the home. Neighbors say—*"

Kalyss reached out and pushed the mute button. They had enough trouble already. They didn't need to borrow more. "It's not my place. That's a residential neighborhood."

"This century seems more peaceful, until you watch the news." He picked up the hamburger and bit into it, frown lines marking his forehead as he chewed.

The silence became uncomfortable again and Kalyss swallowed her food to speak. "I hate watching the news. It's easier to believe there's good in the world when you're not swamped with the bad."

Dragging his eyes from the lettuce and pickles on his meat, he asked, "Do they truly solve all the cases? The news doesn't report that as often as the crimes."

"Not in an hour. Not always even in a year. But many do get solved." She watched him take that in. "You'll get used to the differences."

He polished off the hamburger and wiped his hand on the napkin. "It's not too different. Just more people to investigate, better techniques and slower, more lenient methods of punishment."

She tilted her head in question, surprised.

"We had thieves, rapists, and brigands, Kalyss. Even wife beaters." She looked away. "The men who enjoyed killing usually went to war. Not always, though. And in smaller communities, it was easier to investigate crimes."

"And punishment was swift." She nodded. Perhaps it had been better.

"Swift, yes." His tone commanded her attention again. "And brutal. And often biased. Especially against women."

"So no system is perfect."

He grinned ruefully, his laugh lines deepening. "None that I know of."

She grinned back, looking up at him. Her heart going crazy at his smile. Her breath harder to catch. "So what switched Geoffrey from reading to having you watch TV?"

"The world began to change too fast for mere conversation to keep me updated. So, TV. Thanks to *Sesame Street,* I can read. And thanks to closed captioning, I can read several languages."

"Just not write them?"

He nodded. "More recently, our favorite is the History Channel. It's quite an experience to listen to Geoffrey curse at that one." She laughed with him. "And the Discovery Channel, Animal Planet, and a few select examples of popular culture to understand society and local laws."

"Such as?"

"*CSI, ER, NYPD Blue, Gilmore Girls, Buffy,* and *Angel.*"

Kalyss laughed again. "I can see it now—a thousand-year-old man and his living statue tuning in to watch vampires and high school kids."

"Hey, don't knock Buffy. She's hot."

That kind of sexist remark usually irritated the hell out of her, but it was so incongruous, coming from him, she fell back on the bed laughing harder.

He laughed with her for a moment. "Actually, that show was put together so well, with great acting and writing, I learned quite a bit. Like how to talk to and relate to others."

She pulled a pillow under her head and looked at him. "What else?"

"Well, football, of course."

Her tone dry, she said, "Of course."

He grinned at her again.

"Do you have a favorite team?"

"Of course. I've seen every game, every Super Bowl, ever shown on TV."

She raised her brows, waiting.

"The Raiders."

"What?" she exclaimed. "They're the most penalized losers in the NFL."

He gave her an irritated glower. "They're just penalized because they treat football like war. In war, you only obey the important rules. The rest are inconveniences that could get you killed. I identify with that. I mean, what idiot thought you could fight war in neat little rows, like against Napoleon? In my time, we faced each other across a field, or a castle, clashed and all was chaos for hours."

He growled his disgust. Actually *growled*. She choked back a laugh.

"We fought face to face, strength against strength, like defensive linemen."

"Who begin each organized clash in neat rows."

He ignored her. "We stormed castles with only our courage to hold us on the ladders, our determination to break through the gates. If we'd paid attention to namby-pamby rules—"

"Namby-pamby?" she choked out. "You *are* old."

"—we would have lost. Wars, lands, lives!"

For the first time, she saw him angry. His voice raised, his eyes shooting fire. It should have alarmed her. Instead, she found it funny and cute.

"In my day, there were no referees to halt the flow of battle and institute civilized behavior. And any cowardly dog who dared throw a flag—a flag, Kalyss!—on the ground was instantly marked for death." Dreux stopped, hands on his hips, and looked at Kalyss. Breath blew in and out of his lungs as loud as the bellows she'd mentioned earlier and his chocolate eyes were so hard she couldn't see the sweetness in them.

He paused, staring at her as she lay stretched out on the bed, her hair spread on the hotel pillow. Suddenly all the anger seemed to drain from him and his gaze focused on the bottom lip she was biting to hold in her laughter. Pursing his lips against a smile of his own, Dreux glowered at her. "Who's your favorite team?"

Uh oh. She could just imagine what he'd say. "The Jaguars."

He sniffed in disgust. "They're brand new."

She giggled. "I'm not so old I've seen every game shown on TV."

He pursed his lips, his eyes promising retribution. "Why do you like them?"

She gave a mocking blonde, side-to-side head bob and in her best baby voice said, "'Cause they wear pretty colors."

His glare now obviously hid a smile, but he demanded again: "Why?"

She sobered, but kept it light. "I guess you could say I'm all about beginning new."

He shook his head at her reincarnation jibe. There was too much truth behind it for it to be really funny.

She laughed. "I've just never thought of football in terms of war."

"How did you think of it, then?"

She shrugged, but tingled with a full-body heat flash from just thinking the word in front of him. "Sex."

He froze, astounded, his brow twisted. "What?"

"Typical guy thing. Bust through the other team's defenses any way, any how. It's all about making the score. And at the end of the game, only one team gets the glory."

His voice dropped an octave, becoming a seductive bass. "Oh, honey, you've played with the wrong team."

She arched her brows wickedly, willing her toes not to curl. "Huh, never tried that."

His grin was his only acknowledgement of her joke. "In my mind, after a good game, both teams are glorified."

"Is that what they called it in your day?"

He dropped the sexy tone and glared at her again.

She laughed and sat up, at her limit for playful sex talk. "Since I cooked, you can clean."

"Where are you going?"

She halted and looked innocently over her shoulder. "My turn to get wet and naked."

He groaned. "Now that's just mean. Meanness deserves a penalty."

"There shouldn't be refs in sex, either," she said, smiling, then clicked the bathroom door closed between them.

Imagining his reaction, Kalyss flipped on the light and froze. A wide vanity mirror covered the wall above the sink, leaving nothing hidden. Her eyes twinkled from their playful talk and her cheeks were flushed from the flirtatious undercurrents between them. A wide smile graced her face before it slowly died and, for the first time in years, the man who'd put it there wasn't Alex.

She'd been teasing Alex last night when she'd suggested they do it the easy way and get together, but now she realized that was exactly what she'd forced him into these last four years. They'd worked together, eaten together, watched movies together—always together—and at the end of the night, he'd gone home and she'd slept alone. The perfect relationship—for her.

Maybe he'd urged her to get a life just as much for himself as for her. She'd kept him trapped in a twenty-four/seven relationship. He never had a chance to meet someone new or recover from his high school crush. Most men couldn't be in a friendship with a woman without trying to turn it sexual—but through all their time together, not once had Alex hit on her. Not once had there been a spark of sexual tension. Maybe it hadn't been just her trying to hide from relationships. Maybe Alex had been just as afraid to move on as Kalyss had been.

What would she have done if he'd met someone? Spent more time alone? Met someone herself, eventually? Or been upset and jealous over the loss of his constant attention? What a horrible friend. She didn't want to think that of herself, but that was where all the signs pointed.

Now he was dead and it was too late to free him from the trap they'd fallen into. Yet it was still a step she needed to take for herself. Sober now, she pulled off her clothes and stepped into the tiled shower. The water beat down in relaxing hot streams. She'd just finished washing with the hotel-provided soap and shampoo when she felt it happen.

A slight wobble, a dizzy wave. Her visions had never given her warning like this before. It would be a doozy.

Carefully, she slid down the wall to the tiles, at the edge of the hot spray. And, for the first time in twenty-seven years, she welcomed the burst of colors and sounds, and the knowledge they would bring.

Chapter 12

Without even a groan, the dead man breathed again. Completely freaky and unnatural, but Alex had watched it happen twice now. Did his body fully heal each time?

Alex didn't miss the cold stare drifting over him, taking in the black eye and the split lip Alex kept licking. If it dried any further, it would crack open and begin bleeding again. He tested his jaw, moving it in circles, pleased to find it wasn't broken. It even hurt less than the dozen thin, bleeding cuts all over his chest. Those really stung.

"I see our host has made you welcome," the dead man said. His empty eyes somehow conveyed that, though he couldn't see the cracked ribs and bruises hidden by Alex's clothes, he knew they were there.

"Yeah, but he forgot refreshments. I think he's up getting tea and cakes right now."

The dead man was pretty flushed and tan for a man whose blood pooled around his feet. Alex leaned against the pipe behind him. "So, what are you? A vampire or something?"

"Or something."

Alex looked up to the ceiling again, frustration nearly

overwhelming him. He fought it back but still burst out, "What the hell is going on?"

"It's a long story."

"Then summarize," Alex snapped, allowing his irritation to show. He refused to wait any longer for answers that actually made sense. Assuming a dead man could give some, anyway.

Clearly unimpressed, the other man asked, "What did Kai tell you?"

"The lunatic?" What, was Alex supposed to believe anything the man had said?

Dead Guy nodded.

"That Kalyss is in danger and he would torture me until I told him how to find her so he could save her by killing her." Alex's brain knotted up just saying the words.

"The logic isn't quite all there, is it?"

"Nope." Alex arched his back and winced when it hurt. Was he the only one feeling pain here? Didn't dying at least *hurt*? Alex studied the calm, almost casual, pose of the man before him. If it weren't for the rope around his wrists, it would look like he was leaning against a low beam instead of hanging barely off his toes. "But you gotta admire his persistence."

Dead guy closed his eyes and the right corner of his lips twitched slightly. "Yeah, you have to do that."

"Kai says she's in danger." Not the best source, granted, but still . . .

"No. She's the safest she's ever been." Not a single trace of doubt colored his tone.

"I doubt that," Alex scoffed. She'd been pretty safe with him the last four years. Now she was alone somewhere, hiding and scared.

Dead Guy's empty gaze speared him like a blue icicle. "Don't doubt it. She's where she needs to be."

"Which is where, exactly?" Alex demanded.

"She's with her husband."

"What?" Alex fought his bindings with the brute strength only panic could bring. How the hell could that be considered safe? "You son of a bitch!"

"Not Sam. Her *true* husband," the man calmly interjected.

"She's only been married once." Alex stilled and turned narrowed eyes on the man. If not Sam, who?

"If you keep interrupting, this summary will take even longer than each second of the last thousand years." The man's expression fell into a remote, unblinking stillness.

There was nothing obvious in his manner, but his commanding poise and the fall-in-line-or-get-out-of-my-way drill sergeant look in his eyes said answers were a courtesy—one that could be easily overlooked if Alex didn't behave. Alex instinctively wanted to rebel, but he wanted the answers more—and he really wanted to know where to get a look like that. There were a few students he could see it working really well on. And—

. . . the *last* thousand *years*? Alex raised a brow, blinked, and said smartly, "Sir. Yes, sir."

"A few years after the Norman Invasion of England, William the Conqueror awarded lands to many of his best knights. One piece was a keep along the seaside border of Northumberland. He wanted our leader, Dreux, to defend it from invaders out to help the Saxon rebels. Dreux's task was to take the keep, upgrade it, and settle there.

"That's when he first saw Kalyss. She was the lady of the village. Her family had all been killed and marriage to her would best cement his claim on the land. Local rumors labeled her a witch." The man paused and looked pointedly at Alex. "I'm sure you know why."

Alex nodded, his attention fully captivated by this story. Even told in a dry tone and lacking in description, his mind filled with imagined details. Probably the wrong ones since *Braveheart* was set a couple of hundred years later and set in Scotland, but he could get a picture. And if Kalyss could do then what she did now, no wonder they'd called her a witch.

"But Dreux wasn't bothered by that. There'd been rumors following him as well, saying he'd murdered several women in particularly gruesome ways." The blue eyes looked up and away, focusing inward. "There was nothing in his personality to substantiate the gossip, but the murders always seemed to happen near his location. Kalyss knew this. It scared her, but she was pressured by the villagers around the keep to make the new lord happy. So, they married."

"The love story is fascinating, and I really mean that," Alex said sincerely. Kalyss would've known by touch if her husband were guilty or not. There were more immediate concerns to worry about now. "But, there's this little problem I'm having. It's about the *thousand year* time difference. How'd *that* happen?"

"Kai killed her. She was reborn. Kai killed her again."

"She resurrects, like you?"

"No, she reincarnates, given a hundred years or so."

"Well, that can sure lengthen a struggle. What happens after she reincarnates?"

"I find her, protect her, and help her get to Dreux so she can awaken him."

"And that's when the serial killer steps in to stop her?"

"Exactly," he replied grimly.

"And you just let him?" Alex's outrage bubbled out.

"I tried to stop him. From the moment I first realized . . ." He shook his head and looked away again. "My best guess is that I thrust my sword into Kai as he pulled his blade from Kalyss and sunk it into me. She died. Dreux became a statue. And we were all caught in some never-ending cycle."

"But it can end. You keep her away from Kai and there isn't a problem. It's not that friggin' difficult to protect her from a dangerous guy."

Dead Guy glared, his eyes colder than ever. "It's more complicated than that."

"No. I don't think taking her out of a dangerous situation is all that hard to do. I did fine until you two showed up, drugging me and knocking me out."

"Your fighting last night delayed me and nearly killed her. I'm glad I drugged you or it might have been too late. I *have* to lead her into dangerous situations. She has to free her husband. She's the only one who can."

"He's a statue! He's fine. You could have left him alone, let her live a nice long, happy life and kept her away from Crazy." *He'd* nearly gotten her killed? That was rich.

"And forgotten about Dreux?" Dead Guy shook his head firmly. "That was never an option. He deserves better. And it's the only way to end this, as far as I can tell."

"You mean you don't even know? You risk her for a *theory*?"

"It's not like there's a How-To book about it," Dead Guy snapped. "Besides, even without me, her own dreams and memories compel her. She *yearns* for him her entire life."

Alex slumped and stared at the ceiling. The living corpse had a point there. Kalyss did remember strange things at times. And she was stubborn. If she'd started remembering Dreux, she'd go after him. "Nearly a thousand . . ."

"What?"

"Years. That means she's died, what . . . ?" Alex silently counted.

"Nine times," Dead Guy said flatly.

"And now you want to lead her to number ten?"

"No. That's why we're here, occupying Kai. Keeping him busy, giving her time."

"Did you leave her a map or something?"

The man nodded. "One only she could read."

"Why haven't you just killed him? Ended the threat?"

"Why, indeed," he said, voice dry. "When it worked so well for Kai." Dead guy looked at his blood.

Alex reared back and nearly thunked his head on the pipe. "He comes back, too?"

Dead Guy nodded. "I don't see this ending without Dreux."

"And if Kalyss dies again?" Alex challenged.

"We try again in another century."

Alex pinned the man with his gaze. "What if this is her last chance?"

The man stared at Alex, silent and forbidding. Forget that he was tied and covered in blood. Forget that he had died twice already. Despite these detractors, he still had the appearance of someone who could make anything happen.

"This time, we succeed." His tone refused any other option. That, at least, was a relief.

Alex stared into the hard eyes, quiet, judging. They could be allies or enemies. Whichever would keep Kalyss alive the longest. In *this* lifetime. This situation didn't allow for half-measures and compromises. Seconds went by, marked only by the tinging sound of air rushing through the pipes. Kai had shut and soundproofed the windows hours ago. Other than one dim bulb, the basement was shrouded in darkness.

Finally, Alex exhaled his frustration. It boiled down to the man with a record for killing her or the man who repeatedly failed to protect her. "So you were never even tempted to take her away and keep her safe? Keep her, period?"

The man was silent so long he could have died again. He stared straight ahead; hanging from his arms like it was nothing more than a comfortable stance. Yet his eyes betrayed the first bit of emotion Alex had seen in him. At last, he faced Alex. "Nine times—I held her dying body. Nine times—I dug her grave."

He stopped speaking, as if searching for the right words. His gaze drifted off, to the past. "She never remembered Dreux right away. But given a little time, she'd begin to."

He stopped a moment, gathering memories. "She was so afraid to die. Knowing she'd come back didn't help; it just gave her a sense of inevitability. But once she remembered him, there was no thought of running away.

"She wanted him more than she feared death." He swung his gaze to Alex. "She wasn't mine to keep. And I owe both of them."

Alex hadn't lied when he'd told Kalyss they both deserved better than an easy relationship with each other. They did. But if ever she'd reached for him fearlessly, passionate for him, he wouldn't have turned her down. He wasn't stupid. But *knowing* they didn't belong together, that was something he could identify with. "So you're the protector, the guardian."

Dead Guy nodded. "And you're the best friend."

"Alex Foster."

Dead guy nodded. "Geoffrey Knight."

Alex snorted. "Original."

Geoffrey shrugged, his eyes hinting at laughter. "It was easy to remember."

October 6, 1075 — England

DREUX WAITED SILENTLY, naked and tied, nearly defenseless. Or he seemed defenseless. Kynedrithe nervously looked anywhere but at him.

The fire crackled and moonlight streamed through the tower window. At the very least, Kynedrithe was glad he hadn't let her jump. Her gaze returned to his and her heart gave a hard thump. His intensity was frightening, but he didn't seem impatient. He was a virile, attractive man. Handsome, with black hair and dark eyes. His size invited both fear and a sense of security. She wasn't sure which was intended for her.

"What do we do now?" Her voice came out more timid than she'd wanted.

"We wait," he replied.

She looked around the empty room, then back at him. "For what?"

"For you to do what must be done."

She frowned, puzzled, then shook her head. "I can't do that."

He was unsympathetic, but calm. "Now you know why men usually lead in this."

"Then why don't you?" she demanded.

"You must not fear me. I can only try to eliminate what you fear—my control." His dark eyes held her immobile.

"It's an illusion." She wasn't ignorant enough to believe otherwise.

He smiled.

"But if I believe, temporarily . . ." she questioned.

He nodded. "Then you don't fear me and our purpose is achieved."

"What if I don't fear you now, but do by morning?" Her chin was determined to tremble no matter how she tried to firm it.

"You won't." He was too confident.

"How do you know?"

He smiled again, arrogant.

"It will hurt." She held up that flimsy barrier again.

"That can't be helped." He tore mercilessly through her excuse.

She continued. "And I'm not to fear you?"

"I won't hurt you. You will. You've chosen this task."

"But in the morning . . ."

"You won't know any of your answers until this night's work is done and the morning has risen," he stated abruptly. She couldn't push him further, his voice, his expression said.

She nodded and bowed her head. She had to be brave for this. He was giving her nothing to fight against, no one to blame, except herself. Was she a coward? Yes. Did he deserve a coward as his bride? No. His bravery demanded equal bravery in his spouse. If she was ever to have children, then she would face this dilemma. And other men weren't so kind.

She raised her head, firmed her chin, and faced him. "What do I do?"

He studied her a moment, then commanded, "Stand."

She rose.

He waited. It was her choice how the morning found them. Man and wife or, what? What would happen if they didn't do anything?

"What if we don't—"

"They'd know. You will not shame me."

No. She wouldn't. Looking at his lap, she didn't think he appeared as intimidating as he had earlier. She jerked her gaze back to his and a hot blush climbed her cheeks.

He smiled.

"Now what do I do?"

"Sit."

She took a deep breath and sat on one hard thigh. Her breath whooshed out and she stared around the room. She'd never sat on a man before, let alone a naked man.

Frantically, she searched her mind for something to say. "How old are you?"

"It won't work if you distract yourself." She heard a grin in his voice.

Turning, she stared into his eyes. She licked her lips and watched him focus on that movement as if making sure she did a good job of it. "Why won't that work?"

"It'll hurt less if you're careful and pay attention."

"You'll guide me in this?" She needed the reassurance.

"If you wish it."

"I do." She nodded. Then soberly asked, "It's too late to untie you, isn't it?"

"Yes."

She took a deep breath, turned, and looked him in the eyes and waited, her heart pounding in her throat. The more time that passed, the smaller the distance between them seemed. She lost awareness of the rest of the room as she stared at the charred flecks in his eyes.

"Put your hands on me," he demanded in a low voice that raised prickles on her arms.

Her hands rose from her lap and rested on his shoulders. His skin was rough and weathered. Deeply tanned from the sun. She rubbed her fingers over it, caressing a few silky, black hairs. She'd never touched a man so intimately, so slowly. He'd given her time to revel in this new freedom and she wanted more.

"Where?" Excitement was an undercurrent to her nervousness. Waiting, lurking beneath to suck her into its pull.

"Anywhere." His voice was husky now, tempting her further.

She sucked in her bottom lip absentmindedly, and ran her fingers over his chest. Her heart pounded harder. Leaning closer, she could smell the clean scent of the soap coming from his neck.

Bending close to his neck, breathing him in, she whispered against his ear, "How?"

"Any way you want." He sounded winded.

Taking him at his word, she leaned forward into him and pressed her lips to the curve of his neck. She breathed deeply and realized this was the most comforting closeness she'd ever had with a man.

He hardened against her thigh. She was affecting him. Her power expanded inside her until she smiled against his skin. Opening her lips, she traced her tongue from his neck to his ear. He was salty and warm, a perfect taste.

Breath whistled from between his teeth, but he didn't pull away, so she didn't stop. She scored her fingers through his hair, then gripped it tightly. A passionate ferocity streaked through her. That she could be capable of this—passion in its most elemental form—shocked her.

She pulled away and examined his face, watching the emotions there. The flames in his eyes danced and she knew she hadn't hurt him. If anything, her boldness pleased him. Excited him. She watched him, caressing her bottom lip with her tongue.

He stared at her mouth. She lowered her head and licked at his lips. He groaned and pressed forward. His lips grasped hers, pulling out her bottom lip, tasting it. His tongue entered her mouth and she thrilled to his gentle invasion.

She realized now, her fear had been unreasonable. Despite the visions of blood, with this touch she knew he was not a barbarian—or a murderer. He'd been patient, coaxing trust from her, giving her the chance to explore, herself and him. Her fears and doubts, his strength and power.

Following his example, she plundered his mouth, making him hers. He was hers. She would possess him. He would not leave her for another as she'd seen so many other men do once they were wed. She would not allow it. She grasped his hair and pulled him to her, then let it go and ran her hands all over his shoulders and chest.

"What do I do?" She gasped for breath. Need spiraled inside her.

"Face me. Straddle me."

She tried, but her tunic pulled against her. She stood and lifted it to her knees. Placing a knee on either side of him, she lowered herself and that hard part of him settled against the bare skin of her stomach. She grasped his shoulders for balance and stared at him.

He lowered his head against her cheek, then trailed small kisses down to her neck. She'd never known this gentleness. Hadn't known men were capable of it. This didn't resemble anything she'd heard about happening to women in other conquered villages. Those terrible things hadn't happened in her village and now she knew why.

He might be a conqueror, but he had honor. He fought men, not women and children. He was a man she could respect. A man she would be proud to call husband come morning.

His lips traced her collarbone and his thighs lifted her, just a little. She waited, breathless. His lips trailed lower, his teeth biting at the wool, trying to bare her flesh. When his thighs pushed her up again, she rose up on her knees and leaned forward, allowing her tunic to slip from her shoulders and release her breasts. She watched closely, until his lips closed around the tip of one breast. Her eyes fell shut and she nearly fell off him. He closed around her as much as he could before she grabbed his shoulders and held on tightly.

His hands moved behind her, cupping her bottom. She turned to see his bindings still holding him tight, his hands curved from the wrist toward her. It wasn't right. The bindings rubbed him and welts were appearing on his arms. He was constricted, held back, and her heart nearly broke at the sight.

She kissed him with all the passion welling inside her, then pushed him away and rose. She grabbed his dagger from the floor.

He frowned.

She brought it to his left ankle and sliced through the cord. "Kynedrithe, no."

Ignoring him, she sliced the cord binding his right ankle. "Kynedrithe . . ."

She looked up at him and rose to her knees in front of him. "I feel no fear. And just as you don't want to hurt me, neither do I want to hurt you."

Swiftly she sliced the other bindings and, before they hit the floor, she dropped the dirk beside the chair and climbed into his lap. Pulling him close, she kissed him deep, passion rising with his freedom.

He held still for a while, then his hands closed around her, running through her hair, grasping her back, and coming again to her hips. Her need found its center and she pressed against him. Then his hands were under her dress, clasping her hips and bottom.

He pressed her to him and she wanted more. She held him tightly, kissed his lips, tasted his neck. And he touched her, in the center of her need, caressing firm and gentle. She pressed his head to her shoulder and bit his neck, holding him lightly with her teeth as his fingers stroked her. The spiral of need tightened until her whole body clenched with it.

Then he shifted and the pressure changed. The pain began, but she did not run from it, from him, as his broad tip pressed against her. She almost needed pain to balance the pleasure that tightened to an unbearable pitch, then he was inside her, deep and still. She shuddered and he trembled against her.

"You're mine now." He sounded determined, as if he'd truly fight her if she tried to deny it after this.

She smiled, rubbed the mark at his neck, and whispered, "You're mine, too."

And they began to move, to slide deeper and deeper into each other. Her world narrowed to just his eyes and the heat she found there, and the stretch of him inside her. Tighter and tighter, she gripped him with her arms and her thighs until, with an overwhelmed gasp, she shuddered and moaned her release.

He held her tight to him and shuddered his own release. They were one and the morning would find them without fear, without ill will of any kind. Her husband lifted his bride and took them both to their bed.

Chapter 13

October 7, 2004 — Spokane, WA

FREEZING WATER PELTED her entire body—from the warm comfort of her husband's arms, Kalyss bolted awake on the freezing tile of the shower stall and lunged blindly for the faucet. A few quick twists and she knelt, shivering, on the wet tile. Cold water was one way to assure her alertness, though definitely not her favorite way. That would involve hot coffee.

She grabbed a towel and left the shower, briskly rubbing the thick cotton all over herself. Her body yearned to be back in the eleventh century with a roaring fire and a less confusing relationship with the man who claimed to still be her husband.

This vision had been even stronger than the one she'd had lying at Dreux's feet. And, this time, she'd "read" him without touching him. She'd always had to touch before. Kai, for the first vision in the tower. Geoffrey's hand, for the vision of the church. The statue, for the first half of her wedding night.

Unless she'd read *herself*. Her own memories could be latent, buried deep within her spirit. The spirit that had apparently lived ten lives.

Four visions in less than twenty-four hours and all but Geoffrey's followed a sequence, as though there was a story she needed the full-color version of. But all she knew even now was that Dreux had charmed her then as he did now.

Dreux had said she'd originally had more control and power over the visions. Could she gain that again? Because that would be cool. Finally her gift was starting to sound useful instead of frightening.

Kalyss wrapped the towel around herself and stared at the mirror, finger-combing her hair. A slight click warned her a split second before the door behind her opened. Dreux met her eyes in the mirror before cautiously stepping into the room.

Kalyss met his gaze, trying to forget that only moments ago she'd dreamed of gripping his hair and biting his neck as she rode him.

It was a hard memory to forget.

"You've been in here so long, I was beginning to worry."

"Were you afraid I'd taken the coward's way out so I wouldn't have to deal with you?" She grinned at him.

"Never. You are no coward." His sober voice reflected his sincerity. "You are brave and beautiful."

"You really believe that?"

He stepped up behind her and ran his hands up her arms to her shoulders. She reveled in his heat against her freezing skin.

"I really do," he vowed in his deep voice.

She shivered, unable to look away from their reflection. He settled against her back, warming her, supporting her. Her towel slipped. There was no way she could be laid more bare before this man, so she let it go. The towel caught between them for a moment before it was released. She forgot it as soon as it fell from view of the mirror.

Instead, she watched his face as he gazed at her body. She knew what he was seeing. Breasts not small or large, but in between. A waist not thin, but toned. She'd worked very hard to regain strength there. As she'd expected, he inhaled harshly before his hand settled over the small mound of her stomach, covering the deep scars defiling it.

She could see the defiance in her own raised chin, her vulnerability in the curve of her neck.

"I can't have children."

His liquid brown eyes burned with grief. His right arm settled across her chest, hard, comforting. His head rested against hers.

"I'm sorry."

She heard the words, felt his gentle support around her, but her disbelief was almost tactile. "You expect no children in your future?"

"Expectation left me centuries ago. I am thankful for what I have." His eyes reproached her for her doubt. He may have dreamed of a child, but she was more important.

"Even as flawed as I am?" she challenged.

Irritation graveled his voice. "I am not sorry you cannot have children. I am not sorry you are scarred."

She twisted against him, but his arms tightened and held her still.

"I am sorry for your pain. Your grief. Your fear. The loss of your dreams. Our dreams. But most of all for your suffering, not just in this life, but in all of them."

She froze, staring at the shadows in his eyes and finally understanding them. "You feel guilty for not saving me. Not keeping me safe."

"Of course." His matter-of-fact acceptance of a guilt he shouldn't feel humbled her. He had no control over any of it. He shouldn't bear that burden. "But I can see a higher purpose."

"Where?" she demanded, anger surging up inside her.

"In you, your determination. Your resilience. Your will. These are true strengths."

"Then you are happy with me as I am now?"

"Completely."

"We only had one night. Perhaps, one day, when the newness has worn off—"

"For a thousand years, I had nothing. No wars, no kings, no real family—nothing but thoughts of you to exist on. Nothing else mattered. All else passed beyond me." He tightened his hold around her waist. "Now you are in my arms again. We could freeze, as we are, for many millennia to come and I would be content for all that time."

"You certainly know the right words to say to me, don't you?"

He grinned. "A th—"

"I know. A thousand years to think of me, of . . ." She slowed for confirmation of the truth of her next words. "of how to please me?"

He nodded, a sexy half-smile on his face.

She grinned. Then she grew serious again. "You'll need more." At his frown, she continued hastily. "No, I mean, not another woman, but a job. A hobby. A career."

"Ahh." He nodded. "These will wait. For now, I am content with a simple life. Killing my nemesis and loving you."

"You think loving me will be easy?"

"Yes. Living with you, however . . ." He raised his brows.

She chuckled softly, then she sobered again. "What if he kills you?"

His eyes burned with fiery assurance. "I will take him to the gates of hell with me."

She stared at him. Until now, she hadn't known what to do with him. But the thought she might not have him long tilted her perspective.

"But you'll be dead. He'll have taken all of you. I'll be alone." She spoke to herself as much as to him, the reality of it sinking bone deep. She wanted months to ease into dating, but what if she only had hours to love as she'd always dreamed of loving?

"If my death gave you a chance to live without his shadow darkening your future, it would be a death well served. You're strong enough to be alone. Until you love again."

His sincerity could kill her. The Kalyss of nine centuries past, or the Kalyss she'd been before her marriage to Sam, it didn't matter. This was precious, he was precious, and she couldn't bear the thought of losing him now that she'd *found* him.

"You spoke of partnership. Of strength without loneliness." She turned in his hold, pressing against him. Her arms raised until her hands rested high on his chest. Her right hand settled high over his heart. "Of love. I would prefer that."

"As would I." One hand rose to her neck, fingers threading through her wet hair, his other pressed against her back.

Their lips met, brushing feather light until they were as sensitized as the most vulnerable parts of their bodies. The wet heat of their tongues slipped in to stroke and rub against each other.

Kalyss retreated from his kiss, strategically and thoroughly. Was she really ready for this step with a man? With *this* man? She'd found out just that morning that he considered himself her husband. She couldn't see him deciding not to be anytime soon. Was she ready for that level of commitment?

To hell with it. She was tired of thinking—it was time to go with the moment or lose it forever. And, honestly, she was sick of losing her moments with people.

With a slow, deliberate movement, she snagged the bottom of his shirt and slipped the last button free. Working her way up, she watched him, gauging his reactions.

He stood steady, firm. Not a tremble, not a single sign of impatience. He let her do as she wished.

She'd been forced to submit to a brutally dominating man before, but with Dreux, he would allow her control. His passivity could never be taken for submissiveness, however—when he was ready, he'd take charge. She knew it and gloried in her chance to play.

She reached the top button of his shirt, slipped it free, and spread the sides apart. Trailing her hands down each long sleeve to unbutton the cuff, she inspected his bare skin.

His was not a bodybuilder's smooth skin, tanned and oiled so it shone to perfection, and the men of the WWE had nothing on him for raw strength. His chest was scarred. One of the scars crossed his abdomen, thick and ridged, seemed like it should have been deep enough to disembowel him. It was a miracle he was alive.

Another scar, the width, Kalyss imagined, of a sword as it stabbed, marred his left shoulder. She finished both cuffs, then reached up, up, above her head to his shoulders. Touching only the material, she peeled his shirt back over his shoulders and down his arms, baring him to her gaze.

Awesome came to mind, as in awe inspiring. Her scars were nothing compared to his. Dreux was a true veteran of war. How had she overlooked this in the past? Perhaps battle-scarred men had been too commonplace then. Maybe that's why he didn't mind her scars now.

His skin wasn't pretty, but it *was* intriguing with its high-lighted scars and shadowed valleys. She savored his skin. Over each ridge, natural and not, over each muscle, to his waist.

His skin prickled with goose bumps under her fingers and she read it like erotic Braille. Kalyss had never been one to salivate over a half-naked man, but her mouth watered now.

She brushed her thumbs over his nipples. Her own breathing stuttered when they shriveled to tight nubs. She swallowed once, then again.

"Mind if we do this in another room?"

"Just tell me where you want me." His voice alone made her shiver. He backed from the room, then turned toward the bed.

She followed him, the scarred skin she'd never displayed so openly before bare to his gaze. Somehow it was okay.

From the end of the bed, he picked up the remote to move it. She took it from his hand and clicked the TV off. If she was going to do this, she'd damn well do it right. They'd catch up on the news later.

She set the remote on the bedside table and flipped off the lamp. With the fading sun from the window, they could still see, but the room was now shrouded in hushed shadows.

He stood at the end of the bed, facing her and she strolled toward him, not wanting to rush this moment. It was the most breathtaking excitement she'd ever felt.

He held still for her as she came behind him. She raised her hands and savored his back, from neck to buttocks, and he quivered beneath her touch.

Reaching around his sides, she hugged him from the back, resting her left hand above his heart and her right bracing above his right hip. His back was smooth against her cheek, though it was covered with as many scars as his chest. He smelled of fresh air with an undertaste of salty wood smoke.

Tentatively, she dragged the tip of her tongue between his shoulder blades. He definitely shivered that time, before he reined himself in—a relief and a challenge. She wanted the control this first time in this century. She may have had over nine hundred years of conquering her fears, but she still had a few issues. She liked his aura of strength and power, too. She could never enjoy a whipped puppy of a guy, despite her experience with Sam.

With a slight smile, she tasted him, from his nape to the base of his spine and she gloried in his heart beneath her palm.

She dragged her hands to his hips, caressed both cheeks of his muscular glutes, down the flanks of his strong thighs, and lowered to her knees. Lost in her own sensual enjoyment, Kalyss gave in to an impulse she'd never before had, and wouldn't have admitted if she did. Curling her hands around his rock-hard thighs, she leaned forward and lightly marked one ass-cheek with her teeth.

His hands clenched.

Triumph at this proof she affected him overruled her embarrassment. When she crossed to his front, his eyes were closed, his head tilted back.

This time, as she caressed his chest, she tasted everything that had intrigued her the first time she'd studied him.

She knew what she was working toward and with each drag of her tongue over his pecs and nipples, her impulsive desire warred with fears from the past. She'd had her hair held, had her mouth forced open to accept a demanding, thrusting man before. She'd hated every moment from the first taste to the last mouthful as he withdrew.

She'd hated the humiliation and discomfort and sometimes outright pain. She'd hated her lack of control. Hell, the lack of even having her opinion considered. But this was different.

She wanted him. Wanted his salty smoke taste on her tongue. Wanted to feel his hard length in her mouth. Needed to continue her freedom, her learning of him.

She knew how sensitive he had to be; after not feeling anything for so long, would it be too much for him? Drive him too far?

She'd try, she'd risk. She had to. She sat on the end of the bed, perfectly level with the task before her. She placed her hands on either side of his pelvis and watched as he lowered his head and opened his eyes to watch her.

Carefully, she licked his tip, dragging her tongue around the broad head of his shaft. His hands tightened into large fists at his sides. She stared at them a moment before meeting his reassuring gaze.

She took him deeper inside herself, licking and stroking, loving everything he limited himself to.

* * *

DREUX STARED INTO her wary gaze, fully aware of the gift she was granting him—the gift of her touch, her trust. Glorying in the erotic vision of her mouth widening around him, slowly accepting more and more of him.

He forced his hands open and brought them to her cheeks, but resisted the urge to clench them in her wet, wild hair. He traced his thumbs over the edges her lips, her peachy skin as velvety as the hot inside of her mouth.

Her tongue ran along the ridged vein underneath his erection and he tightened his thighs, forcing back the urge to come. Even as a statue, he'd never been this hard. Even as a human, he'd never felt this needy. His thumbs brushed her lips lightly and they quivered around his cock.

Her eyes shone blue, when she looked up at him, bluer than the ocean at night. Dark with promises. Shadowed with more fears they'd need to overcome. Then her hands clenched against his thighs, her nails biting in, as her eyes closed and she relaxed into her own enjoyment of his body.

The dim light splashed down upon her face, lighting it with a soft glow. He wanted his turn, his time to savor and stroke her, taste her mouth, her breasts, the cream between her thighs. He wanted to bury his face in her cool, water-darkened hair, and raise her up, press her along the length of his body, wrap her legs around his waist, and thrust home.

His fingers curled over her jaw and stroked her neck. She rocked him now, her hands on his hips determining his pace and depth and he couldn't take his eyes off her mouth as he slid deeper and deeper, snowfall-slow, watching himself disappear. He could almost feel the back of her throat before she withdrew. Again and again, she took him into her mouth and pulled back, until she'd swallowed him to his root.

He closed his eyes and forced back his release with a will he'd never realized was strong enough for this.

She'd halted with him squeezed deep in her throat, her tongue curved under him. Reading her expression, he understood that doing this willingly was new territory for her. His lungs nearly burst through his chest with his effort for control, but he could not allow this to finish, not before she was done with him.

With a shaking hand, he gently brushed a strand of hair away from her eyes and praised with a hoarse voice, "Beautiful."

She held him a moment longer, testing him further, before releasing him in an excruciating glide. He choked down the equal urges to beg her for more or to lay her back and take everything he needed. Over and over.

As he left her mouth, her tongue snaked out and moistened her lips to a tempting shine. She grasped his arms and he braced his hands under her biceps, pulling her to her feet.

They slid together onto the bed, his right hand burrowing at last into her hair, cradling her head.

She let him control their descent onto the bed, holding onto his back, another small trust he wasn't foolish enough to ignore. He lowered them gently, settling into the cradle of her thighs.

She widened her legs, opening to him. He reached between them, stroking along her softest flesh, wanting to taste, needing to explore and conquer the trembling flesh before him. But that had to wait.

He spread her creamy wetness over them both and when he was poised at her entrance, hard and hungry and ready to come home, Kalyss reached between them, sliding her soft hand over his rough one, and urged him inside.

She threw her head back, arching. He was in, yes, God, sliding and filling her, stretching flesh that hadn't felt a true lover's touch in nine lifetimes.

What had been a slick, smooth glide warred with his heat until his gentle thrusting burned with an inciting friction, sparking her nerve endings and clenching her muscles around him. He shuddered, stopping as every muscle in his body clamped down and he groaned with the pleasure Kalyss was giving him—and the pain of refusing to just take.

KALYSS CURLED HER hand around Dreux's neck and pulled herself up. Every movement of his body told her of his love, of his *care* for her. It seemed that all he wanted was to give her what she needed—and, deep inside, she felt the last of her fear melt away.

"It's okay," she whispered—and, for the first time in so long, it was true. "I'm okay. You can let go."

He'd clearly been waiting for that moment, that sign, that

trust, and once given, he took her mouth with all the passion inside him. Tasting, feasting, devouring. His right hand clenched in her hair, enough to hold, enough to tug, but not enough to really hurt. His left hand parted her thighs further, pressing up against the back of them until she raised both knees to her chest and spread them wide. His hand moved between them, stroking her fresh cream around and over, finding her sensitive spot and conquering it.

Then he took her, dominated, demanded. His mouth on hers. His thumb on her clit. His cock riding her in one deep thrust after another until they stepped up to the edge of release. Just one more step until they fell over.

She clutched his back, her nails digging in, squeezing her sheath around him as tightly as she could.

"Tell me. Please, tell me," she begged breathlessly in his ear.

Firmly, he gave. "I love you."

She hugged him and fell free.

Then neither could speak as her release triggered his and they held each other with a tight, trembling embrace.

Shadows crept further and darker over the room. Dreux grabbed the sides of the blankets and wrapped them both in a cocoon. Settling back around her, he kissed her forehead.

"It's my turn next."

"Yes, please," she said prettily, then she sobered and hugged him tight. "Thank you."

He nodded against her hair. She'd needed to acknowledge his restraint and regretted that he'd needed to be so careful with her. It wouldn't be that way forever—it would be too much to expect. Her sudden need to hear him say the words told him she'd accept him, love him, and trust him, eventually. If he had enough patience with her until she did. Until she could turn to him in passion, and out of it, with the same words for him that she'd needed to hear.

Chapter 14

The wind howled through the darkness, sending black cloaks flapping like bat's wings. The night smelled ominous, of smoke and fire. It meant nothing good for the small boy trembling at the evil woman's feet. She'd said tonight was the night for the bastard, for Dreux, to pay. His father had hurt her enough by supplanting her with a concubine. She'd never allow Dreux to supplant her son as true heir.

Dreux shivered and huddled in on himself. He'd learned not to defend either himself or his mother. This hateful woman would not hear of how wonderful his mother had been. How she'd filled his belly with hot food every night, before tucking him into a warm bed and kissing his forehead. How she'd smiled and tickled him, playing games and laughing with him.

This woman did not laugh. She did not tuck him in or kiss his forehead. And his belly felt so empty, he wouldn't care if he was given cold food, as long as it was food. But he'd keep silent or she'd beat him again. And he would not beg. Not only did it gain him nothing, but she'd get that horrible look in her eyes. Like she could almost smile and it would be the most horrible sight he'd ever seen in his entire four years.

"Make sure he doesn't come back. I'll not have the shameful

likes of him tainting my hall anymore." The melodic voice was raised slightly to cut through the storm winds that furiously attacked her dress and cloak to reach the group of black knights in front of them both. He had no cloak, no warmth, but he did the only thing he could. He stood straight and absorbed the wind as if it were nothing more than a slight breeze. Anything less would be a mistake with these men. He could sense it.

The evil lady was his father's wife, but she wasn't his mother. His father and mother had both fallen ill and died, leaving him to her mercy—but mercy was a quality she did not have. He knew it and he could tell the rough group of knights she spoke to knew it, as well.

That was why she was enslaving him to them. He was to be theirs, another child they raised with their harsh and cruel ways, to become a mercenary like them. And he knew she hoped he'd die in the process of being with them.

The boy crossed thin arms over his bony chest and struggled with tears. Just a few days ago, he'd been cuddled in his father's lap, full of his mother's delicious rabbit stew. The hearth had thrown gentle light about their small cottage making it a haven of warmth and light, love and smiles, full of peace and happiness. That's how he struggled to remember them. He didn't want the images of them vomiting poison until blood ran from their lips. He didn't want to remember them staring at the ceiling, their chests refusing to rise with breath.

"I tell you, you'll never have to see him again. Just give us the fee and we'll be off," growled the filthy knight, his hair as black as Lucifer's.

"I don't see why I should give you a fee at all. You're getting an able-bodied male child. You should be paying me." The wind lived in the fire of her hair, vibrant and wild.

Oh, he hated this. He might not even live to see another day if they truly made her pay.

"This is how it is done, *ma dame*." The knight sneered the words, as if he doubted that's what she really was.

Her red, thin lips tightened with irritation. Her green, green eyes narrowed at the man. "Very well," she said reluctantly. "Though I believe I've paid enough simply suffering this little bastard to live." She slapped a small pouch in his hand. "Now, be gone with you."

Yes, she had suffered. He was the image of his father, his hair such a dark brown it was nearly black, his eyes liquid brown with golden lights in them. He'd spent many nights staring at his father and mother as they sat before the fire. He knew what the man had looked like and his mother had commented often how similar they were.

And this woman hated it. Hated him. He and his mother had taken her husband, the father of her son, usurping their places in his heart. It was his fault she'd had to kill his parents with her poisons. The only joy she could have was in eliminating him from their lives completely. Or so she'd told him, over and over.

Warm hands surrounded him, their heat so welcome he didn't even mind the cruelly painful grip. The man turned and vaulted onto the horse, pulling his small body into the seat before him. Just as they started to turn away, she walked with a stiff, commanding stride to the side of the horse. The boy stared at where she had been, his attention caught by the sight of a smaller boy, as he had been, so long ago. He had taken after his father, but this small boy with his red hair and green eyes took after the evil woman.

Now the green eyes stared at him, colder than the wind, harder than the man's hold on him. Kai was his name. The woman had introduced them, telling him Kai would have everything and he would have nothing. She'd then told them horrible lies about their father's mistress, Dreux's mother. Horrible lies about their father's oldest son—him.

She reached up and grabbed his leg and he jerked his gaze to her. The emerald gems of her eyes were hard, full of cutting edges. "Listen, boy. No doubt that whore of a mother of yours had fantasies of making you more than the mere bastard that you are. That will never happen. I was his wife. My son is his heir. You are nothing more than a by-blow."

Why was she telling him this again? He didn't want to be a baron. He only wanted to go home and have his mother hold him tight, but this woman had made that impossible. And now he was being sent from the only home he'd ever known.

"I hope you suffer all your days for the pain you have brought to my life." Her lips curled in disgust. "I will more than hope. I have made sure of it. If it takes me forever, I will see your pain and horror runs deeper than mine for the rest of your ill-begotten life." Hatred spewed from her in foul waves. He leaned back and felt the harsh man behind him actually curve around him protectively.

An apology hovered on his tongue. He'd never meant to hurt her or her son. But he knew those words would bring him nothing but a slap and more of her sick smile as she asked if he truly thought those words would help anything.

"He's not for you to worry about. Not anymore." The man's commanding voice cut through her hatred, jerking her gaze to him.

"Worry? I will not worry about him. *He* must worry about *me*." She stepped back.

The boy met her gaze, feeling somewhat protected by the large man behind him. For a moment, he let all the hatred she'd stirred in him—killing his parents and bragging about it, beating and starving him, and now paying these men to take him away—pour from his eyes. It curdled in his stomach, but he let her have it, the only defense he had.

The small boy ran to her side, grasping her skirt. She looked down, then knelt before the child. She grasped his chin and angled him to look up the tall horse to the boy astride it. "Do you see him? That is your enemy. He will take everything from you if he can. Even me. Especially me."

The smaller boy glared at him, his young eyes hardening with a hatred he shouldn't be capable of. The older boy stared back, sickened and desolate, until the horse finished its turn and cantered away. He'd always wanted a brother. But now his only one hated him.

They rode for two days, stopping only to rest the horses. Late on the second day, they reached his new home. Dark and barren, the keep seemed to rise from the bowels of hell itself.

October 7, 2004—Spokane, WA

KALYSS'S DREAM SPLINTERED, becoming short snippets of Dreux's childhood. She couldn't wake, but her mind struggled to. It was the first time she'd been inside a vision with her twenty-first-century self conscious of all that was happening.

She quit fighting the memories and worked on controlling

them, focusing on the things she wanted to know. She watched Dreux grow, begin his training, learn to follow command, to care for armor, to exist on little sleep and minimal amounts of food. The knights who trained him were a band of humorless warriors and it was their task to train more like them—warriors who would follow orders without question, kill in battle with swift, merciless strikes, to march for days and win at any cost.

She watched him struggle against these values. They seemed against his very nature. He'd been raised in a gentle and loving home for the first four years of his life. He'd been raised with peace and affection. And while the knights tried to beat the tendencies out of him, he merely learned to bury them, deep where they couldn't see.

The other children were mostly orphaned by-blows, like him, or children of the very poor. But there were a few that came from the best of families, and those were often the cruelest of all. They tormented and bullied everyone they came across. It was during his first year at the castle that they chose to pick on him. They threatened and pushed him, laughing and mocking, calling him names, until he grew stronger, capable of defending himself against them, even *en masse*. Through this, he gained their fear and their respect, and then he finally became their leader. By the time he was seventeen, he was a fully blooded knight. By his thirtieth birthday, he was noticed by the king, awarded his own keep, and married. He finally had the chance to build the life he wanted, the life he'd had as a child.

Kalyss watched it all. Every battle, every scar, every main event of his life, before the vision released her. She'd never known another person as well as she now knew Dreux. The only question she had was: what was she supposed to do with it?

"So, ANY PLANS to leave this lap of luxury?" Alex blinked blearily at Geoffrey.

Geoffrey checked the pipes and bindings above him again, in case there was something he'd missed the first few dozen times. "Sorry, nothing I can think of."

"You mean you don't have any more tricks up your sleeve?"

"Eternal life not impressing you anymore?" Geoffrey looked past his arms and raised a brow.

"One-trick ponies are a dime a dozen." Alex's voice was slightly thick, slurring his words. Not a good sign. Geoffrey went over his store of medical knowledge, but it all pointed to the same thing. Without a CT scan, he wouldn't know if there was anything more serious happening.

Alex's eyes started to close, so he spoke to keep him awake. "I think talking in clichés is a sign of concussion."

"Nah. I'm distracting myself from the need to pee. Besides, it's the blurry vision that's really telling." Alex blinked at him a few times.

"Don't go to sleep, then." One thousand years of life and that was the only advice he had to give? Geoffrey shook his head and made a mental note in case things went wrong and the cycle continued—he needed to read a few more medical books. Maybe go through the full course and get his license again.

"That's why I need to talk."

The younger man was fighting. Geoffrey had to give him credit for that. To help, Geoffrey goaded, "I think I preferred it when you were quiet."

"We could always go back to when you were dead and couldn't hear me. I don't think Crazy would mind obliging us." Alex grinned a sloppy, crooked grin before cracking a wide yawn—and his lip.

"Is that water running through the pipes? I keep hearing this swish, ssswwwiiissshhh sound." They couldn't be here for too much longer. It was only afternoon, but if the concussion were more serious, like broken bones or blood clots, the wait could kill Alex. The only way to know for sure would be to get a CT scan.

"Asshole." Alex shifted his legs and shoulders, stretching whatever he could.

"Might want to give up. He won't let you free again. Or even bring a cup." Had Kalyss made it to Dreux and figured out how to free him? Geoffrey could only hope.

"I can't even undo my drawstring. That's just gross." Alex rested his head on the pipe. "Why no cup?"

"You can't undo your own drawstring." Geoffrey eyed Alex, analyzing the dilated eyes and fuzzy humor. "Unless you'd want him to aim your prick with his knife?"

Alex shuddered, his eyes falling closed. "No thanks." He took a few deep breaths, trying to rouse himself. "So, your grand plan included being caught by Kai and staying at his mercy?"

"That was part of plan B. Plan A involved staying with Kalyss until she awakened Dreux." For some ridiculous reason, he'd never imagined she'd fight him. She never had before, and it had cost them precious seconds that destroyed plan A entirely.

"And the rest of plan B?"

"When I think she's had enough time to awaken Dreux, for Kalyss to remember the past, and time for Dreux to adjust to living again, then I'll give Kai their cell number."

"How much longer will that take?"

"How long can you hold out?"

Alex sighed. "As long as I need to."

Had Dreux awakened with any memory of the last few centuries? Had he awakened at all? Would he remember anything? Kalyss, Kai, Geoffrey? Would he be able to adapt to the twenty-first century?

There Geoffrey stopped the questions. He'd learned long ago to never underestimate Dreux. If there were anything the man could do, it was adapt. And the mere facts of the cycle told him there was a purpose behind it. He could only assume that purpose was for Dreux to kill both him and Kai. How else were they to die? Dreux must be the key to ending it all.

Footsteps sounded above them and he heard the scrape of the shelf as Kai pulled it away from the door to the basement. Without opening his eyes, Alex spoke in a high-pitched, spooky voice, "He's baaack."

Geoffrey grinned. Alex was hanging in there. Kai pounded down the stairs, purposefully using heavy steps for dramatic effect, he guessed. Geoffrey slumped, hanging heavily from the pipes and dropping his chin to his chest. Kai would see through the ruse, of course, but it was worth it just in case it worked.

"How are my two favorite hostages?" Kai sat a tray on a card table and pulled over the chair from in front of Alex. He took a long look at Alex before walking to his tray. "You're not looking good, Alex. I think we need to do something to refresh you."

Alex glared at Kai defiantly. Geoffrey winced. Bad move to challenge Kai like that. Judging from the tray's contents, Alex was about to suffer.

Kai set out a tall glass and grabbed a full pitcher of Kalyss's iced tea. "Man, Spokane is dry. Makes you long for places farther south. Like Brazil. Remember Brazil, Geoffrey?"

Oh, yes. Geoffrey remembered Brazil, being Kai's prisoner and the great regeneration experiment every time he put his socks on. Dryly, he asked, "How could I forget?"

Kai grinned, unrepentant. "Sorry about the toe. Really thought it would come back. Sacrificing in the name of science is a virtue, though."

"I'm waiting for sainthood any moment now."

Kai held the pitcher high, pouring a long, slow stream of golden brown liquid in his glass. In the nearly empty basement, every drop could be clearly heard. Alex turned distinctly green. Geoffrey nearly laughed. Kai did laugh, at both of them.

An entire minute went by, with nothing but the sound of pouring tea. Then the loud gulping as Kai drained the glass in a few swallows. Alex was staring at the ceiling again, his body rigid. Kai picked up the pitcher and began to pour again. Just as a few drops of tea hit the glass, he stopped and put the pitcher back down.

"Forgive my rudeness. I should see to my guests first. I was just so thirsty." Kai grabbed a brown bottle from the tray and uncapped it as he walked toward Alex. "We wouldn't want you developing an infection, would we?"

Alex closed his mouth and eyes just in time as Kai upended the hydrogen peroxide over his head. It was a rather large, industrial-sized bottle and Kai poured slowly again. In seconds, every single cut made its presence known as the fluid fizzed and bubbled, stinging him unmercifully. The back of his head where Kai had hit him the first time. The side of his temple from his failed escape attempt. The corners of his eyes. His nose. His lips. He couldn't breathe for a long while.

Kai poured until the entire bottle was emptied. Then he strolled back to his tray for a towel and blotted the excess peroxide from Alex's closed eyes. "There. No dangerous infections imminent now."

Alex opened his eyes to see him sit in the chair and pull a

plate of sandwiches close to him. Three sandwiches on Kalyss's home-baked bread, piled high with slices of ham and American cheese. Lettuce, tomato, and pickles, gobs of mayo, and mustard hung over the edges. Kai wrapped a napkin around one and took a loud, crunching bite.

Alex's stomach grumbled, reminding him he hadn't eaten in nearly twenty-four hours. An unheard-of feat for him. Kalyss made the best bread. He'd bought her a bread maker for her birthday a year ago and she'd fallen in love with it immediately. And her tea . . .

"I've raided Kalyss's fridge upstairs, as you can no doubt tell." Kai took another loud bite. "She makes her tea perfect, not syrupy, but sweet. Did you know that, Geoffrey?"

"I had a glass when I checked her apartment a few days ago. She's quite accomplished, isn't she?" Checking her apartment, keeping tabs on her, none of it violated the simple pact he and Kai had made. No direct contact with Kalyss for four years. Amazing, but when Kai gave his word, he kept it.

Kai wrapped a fresh napkin around the second sandwich and crunched his way through it. Between gulps of tea and devouring the food, Kai flipped through a book Geoffrey had never seen before. Judging by the strained worry on Alex's face, though, he tensed up in preparation.

"Is there any part of her life she hasn't documented, Alex? She has pictures of everything, all with lovely written descriptions." Alex didn't answer and Kai continued flipping through the thick binder and eating, smiling in places and frowning in others. "That husband of hers was really a sorry bastard, wasn't he? It has to be horrible, standing by, watching a woman waste her life on someone bad for her, and never doing anything about it." Kai was completely focused on Alex.

Geoffrey stiffened. How could Kai possibly compare Sam's abuse to marriage to Dreux? This cycle would have played out four years ago if they hadn't both been so shocked at the sheer damage done to her the night they finally found her. It was a miracle she'd lived. Geoffrey was thankful Kai had been willing to wait and see if she'd pull through on her own instead of immediately killing her. Dreux would never hurt her the way Sam had, though. There was no comparison between the two men.

Alex stared back at Kai. "I got her away from him as soon as I knew what was happening."

"Well hell, man, all you had to do was check her scrapbook. It's all there, with pictures and everything. Must've been handy in court."

"It was." Alex glared. The last thing he needed was more guilt, no doubt. Geoffrey knew all about guilt for not protecting Kalyss.

"At least you understand how constantly vigilant a man needs to be to protect a foolish woman." Kai wiped his fingers on the napkins and polished off his glass of tea. Then he turned to face Alex, his hands clasped over his knees. "Then you should realize why I need to keep her away from the statue, Dreux."

"Who?" Alex asked in a tone no one would believe.

"I'm not an idiot. I'm sure Geoffrey has filled you in."

"He said she's safe with him."

"No. No one is safe with him."

"I think you're confused. You," Alex nodded toward Kai and spoke slowly, "are the one who tried to kill her."

"Of course I did! How could I not?" Kai raised his voice in irritation.

Alex blinked and shook his head, staring at Kai in disbelief. "Uh, well, I've lived nearly thirty years without doing it."

"Don't be ridiculous." Kai rose and began to pace between his two prisoners.

Alex's eyes widened and he opened and closed his mouth a few times.

"You don't understand." Kai shook his head, then stopped in front of Alex and stared straight into his eyes with a scary, calm logic emanating from him. "I *saved* her."

When Alex's brows twisted in incomprehension, Kai gestured to Geoffrey impatiently. "From both of them."

Geoffrey sputtered. "What? I did nothing but protect her."

"You killed her. Nine times."

Geoffrey frowned and waited for Kai to explain his warped logic.

"It may have been my knife, my hand that did the deed, but look at your own culpability here, old friend. You brought her to her death. You searched her out, found her, and made her remember. You took her from any normal, happy life she could have had. You convinced her she needed to free Dreux. In doing so, you signed her death warrant yourself."

The toughest thing about Kai's logic was that it contained a bit of truth. Geoffrey had never *made* Kalyss remember. She did that on her own. But he *had* searched her out and led her to Dreux. He *had* put her in harm's way. But he would not accept responsibility for her murders. "No one told you to kill her but yourself, *old friend.*"

"I couldn't let her awaken him. I had to guard him. It is my duty—my responsibility. That monster cannot go free!"

Alex cut in. "But Geoffrey said she was safe with him."

Kai turned on him and snarled, "He lied. He may have forgotten that monster's crimes, but I never shall. The fires of hell itself burned it on my mind."

Geoffrey watched the ever-present emerald at Kai's throat begin to glow. He'd seen that glow before, watched it work its will many times. Once he'd noticed the illusion it created, it had ceased to affect him, but how Alex handled it would be interesting to note.

"What did he do?" Alex asked.

Kai stilled, his eyes, bright as the emerald at his neck, staring blankly as he looked into his past. "My mother was a beautiful woman. A strong woman. She survived whatever life threw at her. Wars, endless battles, a cheating husband, raising a son on her own."

Kai focused his gaze on Alex again, determination to make Alex understand clear in his eyes. "In this century, such a feat is commonplace. No remarkable thing. Fatherless children are raised in single-parent homes all over the place. But in 1045, this was much more difficult. My mother held on to the castle, the lands, her son, and her dignity with a strength no other woman of that time had. She survived the cold nights alone, knowing where her husband was. And finally, she survived his death in his mistress's arms."

"I get it," Alex said impatiently. "Your mom was cool. What does this have to do with Dreux?"

"Silence! You will not disrespect her pain or her achievements." Kai's fists curled tighter as he glared at Alex.

Then the very air in the basement seemed to change, becoming stuffy, confining. An undercurrent of energy raised the hairs on Alex's arms. The emerald around Kai's neck glowed brighter, giving off a light that could only have come from within it. "He looks like our father, you know."

"Nope." Alex spoke cautiously, leaning away from Kai, against the pole behind him. "Never would have guessed."

"Do you know what that would've meant in Normandy? Our father preferred his bastard, not yet the embarrassing shame bastardy became by the time I was an adult. It was his bastard who resembled him more than his own legitimate son did, who was born first. When our father died, my mother had to protect me, protect my inheritance. She sent Dreux away.

"She was fair—she sent him to a place where he could grow strong and eventually make a name for himself. And he did. So well, in fact, King William gifted him with land in England. A settlement to rival our father's in size and richness."

Kai knelt in front of Alex, calm once again filling his eyes. "I didn't begrudge him, Alex. He could have what he wanted, what he worked so hard for. All of it—with my blessing." His voice hardened. "But he couldn't have my mother. Not without retribution."

Kai's jaw squared and his brows lowered over his eyes. "Do you know what he did to her? Before he left Normandy, he came to see her. She was tending the grave of her faithless husband when he came upon her. She was a frail woman, despite her appearance. Thin and small."

His words painted a vivid, vibrant picture in Alex's mind. He could see the graveyard on a small hill. He could see the tall tree that guarded the resting places of Kai's ancestors. And the small woman with bright red hair blowing in the wind behind her. He could see too well.

The painting blurred, changed, and he saw Kai kneeling beside his mother, raising her into his arms. Her pain-glazed eyes were blackened and swollen. A line of blood trailed from her broken lips and bruises decorated her delicate throat.

"He has large hands. Just like our father. And he'd punched her over and over, breaking her arm, her ribs. The priest said a rib must have punctured her lung. She died in my arms, gasping for breath, Alex."

Kai stared straight into Alex's eyes. "You know what it's like to hold a broken, bleeding woman in your arms; to watch her struggle for breath, for speech; to stare into her eyes, dry because she's too stubborn to cry—helpless to aid her. Don't you, Alex?"

Alex did. He saw Kai's pain. He remembered his own when Kalyss was in the hospital. He nodded. "I remember."

Kai squared his shoulders. "Wouldn't you keep a man like that imprisoned forever, if you could?"

Alex pictured Sam behind bars, feeling again the satisfaction of when he'd watched the police drag the man from the courtroom. "Damn straight."

"And if someone kept trying to free him, wouldn't you have to stop them no matter what? Who would you blame, the instrument of the monster's freedom, or the man who kept bringing it?"

Alex followed his gaze to Geoffrey. Kai straightened to his feet and started walking away. He picked up Kalyss's scrapbook and turned to Alex once more. "I killed her clean and fast—saving her years at *his* hands. She felt next to no pain. And, it turns out, she came back. Now, who's the bad guy? Me, for ending it fast?" He glanced at Geoffrey again. "Or him, for bringing her to that point *nine times*?"

With a questioning raise of his brows, Kai turned to the stairs and began walking up. "And, Alex? My mother was just his first victim."

He shut the door at the top of the stairs, leaving them alone. Alex faced Geoffrey and their gazes locked.

Chapter 15

October 6, 1075—England

"**Y**ou're not the man I thought you were."

The fire popped and crackled at the end of the bed, its dark glow barely illuminating the naked softness at his side. Dreux trailed his fingers lightly from the curve of her shoulder to the creamy softness of Kynedrithe's breast. The tip formed a velvety pucker against his touch and a possessive beast roared inside him. He knew what she meant.

The lover beside her now was not the knight so feared on the battlefield. He was not the man so strangely beleaguered by mysterious deaths. Nor was he the intimidating new lord of this keep, this land, and these people. No, tonight he was someone else, someone even he hadn't met in a long while.

Tonight, he was the baseborn son of a Norman baron and the leman he'd loved, and he felt the possibility of the starlight, the warmth of the fire, the soft and tender welcome of a woman's arms as he hadn't for a score of years.

He traced the rounded weight at the base of her breast, noticing the prickles along her skin. Oh, how her response to his slightest touch soothed him, and yet, made him ache. Ache to pull her closer, to sink inside her. Soothed because he now knew, at the end of wars and bloodshed, when his body ached with wounds and fatigue, when cries of pain and mourning echoed in his ears without cease, he now had a home to return to, arms to hold him, softness to cradle him, and a tight, wet sheath to sink inside.

He remembered the laughter and friendship his parents had shared. He remembered the love his parents had filled their small cottage with. The teasing glances. The occasional touches—a hand on a shoulder, or soft fingers brushing away hair. He'd felt happy there, safe, secure. Home.

He hadn't felt the like since the day they'd sickened. The day they'd died. He missed them. Missed that home; had yearned for it from that day. But his brief tenure under his parents' tutelage taught him one important lesson.

It was not the building they lived in, a wattle and daub hut, a camp follower's tent, or a keep that created a home. It was the man and woman inside and everything they felt for each other that created the home. And he'd looked and waited patiently for the day he would see the woman he could build a home with.

Then he'd seen her dusting off the bottom of a small child who'd stumbled and fallen in front of her, nursing wounded from a forest attack, defending herself against rough advances. In all her forms, she was beautiful. She'd conquered his heart before it could mount a defense. And God had seen fit to make her his destiny.

His fingers continued the trail down her abdomen to the small dip of her belly button. He savored the texture, the silken feel. He was fascinated by the differences between her smooth, protected white flesh and his sun-darkened, sword-roughed hands. The scars that spider-webbed over the back of his hand and up his arm gave proof to the hard life he'd lived since his childhood had ended.

And yet, as each callus, each scarred ridge brushed her skin, causing her to shiver . . . as a low moan burst from the depths of her throat . . . as he kissed the line between the slight swell of her abdomen and the fur of her pelvis . . . as she arched into his tongue as he traced to the curve of her hip . . . he was grateful for the marks on his body, the life experience he possessed, that they gave her pleasure and would protect and cherish her all their days together.

He would build this castle, these lands. He would spend his

life protecting her people. And he would build a home with this woman.

Stars twinkled through the two windows. The fire burned lower, still hot. He slid toward the bottom of the bed, the smooth wool a cool velvet against his skin. He traced his rough hands over her thighs and between, parting them, opening her.

A glance showed her arms flung on either side of her head, as if she had no strength nor will to move them. The blue depths of her eyes were closed to him. Her back slightly arched. The crinkled tips of her breasts pressed against cool air. Her legs sprawled, leaving her open and vulnerable—the ultimate trust.

You're not the man I thought you were.

"Are you disappointed?" His mouth paused just above that part of her that must be yearning for the opposite piece of him.

Her eyes opened, blazing indigo. He lowered his head and drew his tongue along her opening, and paused to rest on the sensitive spot at the top. Her breath caught and she pressed up to him.

"No. And I feel assured I never will be." She laughed, her voice husky.

A few heartbeats later, she shattered against his tongue, clenching her thighs. He surged up against her, his mouth at her throat, full of pride in a job done well. Then he slid home, her legs around his hips, her arms hugging him, her hands grasping his back.

She inhaled with a sharp shiver and tightened her hold on him. He nipped her neck, pressure building inside him. He didn't want this to end. Not for a long while. He loved being held in her arms, loved feeling her skin slide against his, loved hearing her gasp in his ear, feeling her tight and wet, surrounding him. He pulled from her and slid in again, the friction a building, brewing storm.

She tunneled her fingers through his hair and stared deep into his eyes and whispered, "I'm not afraid."

He shuddered, feeling the warmth of her trust flowing through him. "I never want you to be. Not of me."

She smiled, caring and gentle. He melted into her, his release a waterfall, pouring him into the pool of her embrace. They lay there, still and calm. The night sounds creaked and croaked through the window, a slight breeze welcome over their damp flesh. She cradled him close, her fingers brushing and tugging, feathering and soothing. He sighed.

"I've dreamt of this for so long." He felt her tilt her head toward him and he moved to her side, pulling her close. Their heads shared a pillow and he stared into her eyes.

"You have?"

He smiled. "When I was a boy, I lived with both my parents. They loved each other so much; they filled our home with it."

"What happened?"

"They died. Poisoned. And I was sent away."

She frowned and caressed his cheek. He could see sorrow for his pain in her eyes and it somehow soothed a small ache inside him. She knew what it was like to lose those she loved.

"Who sent you away? Wouldn't the lord send you to another family in the village?"

He smiled, sad. "My father was the lord, a baron. He married a woman with red hair and green eyes and the meanest smile you've ever seen. Maeve. She hated my mother, I realize now. My mother had his love in ways this woman never would."

"Do you think she poisoned them?"

"I can't prove it. But yes, I think she did. Not long ago, she summoned me. I didn't know why, but I needed to put my past to rest. I traveled back to my old home and saw her. She was standing next to my father's grave, furious. I could see this evil hatred twisting her face, her hands. She looked young, much younger than she should have so many years after she sent me away. Her face should have been haggard, wrinkled beyond age, matching her expression." He paused.

"I remember hating her the whole time I was growing up, training to be a knight, training for battle. I'd been blooded by the time I saw her again, killed other men in battle—but never a woman. I asked myself if I could begin with her—for my father, for my mother."

Her eyes were dark, saddened by what he'd gone through, waiting for the rest of the tale. Not judging, not drawing away in horror as she would have mere hours ago. He found comfort in that.

"I couldn't. I couldn't bring myself to that even for vengeance. It wouldn't bring them back, it wouldn't punish her and it wouldn't bring me peace. But when I started to turn away, she shook her fist and I could hear her speaking, though I didn't understand the words. But it didn't matter, she no longer had power over me. I turned away and left. I never spoke to her."

He fell silent again, dreading this final part of his tale, the final test of Kynedrithe's newfound belief in him. Was being patient and a good lover enough to hold her trust in him? There was only one way to know for sure. He stared deep into her eyes, wordlessly begging her to believe in him.

"She was the first murder."

Kynedrithe gasped, and then was quiet far longer than he thought he could live through. Then she met his gaze. "They blamed you?"

"Some did, but there was no proof."

"But who really did it?"

"I don't know." His voice was hoarse. His throat felt clogged.

She snuggled into him, hugging him, her legs twined with his. His arms tightened around her. Night fell in the room, the darkness slowly gathering to the sound of the ocean crashing outside. Wind whistled at the tower, blowing through the window. The fire dimmed to a dull orange glow and the chamber grew cooler.

Dreux pulled the heavy coverlet over them both and sealed in their heat. He'd rise and rebuild the fire in a moment, but for right now he wanted to hold his wife, the only one to believe him unconditionally. He still couldn't quite accept this moment of grace.

"How do you know it wasn't me?"

"The man who held me, patiently charmed me from my terror tonight, could not commit such an atrocity." She held his hand, stroking the rough skin. "I would have read such atrocities by now. I was afraid of the visions of blood earlier, but now I know it's simply the blood of a warrior honorable enough to carry grief and regret for his opponents."

Her arms tightened and she held him closer, snuggling her head into his shoulder. For a long while, Dreux stared down at her, at her tiny hands and body nestled against him. She'd been so afraid at first—understandable considering all the death and horror his people had brought before her the last several years—but she'd fought it with every ounce of strength and will she had.

And now, without a single moment of doubt, she believed in his innocence. He breathed deep, the deepest breath of his life. He buried his face in her breasts, tightened his hold and thanked God for giving him this moment, this woman, this life. The moment of peace swelled and deepened, soothed and contented, rippled and flowed through him.

Her heart thumped slow and thick against his ear. Her chest rose rhythmically. At last, he closed his eyes and fell sweetly asleep.

October 7, 2004—Spokane, WA

ALEX GLARED, BUT Geoffrey didn't seem at all bothered by it. Instead, he looked insultingly unaffected, as if all the accusations Kai had leveled at him were less interesting than even balancing a checkbook. He opened his mouth, ready to speak and make the man pay attention, but Geoffrey spoke first.

"Pretty convincing, isn't he?"

"Are you saying there's no truth to what he said?"

"Of course there's truth. I could have chosen *not* to find Kalyss, help her learn of the past and lead her to her future. I could have left her alone or repeatedly married her myself. We could've escaped Kai, ignored duty to Dreux and lived long, full lives with many children."

Alex nodded at each point Geoffrey made. "Yes. Exactly."

"Why not?" Geoffrey shrugged, appearing to lean against his hands. "Why wouldn't I 'protect' a woman from going after her dreams? It's not like she knew there was a high risk of death. Not like she remembered dying and chose to face it anyway."

Alex raised a brow at the wording, hesitated, but nodded anyway.

"After all, I, a man, should know what's best for Kalyss, what she truly needs."

Alex imagined Kalyss's reaction to that statement and winced.

"Why shouldn't I steal her from the prize destiny has given

her ten lifetimes to fight for? I should have lied, manipulated, and coerced her into ignoring the fate her heart, her gift, led her to. I should have slept, every night, in the bed of a woman who dreamt of, and yearned for, another lover."

Alex sighed and fell back.

"And if she never achieved the great love, and the happiness that goes with it, that she was predestined for, oh, well, at least she lived a half-life."

Alex closed his eyes and sulked. How could he blame Geoffrey when he'd pushed Kalyss on that same issue just last night? He'd wanted her to braven up and search for love, because he thought the steady, calm life she'd attained wasn't enough for her. He had even encouraged her to take a few risks. How different would his advice have been if he'd known the perfect man for her happiness was just out of reach?

"Then there's Dreux—"

"I get the point. You can stop." Alex relented, his anger dying a fizzling death.

"No, you need to know of Dreux."

"The woman-beater and murderer?"

"You've heard Kai's judgment of the man, now you'll hear mine. And later you can decide yourself what manner of man he is."

Alex studied the hard voice, the determined jaw. Geoffrey could be dry, unemotional, downright robotic, but if he felt there was more Alex needed to hear, he was probably right. "So who was he as you knew him? What fated love could an abuser and an abuse victim have?"

"Do you believe everything you're told?"

Alex licked his broken lip and shook his head. What was wrong with him? Was he a hostage with more faith in his captor than his fellow prisoner? He shook his head more wildly, determined to rattle up some common sense. "Sorry."

"No need to apologize. I know what ails you."

"What?"

"All in good time, pup."

"Just don't forget not everyone has as much time as you do, Pop."

The hard line of Geoffrey's mouth eased a bit, before he tilted his head back and stared at the ceiling. "The first time

I saw Dreux, I was a fully trained knight, blooded in battle and past the age of worshiping my superiors."

Alex leaned back and closed his eyes, imagining life in 1066 and beyond. Where men were taught to be strong and capable of defense, and called upon to exhibit it, unlike in this century. Where the ability to fight wasn't a dirty word or a movie gimmick. In Geoffrey's world, war wasn't entertainment. It was a lifestyle. As in I came, I saw, I conquered. Julius Ceasar's words seemed to fit the attitude of many Normans, if he remembered his history right.

It was a distant world from the one he lived in. Police and military did the battle, fools fought against them, and the average American could go his entire life without facing the possibility of a violent death at the hands of a hostile enemy. But a Norman grew up with war and danger right outside the gates of his awesomely built, impenetrable fortress. He knew defense, offense, and tactics that had fascinated scholars for centuries.

"But in our first battle together, our enemy surrounded us and cut Dreux off. I watched him hold off four men, alone, until we could reach him."

At first, this sounded like nothing to Alex. Nothing every action movie didn't show in exquisite slow motion. People could also prepare for battles like that in nearly any martial arts classroom worldwide. Heck, they'd probably even prepared for it a thousand years ago in medieval sword training.

But how different, how much more difficult, would that be if everyone they fought truly meant to kill them?

"Several of us were newly under his command and this act of courage from him won loyalty from many of us. In the following months of service to him, we learned the truth of what manner of man he was."

Geoffrey looked directly at him. "Rape happened during this war. Death came to women and children, old people, disabled people. Everything chivalry says is wrong, it happened many times over with a depth of savagery people of today can't imagine, despite the movies and books. In that time, it was real and common—but not if you served Dreux."

"So he won your respect."

"Simply by being himself."

"Then what went wrong? You haven't told me how this cycle began."

"Yes, I have. Kai killed Kalyss and imprisoned Dreux."

"No. You've told me that and what happens every century, but not *why*."

Geoffrey looked away. "I don't know why."

"Quit bullshitting me."

"I'm not." Geoffrey faced him again "Not really. Not the whole story. I only know my small—" bitterness edged his tone "—part."

Alex's legs cramped and spasmed under the box. "Then tell me your part."

Geoffrey eyed the ceiling again, clearly not even noticing the pipes and wires. The ice in his eyes melted just enough for Alex to see their true color: a bright, summer-sky blue. Geoffrey's jaw hardened until he forced it loose. "My part was to betray them both."

October 7, 1075 — England

"IT IS NECESSARY, Geoffrey. You must know this by now. Your delay in London cost that woman her life."

"It wasn't him. It couldn't have been." Geoffrey shook his head, wishing he didn't remember that one period of time when he hadn't known where Dreux was.

"How naïve must you persist in being? How many women must your foolishness kill?"

"She's his wife. Maybe—"

"She will die like the others and you will live knowing you could have stopped him."

Geoffrey looked away. The dying fire reflected off the emerald at Kai's throat and hurt his eyes.

"You know you cannot risk her. Not another one. His own wife, this time. Killing her would surely damn his soul more eternally than the others."

Geoffrey eyed the stairs to the tower. Dreux had disappeared up them hours ago to be with his new bride. And now Geoffrey contemplated disturbing them—not only disturbing them, but rushing a new bride from her husband's arms and into the cold darkness of this hour just before dawn.

"I'll only take her far enough to draw him away from here and all those he is a danger to. She'll be safe and he will be far from harming any woman ever again."

Kai kept whispering and Geoffrey wished his emerald necklace didn't glow quite so bright, like it was searching for every cloud of doubt within him and, instead of banishing the darkness, intensifying his dark thoughts.

Snoring, sleep-drugged men lounged on the hard floors, wrapped tightly in their cloaks. It was a new hall without the comforts of a woman's touch to warm it. The stone was hard and cold and dampness permeated the air. Yet Geoffrey felt stifled in heat.

"You seem to doubt me. Need I remind you of my mother's fate?"

Geoffrey shuddered. Somehow, deeper than any images of battle he carried within him, Kai's description of Maeve's death had blossomed inside him: each blue-black bruise, each trickle of bright red, fresh blood. Her fiery tresses fanned about her over the ground and her haunting eyes, pleading and pitiful as she grasped desperately for her last few moments of life. No, he needed no reminders.

"Give me a few moments, then follow. I will see if the door is locked and get him to let me in, somehow, if it is."

The man nodded and Geoffrey rose with a heavy heart and trudged up the stairs. Every instinct inside him said Kai was not to be trusted, but if there was any truth to what he said, then the terrified woman he'd escorted to the tower earlier that night was in serious jeopardy. And as much as he wanted to say there was no truth to Kai's words against his lord, neither the tale of Maeve nor of the murdered women in Dreux's trail from Normandy pointed to Dreux's innocence.

Halfway up the flight of steps, just after the narrow rise curved to the left, Geoffrey felt for the small crack in the stones. He'd personally helped Dreux etch out half the hidden stairway to the tower. The tower rested against cliffs that provided protection, support, and a way to escape. This part of it, Dreux had trusted him with. That trust was a heavy burden now as Geoffrey slid into the narrow opening and closed it behind him.

To the left, more stairs curved down and out to an opening

somewhere between the cliffs and the sea. That part Geoffrey had never helped with, had never seen. And now he likely never would. After this night, he'd never be so trusted by anyone again.

He turned up the stairs and trudged his way to the top. Within moments, he stood inside the room with the sleeping couple. If Dreux woke now, there would be no questions. His mere presence inside the locked tower room would signal Geoffrey's villainy.

Despite his loyalty to Dreux, Geoffrey would never risk leaving an innocent woman in danger. He crossed to the door and lifted the large piece of wood barring it. Opening the door enough for Kai to enter, Geoffrey now watched for movement from the bed.

The couple slept peacefully entwined, oblivious to the fate that awaited them. Kynedrithe's face pressed into Dreux's chest, her breathing light and nearly silent beneath Dreux's deep snore. Geoffrey had never heard Dreux sleep so deeply before, as if his mind were completely unbothered by the atrocities he'd committed.

And there should be no doubt he'd committed them. The evidence against him was too damning. Three women in three places they'd been, all killed during hours when he couldn't account for Dreux's whereabouts, all dead in a vicious, brutal slaying that echoed with the violent hatred of Maeve's death. No, Kai had shown him too much truth to be doubted.

He glanced through the crack in the open door behind him, seeing the flicker of approaching light, hearing Kai's tread on the stairs, light and stealthy but impossible to hide completely. A shifting on the bed made it creak and Geoffrey froze, ice prickling on his nape. His heart slammed in his throat and he knew, without a single doubt, that the warrior he'd so admired these past several months would soon send his sword slicing directly through Geoffrey's disloyal heart.

But his heart beat. Once. Twice. Breath entered his lungs and still, no further sign of movement sounded behind him. Unable to bear it any longer, he slowly turned, his heart prepared to stop when he met Dreux's open eyes, Dreux's questioning or furious or condemning eyes.

But when he finished focusing through the darkness of early morning with the fire naught but embers, his leader's eyes were closed. He slept deeply, untroubled with bad dreams, sated by the beautiful woman in his arms. Geoffrey nearly backed through the doorway and let them stay secluded in their marital bower.

Kai had promised no harm would come to Kynedrithe. They were here to protect her. And Dreux would not come to harm. Kai would take Kynedrithe to his lands and when Dreux followed, as sure he must, he would be forcefully brought before a full trial. His crimes would be laid bare and he would serve his punishments before his wife was returned.

And she would be returned. The other women had been unnoticeable peasants. Dreux would pay fines to their families and continue to rule his lands, but public censure would prevent him from killing again. It was the only way to save Kynedrithe. She'd still be married to him, but protected by the public knowledge of his brutality. He'd be unable to hurt her, a lady, without bringing the king's full wrath.

Before Geoffrey could question the plan again, Kai came through the door.

October 7, 2004—Spokane, WA

"AFTER THAT, EVERYTHING happened so fast it took decades for me to truly process it all. Kai and two of his men fought Dreux while I pulled Kynedrithe from the bed. Dreux fought so ferociously, I only had time to wrap a blanket around her before I spirited her away to the deck of Kai's ship."

Geoffrey's voice was low, factual, and all the more poignant for it. Alex could see everything he described, but in a different way than with Kai's description of his mother's death. It wasn't like watching a violent movie, but more listening to the story of a survivor: nostalgic, full of regrets and hindsight.

"She fought against me, struggling to return to the tower, but I was stronger. More convinced I was right and she should just do as I say." Geoffrey's lips curled in a self-mocking grin. "After all, she was only a woman."

"Kai followed us to his ship, his men holding Dreux in front of the window. We could see him when we looked up another twenty feet or so. He was furious, struggling, threatening us with death if any harm came to Kynedrithe."

Geoffrey stared hard into Alex's eyes. "A full-blooded warrior, I quaked in my boots. I never doubted him for a moment. I am dead the moment he is free."

"But you'd resurrect."

"Not from his blow."

"How do you know?"

"It's all that makes sense."

Alex stared at the warrior in front of him. Even death couldn't keep him for long, and yet, he was afraid of the man Kalyss had married. Through all Kai's small tortures, Geoffrey had hung from his arms, his toes barely touching the ground. He hadn't eaten, drank, or gone to the bathroom. He was pale, but still tall and intimidating.

Alex was beginning to fear his first glimpse of Dreux, if either of them lived so long.

"Kai dragged Kynedrithe in front of him, his knife at her throat. I thought the threats he yelled at Dreux were empty, meant to draw him after us. But his tone was furious and hateful, and though the rising sun lay behind us, his emerald glowed."

Geoffrey closed his eyes, his voice dropping lower. "I pulled my sword without thinking, without knowing fully why, but it was too late. In happened too fast. His knife, her throat. Kynedrithe died before she hit the deck. And Kai turned, the same dagger that killed her slicing into me as my sword stabbed into him."

Now he whispered, "So much blood. Always entwined."

Alex breathed in the silence, Geoffrey's regret a tangible presence in the room. Then he spoke again, his words a mere breath of sound.

"You know the worst thing? In the tower room, when I pulled Kynedrithe from Dreux, when he awoke and looked me in the eyes, he knew. He knew that I betrayed him and he was furious. Murderous. But still, he knew I looked out for her. He knew I protected her."

Geoffrey opened eyes tragic with mistakes. "He knew because he said, 'Protect her with your life, Geoffrey.' And I failed, even at that."

From the black depths of the stairway, they heard the metallic click of the door.

SILENT AND SLOW, Kalyss slid from the bed and padded to the wardrobe that housed the TV. She opened one of the cabinets and found a spare blanket to throw around herself. Dreux still hadn't stirred, so she slipped a check card, the one with her name and picture on it, out of his wallet and carried it to the TV setup. The hotel had Internet access for a fee and she was getting tired of waiting for the local news to pick up the story.

Plus, who knew what she'd missed while she'd had the most incredible sex of her life—another big change that she'd have to figure out later. For now, she used the remote to turn on the TV and put it on mute, then switched to the Internet and used the wireless keyboard the hotel supplied to start surfing for news. She was no stranger to the Internet, but she didn't have cable Internet and a wireless connection at home, so this would be kind of a treat.

A frustrating half-hour later, she realized either she couldn't find it or it wasn't there. Spokane wasn't so big they'd miss reporting a double homicide. It would be big news for the larger part of an entire day. Which meant that when the police had inspected the dojo—and she didn't doubt they had—they hadn't found anything, which could only happen if there'd been nothing for them to find.

That left two options. Kalyss Googled a Norman history site as she followed her thought process. Either Kai had cleaned up his mess or Geoffrey had awakened and cleaned it up. What would they have done with Alex's body? If Geoffrey had cleaned up, he would have called—but one glance at the cell phone, sitting quietly on the end table, told her it was still there and not blinking. Therefore, it hadn't vibrated itself off the table and likely had no messages. Getting it, she checked the settings and made sure the volume wasn't muted. No missed calls and it was set to ring quite loudly.

So Kai had cleaned up. Grabbing the keyboard again, she flipped through website after website, researching Norman and Anglo-Saxon history—Dreux's and her history—while thinking about what could have happened. Was Kai still at the dojo? Could he have fooled the cops into thinking everything was okay? Memory flashed through her of his charming grin and large size. He could easily appear at home in a dojo.

So that left, was Dreux ready to fight him? According to her dream vision, Dreux would be fighting his brother. When he'd spoken earlier of taking him to the gates of hell with him, he'd spoken of killing his brother. It was so wrong.

Bone-deep, she felt it, brother could not be allowed to fight, to kill, brother. Not only was murder a taboo, but people went to jail for it. People went to hell for it. There was even a Bible story devoted to it. Not even vengeance for Alex could convince her to condone such a horrible thing. Alex wouldn't condone it, either. But what were the alternatives?

Kai would outlive any prison sentence, any jailer. Boy, wouldn't that raise questions. Was rehabilitation even possible? What would it take to convince him to stop? And would that give Alex or his parents justice? Signing off the Internet and turning off the TV, she slumped back on the couch. With a shiver, she pulled the blanket around her tighter.

"Did you learn anything?" Dreux settled beside her, pulling her into his arms.

She snuggled against him, rubbing her cheek against his warm chest. What should she tell him? That Alex and Geoffrey were likely at the dojo, held by Kai, and have Dreux go rushing off in a male display of power, ready to fight the evil that threatened his home? And wouldn't Kai have moved them by now? She wouldn't know until she checked.

"He's your brother."

"Yes."

"He's trying to kill your wife." She looked at Dreux. "Is it because she's your wife or because he didn't want you freed?"

He thought about it, unconsciously rubbing her arms under the blanket. "Possibly both."

"Vengeance for his mother?"

"Very likely."

"Did you ever . . ." She hesitated to ask the obvious. ". . . tell him you didn't?"

"Yes. Once, before I left Normandy. I guess he didn't believe me."

"She was beaten to death. That takes extreme anger or

someone who loves to hurt people." Or sometimes, a terrifying mix of the two.

"Do you think I am that way, Kalyss?" His heart pounded beneath her ear.

"Any man can fall to extreme anger if pushed far enough." His tension told her it wasn't an idle question. He cared what she thought of him. "But Maeve didn't push you. And no, I don't believe you're sadistic enough to enjoy what happened to her."

Gradually, he relaxed beneath her. "Did you remember more while we were sleeping?"

"I remembered our conversation about Maeve." She twisted to see his eyes as she spoke. "And, more. I saw your childhood, starting with the night Maeve sent you away."

He smiled and brushed her hair back, smoothing his fingers through it. "I wish I could see you as a child."

She grinned uncomfortably and shrugged. "I'm not sure there's any part of my life I'd want to show you. It hasn't been full of goodness, if you know what I mean."

He frowned, his eyes darkening with hurt. "No, I don't know what you mean. You saw mine, in detail. Why would I not want the same?"

"But I didn't want to see it." They were completely different things.

He drew back from her and she rushed to explain what she meant. "I mean, I didn't do it on purpose. I didn't seek to invade your privacy that way."

He still didn't appear to understand, so she burst out, "Who really wants someone seeing and feeling the most painful and humiliating moments of their life?"

In a quiet, dead voice, he answered, "A person who trusts and is ready to open themselves to someone they care about."

She froze, not even breathing until she spoke. "I trust you. That doesn't mean I want to play out the most devastating moments of my life for you."

"You didn't have to. You could have started with a birthday. Your last birthday, if that was happy enough."

She thought for a moment, her hesitance obviously displeasing him further. Placating, she said, "I could share a birthday."

He smiled grimly at her hesitance. "No. I don't want that

anymore." He looked at the bed they'd made love in a short time ago, and then back at her. "You're still testing me. You aren't ready to trust me, still."

She shook her head angrily. "This isn't about trust. It's about personal privacy and now you just back out of the whole thing altogether? That's childish."

"It's about intimacy and that requires trust," he disagreed. "I won't settle for less than everything, Kalyss. I don't want to back out of anything. I'll happily share the happy memories, but first I want to see the devastation." He leaned forward and slipped his hand under the blanket until it covered her scarred stomach.

"I want this." He stared hard into her eyes and emphasized with a slight movement of his hand. "I want to see this."

Shaking her head in denial, she choked out, "I don't want to relive that myself. Why would I want to show it to someone else?"

"Because I'm not just someone else. I'm your husband."

"That's debatable. Why would you want to see? So you can feel guilty for not protecting me? So you can take it out on your loyal knight for not protecting me? It happened. It can't be undone. Why relive it?"

"Because it's formed a large part of you and I want to know you, Kalyss." He shook his head and set her away from him. Rising, he located all of his clothes and began silently dressing.

Kalyss stared at him for a minute, her stomach clamping in anxiety. She'd hurt, then angered him. And she didn't know how to fix it without giving up more of herself than she was prepared to do. What the hell did he expect? He'd been in her life less than one day and already he wanted all of her, body and soul. Did he think she'd just hand herself over without one word of resistance? She'd fought too long, too hard, to be the person she was.

She wasn't going to just open herself up and bleed her pain all over him for him to ease. Is that what he'd thought? That she needed him to heal her, to make her whole again? How would becoming dependent on him for her happiness and well-being make her whole? Only becoming a strong and independent person could do it.

She huffed out her irritation and stormed to the bathroom for her own clothes. By the time she returned, he was dressed and the bed was made. She set the folded, spare blanket on the end of the bed and pocketed the cell phone.

He was silent, staring out the window. Guilt for hurting him swirled with her anger. He expected too much. She wasn't responsible for him, not his pain and not his happiness. She'd apparently married him once, but in eight lives after that, she'd only tried to awaken him. In this life, she'd succeeded. She'd fulfilled her duty.

"I think we should go back to the dojo. They might still be there." Her voice was a little more snappish than she'd planned, but oh well. He could deal.

He turned, his eyes narrowed on her. "Then we should check it out."

She nodded once and collected the keys to the car and the hotel room, then held his wallet out to him. He stalked toward her, his movements slow and dangerous. It made her nervous, but she was too angry to be afraid. Jaw firm, she raised her eyes and stared straight back at him.

His nostrils flared, as if scenting a challenge. "If you're angry, Kalyss, say it. Rid yourself of the venom."

"You're one to talk, with your hurt silence and statue-still poses. I refuse to be manipulated like that. To be afraid of any negative feelings you feel."

He raised both brows. "My feelings are honest, not manipulation, and nothing for you to fear. If I am silent and still, I am dealing with them myself. Not striking at you with veiled hostility, as you are doing. Passive-aggressive, I believe they call it?"

"Better than just plain aggressive and I wasn't about to wait for your silence to turn to that." She pursed her lips.

He reared back like she'd slapped him, fury spiraling up inside his eyes at her accusation. They stared at each other in silence, two powerful, wild animals crouched and ready to spring, to strike out, to defend. She'd watched a man with mercurial moods go from loving to violent in the blink of an eye. Dreux hadn't become violent, but that was only a mood swing away.

Then he shook his head and whispered, "No. We're not doing this."

Her brows drew low over her eyes, the question plain on her face.

He backed a few steps from her and clarified, "I didn't wait that long to be with you only to begin arguing after less than twelve hours. Let's just go."

Chapter 16

Geoffrey came to just as Kai finished tying his left hand to the pipes outside of a building. They were in an alley again, with its strange bluish glow. The clouds were roiling overhead, folding and rolling over and over each other in black puffs. The air smelled fresher than the basement, almost chilled compared to the warmth inside the building, like rain. Thunder boomed distantly overhead, warning of its presence before it arrived.

Geoffrey focused on Kai, his head still swimming. "Chloroform?"

Kai grinned. "Crude, but effective."

"Where's Alex?"

Kai shrugged. "I'll get him when I leave here. I still have a use for him."

"Bored with me already?" Geoffrey asked dryly. "I thought the day would never come."

Kai checked the foot bindings and backed away a few steps. "It's time, old friend. It's been twenty-four hours, already. I'm sure she's awakened him by now. Not that you would ever admit it. Time to retreat to a better location for the final battle. Besides, the game was never truly between us, not you, not Kalyss—just Dreux and I."

"It's not with Alex, either. He doesn't know where they are." Alex hadn't had a moment to speak once Geoffrey's tale was done. Geoffrey didn't have a clue how it'd been received. He certainly felt no relief of guilt, so he wasn't even sure why he'd told him everything. Definitely more than he'd planned to tell. But he hadn't had time to warn him about Kai's emerald.

Kai laughed. "I know. I never expected relevant information from him."

Geoffrey frowned.

Kai clarified, "While Dreux and I are off playing our little game, our sweet Kalyss will need someone to look after her. I had to make sure Alex wasn't a wuss."

One corner of Geoffrey's mouth curled. "He did pretty well, then."

Kai grinned. "Yeah, he did good. He'll look out for her."

"Good thing she got away from you. She has a chance to live now." Geoffrey looked piercingly into Kai's eyes, seeking the truth in his smile.

"She's pretty tough now. Women's lib looks good on her. She's skilled, independent." Kai paused. "I daresay she's the best she's ever been."

Kai finished in an irritating tone close to pride, as if he'd been the one to help Kalyss attain her strength instead of her accomplishing it on her own, "Is that why you didn't kill her last night?"

Kai shrugged. "Ten centuries is long enough. The cycle had to be broken. You did it by stealing Dreux. I did it by saving the fight for my true foe. Dozens of small changes that will hopefully work. Which means . . ." He gestured toward Geoffrey.

"I die."

"You can't interfere this time, old friend."

"How about I just give you my word to stay out of the fray?"

"And I should trust that?"

"Always," Geoffrey lied.

Kai humored him. "Then give it."

"I promise I will leave the battle to you and Dreux," Geoffrey said honestly.

Kai paused, then grinned. "Sorry. But if it makes you feel better, I have another hypothesis I've been testing."

"As long as you don't cut off any more of my body parts."

"Good God, man! Would you get over the damn toe? You didn't even need it for balance. It was one of the middle ones." Kai held his hands out to his sides, palms up.

Each word sharp and precise, Geoffrey bit out, "It was aesthetically pleasing to my eyes."

Kai laughed. Then he sobered and leaned forward. "I kind of have this theory. Cycles and circles, loops and patterns. Decades and centuries. Nice round numbers. But nothing is infinite, right?"

Geoffrey stared, stone-eyed and unimpressed.

"According to my notes, you've died nine-hundred-and-ninety-nine times. What if one thousand is our cutoff?"

Geoffrey raised a brow. Kai took his love of scientific study to macabre levels. The death journal he'd kept all these years was just one example. "Then you have the advantage by a significant amount. I haven't had fun like you."

"No, you haven't killed me as often." Kai tilted his head and grinned. "But that doesn't mean I haven't died."

Geoffrey frowned, his brows knitting together. "You killed yourself?"

"And had others do it. Hanging, guns, fire, drowning. We come back from it all." Kai's eyes lit with scientific zeal. "But, what if, like a cat with nine lives, we have just one thousand?"

Geoffrey twisted his eyebrows. "Yay?"

Kai laughed again. "We're even now. If one thousand is the key, then after I kill Dreux, I'll finish it."

"And Kalyss lives free?"

"Like she always should have."

Geoffrey thought about it a moment. It wasn't like he had a choice, tied as he was. Kai had his theories and illogics, but what if this one was true? He'd never wished to die, but he'd never wanted to live forever, either. Certainly not in this infinite loop of death and betrayal. Not with this guilt. It was the natural cycle for things to come to an end. Even Kai could grasp something as obvious as that. He gave an abrupt nod.

"How do you want it? This last time, I think I'll let you choose." Kai stepped back and stared at the sky, magnanimously respectful in according him a semblance of privacy.

Geoffrey stared at the sky. The normally dry air was heavy with moisture now. For a man who hadn't had a drink in twenty-four hours, it was very welcome. His skin prickled, trying to absorb it. "You truly think it'll be the last time?"

Kai shrugged sadly. "I'm hoping."

The wind slowly began to blow, colder and sweet-smelling. In the distance, he could hear the dancing of the maple trees. The storm merely announced its arrival. The show was still many hours away, however. "I like the rain."

Kai stilled, frowning. "I don't usually do slow and painful, old friend."

Geoffrey met Kai's gaze. "But you will for me."

Kai stared into his eyes, gauging Geoffrey's serious expression. Distaste in his tone, he asked one last time, "You're sure?"

Geoffrey closed his eyes and took a deep breath. "Let me feel the rain."

SILAS CLOSED HIS eyes and clenched his fists. "He figured it out."

"Only partially. He's figured a thousand lives is all he and Geoffrey have. But he doesn't know of the curse."

"He doesn't have to know of the curse. What he knows is damage enough." Silas opened his eyes again, watching the men talk about how Geoffrey should die this last time. One loophole. One crack. That's all there had been in the curse, but it was enough.

Kalyss was reborn every hundred years, but only for the thousand years of the curse. If she died this time and was reborn at the tail end of the curse, she would be a baby, with no chance to save Dreux, and Maeve would kill her. She wouldn't reincarnate after that.

Kai and Geoffrey could resurrect, but only a thousand times within the thousand years. Beyond that, they were dead. All chances spent.

Maeve and Dreux were to be trapped, alone and unable to move, for the same amount of time. Dreux's only escape was for Kalyss to free him and Maeve's only escape was for the curse to be fulfilled, altered, or broken. When the curse concluded, if Maeve or Dreux were still imprisoned, they would

awaken at the same time and, with Kalyss a baby and Kai and
Geoffrey dead from fighting each other, there would only be
Dreux to face a furious fallen angel.

But Dreux was awake now and they had only this one, true
chance to break the curse. Because of the curse, they were all
tied and connected. They all lived or they all died—except
Maeve. The only question with her was how long she slept.

"If any of them die finally and truly before the curse is broken, it's all over." Draven sounded a bit dazed as the realization must have sunk in.

"Yes. Everything is finite. Everything is counted." Dreux
was awake. Kalyss still lived. Geoffrey and Kai each had one
life left. There was still time. Desperation made Silas sick, but
that sickness was all he could feel at the moment.

"Then we can't let Geoffrey die now." Draven's posture
was resolute, the dark tone implacable. Black gloved hands
were curled into fists.

Silas clenched and unclenched his hands. No interference.
The command had been bred into him from childhood. There
were too many consequences, too many ways to unravel the
threads of destiny in God's great tapestry. But if there was
ever a time to break that rule, this was it. There were four descendents trapped in this curse and if one of them died, they
all died, and the world would suffer for their loss. Maeve
would be freed from her curse, from her sleep, and nothing
good would come from all he and Draven had tried to accomplish.

"No, we can't let Geoffrey die," Silas agreed.

In the darkened alley, they heard Geoffrey choose a slow
death. He'd bought them the time to wait, instead of rushing
to him as Kai left, in possession of Kalyss and Dreux's cell
number. His vehicle lights turned on as he reached the end of
the alley, then the three of them were left alone in the freezing
black rain. No light other than the dim glow of the moon
reached them. The only sound the pelting of rain on gravel.

Silas and Draven stepped forward as one, hands out to focus their gifts. They could cross into the human realm and
heal Geoffrey. After three steps, they hit the realm barrier, but
it didn't let them pass—instead it shocked them and they flew
back against the building behind them.

"What the hell?" Draven hissed, unable to move.

Silas struggled against the invisible force that held him pinned to the wall. Geoffrey hung opposite them, blood seeping through his shirt, spreading ominously low over his stomach. No, he couldn't die. Silas struggled harder, reaching with all the gifts at his command, then stilled as the very air lit up, as if electrified.

Dark shadows, blacker than the alley at night, swirled through the air around them before amassing into a large black barrier between them and Geoffrey. The shadows solidified until Silas saw black wings, shinier than a raven's, folded around a kneeling man. Slowly, the wings stretched wide, ten feet to either side of the tall man, completely blocking Geoffrey from view.

The Obsidian Angel rose, taller and larger than any human and most descendents. In the blackest of black faces, his eyes were bright and filled with the flames of righteousness. A two-handed axe was strapped to his back and the head of it could be seen over his right shoulder. The Angel crossed his powerful arms in an intimidating pose that clearly said they couldn't pass.

"But, he can't die. Why would you stop us from saving him?" Draven strained frantically against the restraints.

Silas couldn't move any part of his body away from the side of the building, but he discovered he could move his hand sideways, along the wall. He grasped Draven's wrist, squeezing it in warning. One did not argue with true Angels—ever. Just being so close was awe-inspiring, humbling. As if finally realizing that, Draven became motionless beside him.

Keeping his frustration inside and his tone respectful, Silas asked, "May we return after the curse is broken? Will he live that long?"

The flaming eyes focused on him and it was all Silas could do not to shrivel and look away. No one was perfect enough to face the righteous judgment within them—especially not a genetic mistake who shouldn't exist as all Nephilim were.

His obsidian face expressionless, the Angel gave them one silent, slow nod. The force pinning them released and they were free. There was no time to take relief from that, however. Hands still clasped, Silas and Draven disappeared.

* * *

THE BUILDING KALYSS had always taken such pride in now projected an atmosphere of danger with a dark, spooky, threatening intensity. That pissed her off. This was her home.

"You must use caution, Kalyss."

"Screw caution, Dreux. This is my home. My sanctuary." She gritted her teeth and headed for the back entrance with a determined stride. "I won't allow him to take that from me."

Dreux stared at her squared shoulders, then scanned the area around them. Kai had been here and knew these surroundings. Including the dark alley they headed into. "Why must we enter the rear door first?"

"I want to see if Geoffrey is still here. If there's any sign that he was here." Kalyss stopped by a dark blue door and stared at the ground. "There should be a sign, shouldn't there?"

"I don't know how it works."

"Not a sign he was here, but—" She waved her hands in vague circles, searching the ground at her feet. "There should be something to say a man gave his life for someone else, right here, on this spot. That his body was pierced, his blood spilled. His sacrifice remembered."

"When it's all done, you can build a full scale memorial. For now—"

"It's not even that. His last word was to save me." She shook her head. She couldn't explain all she'd felt as he'd died in front of her. "I can't forget his eyes."

"Eyes can haunt someone's dreams forever." Dreux ran his hand down her arm in understanding and left her staring at the ground. Approaching the back entrance, he ran his palm over the door, feeling the vibration of it, seeking some hint of a malevolent presence behind it. Sometimes those things were as tangible as the door.

"Kai's probably not here anymore." Kalyss came up behind him.

"What makes you say that?" The back door wasn't locked. Good thing since they didn't have keys for it. Dreux turned the knob further and pushed the door open, letting it swing wide before he entered.

"Not high drama enough. It wouldn't be his style."

Dreux grinned. How true. "That's good. You couldn't sneak up on a deaf man."

"I can sneak," she argued defensively. "I just won't sneak here." She followed him into the dark back room, past the shelves and to the main hall of the dojo.

Bathrooms and offices were quiet and empty on the right and practice rooms equally solitary on the left and at the front of the building. Large windows surrounded the outside walls and the lighted streets outside revealed cars and darkened, closed businesses on both the front and sides of the dojo. With the first floor checked, Dreux turned to Kalyss.

"This way," she said.

They headed to the rear again. Absolutely nothing seemed out of place. It only made him more tense. Where was the discordant note, the one thing out of place that would lead them to Kai? Prove that he did, indeed, threaten them still? Dreux liked it better when his enemy was in plain sight.

Kalyss flipped on the light and headed toward a flight of steps leading upstairs. Dreux nearly plowed into her when she stopped suddenly, staring at a metal shelf of uniforms.

"What is it?"

"We blocked the basement so kids couldn't play down there anymore. It's where our tools and heavy storage items are. Could he have found it?" She tugged the shelf back an inch.

Dreux wrapped his hands around the supporting poles, picked up the end, and moved it two feet away from the door that was only now visible. Kalyss reached for the handle, but froze.

Dreux saw it, too. About a foot below the handle of the door was one long smear of blood, dried, but bright red against the white paint of the walls. "Yeah. He found it."

Dreux tugged her behind him and swung the door open, letting it swing into the space over the stairs. Dreux paused in the doorway. He'd given up the idea of stealth, but foolishly walking into traps wasn't an ideal replacement. And it was a good thing. The light caught a glint of silver across the doorway. Bending down, he traced the trip wire from one side to the other. It wasn't hooked to any further traps. He carefully dismantled it and eyed the rest of the stairs.

He edged each foot down a step, sweeping the area across it

and finding it safe before he allowed his weight to follow. His progress was slower, but the confidence was worth it. About midway down, one wall cleared and he could see into the room beyond. Kalyss rushed after him, all but pushing him to hurry. She was hoping for answers.

Dreux eyed the cleaned-up room and knew she wouldn't find any.

"It smells like bleach." He could almost hear her wrinkle her nose.

"Yeah." Dreux eyed the three square foot of concrete in front of him that was whiter than the rest of the floor and the large pipe eight feet above it. Kalyss squeezed between him and the stair rail, heading off to the right, away from the bleached patch.

"It looks like he had Geoffrey tied up over here. He didn't even pick up the duct tape." She shook her head, staring at the tape on the ground behind the chair, and muttered, "Jerk."

Dreux narrowed his eyes and moved closer to examine the area by her as Kalyss stalked off. The dirt on the floor was disturbed. Someone had been tied there. Dreux eyed the bleached spot from where he knelt.

"You *must* be kidding me." Her tone reached new levels of outrage. "He ate lunch." Sheer disbelief filled her voice and she looked to him with wide eyes. "He attacks me, kills my best friend, kills Geoffrey in front of me, then helps himself to my tea?"

"*Now* can I kill him?" Dreux joked with grim humor, approaching her quietly.

Kalyss shook her head, staring around the otherwise undisturbed room. "He's like the Hollywood version of the bad psycho guest. He drinks all your tea, leaves the toilet paper off the roll, makes your house all smelly and, oh, yeah, kills you in your sleep."

Dreux rubbed both of her arms briskly. "You'll go insane trying to figure him out."

"I'm not going to figure him out."

Dreux nodded in agreement.

"I'll leave that to the psychiatrists in prison."

"What?" Dreux's head jerked up, his eyes wide with disbelief.

Kalyss broke away from his suddenly gripping hands and pounded back up the stairs.

Dreux chased her. "He can't go to prison, Kalyss. I doubt one could hold him."

"But just imagine, he's probably the only psycho who really could serve three consecutive life sentences." Or more, if he'd touched anything in her apartment besides the food.

They were halfway up the second flight of stairs before he caught her and swung her to face him. "You know how this has to end. The only way it can end."

Kalyss framed his face and stared straight into his dark eyes. Thank God for high steps to give a woman a little equality. "You can't kill your own brother."

"We don't have a brotherly relationship."

"Not many brothers do. But still, the law frowns on killing, especially your own brother. Every law, political and religious, forbids that."

Dreux straightened, taken aback. "Surely this situation is—"

"—outside the law?" Kalyss shook her head. "It doesn't work that way. This is a new millennium. Justice can't be found at the end of a sword."

"But he killed Alex. Surely you understand he must be stopped."

"Stopped, yes. Killed, no." Kalyss bit her bottom lip, her brows drawn together. "You think losing Alex justifies committing murder, but it doesn't. Rules and laws must be obeyed. We didn't survive the last thousand years only to have you go to jail."

"People kill for justice every day."

"It's nice to imagine, in detail, but vengeance isn't justice. Alex agrees with that." She stared into his eyes, desperate to make him understand. "Why else do you think Sam still lives?"

Dreux's lips closed in a grim line. Kalyss stared at him a moment more before heading back up the stairs. He followed behind her, his silence a savage cloak. Kalyss pushed open the door. He'd make her understand. Eventually.

Entering her apartment, Dreux stopped at the doorway and watched her storm straight up her wooden stairs to the loft above the main living area before looking around. This was her place—hers. With pictures of her and Alex, her books and her art decorating the walls and shelves.

He'd long wondered what she lived like during her lives. Kai hadn't given him that information during his long years in the tower. He'd only tortured Dreux with details of all her deaths. All her valiant attempts to reach the husband so far beneath her.

And so he'd wondered and imagined. Would the Kalyss he'd known love technology? Bright colors? Hard or overstuffed furniture? Would she have fallen in love with one of the lifetimes she'd lived—Victorian, maybe, with the legs and wood and fancy scrollwork?

Now he looked around and filled in answers where questions had only existed before. Kalyss rustled through the room above him, opening and slamming doors. He left her to it, trying to rein in his own temper. Kai would have searched here, invaded her privacy in ways that would make her even angrier than earlier. He couldn't go free. He needed to be punished for all he'd done and imprisonment in man-made walls wasn't enough. He had to die.

Dreux leaned against the bar that separated the kitchen from the living room and crossed his arms. Four comfortable stools lined up along the bar and he could see several modern trappings: a coffeepot, a microwave, and a bread maker. Otherwise, her counters were bare of the accoutrements of a more sophisticated cook. It was a tidy and inviting room where he could picture her teaching him to make breakfast while she drank her coffee. She would sit alongside him, talking, laughing, and discussing their plans for the day ahead. Had Kai pictured them here and hated it as Dreux cherished it?

For a moment, he could see it all too clearly. Right down to the highlights the morning sun from the kitchen window lit around her head. His chest burned with the need to breathe, but he wasn't sure he could just yet. He wanted that future with her. Needed it.

But not only Kai blocked their way. Kalyss didn't fully trust him. Wasn't ready to open herself to him. Yeah, he'd pushed hard and fast, perhaps expected too much, but exactly how long was a man supposed to be patient while waiting to begin his life? How much longer could *he* wait? A thousand years was too long and weighed on him heavily already.

It all began with her—her love, her body wrapped in his arms, her smile, and her gifts. It wasn't self-will or stubbornness that set him on her. It wasn't because she was familiar. He knew, deep inside, had since he'd first seen her, that Kalyss was the woman to fulfill his dreams with. The woman for him to love.

His vision showed him the changes to those dreams, but the essential elements stayed the same. Instead of cuddling before a fire, they'd curl up on her deep, cushioned, black leather couch and cover up with the crimson chenille blanket thrown over its back. They'd watch the respectably sized TV and argue over getting a bigger one.

They'd turn off the lights and light the multitudes of candles that surrounded the room. They'd munch popcorn from the huge bowl in their laps and struggle over the volume of the surround sound he'd insist on.

And when night fell and they were ready for bed, he could see them ascending the stairs to the loft balcony she stood on now. They could walk sedately, with her arms curled around his waist and his on her shoulder. Or he could chase her and make her giggle.

From what he'd seen today, she didn't giggle enough. Or smile. Or laugh. She'd only been playful that once, while they were eating. He'd make it a priority for the rest of their days together. Give her a reason to smile—make her laugh—if they lived long enough for that dream to come true.

He'd help her love and trust again. He wanted that so much he shook with it. Needed the future he'd envisioned. To his soul, he was terrified that future would dry up, disappear, and evaporate like a mirage before he could grasp it. He couldn't continue to be patient. Couldn't wait for her to come to the knowledge he already had. Couldn't allow Kai to kill this chance.

At her pace, with her barriers, he could wait until she died from old age before she came to love and trust him. They'd have to start all over if she was reborn. He didn't like that idea, the idea of another Kalyss. He really liked this one.

Kalyss wrapped her hands on the balcony railing and leaned forward. Her brows were drawn together and her bottom lip tucked between her teeth. The caution she eyed him with was so at odds with his dream that it pained him.

She didn't want him to kill Kai, but there might not be any other choice. His brother was off somewhere, hatching some plan. He still held Geoffrey and Geoffrey wasn't betraying them again. Not if the blood on the wall and the blood cleaned by the bleach meant anything. But why was Geoffrey waiting to have Kai call them?

To give them time. If he and Kalyss weren't fully reunited, then all their sacrifices were for naught. Dreux watched her slap the rails and stomp down the stairs toward him. She shook her head until her newly fashioned ponytail bounced around behind her. He rather liked the way the strands would brush the nape of her neck, soft and feather-light. And her face was left in sharp relief, no hiding except in the depths of her blue eyes.

She stopped in front of him, looking up at his face. This close, standing, he realized again how tiny she was. Her personality was so immediate that any other position they were in or distance between them made her seem larger, stronger. Less vulnerable.

But now, he could see the cost of her strength: the ever-maintained walls, the defensive look in the back of her eyes that never quite went away. As if she expected an attack, was on guard for it and would defend herself with every ounce of power she could muster.

She widened her stance a bit and curved each hand at the sides of her waist, lifting her chin. "You're doing the statue thing again."

He cocked his head to the side. "Sorry. Habit."

She didn't smile, just continued staring into his eyes. "Funny."

"I try." He kept his tone dry, serious.

Her lips did twitch this time before she pulled them in line. "I wish I could read your mind sometimes. Really know what you're thinking."

"Then life would be absent of questions. Wouldn't that be boring?"

She lowered her chin and stared up at him. "Boring could be quite nice."

He looked over her body, imagining the things he'd envisioned earlier, the cuddling and making out, knowing his slight smile would irritate her. Why that seemed like a fun thing to do, he didn't know, but a little devil inside him said it was the best idea ever.

She licked across her top teeth and shook her head, giving him "the" look. Strolling to the fridge, she reached inside, saying, "You know, I just don't understand. For someone who wants to kill me, he sure doesn't seem to be in a hurry."

"You want to die soon?"

She flipped the tab on a Coke and shook her head again. "I just want to get it over with. Either I can get on with my life and do the things I need to do, or I need to focus on this threat."

She took a long drink, her movements suddenly erratic, frenzied. Her eyes darted around the room and her voice became husky. "I need to make calls. Help plan a funeral."

She shook her head at herself. "I need to find a friggin' body. What mother would believe her child was dead if she didn't even see the body?"

Kalyss froze, her eyes widening and darkening with horror. As if she'd just realized it wasn't a nameless body, but Alex's body she spoke of.

Dreux moved toward her, but she darted away, hunching her shoulders and wrapping her arms around herself. Following, he settled his hands on her shoulders, holding her in place in front of him. He smoothed his hands down her arms, warming her with his heat.

He understood the distancing a person instituted out of self-preservation when another died, but he'd also seen war and death to a degree she never would. He'd buried friends, as close as any he'd ever had, men who'd died in moments of high bravery and courage, and sent even more into battle after that. But what was understandable to him disgusted her.

Dreux tightened his arms around her, sorry for every loss of innocence she had to endure. "He'll call. Then we'll finish this."

She pulled away from him and yanked the cell phone from her pocket, holding it in the air between them. "You mean this? It's gonna ring?"

She made a disgusted noise. "How do I know? How do you know? Because a man who says he can come back to life said he'll call? Because he told it to a living statue?"

With an abrupt head movement, she tossed her hair so it bounced down her back in a long, wavy line. "This is so unreal."

Dreux framed her face with his hands and leaned forward. "We're beyond this, Kalyss. It is real and you know it."

Her eyes moistened as she stared back at him. "But it shouldn't be. This isn't the way life is supposed to work."

"So we're complicated people." He shrugged. "It will all work out. We'll find Alex and Geoffrey. Kai will—" she arched a brow, and he smoothly amended "—cease to be a threat and we'll only have to deal with the simple problem of your trust in me."

He quirked one side of his mouth before lowering his lips to hers for a gentle, calming kiss. They'd try to figure out Kai later. Right now, he wanted to enjoy the chance to feel his earlier hurt and anger slide out of him and desire fill him. Kalyss seemed to need the same.

A shrill ring vibrated against his chest and they jumped apart. The ring ended and silence reigned for a brief moment. They held their breath near to bursting, disbelieving the moment they'd waited for had finally arrived, until another ring split the air. Their eyes held as she opened the flip phone and brought it to her ear.

"Hello?" Her heart pounded with hard, painful thuds.

"Kalyss?"

His voice was so unbelievably, endearingly familiar. Tears filled her eyes. "Alex?"

KAI SNAPPED THE phone to his ear. "Sorry to break up the touching reunion, but I'd hate to see my new friend do something wimpy."

Alex scowled at Kai's grin. "Just call me your enemy. I've seen what you do to your friends."

Kai patted him on the head and walked away from the post Alex was tied to, Kalyss speaking in his ear.

"He's really alive? 'Cause if this is another sick game to you—"

"Never a sick game, sweetheart. He's perfectly fine." Kai strode off the wooden walkway of the square, floodlight-lined dock, blending into the shadows of the surrounding cliffs and trees. Idly, he wondered if the sound of water falling in the background would give her a clue to their location.

"Geoffrey said—"

"Don't speak ill of the dead, sweetheart. They can't defend themselves."

"But he's not exactly dead, is he?"

"That remains to be seen, but it's possible. The real question is, are you ready to play?"

"What would I win?"

"Your friend's life not enough?"

"Not anymore. I'm getting sick of the rematches."

"If you'd just learn to accept your losses . . ." he trailed off mockingly

"That's not in my nature."

"Obviously." Kai leaned against the rocks behind him and grinned at Alex. His arms were tied straight out from his sides. Kai had wrapped the rope around Alex's wrists and out to the metal boat ties on either side of him. Now there was no give to the rope, no stretching Alex could do to escape. The strain on his face showed that he knew this.

"I want this over with, once and for all. I don't want to get Dreux back only to have you return for both of us in a few years."

Kai crossed his feet in front of him and used his left hand to prop his right elbow as he held the phone to his ear. As tough as she'd become, he could almost believe she wasn't ready to buckle down and promise him anything for the return of her friend. But he wasn't that naïve.

She could play tough, as long as she played.

"Done." She no doubt tried to hide it, but he heard her sigh of relief brush the phone. He let the moment build, waiting for his moment, then added, "As long as we play by my rules."

"Haven't we always?" Her tone was much too acerbic for

his liking. As if she no longer feared the person she talked to. Kai was a reasonable man. He held strongly to his code, but that did not mean he wasn't a man to fear.

"Careful, Kalyss. Rule number one: always show respect. I will allow no less." He gave it and he would receive it.

"Rule number two?" Her tone was carefully guarded this time, achingly neutral.

"Rule number two is we follow my plan and everyone gets what they want. You and Alex get each other and Dreux and I kill each other. We all go home happy." He paused, listening to her telling silence. "Those of us who live long enough to go home."

"I want Dreux alive and safe, too."

"Sorry, darlin'. You've already set the stakes." Dreux was nonnegotiable, but it spoke of their attachment already that she'd even try to make his safety an issue, which was why the game. If they were to have no rematches, then Kalyss's soul needed to move on after her eventual death. If she continued caring enough to come back for Dreux, then the cycle would never end.

He listened to her heavy silence, knowing this wasn't her last effort on the issue. She'd struggle to save them all, unless he convinced her not to.

"What about Geoffrey?"

"He wanted to feel the rain," Kai said in a dark tone. The wind picked up around him, crisp and cool. He could almost feel the wetness of approaching rain on his face. He raised his chin and breathed deep. He told her the start point of their game and folded his phone closed.

KALYSS LOWERED HER head, resting it on Dreux's chest. His arms surrounded her as he laid his head on hers. There'd been a time when a man's arms had been her prison, but now they were her comfort as she stood trapped by another man's words. She couldn't save them all. That's what he told her. What Dreux had told her, as well.

Denial wailed inside her breast as her will fought the tight bands of control Kai had tried to close around her. Somehow, she'd find a way to beat him. Discover where he was, use any weapon she could devise, and outmaneuver him.

Concern for losing the Geoffrey Dreux had described choked her. The man who'd rescued a statue, only to spend an entire century educating it. The man who'd committed the worst betrayal, only to spend a millennium trying to correct it, no matter the personal cost.

The man who'd known her gift and had not reviled it, but used it to protect her. The man who'd stared into her eyes as the light in his died, and used his last breath to ensure her safety. The way Kai had spoken, he might really die soon—*permanently.* Dreux, Geoffrey, and Alex. Of the three, Kai expected her to choose who would live and who would die.

Dreux kissed her forehead. "What's the plan?"

Chapter 17

The bridge was just as she remembered. Kalyss shivered, forcing back the cold prickling of her skin. It only lacked a dazzling display of fireworks directly above her head. Every 4th of July, people crowded the wide bridges over the Spokane River in the middle of Riverfront Park and stared until their necks, backs, and knees ached as the colored sparks framed the 1974 World Expo pavilion and the trademark clock tower.

Kalyss braced herself on the stone and clenched the steel rails. With dry, unmoved eyes, she stared grimly out over the wide expanse of water a dozen feet or more beneath her. The wind whipped the opening of her jacket against her chest. Stray strands of hair flew wildly around her face, whipping her eyes until they stung and stuck against her lips. She yanked them away and turned to Dreux, who was doing the statue thing again.

She could practically see information absorbing into him like a sponge dumped in a bucket of water. It was surprising his head didn't swell with it all. Hers probably would have exploded.

Kalyss shivered at a sudden chill. It always happened this time in October. The temperature was warm during the day while becoming colder and drier at night. She hadn't owned a jacket large enough to fit Dreux, so he stood with nothing but a cotton shirt between him and the wind. Yet he seemed unfazed by the rush of cooling air around him, just as he seemed unworried about facing Kai whenever his brother finally finished screwing with their heads. As if the thought of killing or being killed was nothing to fear for Dreux. Well, it sure stressed her.

"I don't get why Kai sent me here." She shook her head and looked around the bridge and river again. Her eyes squinted to see what she might have missed.

"His game is not obvious. Look beyond it."

Her brows drew together. She'd been looking. "What are you talking about?"

"Examine the battlefield as much as your opponent." Dreux gestured with one hand around him. "He wouldn't end the game so soon by fighting here. We are in the middle of a wide-open area. We'd seen fighting hand to hand, unconcealed to any who might pass by us and interfere. And he would never do this job from a distance. There is some honor in him."

"So we're not here to wait for him." She looked around again with less hope of seeing something. A neon sign with the words CLUE HERE and an unambiguous arrow would have been nice. Was that too much to ask?

She sighed and leaned against the rail. Could Geoffrey really die? Where was he?

"You're restless."

Kalyss shrugged. "I don't like this place anymore."

Dreux moved behind her, his body providing a nice windbreak for her shivering form. She basked in the warmth, refusing to let past mistakes and regrets color her time with him. Who knew how this night would end? She didn't want to spend it thinking about the past.

"It's beautiful here. Peaceful. Why wouldn't you like it?" His question was innocent, but his tone said he knew this was another bad memory for her and he wanted to test how determined she was to keep to herself, to not trust him.

Kalyss looked at the water and sighed. It wasn't about trust. She truly believed that. But he believed differently. Already, she could feel him stiffening behind her, withdrawing into himself because of her silence. He kept to himself so much, but he made an effort not to with her. He opened himself to her, was honest with her, and he deserved the same in return. She huffed out a sigh of irritation. Why here? Why did Kai send her here, of all places?

"Too bad you can't just see my memories, the way I see yours. This would be easier."

His voice rumbled behind her ear. "It is not a gift I possess. And if it was not a gift you possessed, we'd still have words."

So the limits of her gift were no excuse. She could still talk. She balled her fists on the railing before her and stood silent a minute, listening to the rush of water around her. She'd heard this sound in the phone call with Kai. Was he here? Watching from some hideaway? Was Alex here with him? No, Dreux had said it was too much of an open spot.

They could be hidden in a clump of trees, though. She surveyed the area again, but the park was so large, they could search all night and never find them. And Kai had specified this exact spot. They couldn't move. Not yet. He'd stay hidden until he was good and ready, making them play his stupid game—leaving her plenty of time to face Dreux's demands and her feelings about sharing her most intimate fears and memories with him. Kalyss nearly growled in frustration. What a thoughtful psychopath.

"This isn't the memory you asked for. I don't know if I can share it well. I'm not good with words." She halted, then firmed her jaw and continued, "But I'll try."

Dreux wrapped his arms around her, pulling her back to his front, and rested his hands on the railing beside hers. "It's a start."

Kalyss laid her smooth, pale hand above his rough, sun-darkened one, finding reassurance in the calluses she felt on his hands, reassurance that it had taken strength of character to build them. She closed her eyes and searched for her own strength.

Kalyss opened her eyes to the stars above her. They seemed so close at times, but they'd hidden that Fourth of July evening, hidden behind multitudes of brightly colored starbursts and rocket tails. A different man had held her that evening.

Not so tall and bulky, but stronger than her. His slight build had hidden a deceptive strength, but that night she hadn't known the difference and had gloried in the wonder of a man's love.

She hissed in irritation. As soon as the picture began to form in her head, her inner vision changed it to a memory of Sam's face twisted in fury and viciousness. That night on the bridge began such a series of brutal, heartbreaking events; she couldn't face it as a single memory.

She tried again to draw out that memory, but the same happened. No matter where she began the memory, walking through the crowded park, finding a blank spot among the bystanders to watch the show, or up to the very moment her world had changed, as soon as her memory focused on Sam, the memory changed to a more violent moment in her marriage.

Her head began a small throbbing over her right temple with the strain of trying to see: Past, Present, and Future. They all melded within her, swirling and bursting, piercing her skull until she slumped against Dreux, moisture beaded on her upper lip. "I can't stand remembering."

Dreux wouldn't let her flee the challenge. "Just speak. Start anywhere and tell me the story."

She snuggled his heat to her. How to begin? How detailed should she be? But then, details were what he was looking for. They were his measure of her trust.

She took a deep breath and thought back. "It was the Fourth of July. The day America—"

"I remember," he cut her off, calmly keeping her focused.

She snorted. "Of course you do."

Kalyss began again, picturing as many details as she could remember. The sun, warm on her face as they picnicked among throngs of people enjoying the park alongside them. Special vendors sold everything from hot dogs to charm bracelets, dazzling the nose and eye all at once.

"I'd always wanted to browse through a selection of jewelry and have fun picking something out, something I could keep."

So superficial now, but that day it had meant the world. Sam had set a price limit, but it was higher than she could've afforded on her own for such a spontaneous purchase, so she'd smiled and thanked him for his generosity. Twenty minutes later, she'd walked away, feeling a dainty pair of dangling silver hearts swing from her ears.

Kalyss reached up and felt her empty ears. She hadn't worn earrings for years. They were dangerous when Sam's rough hands had grabbed her, ripping and twisting. But it'd been forever since she'd had to worry about that and she missed how beautiful she'd felt, walking along, smiling, laughing, and holding hands with a handsome man, her heart light enough to float.

"The day was perfect. Peaceful. Even strangers were kind and easily forgiving if we bumped into them. The weather was hot and bright, with only a lazy wind to cool us."

Until darkness fell and they were grateful for their light jackets. Everyone lined up, along the bridges and open fields of the park, at the edges of the walkways, watching their children play in the grass, admonishing them not to climb the trees.

The fireworks began, decorating the sky with bursts of color and light. Sam had pulled her close in a thrilling, possessive hold as they'd stared high into the sky, watching the sparks stream up, burst, and fall into the river below. And just as the last finale rocketed up, Sam had lowered to one knee and proposed.

Like electric feathers along her skin, the memory blossomed inside her, colorful and loud. She felt again her happiness; her honest faith that this was the best gift life had ever given her.

She remembered the joy of well-wishers, eager for yet another crowning moment to top off their celebrations, clapping and whistling and shouting encouragement to both of them. How she'd smiled, thrown her arms around Sam, and pressed her lips to his.

The memory was so real, so present, that it took a moment to realize she'd stopped speaking and was actually transmitting it. She could do that? The shock snapped her back to the present and Dreux's stiff form behind her. Silence reigned for a few moments.

"I didn't realize it was a happy memory that you dreaded here." His tone was her only indication he'd truly seen the flash of memory.

She turned to stare into his eyes. Was he upset? Jealous?

Angry? Disappointed? She swallowed. She wasn't sure she could explain how sick that memory made her when she realized how foolishly quick she'd fallen into the Disney fantasy, believing it was Happily Ever After from there, how naively trusting she'd been, and how thoroughly and brutally disabused of that notion she'd become. She opened her mouth to try when the phone rang. Quietly, heart heavy, she opened the phone and pressed it to her ear, waiting for Kai's voice.

"Amazing how hindsight can change a person's perspective of an event, isn't it?"

"How did you know?" She frowned into Dreux's eyes as she listened to Kai.

"You've entrusted it so well to anyone who reads your scrapbook. Pictures and letters, details galore of everything that has ever happened to you. Thanks for sharing it with me."

"It was never meant for you. For anyone, really."

Dreux's stiff posture screamed his confusion. She'd left the secret horrors of her life where any nosy person could find them, but she wouldn't trust him with them? And now Kai knew more about her life than he did—taunted them both with it.

"Are you sure about that? It seems to be a cry for attention to me, Kalyss."

She closed her eyes and angled her head down. "Why are you doing this?"

"It's the game, darlin'."

"Stupid game. I don't even know what I'm supposed to do."

"But you promised to play. I know Alex would be disappointed, as would I, if you stopped. Now just find the clues if you want to find Geoffrey."

She shuddered at his threat to Alex. "Then what?"

"Go to the southwest corner of the park. You know where I mean."

The line went dead and she turned to Dreux. He stared ahead, his shoulders stiff, his lips grim, his jaw hard. "People hardly ever look through scrapbooks. It was a healing process for me. It was never meant to be shared. I don't even know how he found it."

He stared past her for a moment, then his gaze settled on her face. "I realize that. I just don't enjoy the thought of him knowing you so well when I don't."

She nodded and lowered her gaze to her feet. She could understand that. From the corner of her eye, she caught the flutter of paper on the bottom rails. She grabbed it, intending to throw it away, but froze when she saw tape holding it to the metal. Was this the clue?

Dreux's feet stopped beside her, voicing her thoughts. "Is it the clue?"

Carefully, she peeled it off and unfolded the paper. "I think so. It's a map, anyway."

Dreux paused at her tone. "What does it say?

Kalyss displayed the vague Mapquest printout. "It says Geoffrey's in Spokane."

IN A LONG row that rounded the southwest corner of Riverfront Park, iron statues of runners were mounted on a long cement dais. Some were children, girls with copper ponytails and boys with squared shoulders. Some were in wheelchairs and some were fully grown adults.

On this corner, the inspirational pieces of artwork lined the walkway that ran around and through the park. Dreux stared at it, his brows drawn together, as if asking, *Why would someone want to build art like this and devote it to something as mundane as running?*

"It might not make sense to see this as art . . ."

"Of course it's art." His eyes snapped to her and she closed her mouth. What could she say? She couldn't read him at all, apparently. She had no idea what he might be thinking.

"You were looking at it so strangely." She shrugged the explanation.

"I'm wondering what this spot means to you." He looked at the runners. "Although, I think I can guess. The question is, is this a happy or bad memory for you?"

"What can you guess?" And why didn't he have trouble reading her? Talk about unfair.

"It's motivational. Speaks of drive, endurance, strength." He looked at her, taking her in from head to toe. "Struggle. Determination and stubbornness. I know you were hurt. I imagine it took all of that to recover from such an injury. Is that it?"

Kalyss shrugged humbly, her hands hooking into her back pockets. Her shoulders hunched and she looked at the runners. "Basically."

To know he saw those qualities when he looked at her, touched her. It had taken all that and more to recover from Sam's last attack, and though it was nothing she wanted attention for, it was a defining time in her life. A time when she'd decided what kind of person she wanted to be and how to get there. And Dreux respected her for it. A small treasure chest inside her heart unlocked and opened wide to him.

"In a few months, I went from being a married mother-to-be to an emotionally, mentally, and physically devastated husk of a person. I'd not only lost the child inside me, but the hope of any future children."

His gaze was riveted to her face as he absorbed every word she spoke.

"I didn't know why I was alive. Didn't really want to be."

He made a negative movement and sound, then forced himself to be still.

"I didn't know what to live for. What to do next." Kalyss shrugged again. "Alex refused to let me withdraw from life. He literally pulled me out of bed and forced me to dress and exercise."

The wind rushed a little more wildly around her, shaking the runners and giving them the illusion of movement. "I grumbled and bitched at first, but he took it. And I eventually realized he wouldn't give up on me, so I couldn't give up on myself."

Stepping onto the dais, Kalyss stood behind a female runner with a ponytail flowing behind her. She braced her hands on the statue's shoulders and Dreux could imagine Alex doing the same to her. Pushing and prodding her for her own good. He had to respect the man for that.

"After a while, Alex and I began running here once a week. It's hard to do too often, with parking and daily life keeping us from downtown, but once a week this track was ours. And I began to really care about rebuilding my life." She turned her head toward him. "Then, one day, we paused for breath and stared at the runners, and Alex suddenly said—" She licked her lips and blinked. " 'Kalyss, you're an iron runner to me.' "

Dreux moved closer to her, stopping just inches away. Thanks to the concrete dais, she could look him directly in the eyes and the windows to her soul were wide open to him. "It was a happy memory, Dreux."

He nodded, raising a hand to cushion her cheek.

She watched him with sober blue eyes. "I know why Kai sent me here, Dreux."

"To remind you of everything you went through after trusting a man."

She nodded. "The pain and struggle. The near impossibility of it all. And to remind me of something else."

He looked at her, curious and waiting.

"I'm not the same woman today that I was four years ago. I definitely am not the same woman I was a thousand years ago." She swallowed, knowing her next words would hurt him. "I'm an entirely different animal. Stronger, wiser, independent. I don't need you to survive."

Dreux smiled sadly. "That's a truth I admire in you. And one I hate."

His fingers brushed tenderly over her cheek. No man wanted to hear he wasn't necessary to the woman he loved, but considering their track record, perhaps it was for the best. If he lived through the night, however, he'd work his hardest to change it. To become so necessary to her she found it hard to breathe without him.

She cocked her head, examining his face as if trying to read his thoughts. "There's something he didn't plan on, though."

"What's that?"

"Being here also reminds me there are men I can trust. And I can overcome anything, accomplish anything—" She brushed a hand over his cheek and jaw. "—for something I want."

She held still, as if afraid to commit more to him than her words already had. Her eyes searched his, then her jaw firmed and her chin lifted. It definitely wasn't everything, but it was more than he'd had an hour ago. It was acceptable progress—for now.

"Just keep wanting me," he whispered.

She swallowed, and leaned forward, her lips brushing softer than the wind against his. With a tender skill few warriors had, Dreux stroked his hands around her waist and beneath her jacket, pressed against her bare back. Keeping to light, barely touching kisses nearly drove him insane with need.

A car passed by and they separated. Now was not the moment to get distracted. Kalyss turned back to the runner with the ponytail and pulled a taped piece of paper from it. Unfolding it, she showed him another map of Spokane. It was only slightly more detailed than the first one. Kai wouldn't let them figure it out until he was good and ready.

The phone rang.

Chapter 18

Many people had nightmares about high school, but Kalyss's experience had been positive. Kai was likely leading her to another happy memory, almost assuredly one with Alex. Did Kai think Alex was the only man she should trust?

Heading back to Geoffrey's SUV, they stopped for a moment to stare at the world's largest Radio Flyer wagon. The red wagon a generation of *Dennis the Menaces* had pulled along behind them now thrilled kids in a new way. Kalyss and Dreux watched in the dim light as a couple of older kids climbed the ladder in back and slid down the handle/slide in front. The kids laughed and playfully chased each other back to the ladder.

Kalyss smiled. "Sometimes, it's too easy to forget the good things in life."

"I remember the commercials for those. They made them look fun."

Kalyss frowned. "It's sad. If you and Kai had been born in this century, no one would have cared if you were illegitimate. You probably would have been raised together, played together, and had a much better relationship."

Dreux's stillness alerted her and she looked into his shadowed eyes. He turned toward her and, for an instant, the light made his eyes shine bright, then it was gone and he stared at her with flat black eyes. "I know, Kalyss. But some things were meant to be. He and I were raised apart. He was raised to hate me and I was raised to be a warrior."

Kalyss stared up at him as he towered over her, suddenly as big and dark and forbidding as he'd been the night before in the dark basement. "Kalyss, I can't allow him to continue attacking me or those I love. He must be stopped and I'm the only one who can see to it."

"I'm not exactly his fan, being his favorite victim and all, but he's your brother." She shook her head, searching for the right words to describe the feeling of wrongness that swamped her when the thought of them killing each other was mentioned. "I mean, there has to be another way. A way to save you both."

"If Geoffrey were meant to end Kai's life, he would have long ago. No one else can stop him." Dreux looked away and sighed. "I know what you're saying is right, but he's my responsibility. My task to see finished."

"But—"

He took her hand and guided them back to the sidewalk. "It's done, Kalyss. This is who I am, what I was raised to do."

"Be a killer—a murderer—of your own brother?" She shook her head in denial again. "I can't see that being something God would want on your conscience. Your grand destiny is to repeat Cain and Abel? I don't think so."

"What else is there to do?" he asked impatiently.

His snapping tone made her heart stop for a full beat. He'd never been less than absolutely patient with her, but at this moment she saw the bullheaded maleness of him. His strides were quicker, longer, and she had to pick up the pace to stay beside him. Maybe he didn't like the responsibility he insisted he had, but he'd still see it through to the finish he thought it needed.

"I don't know what else to do," she admitted quietly. But she'd damn sure figure it out. What was it that made Kai, Dreux, and Geoffrey think death was the key to ending the cycle? As much as she hated being a victim, Sam's or Kai's, she still wasn't immediately for the death penalty—especially if it meant brother killing brother.

Kalyss eyed the roiling black and gray clouds above them. Hopefully they'd finish this traveling trivia game before it rained. Something about the ominous heaviness in the air triggered an anxiety that was hard to control.

Everything seemed to stem from Maeve's death, who had killed her and the women after her. Murders from so long ago even *CSI* wouldn't be able to find enough forensic evidence to solve them. Which left he said/she said, the most worthless of evidence. You never knew who was lying, mistaken, or conned. The truth of Maeve's death could only be told by her and her killer.

And Kalyss couldn't just pick a moment in history, think about it, and boom, there it was like a movie in her mind. It would be cool if she could. So many answers to so many questions could be solved that way. Who really shot JFK? Did Marilyn Monroe really commit suicide? Had there ever been a moment when Sam loved her, or had he cared too much about control to be capable of love? Had she been duped once by a good con artist or was she doomed to repeat her mistakes with regards to men?

Dreux wanted her to show him her past, her memories. There'd been an intense second where she might have transmitted something due to her own emotional reaction to her memories, but the flash had been brief and difficult to produce. Her gift was iffy, sporadic, and unreliable. She couldn't tap into her *own* memories at will, let alone someone else's.

But what if that was the answer? What if she could use this ability to go back to the night Maeve died and pull enough information from both Dreux and Kai to solve the mystery and end the cycle? Was she strong enough to expand her gift? Or was she already at her limit?

She shivered and tucked her hands in her jacket pocket. They turned at the corner across from the opera house and its water fountain. The tall, metal fountain drowned out every other sound for a good block. "They're somewhere with running water. I can hear it when he calls. I've looked around at the bridge and here by the fountain, but I haven't seen them."

"He hasn't been close. I would have known."

She hadn't noticed before, but now his vigilance hit her hard. She shouldn't be surprised, but she was. Of course he'd looked around them, but she'd thought it was curiosity of the world. He'd been looking for Kai the entire time. She unlocked the SUV and they climbed inside.

She drove a few blocks and stopped on 4th Avenue, right in front of Lewis and Clark. LC made a great first impression. She paused and stared at the tall, oak-shaded building. The grand, wide staircase to the double doors was farther to their left, but straight in front of her were the benches and flagpole that graced the often-used side entrance.

"Is this it?"

"Yeah." She unbuckled and opened her door. "This is where he said."

The flagpole stood in the middle of a circular, wooden dais. Like the saying goes, as long as there are tests, there will be prayer in schools. But when she'd gone to school, they didn't pray only on test days. Many of the Christian students would hold hands around the flagpole and pray as a beginning to their day. It was not required and not led by any adult and she'd loved it.

That was how she'd met Alex. They'd held hands for the morning prayer when suddenly, without any control, her gift had reached for his memories and she'd seen Alex's first enraptured glimpse of Beth Ann Raines, his high school crush. Papers had fallen from his hands, one carving a nice slice in the palm of his hand. In the vision, she watched the skin seal closed.

He wiped the red streak against his jeans and his hand was as good as new. Later, when she'd talked to him, they'd discussed all the psychics and witches and magicians in the world and how they were often considered frauds. Most probably were, but neither she nor Alex wanted to put themselves in the position to be judged or targeted because of an ability they had no control over. It was then she knew her secrets were safe with him. She'd been as faithful with his—until now. She had to share them with Dreux.

Kalyss stared at the flagpole, refreshing the memory in her mind. Starting at the rim and working in. The bright sun shining over the field beside LC; the drone of many voices punctuated by a laugh or shriek as some people were playing; the reverent prayer just before the bell rang, shrill and commanding. Then she focused on the feel of Alex's larger hand clasping hers and the shock of reading his memory. Her amusement and his surprise as he'd thought she'd shocked him with static electricity.

She built the memory, filling in the details as she had at the park. When she was sure she had it, she reached for Dreux. His attention snapped from their surroundings to her when she grasped his arm, then he held still and waited.

She lost focus when she reached for him and had to build it back up. She wasn't starting fresh, so it wasn't hard to do, but then she worried about it not working. Who would die if she didn't master this? That thought froze everything and her mind blanked.

She sighed and slumped. "I thought I had it."

Dreux's eyes narrowed, as he realized what she'd tried to do. "You're fine. Try again."

His intent encouragement bolstered her and she faced the flagpole. Detail by detail, she built the memory yet again. This time, when she reached for Dreux, she felt the electric shock, and knew, without doubt, that he could see her memory as she'd seen it.

They held still, breathless. She was afraid to think of anything else in case it broke the link. Then, in her mind, the school bell rang and the memory ended. Eyes burning, Kalyss spun toward Dreux with an exultant laugh and he hugged her to him, laughing with her. She buried her face in his shoulder and held him tight. With her nose in the crease of his neck, she breathed him in. She hadn't thought she could do it, but she had. She could again.

The phone rang, cutting into their celebration. Stiff, she pulled away from Dreux and answered the call.

"How's IT GOING?" Kai sounded happy. Relaxed and amused. It scared her.

"I want to talk to Alex again."

Kai chuckled and drawled, "Sure, I'll get right on that."

"I need to know he's still alive while I'm jumping through your hoops or I'm not playing." She infused her voice with hard determination. This was nonnegotiable. He could barrage her with happy memories, even horrible ones, all night if it kept Alex safe.

He sighed, then the phone moved and Kai's voice sounded distantly from the mic. "Say hi so she knows you're alive."

"Waterf—" Alex rushed out urgently. The phone moved again and a loud splash crackled through the earpiece. She heard Alex choking, then Kai's grim voice.

"You abuse the privilege, it's gone. Don't be such a bad boy." Air brushed the mic again and Kai spoke clearly in her ear while Alex coughed in the background. "Now, back to the game."

"What did you do to him?"

"Not as much as I will if you two don't behave." He paused. The silence stretched too long and she realized he was waiting for her promise.

"I've done everything you asked, not that it makes sense."

"It makes sense to you, Kalyss. Don't lie to me." The silence stretched again and she heard the rushing sound of water in the background.

Waterfall, Alex had tried to say. She tried to picture all the waterfalls in Spokane. It was a big clue that he hadn't said fountain. There was a waterfall at the Spokane Falls and at the YMCA in the valley.

"It's all about trust, isn't it, Kalyss? If you trust too quickly, too easily, well, you remember what a mistake that was." The manipulation in his voice was a weapon she'd become immune to. It sickened her, but she couldn't deny the truth in his words.

"One mistake doesn't mean I'm destined to compound it." She avoided Dreux's eyes.

"You already have. Who do you trust now? Who's really come through for you?"

"Certainly not you." She set her jaw at a stubborn angle.

"You've never been stupid." Was he agreeing she shouldn't trust him or telling her she was being stupid now? Kalyss shook her head. "There's only one man you trust, isn't there?"

Just get to the point already. She shifted impatiently, trying to use this time he gave her to get on top of the situation, but he was like quicksand, drowning her slowly but surely whether she struggled or not. "Why do you care who I trust?"

"It's between me and him, Kalyss. It's time you quit interfering."

"Hey," she snapped angrily. "I didn't start this crazy day, damn you. Don't blame me."

"But it's your fault. If you'd quit coming back and searching for him, attempting to free him, then he and I could settle this and it would be over."

"Last I checked, I don't control reincarnation."

"But you control who you trust, who you love. I'm telling you to choose wisely. Geoffrey won't be around to influence you next time—"

"Why? What did you do to him?"

"—so it's all up to you. Break the chains that have bound your spirit. Forfeit the game."

"Where's Geoff—" The line went dead.

She stared blankly at it until Dreux took it from her hand and closed it. Mouth grim, he tucked the phone into her pocket and placed the third vague map in her hand.

"What did he say?"

Chapter 19

Kalyss's old house nestled in the older section of Browne's Addition, shrouded by huge trees with huge roots that pushed up the sidewalks until they were riddled with cracks and broken into large sections. Once a symbol of wealth, the neighborhood had become synonymous with cheap rent and old mansions-turned-apartment buildings—luxury on a budget. She and Sam had scrimped and saved for a two-story fixer-upper in one of the worst sections.

His parents hadn't wanted them to marry just out of high school and had withdrawn monetary support for the first year, waiting for it all to fall apart, but when it became apparent they were serious about their marriage, his parents re-entered their life the only way they knew how: by manipulating Sam with money and a higher paying job offer at his dad's building and supply company.

On weekends, they'd scraped and painted, installed a fence around the backyard, and rebuilt the gardens. The inside had been in relatively decent repair then. They'd furnished and decorated, smiling and loving both each other and the home they were creating.

Now, Kalyss and Dreux trudged through the knee-high piles of leaves to the back door of the shrouded, lonely house.

After winning it in the divorce, she'd sold it and later used the money to finance the dojo.

Apparently as a symbol of hope their son would soon come home, his parents bought it and left it closed. Waiting. Kalyss reached under a pot of dead shrubbery for the key no one but she and Sam knew of, then stood and stared around at the dark, overgrown yard. Once familiar and comforting, it was now strange and threatening. Full of blackness and sour memories.

"Do they blame you for the attack?"

She stared at Dreux a moment, her eyes vague and unfocused as she looked into the past. A breeze brushed by, chilling her through her jacket. It was a necessary link to the present as she felt her mind slip further and further into the past.

"WHAT DID YOU do to him, you slut? He'd never have done anything wrong if you hadn't made him!" Sam's mother screamed from across the courtroom as the bailiff cuffed Sam.

Sam's father, lost and confused, put an arm around his wife. She broke his hold and, moving faster than anyone suspected she could, streamed across the courtroom and slapped Kalyss. Pain exploded across her cheek and blood roared in her ears, deafening her to the woman's screams and curses.

Before the bailiff could cuff any more of his family, Sam's father caught her arm and dragged her from the room. She fought him, struggled to reach Kalyss again, but she'd never been a strong woman. Her husband closed his thick, long arms around her and they disappeared through the courtroom doors.

Kalyss stared after them, frozen in shock and disbelief. The blood pounding past her ears had protected her from the rest of the woman's hateful words, but as she watched her ferocious red lips form them, Kalyss couldn't help but get the gist. She could only rub her hot, welting cheek and try not to shrink under Sam's furious, promising green gaze. She'd done nothing wrong, but they were determined to punish her anyway.

* * *

DID SAM'S PARENTS blame her? Kalyss stared into Dreux's dark eyes, and as leaves swirled through the air around them, she muttered, "You could say that."

His thumb brushed gently over her cheek and his fingers curved, warm and comforting, around the back of her neck. "Then they are fools."

His quiet faith in her touched her more than any of Sam's grand gestures ever had. She brushed the back of his hand with her fingers. "Thank you."

One deep breath and a bracing of her shoulders and she turned to face the back door, the old key burning its imprint into her hand.

"Kai's reminded me of happy things so far. I'm not sure where he is in the scrapbook, but there's one memory I'm sure to show you." And she still wasn't sure how she felt about that.

Parts of that last night were still blank. Would they fill in? Was she ready to see that night in its entirety? To relive it? Despite Dreux's assurances, was he?

His eyes piercing and steady, full of shadows and mystery, Dreux looked down into her eyes. "I would share everything with you, past, present, and future."

How was he real, this man who'd been a statue and a medieval warrior before that? A man who appeared from nowhere to care for her, be endlessly patient with her hang-ups, and simply stride over all her insurmountable barriers like they were no more than speed bumps.

He made life seem like a possibility again, an adventure where it had become an obstacle course. An endurance test for those who learned to thrive on challenge or a grave of buried dreams for those who didn't. She'd been the one, struggling to become the other, when he'd come along and made the world, and the troubles in it, smaller and more dealable.

Ironically, that only made him scarier. He made impossible, dangerous promises that most men couldn't begin to fill. Promises she couldn't let destroy her when he broke them.

"Okay, then." She took a deep breath of sweet, musty air and squared her shoulders. Dreux held out his hand, palm up. She stared at it for a long moment, imagining what it would mean to share everything with this man. Leave nothing out. No hiding, no secrets, no privacy screen between them.

Briefly, the thought was a clawed pressure grasping at her throat, choking and overwhelming. She forced the panic down. This house was a memory. The past. If they couldn't handle sharing this, then there would be no future for them. Determined, she firmly placed her hand in his and tried not to choke on her fear of the symbolism.

As soon as she turned to the back door with the key in her hand, Dreux's hold on her other hand became her only link to the present. A chilled warmth ran through her, like sweat freezing on hot skin, and her mind traveled back until she was a ghost walking through her own memory.

On October 7, 2004, she slid a key into the rusty lock of a scratched and faded door. But in her mind, it was a bright, sunny day—October 6, 2000, now that she thought about it.

The last flowers of summer sweetened the air and the door in front of her was freshly sanded and polished. The locks were new and golden. When she pushed open the door, there was such a smile on her face and a spring in her step that one bounce and she could fly through the roof.

Three months. She grinned and started whistling. With a small rub of her rounded stomach, Kalyss dropped her keys in the bowl on the table by the door and rushed to the kitchen with a bouquet of multicolored flowers and the bag of groceries for tonight's special dinner.

Kalyss pulled Dreux into the dark house behind her, absently dropping the single key on the empty table as she watched herself, at once full of color and vibrant, then transparent and echoing like a ghost in this house of haunted memories.

Her gift seemed to grow stronger the more she reached for it. She could feel the electric current running over and through their linked hands and she knew Dreux could see with her.

The Kalyss of old wore a spring blue dress that day. Probably impractical for what she'd had to do, but her very first ultrasound had seemed occasion enough to warrant it. In the end, it had worked out. She'd simply unbuttoned the buttons over her stomach. She filled a canning jar with water and flipped her long hair over her shoulder before arranging the flowers.

It was a slow day, happy and almost lazy. Sam didn't want her to work while she was pregnant, so he worked early to evening while she made their house the best home possible. Kalyss placed the flowers in the middle of their scratched table and adjusted their angle.

Their home was not perfect, as her mother-in-law was always quick to point out, but it worked for them. And maybe Sam's mom would be happier now. She'd insisted Kalyss wasn't a real wife until she'd given Sam a child. Maybe there would be less interference from her once the baby was born.

At least it was one directive Kalyss could be happy with. Striding comfortably, she returned to the kitchen and gathered utensils and ingredients for their spaghetti dinner. One glance at the microwave told her she had plenty of time. She picked up the pace anyway. Sam liked dinner on the table when he came home. He was always hungry and didn't like to wait.

Once she'd gotten pregnant, he'd mellowed. His moods were less mercurial and he was less demanding. Everyone said the first few years of marriage were rough and they'd been right, but everything was getting better. After their first year, when he'd gone to work for his dad and taken on all that pressure, they'd fought—often and painfully.

She'd even imagined him cheating on her. False, of course, but it just showed how crazy the first few years had been. But now the shouting was silenced. The bruises had healed and she could let the whole memory slide into the past. It was just a rough beginning.

All she needed to do was make dinner and keep a lid on her excitement. Sam didn't want to know the sex of the baby. He said he wanted to be surprised. She'd have to paint the room in different colors, no typical pink and blue, or lace, or sports stuff. She'd have to play it neutral with everything.

Kalyss stepped back from the kitchen door, one hand over her flat stomach, one still clenching Dreux's hand, until she felt Dreux's solid strength brace her back. Sweat dotted her forehead and nausea churned inside her. For that brief moment in time, life had been perfect. She'd had a home, a husband, a baby in her womb, a smile on her face, and the raindrop song from *Bambi* playing in her heart.

"This is too cruel." Her voice shook. She turned her head aside and closed her eyes. "I can't do this, Dreux. I can't stand to relive this, let alone make it clear enough for you to see."

Sounds from the kitchen changed from pots and pans, running water and chopping to a dark wind slapping scratchy branches against the windows. Dreux wrapped an arm around her waist, keeping their hands linked. "You are not alone, this time. I am with you."

Irritation snapped in her voice as she looked over her shoulder at him. "I said no. I can't do this. It isn't a trust issue."

"I realize that, but you have to." His eyes were certain, unwavering. "There is something here you need to see, or the vision wouldn't be so strong."

His calm, reasonable tone only angered her more. "I don't care!" Her voice rose. "Maybe you can face everything life deals you with Mr. Statue stoicism, but the rest of us actually have feelings."

His lips tightened and he shook his head, turning her to face the kitchen again. "This isn't about me. Face your fear, Kalyss, so we can all move beyond this moment. Don't let it trap you anymore."

Even with his firm support, she still wanted to run. But he was right—she had to face her past. But she knew what was coming and she wanted to scream at her ghostly memory to run. Run fast, run far, and never look back.

Past Kalyss hummed as water bubbled in one pot and she dropped chopped vegetables into another. When steely arms encircled her, settling over her tummy, she jumped and splashed mushrooms into the sauce. Looking over her shoulder at Sam, she caught sight of the microwave clock. He was home early.

No. That sounded accusatory.

"Expecting someone else?" Sam joked with raised brows. The problem was that ever since that night a month or so ago, when she'd called out some strange name in her dreams, he'd always seemed to fear there just might be someone else.

She grinned sweetly and assured him, "No, of course not. I just didn't realize it was so late."

He kissed her cheek and moved away. "I got off early. Dad remembered your ultrasound and wanted me to hear the news. So how's the baby? Healthy?"

And just like that, she'd relaxed and smiled, convinced the world was a good place and tonight was the night to enjoy it.

Sam was a little controlling, a little overly jealous, but it wasn't anything too serious. She just had to keep the baby's sex to herself and he could have the surprise he wanted. Sam wanted children, boys and girls. And it didn't matter which came first, so it was a safe surprise that he was comfortable with.

Now Kalyss could see how the small signs of Sam's issues heralded bigger, worse problems. But at the time, there had been no indication of just how horrible it could get. And as she watched her past self set the table with candles and a full set of silverware, she reached for Dreux's hand and held on tight.

Small talk, easy banter, and smiles and blushes character-ized their meal from salad to main course. Even to the cherry-topped cheesecake that she'd chosen for dessert. For all that sense-memory could do to a person, she was amazed that still remained an enjoyable meal for her. Perhaps that was due to the earlier memory of a happy time with her parents, when her mom had made fresh bread and they'd eaten at the table.

As she watched the past figures climb the stairs to their room, Kalyss's stomach twisted tighter. Her legs weakened with every step until Dreux had to support her up the last few. They edged down the dark hallway to the doorway of her old room. Inside, the bedroom waited like the deepest depths of a dungeon. Shrouded furniture cast shadows from one corner of the room to the next, highlighted only by weak beams of moonlight shining through the horizontal blinds.

Kalyss leaned against the doorway, breathing heavily, hold-ing her cramping stomach. In her mind, she could hear herself screaming. *No!* She didn't want to see this, but it was too late. Kai had shown her happy memories earlier, even a happy one here. Maybe that was where he'd intended it to end—maybe in a parallel universe where he wasn't the bad guy.

He wanted her to see this, to remember and feel it again. She'd trusted two men in her life: Sam and Alex. One was a wise decision and one was the worst possible. Kai wanted her to remember the consequences of a bad choice, the betrayal and pain and cost that seemed to only climb higher, even when the moment of crisis was over.

How could he be so horrible and make her relive this? How

could Dreux? This wasn't about trusting him with her secrets. There was no secret here, only tragedy. She gasped and her eyes prickled with her frustration. So many factors in her life making her experience things she'd never wanted—men, controlling and pushing, forcing what they wanted.

Her anger built, seething inside her and gathering force. She could leave, walk away, never see this, never know . . . but it began again. An electric current zinged from her hand to Dreux's where she still gripped it. If anything, her anger seemed to feed it until all that was ghostly was stronger, brighter, more real and solid than the abandoned house of today.

They were pushing her. Even she was pushing herself, like she'd flipped a switch when she'd begun to use her abilities, and now that part of her controlled her conscious self. Or something. All she knew was she wanted to run. She wanted to scream and hide, cringe into some darkened corner, hold her breath, and wish it all away. But she couldn't.

So she gave up. She quit fighting. She took a deep breath and threw Dreux's hand away from hers, ignoring the one on her shoulder. She walked into the room and allowed it all in. Everything, until the Kalyss of today dissolved and she saw again through the eyes of the woman she used to be.

Already the beams of moonlight were brightening the room until the furniture was clear and distinct. The broken mirror of the vanity became smooth and whole. The bed was freshly made and the carpet freshly vacuumed. She'd prepared for tonight before she'd left for her appointment. French vanilla scented the air, sweet, rich, and creamy. Once her favorite, now it made her nauseous. Inside, she was tense and angry, ready to explode, but she pushed it away, opening herself to the full horror, and settled on the bench in front of the vanity mirror.

She'd always wanted one. In her mind, it symbolized the grace and beauty of the women who'd lived in the early years of films and movies. She picked up the hairbrush and watched Sam through the mirror. One hundred stokes to keep the strands silky and shiny. To eliminate tangles and provide a slow, soothing glide from top to bottom.

Kalyss's eyes captured her attention in the mirror and she stared into them, thinking and dreaming. They were the soft

blue of a cloudless day, calm and peaceful. Someone to name.
To hold and love and claim, forever. She'd always dreamed of
this moment, this special time. She was a woman in every
sense of the word—natural and beautiful, glowing and happy.
She didn't have the nausea and weakness a lot of women com-
plained of—at least not yet. Everything was going perfectly
for this first pregnancy and she enjoyed it to the fullest. She
was nature, earth mother, a goddess.

And Sam's smiling glances confirmed it. He liked her pregnant, he'd said. Liked how happy and settled it seemed to
make her. Kalyss smiled and lowered the brush, her hands going to her stomach and rubbing it. Elation filled her heart in
ways it never had, expanding her lungs until she nearly
floated. She hadn't been this happy and excited about the future since before her parents died. All the possibilities of the
universe stretched before her. The love she already felt for that
tiny, fuzzy, black-and-white ultrasound image was enormous,
engulfing.

"I was thinking creamy yellow walls with royal purple bedding for the crib." She met his gaze in the mirror, searching
for his approval. Neither of them really liked pastel colors.

He pulled the covers on the bed back and fluffed the pillows
against the headboard. Leaning against them, he smiled
through the mirror at her. "You might find it difficult to find
royal purple baby bedding."

"I could sew it. Your mom could teach me." She'd always
wanted to sew and she'd take lessons from the devil herself if
it would decorate her baby's room perfectly. And if it brought
her and his mother closer together, made her happier about
their marriage, then it was worth it.

"That sounds like a plan. Do you want me to pick up the
paint for this weekend?"

"Yes, please. And I think I'll go shopping for the material."
They'd already picked out the furniture and had it on layaway
at Target. If all went well, they could have the basics put together by next week and she could nest to her heart's content
for the next five to six months. She grinned and smoothed the
dress over her belly.

"The doctor said I should feel the baby kick in about a
month or two."

Sam raised his head from the headboard and smiled patiently at her.

Looking at her reflection again, she mused, "I wonder, will the baby be blonde or brunette?

Sam smoothed his hand over his hair. "I think darker is usually dominant, but you never quite know."

"Yeah, I know." She shook her head. People had all kinds of stuff hiding out in their genes. She'd be lucky if her kid didn't end up with green hair and orange eyes. Of course, purple with her blue eyes wouldn't be too bad. But a blonde, and . . . "I hope she has brown eyes, like her father."

And like a bass boom of thunder, her heart pounded once, hard, then stilled for an endless second. What had she said? It was so wrong, so horribly wrong. Had she spoken out loud? She didn't want to raise her eyes—didn't want to know. But her skin vibrated with warning and her hands gripped protectively over her stomach. Dread weighed down her eyelids, but she forced them up to the mirror as a hand threaded under her hair to curve over the back of her head.

For one long, silent instant, she stared through the mirror into Sam's emerald green eyes. Bright, bright green. Ireland green. Shamrock, St. Patrick's Day, March green. March, the month her daughter was due to be born with green eyes, if she was like her father.

Kalyss opened her mouth, barely finding air to speak. "I-I didn't mean . . ."

"I'm sure you didn't." The hand against her head tightened, gripping her hair and pulling her to her feet. Sam's mouth had tightened to a grim line and his eyes were flat, dead.

"Really, I don't know why . . ." Her rush of words ended in a scream as he whirled her behind him, barely releasing most of her hair as she spun onto the bed.

That horrible hot flash was back. The one that burned her skin while freezing her insides. Her scalp hurt. Dizzy from the spin, she could only stare at him through hot, prickling eyes. Wounded eyes, she knew from all the times she'd inspected her face after a sudden storm like this.

And why wouldn't she feel wounded? This wasn't supposed to happen anymore. He'd promised. She was pregnant. It was getting better. He was getting better. Maybe if she reacted

differently, found a way to reach him through his anger, instead of huddling in on herself, it would work out. Sam hated
when she acted like a victim. He said she manipulated his
guilt.

His eyes were ice green, furious and cold. His harsh breath
was loud in her ears. His hands fisted and his jaw locked. He'd
stopped, frozen in the middle of the room. He'd never shown
this much control before. It gave her hope. They could fix this.
It was just a misunderstanding. She loved his eyes, had been
thinking green. Why brown had come from her mouth, she
had no clue.

She raised a shaking, beseeching hand toward him, begging. Her eyes burned and her heart tried to jump through her
chest. She swallowed. "Sam."

His name from her throat was garbled. She swallowed and
tried again. "Really, I don't know why I said brown. I was
thinking of you."

He scoffed. "Cut the crap, Kalyss. Who is he?"

"There isn't a he. There's no one. Please, Sam, I promise."
She inhaled shakily, silently praying. Please, God, just let him
calm down. There didn't have to be a problem tonight. She'd
done nothing wrong.

He stood, braced at the end of the bed, looming over her.
His fists clenched and unclenched, his breath harsh in his
chest.

"Please, Sam, don't be angry." She kept her hand up, offered to him as she begged. "I love you." Tears filled her
throat. She blinked rapidly, cleared her throat and tried again,
putting her heart in her voice. "I love you. Only you."

In the darkened room with only a small glow of light
through the window blinds, Dreux watched tears stream down
Kalyss's face, both past and present. He stood somewhat behind her, his hand forgotten on her shoulder. She didn't even
know he was there anymore. She simply stood behind and
slightly to the side of a ghostly Sam and stared at herself,
sprawled on the bed and begging.

Dreux clenched his free fist and locked in his own rage.
Only glancing from the past Kalyss to the present Kalyss kept
him sane. Otherwise, he'd step between the ghostly figures and
fight the man his wife feared. Destroy him as he'd destroyed

the woman on the bed. But he couldn't fight a memory, could he? He couldn't swing at a ghost. He couldn't protect a woman that no longer existed.

That woman, that terrified woman on the bed, full of tears and pleading, abused and terrified, that woman was the one he'd married. The woman he'd vowed to cherish and protect. The woman he'd been so patient to seduce. The woman he'd wanted a future with. The woman he'd failed, Geoffrey had failed, and Sam had failed. Three men had broken their promise to that woman and she'd died.

Not just a thousand years ago, or the centuries in between, no. She'd died four years ago and risen again as the woman beside him. As someone who didn't need him to protect her, didn't want promises. Didn't believe . . . in much of anything anymore.

Dreux watched Sam loosen his fists and move to the bed. Tense, still angry, he braced himself over Kalyss with one knee on the bed and a hand on either side of her head. Slowly, all control and leashed fury, Sam lowered himself over Kalyss until she was pinned under him in complete submission.

He nipped at her lips with quick, hard kisses. Her hands fluttered to frame his face as she apologetically, tentatively kissed him with quick, gentle butterfly kisses along his lips and jaw. Still begging forgiveness for a crime she hadn't committed.

Anger was a furious beast and Dreux held tightly to the leash. He'd demanded to see, to know. Sam reached down and snagged the hem of Kalyss's dress, dragging it up with firm menace, baring her calves, knees, then thighs. Dreux's stomach tightened as he held in his fury, his own righteous anger. Right or wrong had no place here, in this time. No man should rape his wife, take her in anger and control—but this was the past, not something he could stop, prevent, or change. He hadn't been there that night. He couldn't protect that Kalyss now.

But neither could he look away, ignore the snap of Kalyss's underwear. This had happened to her. It was her horror. Her nightmare. Her pain. And he'd demanded to see it. Looking away when he'd forced her to relive it would only betray her further.

The ghosts were more solid now, he realized. They'd been nearly transparent in the kitchen. They'd been dull with color earlier. Now some of that color brightened, solidified the images as if they became more real the longer Kalyss lived in this memory.

Sam pulled her arms from his shoulders and pressed them over her head, against the bed. Another adjustment and he pushed inside her body. Her dry body, if her pained gasp meant anything. He stilled over her, his eyes boring into hers. "Mine."

"All yours." She confirmed obediently. Then she bit her lip as he buried his face in her neck and thrust.

Her body rocked, pressed up and released, as he pushed vigorously. She kept her hands in his, above her head with no struggle, and stared behind him, to a corner of the ceiling with eyes that lost their shock and pain and became empty and dead, instead.

Dreux watched her leave her body as she had when she'd died in front of him. It was obscene that her body breathed, rocked, received a man, when she was dead. He wanted to turn, to hide from the horror in front of him, but he couldn't. He'd pushed for this. Demanded she open to him. He'd wanted to heal her. But was she already as healed as she could get after this?

The real Kalyss, the one beside him, sniffed. He was relieved, for a moment, to look away from the bed, but facing her pain at witnessing what she'd already lived through was worse. He shifted to fully look in her eyes and sucked in a breath. What he'd mistaken for pain, he could see more fully now.

It wasn't pain. It was hatred. He followed her gaze back to the bed and the woman half-hidden by a man's body. Self-hatred. Self-disgust. His heart twisted painfully in his chest. He looked back into her eyes and heard the words her mind shouted at her. Weak. Fool. Pathetic.

The light in the room flickered, turned off. The memory changed. Dreux faced the bed again, afraid of what he'd see. This was the night she'd received her scars. Lost her child. He didn't want to see it. Every particle of him begged to run, hide, but looking at both women, he knew he owed them more than cowardice.

Sam lay on his back, his hands under his head, staring at the ceiling. Kalyss lay on her side, facing away from him and gripping the edge of the bed. Her tears were silent, her shuddering breath nearly so, but each sob shook the entire bed.

Dreux turned back to the Kalyss of today, the one he could help. Bitter hatred turned to rage and twisted her lips.

"Kalyss, no . . ."

She stormed past him and he followed, gripping her shoulder, desperate not to break the connection. He had to see what she saw. He had to stay with her. He couldn't leave her alone to face this, not again.

Kalyss stopped, poised over the crying woman and screamed, "You stupid bitch, get up!"

She didn't move, just cried her broken tears.

Kalyss tried to grab her, but her hands went through the memory woman to the real bed beneath. Her fury spread around her like a dark cloud, a pulsing aura. Her voice deepened, raw and raging. "Don't just lay there, you damned victim, get up! Leave. Flee. Run."

The image didn't respond and Kalyss bent at the waist and reached through her to shake the bed furiously. "You fucking idiot! Get up, get up, get up!"

Her voice pierced higher and louder in her anger, but the woman still didn't move. Logically, she couldn't influence her memory. Couldn't change the past. But Dreux let her scream, knew the words needed to come out. Kalyss fell to her knees beside the bed and Dreux knelt beside her. She leaned over until she was eye to eye with herself, anger deserting her. Taking its strength and leaving her shaky. Her fingers twisted and tangled in the dusty bedding and her voice was a wobbly whisper.

"Please, don't stay," she begged herself, still trying, against all logic, to change the outcome. "Just get up, go."

Her tears soaked the bedding where the memory tears had dried. Dreux reached for her, one hand grasping hers and the other reaching across her back. Her tears broke him inside, another part of that failure so long ago.

Tremors racked her hands, her arms, as she reached for the blond hair in front of her. Stopping just short of sinking through the memory, she skimmed one shaking hand over the soft waves. Then Kalyss framed her face, kneeling so she could look into her own eyes.

"Please, don't . . ." Her voice broke and she tried again. "Please, Kalyss, don't dream."

A freezing chill ran through Dreux and the hair at his nape stood straight. No, not that.

"Don't dream."

But her eyes drifted shut, her breathing evened, and the Kalyss on the bed had cried herself to sleep. Kalyss straightened, looking over the memory of herself to the man behind her. He didn't move, didn't say anything, but neither did he sleep. He just stared, silent and dark, at the ceiling above him. The light flickered again.

Dreux nearly missed the change. The people on the bed hadn't moved. The only difference was the bright red numbers on the alarm clock by Sam. It was four hours later. Dreux pulled Kalyss to him, holding her tight. She whimpered, terrified, hopeless and Dreux understood. She'd tried to outrun the boogeyman only to find she wasn't fast enough.

Sam moved toward Kalyss so suddenly, Dreux nearly thrust her behind him. He did pull her back, his arms surrounding her. Then he realized Sam didn't see them, either. Sam's hand curved over sleeping Kalyss's arm, brushing down strands of her hair. He formed to her back and placed his mouth to her ear and whispered, "Kalyss."

She shivered and mumbled unintelligibly in her sleep. Sam squeezed her arm gently. "Kalyss."

She sighed and mumbled, "Dreux."

Sam froze. Dreux tensed. Kalyss screamed against her fist.

Chapter 20

It felt as if the very room held its breath in silent terror. No one moved, not even the black shadows in the gray light. Sam poised, still as death, over Kalyss. Dreux held Kalyss's shaking body, the tremors racking her head to toe.

"Drew?" Sam questioned in a deadly whisper.

The room exhaled in a rush of violence, an explosion of sound and color. Sam grabbed Kalyss's hair and pulled her to her back, jerking her suddenly wide awake. "You fucking, lying bitch!"

The accusations came, followed with more desperate pleading and tears. Dreux couldn't grasp the exact words through the ringing in his ears, but it didn't take a genius to figure them out. He focused on Kalyss.

She rocked herself against him, wincing with each slap as Sam got angrier and angrier. Her body tensed as she watched herself, knowing what she'd done, what actions she'd taken that night, but dreading the fact that they hadn't helped. She was locked, trapped in that memory, unable to pull away until it reached its obscene, nightmarish conclusion.

Dreux tensed his hand on hers, grimly holding on for the duration, as Kalyss rolled from the bed, not quite fast enough to escape her raging husband. One hand grabbed her hair again and Sam threw her into the vanity mirror at the end of their bed. It shattered in a silver-backed spray of glass shards. Red streaked off her forehead and welled to the surface of her hands. Before she could run again, he had her in hand, shouting, cursing, accusing.

Her breath shuddered through her as she gasped in helpless terror. Her uncontrollable shrieks were barely loud enough for them to hear through Sam's thunder. Sam pulled her straight in front of him, holding her by her hair, and screamed into her face. Ignoring her ineffectual struggles, he smacked her again. She flew back from him, strands of her hair remaining in his hand. She landed against the vanity, falling to her knees, scratching bloody streaks on her hands and legs.

Instead of rising, she crawled away, one bloody hand with a shredding grasp on a long, wicked shard of mirror. Scrambling on her knees as fast as she could, she thrust to her feet and exited the room just slightly too quick for him to grab her again. His fingers scraped her back as she escaped down the hall.

Her screaming breaths still loud in the room, Kalyss pulled to her feet and rushed away from Dreux too fast for him to hold.

She was out the door and down the hallway before he rose to his feet. What if he couldn't reach her before it was over? What if the connection was lost and he couldn't recapture it, regain the memory in time? What would happen if she had to relive this moment, by herself yet again? It couldn't happen.

He rushed over the shards of glass as they melted into the carpet. One hand slapped the door frame as he spun out of the room and down the hall, hearing Kalyss's screams and not knowing if it was memory or real. Down the stairs and turning again, he faced the living room and stopped against the wall, grabbing his chest from the sheer agony of what lay in front of him.

The memory still projected. Even without touching Kalyss, she showed him what had happened that awful night. It was so horrific, so traumatizing, and she'd been in the memory so long, it now had a life of its own. A table lay on its side, its contents scattered over the floor: a plastic cake top, the bride splattered with blood, a broken unity candle, a gleaming silver service set. In the center, Sam straddled Kalyss's legs, one hand holding hers above her head, imprisoning her in his unbreakable hold. His free hand fisted and pounded into her defenseless face. How was she still conscious?

Blood pooled under her hands, bathing the shard beneath them. She hadn't even been able to use it. Kalyss fell to her knees beside the struggling images. Tears carved violently down her face and her body shook with sobs. Her hands overlapped themselves around her waist and keening screams broke from her throat, long and loud, over and over.

Everything suddenly seemed in slow motion and Dreux watched for years as Sam's fist slowly descended in punch after punch. He had an eternity to witness as Sam's hand clenched around the silver cake knife and raised it. Eons, as his stomach churned with nausea and his mind screamed in denial of what was happening, to see it rise and fall, thrusting into her stomach seven times.

Kalyss screamed one long, broken, jagged shriek as she watched herself fall unconscious. Watched blood pool in scarlet lakes over her stomach. Watched Sam lean back against his knees, his hands falling to his sides, his fist still tight around the knife as his face twisted in hatred and fury. The image froze.

The only signs of life, of movement, of sound, in the dim, gray room were Kalyss, sobbing and rocking, and Dreux drawing deep breaths to hold back the vomit. The aftermath of battle had never been this sickening.

The vision paled to transparent, Sam straddling an unconscious Kalyss, then it was gone. Still burned into his mind, but otherwise gone. Only a dark spot on the floor in front of Kalyss, easily overshadowed earlier, lay as mute proof of what he'd just seen.

Her voice was raw, nearly hoarse. It croaked from her chest in deep cries. Tears clung to the grooves in her face they'd created and she rocked. Back, forth. Pitiful, broken cries that shredded his heart. He hadn't prevented it, then he'd forced her to relive it. In detail. In full, Technicolor, Dolby Digital Surround Sound detail. The common definition may have changed over the years, but he was still a bastard.

Dreux approached her, hesitant. How could he possibly comfort her? What could he possibly give her? Her attacker was behind bars, her marriage to him dissolved. She'd lost her child and wouldn't have another—couldn't have another. Her body had healed the pain, leaving only seven scars as savage testament. Her heart and mind had reached a peace, a plateau, until he'd ripped her from it with his centuries-old drama.

And now she huddled, broken again. Shattered. So small. So defenseless. Her narrow shoulders shook. Her fragile back bowed over until her forehead rested on her knees. Her black tank top rode up her back, exposing the delicate knobs of her spine. Her black jeans encased slim hips that had never grown wider from a full-term pregnancy. And her long tail of blond hair fell forward, over her head, until it flowed onto the floor in front of her, strands of it barely touching the edge of the blood stain.

He lowered to one knee behind her, his hands curving over the chilled bare skin of her lower back. He whispered, "Kalyss?"

Her spine tensed, her sobs silenced. Slowly, she straightened until he could whisper in her ear. "I'm so sorry."

Quick, deadly, she spun from the waist, her elbow cutting high in the air behind her until it connected solidly with his jaw. He landed back, away from her, his teeth fused to the flesh of his cheek, blood pooling on his tongue. He braced one hand under him and watched her rise, facing him fully.

Tears stained her cheeks, but dryness, and a beam of light through the shadows, froze her blue eyes crystal. In a low, growling voice a woman should never be capable of, she asked him, enunciating slowly, "What the *hell* makes you think I give a *damn* if you're *sorry*?"

In the darkness, he rose. His heartbeat taller than her head. His arms thicker than her waist. His body more solid and steady than the thickest of oaks. His time with Geoffrey hadn't been all books and TV shows. His mind knew the moves of thousands of fighting styles. His muscles, trained from birth, could respond to any one of them with lethal force.

His mentors hadn't just been the strongest, the biggest, or the most ferocious of all the warriors of his time. They'd also been the most cunning, skilled, tactical minds of their day. As leaders, teachers, foster parents, they'd been unmerciful. He'd faced many a battle. Sent many men to their deaths, at his hand or by his command.

She knew this.

Yet, her eyes didn't flinch. Her lip didn't quiver. Her hands didn't shake. She moved into a beginning posture, balancing evenly. Her body strong, her posture flawless. Many gazes had promised him death, but hers was the promise death might keep.

For all his knowledge, all his training, none of it would he use against her. He would allow her to kill him before he'd harm her. His beautiful, broken warrior. It was obvious what she needed and he would give it to her. Because this battle, this fight to conquer the memory that imprisoned her, *this* he could give her. He narrowed his gaze and nodded his acceptance.

He broadened his stance and raised his hands. She spun in a powerful roundhouse kick that he caught, bracing her ankle so it wouldn't bend as his chest absorbed the blow. His breath stuttered, but he regained control of it as she fell back in form.

Her arms tensed, sleek muscles bunching. She was tight, from the bare skin of her shoulders to the naked, lean strength of her waist and down to the bunch of her thighs under her tight jeans. She was bottled fury in a sleek package. He caught her punches, throwing her off balance just enough to give her something to fight against.

His heart wasn't in the battle, so his mind wasn't a bit clouded. He calmly watched each move as if it had years to complete, providing the perfect counter to any blow she could think to land, discarding the counters to blows she wouldn't know how to land. Admiring her skill even as he mourned the necessity of it.

She stunned him with her strength. With the power of her strikes. Her eyes were wide and wounded. They stole his breath and damaged him more than anything she did physically. But he kept her moving, kept her trying, gave her an outlet for her anger. Her rage.

Gave her something to fight now that she knew how. Something she could injure back, since her memories were impervious to harm.

"I don't need you."

He nodded, drinking in her feminine beauty, her dangerous appeal. "I know."

"Not in my life, in my bed, and definitely not in my heart."

He absorbed her words, and her kick, in silence. So strong, his warrior.

"No man will have that power, that opportunity, again." Her voice was still that low growl of fury. Gorgeous in all its forms.

He couldn't doubt the truth of her words. She'd never allow herself to be that vulnerable again. Never so fully, even if a man, even if *he*, were to break through most of her barriers trying to find a permanent place in her life. The vulnerable, trusting woman he'd married had died.

"It's all your fault." She spun to his side and backhanded him. His head snapped back.

Again, he couldn't deny her truth. He hadn't protected her. He'd married her and dragged her into centuries of pain and sacrifice all for the mere memory of him. The same memory that drove Sam over the edge and lost her a precious child. "I know."

She ignored his words and hurled hers like a poisonous-tipped spear, "Your eyes that are brown."

The spear pierced straight to his heart. A heart that beat because of her kiss. Because of her strength that freed him. And his name on her lips, him in her dreams, had nearly destroyed her. "I know."

"Your name that I mumbled in my sleep."

The poison spread like fire in his veins, weakening him. His vows to cherish and protect her had brought her nothing but pain. In a lifetime of war, he'd found one woman that meant family. And crushed her. "I know."

Her voice rose. "What I dreamed of in my marriage bed, and why?"

She quit trying to fight by a style and simply shoved him with both hands to his chest. "Why? Because some medieval asshole wanted to hurt you and used me to do it."

He collapsed to his knees before her, his hands by his side, and faced her, defenseless. It was fitting. In an age without kings, where he must bow to no one, he offered his life to her. His love, his loyalty. She was everything he'd fought for. Striven for, through decades of violence and bloodshed. And she was more. She was his warrior.

More than the gentle soul he'd dreamed of during his im-prisonment. More than the tragic sacrifice to an old woman's hatred. More than a survivor of horrors that crippled others.

"I am sick of dying for your cause." Her voice was raw, ragged.

He couldn't breathe and his chest hurt from the clenching of his heart. She twisted her fists in his shirt and stared straight into his eyes.

"I will not be trapped in a marriage with a statue just be-cause he woke up and said he's my husband." She shook him hard. "I don't need a preternatural court of law, because I live in this world. In this time. And by these laws, which say I be-long to no man."

She was an angel of fire, a Valkyrie, a warrior woman of legend, a phoenix risen from the ashes. She was all of them, and more. She'd earned her freedom.

All his previous knowledge of women, of her, dissolved. She wasn't the wife he'd married. He had no claim on her, by her own decree. She wasn't a symbol of the family he'd lost. She wouldn't give him back the sense of home and warmth he'd lost as a child. She wouldn't be his safe haven in a life that had stranded him away from everything he'd ever known.

She wasn't the wife of his expectations. She was a stranger to all he'd known before that very morning, when she'd awak-ened him. She wasn't just different, she was new. Not just changed, but a different person altogether. All his thoughts, feelings, dreams, and expectations involving her were dust.

But he loved the woman in front of him with a purity of emotion he hadn't known existed past childhood.

"Tonight, I find Alex. Alive or dead, nothing changes." She held her face close to his, stared straight into his eyes. "You've lost me."

Dreux met her hard eyes, cobalt in the darkness, with all his love in his gaze and said, "I know."

Chapter 21

Nothing more needed to be said. Or, if it did, she couldn't think of it. All the anger, the violence, the sheer grief she felt spread from her like black tendrils into the air around her. Pushed against the walls until it seemed they should curve outward, ready to explode.

The uncontrolled fury, the wild pain, burned through her until she shook with the ferocity of it. If she had the super-powers of any of her favorite comic book heroines, the destruction she could cause would be terrifying. But she didn't and the feelings left her gasping and fighting the utter lack of control. If unleashed, she could only ultimately hurt herself and the damage would be too extensive to repair.

Tendril by tendril, she pulled in each onyx thread of emotion until it painfully expanded her chest and strangled her throat from the inside. Deliberately, she unclenched each fist and released Dreux, stepping back and avoiding his gaze.

She could become trapped in his eyes forever. She'd already spent the entire day seeing the world from his perspective. It was past time she returned to her own.

Back straight, each movement scrupulously controlled, she circled around him and headed straight for the back door, grabbing her jacket on the way out. Like a solid presence, he rose behind her. Her heart gave a few extra hard thuds and she rushed through the doorway, her mind blank, flinching from dealing with thoughts while her feelings raged and tore inside her.

She strode past the back patio to the side of the house. Behind her, she heard Dreux grab the key, shut the door, and lock the evil of her past inside.

The phone rang. She pulled it from her pocket, flipped it open, and said, "Not now."

One more flip and it was off and sliding back into her pocket.

When she reached the SUV, she stopped and stared at it. What the hell—dying without ever having driven was as bad as dying a virgin, wasn't it? And if she drove now, it just might kill them. She pulled the keys from her pocket and when he stopped beside her, crumpling probably another slightly more detailed map that would tell them nothing, she tossed them to him.

Silent, they got in and buckled. Without hesitation, he slid the correct key into the correct slot and, with only a minimum of awkwardness, drove to the end of the block. She mentally shrugged. He may have been cautious, even ignorant, at times today, but never had Dreux been lost or incapable. Geoffrey had educated him well.

He paused at the end of the block and glanced at her.

"Left. To Sprague." The Mirabeau Waterfall might not be the right location, but it was worth checking out. He complied and she eased back into her seat and stared out her window.

SILAS WATCHED DREUX follow Kalyss from the house, his heart so heavy he couldn't move immediately after them. How had things gone so very wrong? On top of the situation one minute, now Geoffrey was dying, threatening all of them, and—

"I can't believe she just walked away from him." Draven's fists were clenched almost tight enough to pop the seams of the black leather gloves.

"She is still too scarred from that night to face love with any degree of rationality." Silas's voice was low, almost monotonous. He understood. He felt her pain. Remembered his own horror the night it happened and he'd watched it, unable to physically do anything to stop the beating, the knife, the blood. Maybe they expected too much of her, but—

"Well, she needs to get over it."

Silas blinked in surprise. Draven hadn't been there. Hadn't seen and feared the way he had. Draven had only seen the memory Kalyss had shown, but still. It was horrible. Were scenes like this so commonplace to his companion that the tragedy of Kalyss's memory didn't even faze Draven?

"Are you honestly trying to say you don't understand her fear? She nearly died because of an alternate life, a destiny she didn't even remember. The worst moment of her life, the worst loss, her nightmare tragedy is now tied to the grand love she's spent all day trying to trust." Silas stared grimly at the blood-stained carpet. "You're surprised she wants to run? I'm not."

"Boo hoo," Draven mocked callously. "She's about to risk more deaths just because she can't deal with a few bad memories."

"She doesn't know she's risking others." Silas glared down at Draven. "Are you upset about them, or yourself?"

"And you're not worried about yourself?" Draven challenged him. "If the curse isn't broken, everything we've risked has been for nothing. Maeve will kill us for our interference in her curse and our good deed will only be so much dust. Our chance for redemption forfeit."

"Your positive attitude is always such a comfort." Silas scowled.

"They can only succeed by working together. She can't delete herself from the equation now." Draven's black fists clenched.

"She can do whatever she wants. Free will, remember?" Silas helplessly motioned toward Kalyss.

"Screw free will, Silas. I refuse to allow my future, *my forgiveness*, to depend on unreliable humans," said Draven with a dark, hard voice.

"We have no choice. You *saw* him, Draven. We cannot interfere," Silas reminded.

"So we just sit and wait? Is there even any point to watching? Or should we just try to get a good night's sleep and hope we wake up in the morning?" Draven asked sarcastically.

Patience lost, he demanded, "This is good work. Remember? Those were your words."

"If she's just going to give up—"

"We won't allow it." Silas took a deep breath and drew strength from his righteous anger during that tragedy four years ago. Kalyss had suffered too much, sacrificed endlessly. She couldn't walk away from the prize now. He wouldn't allow all her pain to be for nothing. "We can still whisper suggestions and influence."

"She won't listen. You saw her. She is completely closed. As our only weapon, suggestion is a weak one."

"Not when it's used correctly." His voice lowered hinting at a deeper meaning.

Draven froze a few long seconds, then whispered, "What did you do?"

Silas waved a hand, drawing on the energy of the house and the tragedy it had concealed. Once again Sam knelt over a helpless Kalyss in the middle of the floor, a bloody knife grasped in his raised fist. "Sometimes, to avert a tragedy, it's best not to go to the source."

As they watched, a ghostly image appeared over Sam's shoulder. Slowly the form became visible to them, an echo of Silas's presence four years ago. Silas's lips moved; whispering words in Sam's ear that didn't even make him pause in his attack.

"She could've died while I tried to convince him to calm down and listen to reason. So I left." Silas's ghostly form disappeared from behind Sam. The memory continued to play, as if psychic echoes from the house itself kept the tragedy alive.

"Where did you go?"

"To the neighbors. They had heard her screams. They always did. But they were closed off and didn't report things the way they should have. This time I filled their minds with worries and inundated them with fears until they had to act. The woman called 911 while her husband snuck to the back door to peek in the window."

The face of the neighbor appeared in the back window. His eyes widened and his mouth fell open. Then the man crashed through the door and grabbed Sam, fighting him to the ground and screaming for his wife at the same time.

The woman appeared at the door, then ran to Kalyss. Her

eyes poured tears and her hands shook ferociously, but she knelt by Kalyss's side and did her best to staunch the blood. Amazingly, she hadn't sickened or fainted.

Slowly, like the dawn just before the sun can be seen over the horizon, Kalyss's body and the woman beside it lit up, glowed. Astonished, Silas stared as a form began to appear. Bright white shot with soft, vivid colors like a large mother of pearl shell, the form slowly solidified, showing someone bent over Kalyss's body

Enormous white wings, soft as a baby's cashmere blanket spread behind her, reached from one side of the large room to another. The face was solid, glassy almost, with soft colors swirling beneath the surface. As with the Obsidian Angel they'd met earlier, this Angel possessed fiercely glowing eyes. At the moment, they weren't righteous or judgmental, but focused on Kalyss with a gentle, determined strength.

Silas stared in awe. This Angel had a sword strapped to her back and one to her side, prepared and capable of a good fight, yet she emitted a feeling of comfort, of healing and gentleness. This one was more a healer than an intimidating warrior like the Obsidian Angel in the alley.

With hands that were glass and color at once, like the Angel's face, the Pearl Angel held onto Kalyss and the neighbor woman, feeding them both with strength.

Draven inhaled a shaky breath and spoke in a whisper. "You never told me about this."

Silas returned the whisper. "I didn't know."

"You saved Kalyss. By suggestion to a cooler, calmer mind, you influenced someone else to save her. And your actions were approved."

"It's not interference if it's their destiny to be saved."

"Once the curse no longer holds destiny for ransom, anyway," Draven agreed. "What does this mean?"

Silas held his hand out for Draven's. "It means we talk to Alex."

A split second before they blinked from the room, the Pearl Angel turned to them with a gentle, encouraging smile. "Continue."

* * *

SLOWLY, THE STRANGLEHOLD of fury trickled away, shrinking smaller and smaller and sinking down into a roiling pit inside her. Kalyss's eyes prickled with the need to cry for the sheer release of it. She ruthlessly blinked them back. Nothing was worse than crying like a wuss when she was ticked off.

Images flashed randomly across her mind: Sam throwing her into the vanity mirror; raising the knife high above her while he held her helpless; Kai at the dojo, knife in his hand, rising after she'd thrown him over her shoulder; St. John's Cathedral from a distance, then up close, double doors arching; Dreux as a statue before she'd kissed him.

Out the window, wild wind rushed across the black sky and whipped the trees into a clapping fury of snapping leaves and branches.

Then she saw eyes: green eyes, brown eyes, hazel eyes. Each color inspired a different emotion: green for violence, for jealousy—and for terror. Brown was for melting, promising a home, a comforting embrace and warm security until she drowned from it, barely struggling. Promises that coated her like thick, hot chocolate until, after coaxing her to a false peace, she would disappear. Never again free, never again herself.

And last but never least, hazel eyes for truth and honesty, for friendship and loyalty. Like a silver rope in endless darkness, while she rolled and fell through space like an astronaut without a suit, hazel eyes gave her something to grab.

Alex. She needed to pull away from this—the violent mix of histories, the logic-defying search for truth in the midst of madness. Alex needed her.

Prince Charming lay trapped, waiting for rescue. It was a joke in high school, a nickname with a role-reversal twist. They both knew she couldn't be his Cinderella if she prayed night and day for it, but even Prince Charming needed a friend. Kalyss was that friend.

He was stability and goodness, the last knight who ranked the code of chivalry right up there with the Ten Commandments. Honor and faith, love and loyalty, like an obelisk piercing the sky, he was her compass when life lost its polarity.

Two blocks from the light, she said, "Right on Sprague."

She'd let Dreux figure out how to drive on major roads

before attempting the interstate. Sprague was a parallel road to the valley, anyway. Without a glance to her, or a pause, he eased to the right side of the road and made the turn when the way was clear.

It had to be a trick. He seemed to follow directions so well. No argument, no debate, but she knew he had certain goals in mind. Goals that included her, despite his apparent acceptance of her rejection.

For the first time all day, she felt strong. Sure of her own opinion, instead of swayed by the emotions Dreux stirred in her. Her anger had been a cleansing fire, devastating while it raged, but ultimately unsustainable. Left in its wake were only the most basic foundations of who she was. What she built with them was her choice, her design.

Determination was a cooling core of bright steel that filled her inside, from toes to ankles to calves. It hardened to a cold, shining clarity. She built the picture in her mind, filling her knees and thighs with the image of solid, unbreakable strength.

Her life was hers, hers to direct, hers to control. There were no ties binding her but the ones she allowed. The core of strength calmed her stomach, braced her spine. She wasn't beaten. Her past would only affect what she allowed it to affect.

Kalyss rolled down the window and drew slow, deep breaths, one after another, letting the cool breeze brush away every cobweb, every speck of dust that clung to her mind. She opened the scuffed and dented chest in her heart and stuffed the past inside, slamming the lid and jerking the padlock tight.

The future would take care of itself. It was the present she needed to concentrate on now. The present and the important things she chose to build on her foundation.

Calm now, she directed the SUV to the parking lot of the valley YMCA, eyeing the dark, paved path that led to Mirabeau Waterfall. It had been a long day. A long journey, but she'd finally arrived. The phone rang again. She took it from her pocket and set it on the dash. Ignoring it, she unbuckled.

Dreux exited his side of the vehicle and she took a moment to breathe in a bit of solitude. She hadn't truly had one all day. Not even when she took her shower, since she'd been overwhelmed with her past. The past when she'd claimed Dreux, body, mind, heart, and soul.

Kai wouldn't hurt Alex because she didn't answer the phone, not this late in his game. But they were no longer playing by his rules, so maybe now it was her game. As if realizing this, the phone stopped ringing and the silence was loud.

With a click, her door opened and Dreux stood there, no longer willing to be ignored. Large and determined, he blocked her doorway. Kalyss put her feet on the bottom rim of the car and eased down, putting the rear door at her back. She wouldn't claim him. Not anymore.

Dreux leaned one arm on the top of the SUV and brought his face to hers, his eyes direct, his gaze encompassing all of her. He loomed over her, intimidating in size and serious mien, but she wasn't afraid of him. He wouldn't want her to be.

Nevertheless, she firmed her chin and faced his gaze head on. It wasn't stubbornness, bracing against her fears or even defiance. It was pure clarity. Not anger, not vengeance. Just a calm acceptance of herself and her feelings and the way she needed to do things.

DREUX SEARCHED HER face, worried at first, then calming as he read her. No longer crushed by grief or blinded by rage, she had bounced back. Resilient. Strong. Strangely dispassionate, as if the overwhelming maelstrom of emotions nearly crippling her had seeped away, leaving cold logic to take its place. He could accept cold logic.

His finger traced her cheek. It was hard and cool to the touch, like porcelain. But porcelain was fragile and he knew now that any appearance of fragility in her was deceptive. If there was anything he'd learned today, it was that she was unbreakable.

"Rescue your friend, Kalyss. Save Alex. Then leave. Forget about us. Especially forget about me and I will do all I can to keep this from touching you ever again."

Her brows drew together. No doubt she'd intended to see this through to the end. Ensure that it was over. He smiled a little and brushed the back of his fingers over her cheek.

"Please trust me one last time. I'll stop Kai and find Geoffrey. I won't fail you again."

She swallowed, her jaw working as if she rolled his words over her tongue as she considered them. Finally, she nodded.

He contemplated her face, feeling seconds of the night tick by. Breezes rushed by and through him, caressing him as they hadn't for centuries. He allowed himself to enjoy them while he soaked in the sight of her. This last look had to warm him forever.

Her blue eyes were large, dark, and much of their sparkle was gone. Her skin was soft and warm beneath his touch. Her lips looked tender and welcoming, but that was just appearance. A kiss now would comfort only him and he just wasn't on the priority list. She deserved more than for him to take yet another thing from her.

Despite that knowledge, he still wanted that kiss. The connection made. He needed the moment where anything was possible if they could only keep kissing.

Stray strands of hair blew into her eyes and he tucked one finger under them and pulled them away. He had a lifetime's worth of things to tell her, share with her. Things he'd wished he'd said, then planned to say if he ever again got the chance. He settled for just a moment's worth.

"I need you to know, you are everything I never knew a woman could be. I've seen them strong, resourceful, resilient, but your heart, mind, and body are incomparable. You were right. About all of it. I lost the woman I married long ago."

He licked his lip and breathed deep. "She was sweet and gentle and kind. For that one night, I was the happiest I'd ever been. I would have been happy with her forever."

She nodded, glancing away, as if his words struck her some way. He couldn't figure out how, so he continued. "But you have suffered beyond belief for me. That suffering has created a woman of such spirit and beauty . . . no."

He shook his head, as if erasing what he'd said, and began again. "You. You took that suffering and created spirit and beauty from it. I am honored I had a chance to learn the woman you've become. The woman you are. If I could, if it wouldn't change you, I would erase or prevent all your pains. But you're too precious to want you different than you are. I will cherish this day always, as I will mourn the loss of you with each beat of my heart."

Her eyes were wide, searching, as if she wondered if she could believe him. A thousand years and this was all he could say? His words were so inadequate.

But then, was there a satisfactory way to say goodbye?

He swallowed, stared at her lips, caressing the side of her face with his thumb. One kiss to last him forever. His thumb brushed her bottom lip once, then he backed away, looking straight into her eyes. "I love you."

KALYSS STARED AFTER him, her lips quivering. Her future was hers to make. Would it be a mistake to not let him be a part of it, to send him away? Or would it be a bigger mistake, a larger danger, to continue opening herself to him? She shook her head, straightened her back, and squared her shoulders. It was her life, her choice. And she chose to be free.

Dreux opened the back of the SUV and pulled out a sword longer than she was tall. It glimmered in the parking lot light. She hadn't even known it was there. Figured.

Kalyss yanked her jacket straight to her waist and they began to approach the waterfall.

HIGH ON A walkway even with the top of the waterfall, across from where Kai stood, Silas and Draven watched. Kai tensed, folded a phone, and put it in his pocket. Water streamed around the boulders at his feet, over the edge, and straight down to the shallow, rocky bottom of the man-made pond below.

Below them, a square deck perched over the water. It had no rails, only low support posts that rose two feet above the deck at each corner and once in the middle of each side. Halfway between each of the posts, there was a metal boat hook, like those for tying boats to docks, though there would never be a boat in this pond. Small garden lights positioned at intervals around the deck lit the whole area.

At the center post closest to the waterfall, Alex slumped. Each arm was pulled straight away from his side, a rope stretching from his hands to the boat hooks. He didn't struggle or look around, as if he'd learned by now that it was futile. He was not going anywhere until this night's work was done.

Moments ago they'd whispered in Alex's ear. He'd worried about Kalyss all day, but he'd also heard the story. They suggested he keep his eyes and ears open. He knew her better than anyone. When she was ready to fight and when she was ready to run. He needed to encourage her to fight so she no longer had to run.

Now they could only wait. And watch. And prepare to step in if they saw an opening. Draven's hands were clenched around the bridge rail, the leather gloves squeaking against the metal. Silas folded his arms, holding in his own tension.

They'd never made it so far, before. All four of them so close to discovering the origin of their curse, the truth of Maeve's death, and therefore breaking the spell. Kalyss had built her strength and her gift. She could finally accomplish what was necessary. If only she reopened what her last vision had closed—her heart—then she would be able to see what she needed to see. As trite as it sounded, in this case the truth really would set them free.

Silas and Draven had done all they could. It was up to Kalyss and Dreux now.

THE PAVED WALKWAY was dark, lit only by periodic streetlamps. All was quiet. Cars passed infrequently in the distance. The bright parking lot across the street held the cars of a few people out to stroll the walking and biking trail that led in a wide, wooded loop.

But the path from the YMCA to the falls was dark. Quiet. Kalyss and Dreux approached in a straight-forward walk. If Kai was here, he was watching. Stealth would be impossible. Besides, this is what he'd waited for. He wasn't hiding. He wanted them to come to him.

By the time they reached the picnic gazebos, they could see part of the deck. Kalyss's eyes searched every tree, boulder, and shadow, unwilling to be surprised again. Alex was tied at the end of the deck closest to the waterfall. She stared at him a moment.

The only ties in her life would be the ones she allowed. From that core of steel strength inside her, an imaginary bright silver cord formed and flew from her to wrap around Alex. A tie. A connection. She wouldn't let him go.

She wanted to run to him. Hug him and make sure he was okay. Dreux could take care of Kai, as he'd promised. But she didn't want to risk being blindsided and caught in the middle of the battle to come, so she stayed by Dreux's side up to the edge of the deck.

She stepped onto the wood walkway and stopped, looking past Alex, up the waterfall to the tall man standing still on the rocks, watching them all. For a moment, she froze. Then she turned to her left to find Dreux already bounding around the edge of the pond to a small stream that ran from the back of it, at the bottom edge of the cliff.

Two steps sprayed water up his legs, then he was over the stream and climbing the sloping cliff toward Kai, his sword in one hand while the other braced against the rock. Kai stood above him, his own sword held at his side. When Dreux reached the top, Kai backed away and they both disappeared from view.

Kalyss looked at Alex, at the knife two feet from his tied feet, then met his familiar gaze.

He arched a brow. "What can I say? He's got a wicked sense of what's not funny."

Choking on a laugh, Kalyss fell by his side and threw her arms around him. The cord that bound them solidified, tightened. She had the foundations of the person she wanted to be and now Alex. What else could she need? "I've missed you."

DREUX STOPPED JUST out of sword's reach and inspected the man who'd killed his wife. The man who'd imprisoned him for centuries, forcing a helpless statue to listen to all his odd ramblings. The one moment he remembered the most clearly, was the sight of Kai racing toward the tower window Geoffrey and Kalyss had just jumped from. The rising sun had glinted in his dark red hair, highlighting the satisfaction on his face as he'd turned to Dreux. *"Looks like we get another century together."*

If for nothing else, Dreux owed Geoffrey for saving him from Kai's promise.

"You look quite different when you're not all gray." Kai's lips tilted in that grin Dreux had come to hate.

"And you look quite different not covered in my wife's blood."

Kai's grin died and he eyed the sword in Dreux's hands. His hand gripped his own. "I'm glad you brought that. I've always wanted to best you in a true battle."

Dreux inclined his head. "I remember."

Kai's eyes widened a bit. "I wondered if you would."

The pleasantries were over. They both raised their arms and their swords clashed in a loud grind of metal that announced to all that the battle had begun.

KALYSS JERKED AWAY from Alex and stared up at the waterfall. They weren't close enough to the edge for her to see them, but she heard their swords ring. The first clash was loud, long, uninterrupted, then the battle was on with a series of quick scrapes of metal against metal, blow after blow.

The wind picked up, suddenly sending icy shards through her jacket, through her shirt. It whipped strands of hair around her face, stinging her cheeks. With one shaking hand, she brushed them away from her eyes.

"Let's get you out of here." Kalyss turned and grabbed the knife from the deck. "Why haven't you healed yet?"

"Drugs, I think. And having my hands tied. Plus, he hurts me faster than I can heal."

Kalyss brushed hair from his eyes. "Makes sense. I'm so sorry."

"Not your fault." Alex searched her eyes, examining the differences a day had wrought. He knew what his day had entailed, but what about hers? "I heard Dreux was a statue."

"At least it's better than ex-con, right?" She ducked to his right and sliced the rope carefully away from his hand. His wrist was bloody slashes where the strands had rubbed.

"How is he not a statue?"

Alex's hand free, Kalyss sat up and faced him briefly, shivering, her face flushing. She gave Alex a quick, uncomfortable smile. "I kissed him."

Alex's brows rose as Kalyss quickly averted her gaze, stood, and crossed to his other hand. He hugged his right arm to his side as he looked at her again. Kissing wasn't something she did lightly. Hadn't Alex tried to convince her to change that just last night before Kai's first attack? Of course, he'd pushed her to kiss a man made of flesh, not a statue made of stone. "There's a lot I don't understand about today."

"I know." She ducked her head to her task, avoiding his gaze and ignoring the battle above them. "I'm sorry you got hurt because of me. I thought you'd been killed."

"Yeah, there's a lot of that going around." Geoffrey dying and resurrecting, the story of Kalyss's lifetimes. She looked at him, her brows together. He shrugged and hugged his free arm to his chest. "There's this guy, Geoffrey—"

"Where did Kai take him? He said he left him to die." Regardless of their history, Kalyss owed him for last night. He'd died protecting her. It wasn't something a girl forgot.

"I wouldn't worry too much. It's apparently Kai's favorite episode and he replays it over and over. But I don't think anything can kill Geoffrey for good." Alex considered the anxiety in her gaze. Whatever she'd remembered hadn't left her as untouched as she first appeared. She cared.

Kalyss freed Alex's left wrist. Geoffrey might resurrect again, but as Genie had said to Aladdin, it's amazing what you can live through. And, somehow Kai suddenly seemed sure that this would be the last time Geoffrey was with them. She grimaced. "That's not comforting."

His lips twisted and he rubbed his face in a tired motion. "Sorry. I think Kai's humor warped me. I'll never look at a dead man the same again."

Kalyss glared at him.

Alex shook his head ruefully. "I don't know where Kai left him. He put a cloth over his nose, knocked him out, and dragged him upstairs."

Kalyss watched the top of the cliff. The swords sounded more deadly every second and branches whipped around above her head, mimicking the clash of battle. It twisted her stomach though she tried to ignore it. "He's probably near the dojo, somewhere. We'll find him."

"Do you think he needs help?" She turned back to see Alex examining her face.

"Dreux?" Kalyss frowned, setting the knife aside. The knife was sharp and she wasn't exactly at her most calm and focused.

Alex nodded.

"No." Even if Dreux did, it was no longer her responsibility—she was freeing herself from the ties that bound her to him, to this dangerous cycle. Maybe if she kept telling herself that, the chill along her spine would go away. "Where are you hurt?"

"Just about everywhere in differing degrees. Don't worry. I'll heal." He sucked in his breath as he pulled both arms in front of him for the first time that day. "Eventually. Where are *you* hurt?"

She ducked her head, grabbing the knife to cut the rope binding his feet. "I'm not."

Alex scoffed. "Don't lie to me."

She stilled and raised her gaze to his. "Physically, I'm fine."

He nodded. "But emotionally . . . your eyes are swollen and strained. Your face is pale. What has that jerk's game done to you?"

Kalyss thought back to earlier that night, what she'd seen, what she'd felt. The emotions she'd locked in a chest inside her heart jumped and stormed against the lid, fighting for freedom. She forced the lid back down, but her voice was quiet, vulnerable. "He made me go back there."

"The house?" Alex's face softened with sympathy. "I know. I heard . . ."

She shook her head and strengthened her inner defenses, determined the lock on her emotions would hold. She massaged one of his arms, letting him stretch out before trying to move him. "No. Kai forced the house, but Dreux made me go to that night. He wanted to see."

"You mean actually see?" His face twisted in horror.

Her fingers dug into his muscles through the shirt. "In living Technicolor."

"You can do that?" His whisper was almost awed.

Funny, huh? Too bad she wasn't as impressed with herself. "Apparently."

"Wow." He looked at the water, taking in this new turn in her gift. She took his other arm and worked down from his shoulder to his wrist.

Suddenly the swords sounded closer and she looked up, to see Dreux and Kai at the cliff's edge. Her heart crawled into her throat.

DREUX TURNED BEFORE Kai could push him over the cliff. Their swords clashed and held, each of them straining to throw the other off balance.

Kai's eyes glittered like wet grass in the moonlight. His head tilted to indicate Kalyss and Alex below them. "Cozy. I bet she's glad to have her lover back."

Dreux refused to fall for the distraction, but used his irritation to push Kai away. "They were never lovers."

Kai paused, his sword up at a defensive angle. His lips quirked in a small grim smile, an almost pitying smile. "Are you sure?"

This time, Dreux found it impossible not to look. Kalyss leaned close to her friend, her face animated as they talked. Her hands rubbed down Alex's arm with a familiarity that didn't sit very comfortably in Dreux's mind.

"Burns, doesn't it?"

Dreux snapped his gaze back to Kai in time to respond to his blow. Their swords clashed again.

"I feel no burn. They are friends. I know she loves him."

"Still has to hurt." Kai swung viciously. "You can't tell me you pined for over nine hundred years for your passionate—" He swung again, knocking Dreux back. "—loving—" He kicked on a back swing, catching Dreux's left hip. "—wife. Only to wake up and find she's moved on. Shacked up with some other guy. You can't tell me that don't juice up the old green-eyed monster."

Dreux glanced down at Kalyss again. When he felt Kai follow his gaze, he struck. Kai was caught off guard by his own distraction and fell back a few feet from the cliff's edge.

"There's only one green-eyed monster around. Until I kill him, anyway." Dreux swung at Kai again. "She is free to be with who she wants."

Even if the mere thought of it killed him. She'd suffered too much for him already. If the best way to repay her was to set her free, then he loved her enough to do so.

"Quite the selfless sacrifice for love, *big brother*," Kai mocked.

"I pity you that you've never felt such a love, *little brother*." As he would never again, either. Dreux's mind was rational, logical, but with that thought, his heart chose that moment to rear up and choke him with an overwhelming desperate need and possessiveness. It was his heart that roared, *Never!*

Never would he be able to accept the loss of her, let alone someone else loving her, touching her. Spending a lifetime anywhere nearer to her than he could be. But now was not the time for these thoughts. He needed to ensure Kalyss's safety. She was the priority. Not him.

KALYSS WATCHED THE shadowed cliff where the battle raged. This wasn't the movies where a swordfight lasted five minutes or so and was over. Dreux and Kai were two medieval warriors who'd trained to battle for hours, even days. It could take all night before they found a weakness to exploit. Of course, Dreux had been frozen for centuries. How battle-ready was he? Kai'd had time to practice in many styles. He'd have a leg up in knowledge and flexibility. Yet, Dreux had rage on his side, vengeance, and the instinct to protect.

But so did Kai.

She shook her head, all the "buts" hurt her brain. Cold rain had a scent, and it was all she could smell. She welcomed the breezes, the weather's tension in the air. Maybe when the storm released its fury, she would feel the release, too.

Maybe as long as they stuck to swords, all would work out. But she had to stay here until she knew for sure that Kai was defeated and Dreux lived. Maybe she shouldn't care—she was free of him *and* his mess. Yet, strangely, she *did* care. She didn't want him hurt.

"That bastard," Alex said. She swung her gaze back to him. The brown flecks in his eyes were hard, the green bright. "He made you relive it."

"Don't call him that." She gazed at the cliffs, massaging his hand. "It's a painful truth."

The sudden silence between them felt so heavy, Kalyss

turned back to Alex. His eyes were dangerously speculative. She so did not want to face that look right now.

"Geoffrey said you were destined to love him." His gaze narrowed on her, demanding total honesty. "Do you?"

"Everything I suffered was because of him. Even he admits it's all his fault. How could I love him?" Despite all her anger and pain and grief, there was a little part inside her that hoped to be convinced it was okay to love him, a gentle part that wanted happiness so desperately.

Probably the same slutty part that slept with him, her bitter self blasted. It was time to move. She pulled Alex to his feet and braced him when his knees didn't quite hold him up.

"Last I heard, *Sam* was the one who hurt you," he gritted through clenched teeth, clearly grateful for the distraction from his painful weakness.

She shook off that logic. "I dreamed of Dreux that night, said his name in my sleep. I wanted a brown-eyed baby. Dreux's eyes are brown. Sam's are green. It's what set Sam off."

"So? You could have talked about yellow eyes, dreamed about shamrocks, and said Patrick, and it still would have been Sam who killed your daughter." Alex's gaze said he wouldn't let her escape herself this easily. Kalyss half-dragged his limping weight off the dock, to the paved walkway.

She swallowed the lump in her throat. "I've died nine times because of Dreux."

"From what I heard, it was Kai and his hatred that put a knife to your throat. It was Dreux you married then, Dreux you kissed awake now."

"Oh please." She rolled her eyes. "Who's going to uphold that marriage certificate now? If they even had certificates then. We're not still married."

"But you kissed him." She froze, her eyes narrowed. Alex held on to her and tried to catch his breath before continuing. "You two are the only ones who can choose to uphold those vows. As for a certificate, vow renewals aren't unheard of. Nor are weddings. So the question is, if you want nothing to do with him, why did you kiss him?"

"I don't know. It just seemed right at the time." She wanted to look away, but couldn't.

"If you want him out of your life, why do you keep looking up at the battle?"

She looked at the picnic table a short distance away. This question she could answer. "I have to know it's over. That we're not in danger."

"Why can't I call him a bastard? What does it matter to you if it causes him pain?"

She did look away this time, up to the storming branches and farther, to the black movements above the cliff. Even she knew it wasn't logical to defend Dreux when she blamed him, but she couldn't stop the instinct to protect him. "He's suffered a lot over it."

"So? He suffered a thousand years ago because some meanies called him a bastard. Life's rough. You get tough or you die." Alex's voice was hard, piercing. "You're running."

She closed her eyes and winced. Alex wouldn't let her rest, wouldn't let her hide from the truth inside herself. He never did. She dragged him to the table, feeling the cold logic that had given her such strength fade beneath the emotions she hadn't locked away in her heart.

The peace when Dreux had held her hand. The empathy when she'd remembered his childhood. The moment of clarity when she'd finally understood what he'd endured as a statue. "That's not all he went through because of it. It's not even the worst."

"So he had a rough life. You've had ten. All tough, tragic, while he what? Slept?"

She tugged him the last few feet and pushed him to the bench. This wasn't strength, this confusion of thoughts and emotions. It wasn't strength, but even in her mixed-up mind she recognized that it wasn't weakness, either.

It was *humanity*.

"No. Being a statue wasn't easy, either. He was awake the whole time, remembering my death. Feeling pain. Going insane."

"So, he's crazy, too."

"No!" she shouted.

"I see."

She froze and even the trees seemed to still briefly at his

tone. What did he see? Did she want to know? Did she want to face the hard truth that he seemed to be building toward?

"You want him gone because he's just not worthy of being loved by you."

She inhaled sharply, her insides rebelling against the nasty allegation. It wasn't true.

"He's not good enough for a strong, independent, forceful Kalyss."

"No—"

"He's controlling? Weak? Not safe? Which is it? Are you afraid of him? Do you think he'll attack you?"

"No," she shouted again. The only one attacking her was the best friend she'd mourned most of the day. "I don't think that at all." She clenched her fists and ignored Alex's raised eyebrow. "He's gentle and tender and intelligent and sexy as hell."

"Then you're a coward." Like a lethal dart, his words flew straight to her heart.

She gasped, collapsing to the bench beside him. Truth hurt, but she had reasons for her fear. "I just don't want—"

"It'd be a shame to lose the one man God and destiny gave you simply because you're confused."

Arguing an independent life with Alex would never work. He never saw love as a chain to freedom, but it was all she had left. "He wants all of me. Everything I am. Even showing him my past."

"Even your morning breath?" he mocked. "The bastard."

Her face twisted between irritation, fear, and humor. "It's not funny."

"Not when he's about to die. You're right. Did you even kiss him goodbye?"

Her eyes widened. She hadn't even thought about kissing him. She'd been too busy trying not to melt all over him. Melting and wallowing in confusion were not part of what she wanted to build on her new-life foundation. She'd end up with the same rickety structure to her life she'd had before. "I can't give him me. I don't know how. I don't know—"

"Is there anything you *do* know?" he challenged.

Sudden silence reigned from the cliff. Kalyss stared up in horror. Even her heart held still in her throat. Was it over already? Was one of them dead? Could she have prevented it? Her thought from earlier that day came back to her: *"Brother shouldn't kill brother."*

The branches waged war again, leaves striking death blows in an explosion of sound that raised life from the darkness all around her. Then she was up and running.

Chapter 22

A lex rose to follow Kalyss, but his legs buckled beneath him. Damn it—now was not the time for him to be weak. She needed him. He watched her climb the cliffside, her movements a little slower and more cautious than Dreux's had been. His best friend was heading straight for danger and he couldn't help.

But he had to help. She needed him. Alex worked his way back to his feet and stumbled to the base of the cliff. Between the concussion still pounding in his head and all the tight muscles from being tied up and poked at, he was very unsteady. Once he got both hands on the hard rocks, though, he was able to balance himself. Carefully, Alex began to climb.

FURY AND RAGE powered each stroke of Dreux's sword. No doubt Kai had expected him to be weak, stiff, from his time as a statue—Dreux had as well. But, strangely, he felt physically rejuvenated, as if his mind had been active while his body slept, waiting for his wife's kiss.

A kiss that had been torturously delayed for lifetimes in which she'd needlessly suffered tragedies that would fell giants.

Dreux loosed a swift rain of punishing blows onto Kai, each one a vicious demand for retribution.

There had been a chance, once, the night he'd held his bride, made love to her, and earned her trust. A chance for them to be happy—to have a home and family where they could dwell in love and healing, a feat that would have been hard enough after so many years of war and destruction. But the promises made that night had been shattered by a demon even more diabolical than Dreux had ever been accused of being.

Their swords clashed as they circled around the wet boulders above the waterfall. Struggling not to slip, Dreux stared into the glittering green eyes of his father's youngest son and became again the warrior he'd been raised to be, by the men Kai's mother had sold him to. Striking fast, Dreux slashed hard enough to knock the sword from Kai's hand and landed a kick to his stomach that thrust the man back and to the ground.

Dreux raised his sword for the killing blow as Kai knelt before him. Kai looked up from his position close to the ground, his wet hair straggling around his face, emphasizing again the green of his eyes just as it had that night so long ago, when young Kai had stepped protectively in front of his mother.

Not that he'd ever be believed, Dreux had to say it again. "I did not kill her. I never touched her, which is not something you can say. For that, you will die."

Just then, a scrabble of rocks falling from the cliff's edge announced someone's arrival. Kalyss rushed over the edge of the cliff, freezing behind Dreux and gasping for breath.

Dreux spared her only a moment's glance over his shoulder, but it was all his enemy needed. Kai rose to his feet, sword in hand, ready to fight as Dreux turned, his sword raised at a defensive angle perfect for another slashing attack.

But Kai didn't slash. He thrust, his left hand grasping the hilt, his right palming the pommel. The tip of Kai's sword evaded Dreux's block, and sunk deep into his side. Pain exploded through his body and blood roared past his ears.

Kalyss screamed and rushed forward, Kai's knife in her hand. Before Dreux could warn her of Kai's greater experience or lift a finger of his own to help her, Kai grabbed her knife hand, twisted, and spun her into his arms, her back to Kai's front and his hand once again holding a knife to her throat.

Dreux grasped the sword to pull it from his side, his eyes wide and horrified. No, this couldn't happen. He could not watch her die in front of him again. Kalyss met his gaze, her beautiful blue eyes full of panic and apology.

Kai braced on Kalyss's body and kicked Dreux square in the stomach. Dreux stumbled backward, struggling to lean forward and catch his balance, but the heel of his boot went off the edge of the waterfall.

He might have been able to regain his balance before he fell completely, but the awkwardness of the sword slid half into his side made that impossible. Dreux flew back, his gaze solely for his wife. More than anything, Dreux wanted to reach out, grasp Kalyss's outstretched hand, and hold it tight as he had just that morning. His side burned. His balance was off and he couldn't regain it. Couldn't pull Kai's damned knife away from her throat.

He'd failed a second time, and she would die.

Dreux heard her screams as he disappeared over the edge of the fall and down to the pond more than thirty feet below. Water rushed and thundered around him, under him, waiting to swallow him. Blood roared through his ears and his side was a raging inferno. He couldn't move, couldn't scream. His body stiffened in a familiar paralysis he couldn't fight. He could only listen and watch.

And think.

She'd returned for him.

KALYSS REACHED OUT a hand, straining against the knife, and screamed. Ferociously, she grabbed for that steely strength inside her to form another cord, another unbreakable tie—this one to throw around Dreux and hold him safe. She didn't know what to do with him, yet, but she knew one fact without a doubt: she wasn't ready to let Dreux go.

As hard as she hoped, as far as she stretched against Kai's arm at her waist, reaching until it seemed her fingers might actually brush him, it wasn't enough. She wasn't enough.

Dreux disappeared silently over the edge—the only noise the loud splash a few seconds later as his body hit the pond.

Kai laughed against her ear, a strangely bitter sound. "Don't worry, love. It's not over yet. That would be too easy."

Kalyss swallowed against the sharp knife once again at her throat. Desperately, she searched the edge of the waterfall, hoping against hope, but all she saw was one familiar set of hazel eyes peeking over the cliff. He looked down, then at Kalyss as Kai pulled her back.

Kalyss stared into his wide eyes, silently begging him. He knew her better than anyone. He had to know what she'd want.

"Please," she begged.

SILAS STARED DOWN at the pond in disbelief, while Draven slumped against the railing. So close, so very close. How could—

"Wait," Draven said in a disbelieving gasp.

Silas raised his head and followed Draven's pointing finger to the pond below—to the boulders and the bubbling water, swirling and frothing where the waterfall crashed down. Ahh, there. He could see.

Once a descendent followed certain connections in his mind, the path was forged. It became their gift and could be followed over and over. The curse had set no limits on the number of times Dreux could make the change, so when he had followed his path, he once again became a statue—an unbreakable man of stone. Silas smiled.

"But it's raining." Draven's palm cupped the falling droplets and they both made the connection at once.

"Geoffrey," they said.

Resurrection was not his gift. Not yet. It was still tied to the curse, with all the limitations that implied. Silas backed away from the rail. "I'll check on him. You go with Kalyss and Kai."

"What about them?" The black gloved hand pointed down to Alex and Dreux.

"It can't be helped. They need to figure it out on their own."

* * *

THE ROAR IN his head faded, leaving a blessed moment of silence, one last moment of clarity. Geoffrey blinked open his pain-clouded eyes. Still here, still dying—almost done. It was fitting. They'd finally reached the end of their long journey.

For good or ill, whether all his efforts were worth something or not, the finale was here—assuming Kai was right in his predictions and he would die permanently. But, even if Kai was wrong, the rules they'd lived by for so long had changed and Geoffrey had no assurance that he'd resurrect this time. Actually, he'd never felt *assurance*, anyway— capricious destiny could have banned him permanently to hell at any time.

But they'd never made it this far before.

They were fighting, or had already fought, the final battle. He didn't know who won. For a brief second, the injustice of that cut deep. He'd died for them. Never daring to hope he'd be forgiven, he'd simply tried to make it right, to give Kalyss and Dreux a life together, the life they would have had if he hadn't taken it from them.

There were many things he could have done with ten centuries. Many goals he could have met. He could have settled down with a woman who loved him instead of a dream- memory. He could have had children and made sure they prospered for generations. Built an empire, a legacy.

But he hadn't done any of those things. Instead, he'd been burdened with a purpose, an impossible goal that he had to see through. He hadn't rested, hadn't quit. Not when they failed. Not when Kalyss died. Not when he buried her.

He'd adjusted his strategy and moved forward, learning all he could, gaining as many resources as he could possibly use. He'd abandoned hope, sympathy, guilt, every emotion in a re- lentless drive to accomplish his task. He should have at least earned the right to see the end.

He knocked his head back against the building and stared at the whirling black sky above him. The first freezing drops of rain knifed into his cheeks. He laughed, dry, humorless. At least he'd gotten to feel the rain.

His head dropped. He no longer had the strength to hold it up. His eyes closed. Icy rain soaked his hair, his clothes. He was still thirsty.

He had no regrets. He'd followed the only course he could and still retain his soul. Dreux and Kalyss should be together. They deserved the life he'd stolen from them.

But he wished he'd seen their victory. That last thought followed him down those long, dark, spiraling stairs. Those familiar stairs. He remembered them well. Knew where they ended. Knew this time, if Kai was right, he wouldn't come back up them.

KALYSS WATCHED DREUX fall back, flying into the air in a slow arc, arms outstretched, legs extended, sword protruding from his side. Everything ended here. He'd never hold her, never kiss her, and tell her he loved her. Never hear she loved him, too.

She'd pushed him away, rejected him and the love he'd offered. She wanted a life free of men, and now she had it.

All this she thought in that endless moment when he lay upon the sky, his eyes all for her. Then he dropped below the waterfall's edge, gone. A chance irrevocably lost.

Kalyss's befuddled brain recognized it was trapped in a dozing nightmare, but she couldn't fully break free from it. Instead, the tape rewound so she could watch his fall again.

Feel the terror and foreboding as he flew back. That split moment of hope, as he froze in the air. The hope that if she disbelieved what was happening, enough to rewind time even, she could still change it.

Then the irrevocable loss as he descended. The hot-flashing instant a second after he disappeared when she had to accept what she saw.

The tape rewound repeatedly until she screamed, long, loud wails that pounded inside her head. Her hands clawed at the gauze that shrouded her mind, trapping her in the drugged sleep Kai had forced for them to easily leave the waterfall. She sobbed and struggled frantically to awaken. It had to be a nightmare. It couldn't be real.

She could still fix it. Please, God, let her fix it.

ALEX MENTALLY KICKED himself with each stumble back down the side of the small cliff. Every best friend instinct said to go after Kalyss. Kai might be armed and skilled with a thousand years of training—to the death, even—but Alex should have at least tried.

So his instincts said, but the look in Kalyss's eyes had clearly directed him to the highest priority. And, honestly, he wasn't strong enough. He was still weakened by wounds he would have already healed if it had been any other day. Any other day he wasn't drugged.

Kai had promised she'd live if Alex could keep her out of the way during the fight. But she hadn't stayed clear and the deal might be forfeit, unless Dreux's death balanced it?

If Dreux was dead. Should he hope Dreux was dead? It seemed like Dreux was integral to stopping Kai and regaining their life. If he wasn't dead or paralyzed, his presence could end all threat to Kalyss. His presence could fully heal Kalyss's heart.

Alex had to save him.

Alex's feet splashed in the stream at the base of the cliff and he slipped on the wet rocks. He was able to regain his balance in time to prevent a fall, but his head tilted and his vision blurred. On the grass again, he sunk to his knees, his hands pressed to his head, trying to steady it. Damn it, he wasn't used to being ill. Not to nausea that crawled up his throat and burned his tonsils. Not to skull-pounding headaches or aching lungs that couldn't fill with enough air. Especially not used to the inability to think when he needed it most.

Alex clenched his fists in frustrated fury, calling for some form of control over his own body. He didn't have time for this. Kalyss was in danger. Kai had done something to Geoffrey and Dreux was somewhere in the pond, dead or dying. Alex was the only one free. The only one left to help. Without this damn drug in him, he could heal the concussion that slowed him down. He pounded the ground with his fist.

Stabbing needles jabbed his brain until he nearly screamed. Every cut and bruise in his past that had disappeared almost before it formed, now mocked him. Every cold or flu that hadn't eaten him alive, now taunted him. He'd healed those. But now, when he needed to heal most, he couldn't.

Alex clenched his fists and strained against his limits. He wanted the damned drug *out* of him. *Needed* it to flee every cell it infected. It *would* expel, damn it. He'd make it.

A warm heat rushed through his body, fueled by anger and desperation. Then the heat became wet and Alex stared at his arms. A clear liquid broke out and trickled down each limb like sweat, but thicker. He stared in disbelief. What the hell?

More of the liquid oozed out of his skin and he would have thought he was dying if he wasn't suddenly feeling so much better. The nausea cramping his stomach eased. The shaky soreness disappeared, nearly leaving him vibrating with a strange energy.

The pressure of Alex's brain expanding against his skull let up, clearing his mind and allowing him to think normally. The gash over his eye closed as he rose to his feet. His lip healed with the first step to the pond. All he'd had to do was want the drug gone and it would have been?

No. He'd wanted it gone all day. But until this moment, he hadn't *willed* it away. A slight distinction, but apparently it made all the difference in the world. And now, with it out of his system, his body could absorb the damage it had taken during the last twenty-four hours and eliminate it.

Alex took a deep breath and braced at the edge of the pond. It was time to go to work. He needed to find Dreux. Alex released the breath, slow and focused. The light from the deck didn't extend into the dark water very far. Add the rain that blurred the sky and he couldn't see much of anything. There was no other option but to wade in.

One step into the liquid ice and he couldn't breathe, it was so cold. He pushed forward, deeper, the water reaching higher. His pants wrapped tight around his shins, knees, and thighs, shrinking them against his skin. He was in to his waist when he thought he saw something around the edge of a boulder.

Whatever it was, it wasn't moving. He rushed forward.

When he rounded the boulder, he expected to find Dreux struggling to hold his head out of the water, or with his head out, but the rest of him too broken to move—or even unconscious, or dead, and floating face down in the water. But instead of a broken and near dead human body, Alex only saw stone and more stone. It took a moment to make out the head resting against the boulder, dark water lapping at his neck. The eyes were open and full of sorrow, the lips twisted in pain.

The hilt of a sword was held firm in front of him, pointing

at an angle away from him. Alex braced in front of those eyes, hands clenched, eyes narrowed. It didn't matter if the man inside the statue could hear, understand, feel, or not. He would only give him one chance.

"She's alive, but still in danger. We don't have another millennia for you to hide in stone. Fight your way out and help me rescue her, or give her up for good." Alex leaned forward and stared straight into the blank eyes. "Either way, Stone Grey, *I* am *not* kissing you."

DEEP INSIDE THE stone, Dreux raged. He fought an endless, tireless battle in a place where time had no meaning. His mind had to be stronger than this. He couldn't be trapped again. This wasn't the way for it to end. He couldn't give up and allow Kai to kill her. He couldn't spend eternity waiting for her rebirth, if they even had another chance. His mind would never survive this entrapment, not again.

Panicked, he struggled harder. She'd freed him with a kiss, but she wasn't here to kiss him now. This time, *she* needed the rescue and he couldn't allow his imprisonment to keep her at risk. But nothing moved, not a finger, not a toe. His earlier freedom was only a dream now.

Suddenly, Alex stood before him. His eyes glared like hot iron prods, merciless. They cut through Dreux's rage, stilling his mind, freeing his senses. It was suddenly disturbingly easy to slip into the sharp focus he'd perfected in the last hundred years, the focus that was a pure, sharp synergy between mind and heart and, now, something new—his senses.

All six of them.

His clothes plastered to his body, Alex wasn't the helpless victim from the deck. His voice slightly muted by the thundering water, he said, *"She's alive, but still in danger."*

There was hope. Kalyss had solved this puzzle and freed him the first time. Now it was Dreux's turn to free himself, to rescue her and keep his promises, to never allow her to push him away. They had a future together. He refused to lose it again.

"We don't have another millennia for you to hide in stone."

No, they didn't have that time. But Dreux didn't need it, either. He only needed to remember that morning, that moment when Kalyss's lips had touched his—the flashing heat, the electrical charge, that lightning path that had charged through his mind.

"Fight your way out and help me rescue her, or give her up for good."

Not an option. Dreux mentally clenched his jaw and narrowed his eyes. The kiss had forged a path. Now he'd simply follow it.

"Either way, Stone Grey, I am not kissing you."

Well, thank God for that.

Alex gripped the sword handle, braced against the rushing water, and pulled.

Chapter 23

Choking on her tears, Kalyss fought her way through the shroud. Her fingers mentally stretched the gauze, peeling and prying it away from her until she broke free. Which sounded great, except she wasn't truly free. She was in a car.

She blinked open her eyes, the rest of her body still feeling numb and hanging inside her seatbelt like a dead weight. Rain pelted the windshield like a hail of bullets. Water splashed against the outside of the car, like crashing waves in an angry sea. The wipers rubbed reluctantly at the glass, groaning at their futile efforts.

She had no idea where they were going, but from the darkness and long stretch of wide road, she'd guess they were on Newport Highway, heading north. Kalyss took a deep breath, struggling to raise her hand and wipe tears from her face.

"*Why?*" Her word was a breathy sigh, full of helpless grief. It was the only question she could pull from the maelstrom and, for a long time, she thought he wouldn't answer.

"I own land out here. We can finish this without more interference."

Kai knew what she meant. He wanted to force her to say it out loud. Heartless jerk. "No. Why did he have to die?"

"That's what I asked when my mother died in my arms." For once, his expression wasn't full of crazy good humor. It was serious and dark, like his tone.

"Are you sure Dreux murdered her?"

"You honestly believe I'd spend a thousand years vowing vengeance on an innocent man?" He sounded so logical, so sane.

"But he didn't. I saw . . ." Now she'd sound insane. Kalyss snapped her mouth closed.

"I saw her bloody, bruised lips speak his name with her last breath. I saw the rest of his victims." His jaw clenched.

The rest of his victims. Kai wouldn't believe her. No matter what she told him, all she had was words. She couldn't show him the truth of the past. She'd taken Dreux to a past memory, but she'd been the link. She'd lived it, in the very house they'd stood in.

Could she convince Kai to take her to Normandy? Would his castle still be standing? Or even the tree by his father's grave? Could she access the memory through location?

Kalyss closed her eyes. It didn't matter. Dreux wasn't safe inside a statue anymore. She'd awakened him and he'd died. Whatever she could piece together of this mystery, it would still be too late. She'd failed. Again. Catastrophically.

She'd made love with a man today. For the first time in four years, she'd opened her heart to the possibility of love. Now it was over. And it pissed her off.

"I didn't ask for all this crap to happen," she exploded.

He calmly continued driving.

"Damn you!" She hit his arm, looking for a reaction. Any reaction. "You brought this to me. I was fine, living my life completely separate from you. I didn't even remember anything. Why didn't you leave me alone?"

"That wasn't the game, Kalyss." There was cool resignation in his tone.

"Screw the fucking *game*, Kai. I had a *life*. Plans for a future. I was doing things."

His gaze flicked over her dispassionately. "So? Go back to it."

She stared at him, speechless. Like it was so easy. Like she could just forget everything she now knew. Forget Dreux? Forget his last words to her? *I love you.* "What? Jump out of the car now and pray I don't die before landing on the asphalt at sixty miles an hour?"

He snorted. "Don't be ridiculous. I'll drive you back home after a while. I just need to make sure—"

She spluttered, nearly choking. "You'll drive me back home? Like a prom date, walk me to my door and just say goodbye?"

He grinned. "I'll kiss you before I leave, if that makes you feel better."

"Un-friggin'-believable!"

"What else do you want me to do or say, Kalyss?"

"Sorry would be a decent start."

"I'm sorry I killed you—*nine times*?" He raised a brow. "There's a paradox in there somewhere."

"Show regret, psychopath." She crossed her arms and looked out the window.

"And you'd believe me?" He shook his head. "Besides, it was necessary."

She snapped her glance back to him. "Necessary? To kill me? To attack me today? You could have left me alone."

"By reaching you first, I gave you a chance to be done with it early, without this confusion. Otherwise, Geoffrey would have convinced you to involve yourself again. I tried to stop his influence on you. It didn't work, though." His gaze swiveled from the road to her. "Has Geoffrey ever contacted you before last night?"

"No." He thought she was just confused? Maybe she was, but not the way he thought.

"Then how did you know where to find the statue and what to do?"

Her hands twisted in her lap. "Geoffrey gave me the keys to his car. Everything I needed was there."

"Then you only have yourself to blame for following his directions."

She chuckled furiously, shaking her head. Up was down and down was up with him. "Nothing is your fault, is it, Kai?"

"Should something be?"

"Yes, you freak. You hurt Alex." *You hurt* me. She'd been falling in love with a man who loved her, truly cared, would never hurt her. Then the mind games had wrecked all of it, not that she could ever admit that to Kai.

"He wouldn't give me any information without pain. That was his choice."

"You killed Geoffrey right in front of me." Turning her life upside down with one thrust of his sword. She could've moved on after being attacked, but not after watching a man die while trying to save her.

"Not like he didn't come back from it."

"You took me back to my past!" Invoked her most painful memories to make her turn on the one man who'd treated her like she was his world. Kai had resurrected her fear and she'd used it to reject Dreux.

"Those were your memories, Kalyss. They made you who you are, not me. I just reminded you." So logical, so cold. How could he honestly deny any fault was his?

"You made me see it again! In living color, I had to relive every moment of that night, helpless. Totally helpless." Remembering details she'd forgotten. Details that pointed to a past love. Her memories of Dreux had tried to surface four years ago, but the tragedy of that night had pushed them away.

"Were you always such a drama queen? You had to walk into an old, empty house. If that was so hard, then you obviously needed to deal with some things." He glanced at her. "Relax. It'll only strengthen your character."

That did it. She shrieked. "Uuuggghhh. My character is strong enough, thank you. You have no idea what you did."

"I made you face two choices you've made in your life—one good, one bad—and the consequences of each. I'd say you still need the reminder."

"Why is that?"

"Because you keep abandoning the good choice and chasing the bad. You had Alex and your freedom. You chose to give them both up to interfere in our battle. Why?"

"Because brother shouldn't kill brother."

"Says who?"

"The sky is blue, the grass is green, whether you agree or not."

"Is that the reasoning that will let you sleep at night?"

"What?" By God, she'd kill him herself before this night was over.

"Face facts. You were so happy with your independent future

that you fell for the first strong man with a pretty face you saw in order to avert it."

"Not true."

He smiled charmingly. "Meaning you saw me first? You think I'm handsome?"

She graced him with a withering glare. "Geoffrey is very good looking."

His raised brows lowered into a pout. "Was."

"What did you do with him?"

"I let him feel the rain."

There was no reason for his seemingly innocuous words to freeze her to the bone, but they did. "Cut the crap. Where is he?"

"Not far from where I killed him last night."

"In the alley?"

"And down around the corner a ways—just far enough to have kept you from finding him easily when you went to the dojo earlier tonight."

"You're sick."

"You have a bad habit of name-calling."

"Much as I appreciate you *psycho*-analyzing me, I'd rather take advice from a professional."

"But, my dear Kalyss." He smiled mockingly. "You *are*."

She groaned. "You studied psychology?"

"What else was I to do with my time?"

"Die from old age?"

"Sorry," he stated cheerfully. "Tried that. Didn't work."

She rolled her eyes. "Nothing gets through to you, does it? You use logic like a force field, bouncing everything off it, even the concept of right and wrong."

"As a plan, it's proved infallible."

"Then I'll just have to prove your logic wrong."

"Logic has been my strength for over nine hundred years. Don't be too disappointed when you fail."

Kalyss looked away, staring out of the window at the rain and swaying trees. Talking to him would get her nowhere. It was like part of his mind was missing—the conscience part.

They drove farther north, where the houses grew farther and farther apart. This was mountain farm country, where people took pride in their self-sufficient distance from town.

Where they could have as much peace and quiet as they wanted, or do what they wanted, and no neighbor could hear. It wasn't a comforting thought just then.

He turned off onto a small road and followed it a ways, going higher and deeper in the mountain, where trees gathered close, shrouding the night in a deeper black. After a maze of twists on unclear roads, he selected one long dirt road. They drove through an open fence, continuing past trees and more trees on a narrow, rutted path until they reached a clearing. Kai pulled to a stop at the edge of the open field.

"The original plan was to build a house here when the cycle was finished. I find I really like the natural feel of it." He shook his head regretfully. "I think, after tonight, I'll need to find somewhere else. Too bad, but not even I could build on the land where someone died."

Her heart lodged in her throat and she couldn't swallow it down. "It's not too late. Don't kill anyone and your plans aren't wasted."

He stared into her eyes, as if actually considering her words. Then he smiled mockingly. "Where's the fun in that?"

Her eyes crossed until she saw spots. He chuckled and climbed from the car. There was no talking to him. Who did he plan to kill? If she was free to go, then who would die?

Before she could calm the terror inside her, he opened the door, bent in, unsnapped her seatbelt, and pulled her from the car. What kind of freaking idiot was she to believe a man who'd killed her before? To trust, even when he promised her so reasonably, that he'd let her go? Oh, she was too stupid to live.

They got around the edge of the door, Kalyss walking calmly, pretending to be clueless to his lies. When all was clear, she broke away, running for the trees. Her brain fired rapid thoughts and adrenaline forced her body to move fast. But she didn't get far.

He'd been more prepared for her escape attempt than she'd given him credit for. One minute she was running full out, the next he tackled her and they slid, face down on the wet grass. She felt him above her, his chest heaving with the laughter that escaped his lips.

She swallowed. "Let me up. I won't—"

"Don't bother trying to make deals with me, Kalyss. I'm not that much of a fool." He tugged her arms behind her back in a hold she couldn't break, then pulled her to her feet. "Would you believe me if I said it wasn't you I planned to kill here?"

"No. That's not exactly reassuring." She looked back at him, frowning.

"Quit worrying. Your life will not be forfeit tonight."

His tone didn't reassure her. He'd emphasized the *your*. Whose life was, then? "You can't kill Dreux. He's already dead. You've eliminated Geoffrey. Why kill Alex?"

He calmly walked beside her, guiding her. Panic rose inside her. Her heart pounded. "Please. Kai, don't hurt him. He's suffered enough. He's had so little chance to live, really."

He looked at her, one brow raised.

"You've had a thousand years, so much time. You can't . . ." She choked. Tears began to gather in her throat. "I love him. I trust him. Please don't take him away from me, too."

"You plead so prettily." He paused next to a tree that had split near the base. One trunk led up as high as her neck, then four large branches sprouted from it—a chestnut tree, judging by the large shelled seeds on the ground. He pulled cuffs from his jacket pocket, unhooked one cuff, and put her back to the tree.

She couldn't let him do this. She kneed him.

He grunted and lost his hold on her, freeing her hand. She swung at him and connected, knocking him back a step. He kept underestimating her. She shook her head and kicked him square in the stomach. He landed on his knees, winded. She sprinted past him, toward the car. She could lock herself in. Unless he'd left the keys inside of it, then she could drive away.

Before she reached it, he grabbed her ankle and she went down. He landed atop her back, panting for breath. Now she couldn't breathe. They froze a few moments, Kai regaining his breath, Kalyss losing hers.

"You are really starting to piss me off." He raised her cuffed arm above her head and brought her other up, but left it uncuffed. When she was near dizzy and ready to pass out from the lack of oxygen, he rose and pulled her up to his chest, her back to him, one hand trapping hers behind her head. His free arm surrounded her waist and he dragged her toward the tree, impatience in each movement. "Now, stop fighting."

But she couldn't. She struggled, kicked at his legs, stomped on his toes, twisted her arms, and dug her nails in his hands. Nothing worked. His size guaranteed his success. It went against all she'd taught, all she'd learned—but in this kind of up-close battle, she didn't stand a chance. She swung her head back, hoping to get his nose and loosen his hold. It didn't work.

Tears came fully now, her heart pounding with a sickening sense of dread. She could breathe, but dizziness still assailed her. Her arms ached from being stretched so firmly above her head. His arm cut around her waist, squeezing her, allowing only shallow breaths. He was strong, balanced, and firmly in control. She couldn't shake him off. She was helpless as she hadn't been since Sam—as she'd never wanted to be again.

All her training, all her books, all her attempts to be in control of her own life. They were in vain. She wasn't in control. She was still vulnerable. She was still alone, still needed someone to come to her aid. Someone she could trust. Someone she could believe in. And for once, the face that came to her mind wasn't Alex's.

Kai reached the tree again, turned her, and used the bulk of his body to press her back against it. She tried to knee him, but he was prepared and blocked her with his thigh. She could do no damage. He held her cuffed hand to one side of the tree branch above her head and pulled her other hand to the opposite side of the branch, raising her to her toes.

The cuffs clicked and she was stuck. The trunk angled up into a series of branches and smaller branches. She was trapped, her back to the trunk, her arms over her head, until the cuffs were removed.

He stepped away, breathing heavily. Her one consolation was she hadn't made it easy for him. He held up the key to the handcuffs in front of her. In a dry, flat tone, she said, "You should have been a comedian."

He grinned and slipped the key into the front pocket of her jeans. He was *so* not funny. She raised an eyebrow, her voice deadpan. "You're killing me."

"Not this time." He leaned closer, his face inches from hers. "I'm glad I had this chance to get to know you, Kalyss. I'm finding I actually like you."

DREUX EXITED THE bathroom, one thick towel tucked around his waist while he rubbed another over his head. He stopped abruptly and eyed Alex. Kalyss's best friend sat on one corner of her bed, his elbows on his knees, his brows twisted in thought. They'd taken turns showering and looking for Geoffrey. It didn't look like Alex had had any better luck finding him.

"I don't understand," Alex said, frowning. "Kai wasn't gone that long. He couldn't have taken him far."

"He wouldn't want to risk us finding him. Geoffrey would interfere too much. Thus the vague maps. We won't find Geoffrey until Kai allows it." Dreux tossed the towel over his right shoulder and pulled clothes out of another bag he'd grabbed from the back of Geoffrey's SUV.

Alex sighed and looked up, then his gaze froze on Dreux's chest, on the blood red handprint over his heart. Dreux saw his glance and quickly averted his face. The handprint stirred a mixture of pride, satisfaction, shame, and horror in him. He'd stared at it in the mirror twice today, trying to reconcile his feelings.

Kalyss had marked him, branded him hers with her bravery, courage, and sacrifice. An honor he could be proud of. But the memory of her death, of her sacrifice, horrified him and shamed him. He hadn't protected her. And now she was unprotected again. Alone with Kai.

He ripped the tag from his shirt and unbuttoned it.

Alex nodded toward the handprint. "That's hers, isn't it?"

"It is." Dreux tugged the shirt up his arms and straightened the collar.

"Are you hers?" It wasn't an idle question. Her best friend was testing him.

Dreux paused at the second button. He met Alex's gaze squarely, his expression solid, implacable. "I am."

Alex eyed him a silent moment, then he nodded. "That's all I needed to know."

"You heal?" The gash to Alex's head and the split on his lips had disappeared since Dreux had seen him on the dock—further proof after Kalyss's vision of Alex's ability.

Clearly deciding a statue-man had no room to judge him for being weird, Alex admitted, "I do." His lips twisted ruefully. "When I don't hold myself back."

"Others?"

"Yeah, I can heal others."

"Then why is Kalyss still scarred?" Dreux made his gaze direct but not accusing. Alex cared too much to do nothing. Something had prevented him from healing Kalyss completely.

Alex looked down, shame and regret on his face. Then his eyes met Dreux's again. "Sam was possessive. And like a typical abuser, slowly alienated Kalyss from her friends. I thought she was wrapped up in being happily married and allowed myself to focus on college."

Alex looked down at his hands. "I didn't know about Sam's abuse until a few days after his last attack, when Kalyss was awake and coherent enough to call me. By then, she'd had surgery. Stitches. I healed her all I could, but the scars never left."

Dreux nodded. Alex had done what he could. That was all anyone could ask. The cell phone slid on the pile of clothes as he grabbed his jeans. "How long do you think he'll wait?"

The phone rang, echoing in the nearly empty apartment.

Alex smiled tensely. "Not too much longer."

Dreux flipped open the lid, pressed OK and raised it to his ear. "Where is she?"

"Ahh. Brother dear, I'd wondered if you'd survived. How intriguing."

"Where is she?"

"Just outside my car, right now. Get a pen and I'd be happy to give you detailed directions. Perhaps this time we can finish without interruptions."

Dreux looked for a pen and paper, found them on the end table, and gave them to Alex. "Have you hurt her? Is she still alive or will I arrive too late?"

"That would be too sad for words, wouldn't it?"

No matter the provocation, Dreux refused to give in to it. Kai would only be amused. "Let me talk to her."

There was silence until Dreux thought Kai just might put her on the phone, but then he came back. "I don't think so. This doesn't look like the right time."

"What are you talking about?"

"She appears to be communing with nature right now. It would be rude to interrupt, don't you agree?"

Dreux scowled at the ridiculous answer. "This is between us, right?"

Kai was silent a moment, but Dreux knew he understood the question. "As I promised her friend, she will go free regardless of this night's work."

"Tell me where."

Chapter 24

What was he doing? Going to his car? What was in it? Would it hurt? Kalyss stretched and twisted, but nothing worked. It was dark and she couldn't see around a few of the trees to the inside of the car.

Great. He'd brought her to the middle of nowhere, tied her to a tree, and left her with no way of watching him. No way to prepare for what he intended. As far as she could stretch only showed her the very front of the dark blue Dodge Durango. It was too dark to see inside it.

Kalyss slumped against the tree, her mind nearly blank. Despair crept to the edges of her emotions, testing her defenses. She was so tired of fighting, of spending so much effort to push herself every moment. Go, go, go. Keep going. Don't quit. Tears filled her eyes.

She'd struggled so hard to reach this level in her life and look at it—wet and cold on a dark night, far from anywhere, with only a man who might kill her for company. Or kill Alex. Then she'd be left with even less than before she'd awakened Dreux and fallen into him.

Suddenly, the last four years of struggling for strength and independence didn't seem like anything. She was back where she'd been the night Sam had taken their wedding cake knife and murdered their baby girl. Cold, helpless, and at the mercy of a man who had none.

No. She shook her head and blinked her gaze clear. He wouldn't get her that easy. She twisted her wrists, pulled against the cuffs, and again examined the tree she was tied to.

Thick roots formed a tangled web at her feet. A thick branch stretched her arms above her head. The cuffs were on the upside of that branch. The key to the cuffs, Kai had mockingly placed in her front jeans pocket. Never before had three feet seemed such a great distance.

She groaned and let her head fall back against the tree. It was three in the morning on a dark, wet night. The rain had eased up as they'd arrived here, but she was still soaked and chilled. It was too black to see anything this far from street-lights and business signs. Even the moon and stars wrapped themselves in clouds.

She'd been warm once. Just a few short hours ago, in fact. Standing on a bridge, the love of ten lifetimes had wrapped his arms around her and protected her from the wind.

Kalyss shook her head and laughed at herself. *The love of ten lifetimes.* She looked to the trees to share her humor, but they only swayed mockingly above her. She sniffed in disdain, but only inhaled the smell of dark, rich soil. Wet leaves caressed her face, soft, compassionate, until they brushed the grass burn on her right cheek.

Even the leaves felt sorry for her. Tears gathered inside her chest, pressing, expanding until she wanted to explode, but she gathered them back and yelled to the sky, "What do you want from me?"

The wind stole her words, sending them amidst the clapping leaves and dancing trees. She doubted Kai could hear her from his warm, windless seat in the car, but that was fine. She wasn't talking to him anyway.

"Haven't I been through enough bullshit? Suffered enough for your enjoyment?" She shook her face wildly, refusing the false comfort of the leaves against her cheeks. Maybe she was wrong and the God of love and light didn't enjoy her suffering, but she'd had no evidence of it so far.

"You're supposed to be about love. The God of the living. You created all this and declared it good. But you keep taking it away from me." Tears did come then, soaking her face, coating her throat and she stomped her foot ineffectually against the base of the tree.

"I grew up in foster homes after you took my parents from me, leaving me alone for so long. But still, I trusted you." She dragged air into her lungs, the path as rough as an uneven gravel road full of holes.

"You sent me Sam to love, to honor, and I did. He hit me and I forgave. He cheated on me and I forgave. I stayed married and faithful and you gave me a daughter."

Angry sobs shook her, swinging her against the tree. "I trusted him. I trusted you. And you let him kill her. You took her away from me forever and I couldn't forgive that. I can't forgive that."

Her voice clogged closed and she choked. She coughed to clear it. Her mind was a jumble of furious half-formed thoughts and images. She didn't even know what she'd say until she heard it leaving her mouth.

"Gone. It's all gone. I tried to do it the right way. I didn't have a family, so I tried to make one. That blew up, so I tried to make something else. A business. A strong life. I help others, even. Why isn't it good enough?" she gasped. Every time she wanted just a little more than she had, she got smacked down.

She tossed her head back and screamed as loud as she could. "Why do you hate me?"

She laughed harshly. "You want me to believe the fucking impossible. Resurrection, immortality, reincarnation . . . please. I'm not John. Elijah hasn't come alive in me. Geoffrey certainly isn't Jesus and Dreux is not Kingdom Come! But you did promise love. How can I believe in the rest if you won't let me believe in love?"

There was no answer. Not in the trees, not in the wind. She was still fighting a losing battle. She slumped, hanging from her wrists, and quit yelling. "What possible good can come from ten lifetimes of failed attempts at love?"

Like a memory in the distance, she heard her voice. *"May God make me strong, Geoffrey."*

"What?" she shrieked. "Is this supposed to be your idea of an answered prayer?"

Like a movie, she saw herself nine-hundred-and-twenty-nine years ago with one leg thrown over the tower window, praying for courage.

"Ugh." She raged in disgust. "You definitely made men in *Your* image!"

Wouldn't Kai just love to know he'd been doing God's dirty work all this time? The wind laughed at her. She burst into a frenzy of struggles, jerking against the handcuffs, scratching her arms and digging bloody grooves in her wrists until the dark liquid trickled down her arms in small, black drops. But there was no escape. Never any damned escape.

The pain shocked her, her mind clearing a fraction. She stilled, her body stiff and frozen from head to toe. Then she sagged against the tree, defeated. There was no way out. She was trapped, again. Why did it always come back to this? Why couldn't she win, just once? Cold breezes cleared away the clutter in her mind, in her heart. This time, she whispered.

"I get it." The night snorted. Resentment nearly silenced her. "I do. I'm helpless, small in the grand design. You've got a plan. You're going to make it happen when you're ready and not a minute sooner. I can't push for it. I have to quit. Give up."

She sucked in a breath, trying to do that one thing that was so against her very nature. Gradually, resentment gave way to fresh understandings that trickled into her mind slowly, like each realization needed a full moment to itself, lest it be forgotten. "I can't have love if anger and bitterness are filling my heart up. There's no room for it to move in. I get it."

She stared at the ground, huddling in on herself as much as she could. Had Dreux felt the cold, the rain? Had he huddled inside his shell and raged at God?

Tears slid softly now, soaking into hair the wind blew against her face. "What do you want? I thought it was love. Trust. I was working up to that. Was I too slow to accept it?"

Probably. She'd done fine until the vivid reminder of her past, then she'd pushed Dreux away, rejected him. As Alex had reminded her, she hadn't even kissed him goodbye. So much for begging for a grand love—she'd had it in her hands and shoved it away.

How could a woman spend ten lifetimes trying to earn love

without learning how to accept it? Believe and receive it? Trust it?

"I was wrong," she whispered humbly. "I'm so sorry."

Anger didn't earn her love. No wonder Dreux had been taken away. "I'm done trying to do it my way, done fighting you. This love you've promised me is worth everything, anything. He's worth it. I'll wait for you. Another hundred years . . . another thousand . . . please, God, let there be another chance."

Tears streamed down her face steadily. "I'll do anything."

Much as it defied all logic, much as she dragged her heels and didn't want to, she knew what she had to do. There had to be room for love. She had to make that room before she died. She threw the door to her soul wide open, stalked determinedly to that treasure chest she'd stuffed her emotions into, threw open the lid, and let them fly free.

Hatred, distrust, bitterness, anger—she'd held them all inside that locked chest in her heart. She'd thought only pain was in there, but no. The rest had clung to it. Stored away and carefully preserved like the finest family heirloom. No wonder there had been no room for love.

The poisonous emotions swirled above her and she finally recognized them for what they were. All her attempts to push away Dreux? Fear. Refusing to believe what he and her dreams told her? Distrust. Expecting him at some point to turn and hurt her, by word or deed? Bitterness and cynicism over a past she wouldn't let go.

One by one, she catalogued the events of the last day and a half and matched many of her "logical" actions to a negative emotion. When she finished, she saw herself in a new light.

Not Kai's skewed light, though.

Too bad these realizations were so late. Would she carry them to the next life, if she had another? Would there be another? She'd watched him die. Didn't that signal the end? The game was truly lost wasn't it? But if there was some chance, some remote possibility, clearing her soul in this life saved their love in the next life, then it had to be done.

"Faith tiny as a mustard seed, right?" Her lips trembled. "Okay. I'm letting go. I'm forgiving—"

Kai's headlights flashed on and cut through the darkness,

blinding her, stopping her heart. His door slammed and he walked toward her, a large, black silhouette. She blinked her eyes closed until he got close enough to block her from the worst of the glare.

When he stood before her, before he could speak, before she could doubt herself, she said, "I forgive you."

Like a subway rushing to a silent stop, he halted. His eyes widened, the green very dark, very surprised. He shook his head sadly and softly said, "Oh no, sweetheart. Don't do that."

She shook her head, refusing his refusal, then nodded. "I do. I forgive you. All of it. Everything."

She felt raw inside, her eyes still full of tears. This wasn't a manipulation ploy—I'll forgive you *if*—he seemed to recognize that. She cleared her throat, but he placed two thumbs on her lips, his fingers cradling her jaw.

"Shh. It's almost over, sweetheart. Almost done."

She struggled to repeat her words, make him understand, but he shushed her, pulled a blanket from his shoulder, and draped it around her.

"But—"

He pulled her face to his chest and wrapped his arms around her and whispered against her hair, "We'll be done soon, sweetheart."

She could only hang there against him, his body supporting her weight and warming her.

SILAS APPEARED BESIDE Draven in the trees at the edge of the clearing. The rain still fell in a drizzle, soaking everything that was already chilled. Draven looked at him. "Geoffrey?"

"Unconscious. He doesn't have much time." Silas looked to Kai and Kalyss and frowned. "What is he doing?"

"Keeping her warm." The logic to Kai's nurturing action would likely only make sense in his own mind.

Silas raised a brow. "Cozy."

"She forgave him." It had been a difficult, but necessary step in their progress if they were to break the curse. How else would they succeed without killing each other?

"Did she really?" Silas asked in wonderment. For the first

time that day, his expression eased and he seemed less tense, more pleasantly surprised. Then his expression darkened and he eyed Draven suspiciously. "What on earth would make her do that?"

Draven shrugged innocently. "She vented all her anger, all the poisonous feelings she'd held inside, to God."

He stared accusingly.

"I just watched." Draven huffed in irritation, then faced the clearing and mumbled, "And listened to the wind."

"IS THAT HOW you get all your women, *brother dear*?" Dreux's voice cut across the clearing. "Tie them up and take liberties?"

Kai pulled away from Kalyss slowly, then turned. Light spilled across his face, highlighting his charismatic eyes. He sauntered to the center of the clearing, a baiting grin on his face. "Just keeping her warm."

Dreux entered the circle of light, his eyes seeing to the edge of it where Kalyss hung from a branch as thick as her thigh. Her eyes were wide upon his face, caressing, loving. Wishful thoughts now could only distract him and get them both killed.

He jerked his gaze from the woman he loved, thankful she still lived, and focused on the one man who would change that if he deemed it necessary. Dreux wouldn't let that happen. Not again. Never again. His eyes narrowed as he tossed Kai's sword across the clearing, now clean of Dreux's blood, and tightened his grip on his own sword. Kai picked up his sword and braced in the clearing, a slight grin covering his face. A sudden sound behind him made Dreux pause.

Dreux carefully glanced behind him to see Alex at the edge of light, trying to step inside it, but unable. As one, they both looked toward Kalyss. The edge of light covered her and the tree that trapped her. Alex couldn't reach her and Kalyss couldn't leave the circle. Fury beat inside his chest, but Dreux pushed it back, using the adrenaline to energize him.

"Don't worry. The barrier spell will end when the battle is over. Light bends around us, invisible but solid, blocking all entry and all exit until one of the hearts trapped inside quits

292 JAMIE LEIGH HANSEN

beating. Not too soon, just too late. It's a little trick my mother taught me." This time Kai's grin was edged in bitter humor. "Kalyss will be safe and unable to interfere until either you or I die. Then her friend will be able to reach her."

"No!" Kalyss cried out, pulling at her bindings.

Kai glanced at her. "Must you be gagged as well?"

Dreux took advantage of his distraction, as Kai had earlier. There would be no playing this time. He brought up his sword and struck. Kai turned back just in time to block and the long, loud clash to signal battle was struck.

THE CLASH OF swords was much louder this close to the battle. Tears sprang to Kalyss's eyes. Dreux was alive and he'd come for her. She drank in the sight of him, his strength, his determination. Her prayer for another chance had been granted. She'd have this one chance to change their fortunes. Just once, because there was no way in hell she'd risk not having another.

No more playing. No waiting for centuries, dying and wishing and living on nothing but dreams and memories. They were going to crash this cycle. Destroy it. And the next time she crawled into bed, it would be to move straight into Dreux's arms.

The men circled and clashed. Sparks flew from their swords. It wasn't musical to listen to. No heavy metal ballad from Queen played in the air. Dreux and Kai weren't moving like they were dancing. Instead, each strike was a limb possibly lost. Each discordant note was a life possibly ended. It wasn't beautiful. It was terrifying. They needed to quit fighting. This wasn't what needed to happen. This wasn't how it should be. It couldn't end this way.

Dreux's brown eyes darkened to black against the night and the glare of lights. His face was hard, his lips grim. He was death. It was a promise in his eyes, his stance. For the first time that day, she felt fear. Not fear for her heart, but fear of a more tangible danger.

They moved, circling around each other and she could see behind Dreux to the spot where Alex had been. Alex wasn't there anymore. She searched for him, one eye on the battle in front of her, but couldn't see him until she turned and glanced over her shoulder. Her heart pounded. She had to get out of this. She had to stop the battle.

Alex halted at the edge of light, testing it for a weakness that would allow him to enter. She held her breath, hoping against logic, but he couldn't break through. She slumped. The swords clashed. Her attention switched, riveted on the two men. They were going for death. This time the swords rang more clearly, the blows fell slightly harder, the steps were faster than she'd ever seen.

First blood was drawn when Dreux's sword sliced into Kai's arm. Kalyss flinched, sickened. Violence filled the air, swirled and pulsed. This was not a training exercise. They were out for souls.

She cried out, hating being so damn powerless. This wasn't how it had to end. It wasn't how the cycle would break. They needed love and forgiveness. She could see it so clearly. Maeve's death had happened so long ago. No one could even know the facts and events for sure. They were all clouded by opinions and perceptions. It didn't have to affect life today. Or death.

But Kai would never let it go. The best she could do was show them the past as they each saw it and hope that would be enough. She couldn't lose Dreux now. Not now that she could finally admit how she felt. Not now that she could accept him in her life, in her apartment, in her future. Her body, her heart, her mind cried out for the chance to have the marriage they'd whispered about that long ago, dark night—the marriage of her dreams.

Kai was Dreux's brother and it would be a tragedy if either were to kill the other. That was a curse to condemn them all. She could feel it, see it.

They stared into each other's eyes, focused and unemotional. Chilling. Two warriors blooded in battle. They'd killed before and their swords clearly snarled that they wouldn't hesitate to kill again. Her heart crawled into her throat.

"Kalyss," Alex whispered, hand against Kai's light barrier, attempting to draw her attention without distracting Dreux.

She turned to him. Had he thought of something? She sighed with relief. He had. She watched every motion he made with his hands, then looked above her, considering. He whispered encouragement and directions so only she could hear.

She nodded and squared her shoulders, twisting and stretching the kinks out from hanging so long. Standing tall, she grasped the branch above her with both hands. With all her strength, she lifted her knees and hung from the branch.

She tilted her chin up and used the extra angle to help curl her abdomen, bringing her knees to her chest, her feet to the branch. She pressed her head farther back, her forehead almost to the trunk and curled her legs around the branch.

She now hung with her back down, both her hands and her legs holding her to the branch. Kalyss paused, keeping her breath even. Her wrists felt their first relief in over an hour without her weight pulling on them. Wedging her foot between two branches and grabbing a third, she used them for leverage to pull herself around, sitting on the main branch and looking down. Now her hands were on the bottom side of the big branch.

She stilled and looked at the men. They were still hacking and slicing, feinting and blocking. Graceful as ballet dancers, they were home. They knew this. It was their song. But it wasn't a musical to her.

Kalyss shook her head and gripped tight with her thighs and arms. Alex stared at her, a proud, encouraging grin across his face. Another day, she'd have basked at his confidence in her, but they didn't have time.

"You're doing great. Now—" Alex motioned with his hands.

She nodded, seeing where he was going with his instructions. She stretched her hands to her left as far as she could. Then she loosened her left leg, letting it hang toward the ground while curling her right as far around the branch as she could. She stretched, reaching, reaching.

Finally, she grabbed her belt loop with her right pointer finger and pulled at her jeans, dragging her pocket to her hands and opening it. She quickly stuffed her left hand inside and grabbed the key tightly.

At that moment, unbalanced on the wet branch, she slipped. She grabbed for the one small branch with her right hand again, trying not to fall all the way down. She gripped the key so tight that it cut grooves deep into her left palm. Carefully, she pulled herself upright again.

Leaning down and holding the branch with her arms and legs, she turned the key in her hand, got it in the lock, twisted, and one cuff sprang free. It was all she needed, but she took the time to undo the other one and tuck both the key and cuffs in her back pocket.

"Good girl." She grinned at Alex. "Dreux noticed you were gone. He's keeping Kai's back to you."

Twisting, she examined the battle. Dreux knew she was coming this time. She plotted her advance, then froze. The realization hit her so hard she nearly fell from the tree.

He trusted her. Not just in the you-won't-cheat-on-me way, but in the you-got-my-back way. Her strength, her skill, he trusted them. Though she'd screwed up at the waterfall, he trusted her not to make the same mistake twice. She smiled and a glow blossomed inside her.

Or he was just afraid to have her behind him, distracting him again. She sobered, gulping. She wouldn't make that mistake a second time.

Silently, she dropped to her feet at the base of the tree, crunching chestnuts. She winced and stood slowly. The noise hadn't alerted them. Now, no sudden, distracting movements and this might actually work. Raising her hands, palms out, she waited for Dreux to notice and realize what she wanted.

When he nodded, without looking at her, she knew it was time. Kai sensed her movement behind him and turned, as she'd expected. Dreux tossed down his sword and brought his arms around Kai, holding tight long enough for his arms to harden into unbreakable stone.

Kai looked down, his eyes wide, then met Kalyss's gaze.

"You're not the only one with a few tricks, little brother," Dreux said against his ear.

Kalyss smiled.

Chapter 25

With Kai held tight, it was easy for Kalyss to disarm him. She paused a moment, staring at the stone that hardened all the way up Dreux's body, leaving only his head free to move and speak. The rest was unshakable and indestructible. Kai struggled futilely.

"Wow," she whispered in awe. Shaking her head, she raised her arms and stood on tiptoe. Placing a hand against each of their cheeks, she whispered, "Hold on for your life."

"What is she doing? Make her stop." Kai fought wildly, his eyes panicked.

"She's searching for truth." Dreux met her eyes, calm, ready.

She didn't have a memory to immerse herself in, but she did have that dream of Dreux the night Maeve sent him away. She imagined a path to send and receive between them all and, amazingly, there it was. As soon as she accessed the dream, however, the images shifted.

Instead of Dreux on a dark night in front of a cold woman, she saw a much smaller, younger Dreux, sitting on a dirt floor by a warm fire, holding a wooden toy. Cuddled on a seat, his mother and father watched him, love for each other and him clear in their eyes.

Without warning, the memory altered again. This time it was Kai huddled in a corner as his mother and father argued.

She grabbed the big man's arms, pleading, "Please. Forget her. Forget them both."

He shook his arm free. "Don't you realize what you're asking? No."

She reached for him again, but he shook her off and turned away. Maeve's face twisted with hatred and she screamed at him. "Then go to her! Go to her and die!"

Their vision turned black, then brightened on a different scene.

Four-year-old Dreux huddled in a dirty corner of a filthy cell, his clothes in rags, his bed occupied with rats. He wanted to cry, but he'd been warned. His cheek was still bruised from giving in to his tears on his way to this new hell.

The heavily armored man who'd shoved him in there barked gruffly, "Fight for your place or die. We don't waste time on weak little bastards."

The cell door banged shut, sealing him in darkness.

The next memory was Kai's . . .

He sat stiffly at a banquet, food overflowing the tables, men and women in rich dress all around. He'd watched his father buried this morning and tonight his mother laughed and flirted. Every few moments, Maeve would pull him to her, surrounding him with her softness and perfume.

When there was a lull, she took him to his room and tucked him into bed. She looked into his disapproving eyes. He'd always adored her, but now her behavior made no sense to him. "Don't you miss Papa?"

Straightening his covers over him, she asked, "Why would I miss that heartless cheat?"

Tears filled the three-year-old's eyes and his lips trembled.

Time fast-forwarded, to a night when he was twelve and opened his mother's door to find her bed occupied. The man paid him no notice, but his mother calmly met his eyes.

He'd been called here by her. It was arranged.

The man grunted, gasped, then heaved his adulterous body off Kai's mother. As planned, he was shocked to see the lord of the manor, even a twelve-year-old lord, trapping him in such a compromising position. In a few years, the boy could easily remember all he'd seen and use it to blackmail the man or outright kill him for defiling Maeve.

The man bargained for secrecy, but the deal was quickly understood. If Kai's keep was attacked, the man's knights would protect them. He left the bed, grabbing his clothes and hurrying to dress. The covers slipped, revealing Maeve's milk-white bounty. The man froze in place and stared hungrily, licking his lips. Maeve bit her lip suggestively and lazily pulled the covers up. Her hair pillowed around her, a cloud of red temptation.

He forced himself to look away, accidentally meeting the gaze of a twelve-year-old with the coldest eyes he'd ever seen. He dressed quickly and left, without stealing another peek.

Kai met his mother's eyes. She pouted. "Don't look like that, you know it was necessary. The difficult things always are. Now," she smiled sweetly. "Come thank me."

Kai walked to her side, kissed her cheek, and said solemnly, "Thank you, Mother."

The image wavered again. A bloody battle like she'd never seen before filled the courtyard of an austere keep. The horror of it was, the warriors were all children.

Thirteen-year-old Dreux faced the crowd around him, taking them all on at once. Deadly, brutal, their swords the sharpest wood could be, they piled on him. A group of knights watched, arms crossed, their faces serious. One said, "He's getting better."

"Aye. Yet if he isn't willing to make the killing blow, he'll still be the first to die."

Just then, they heard a loud, low snap they all recognized. One of the boys screamed and the others backed away. They watched Dreux release the kid's arm, standing braced and ready to defend as the kid collapsed, hugging his broken limb.

"An improvement," the first man said.

"It'll do. For now." The second knight nodded to Dreux and the sober-faced lad silently nodded back.

The boys rushed him again.

Tears poured down Kalyss's face, from effort and an overwhelming bleak despair. Her mind swirled relentlessly, making her dizzy and weak, but she couldn't quit searching for the memory that would save them. Save them all.

"Mother, no!" Kai threw himself forward and bounced back from the barrier of light. His mother sat in the center of it, his first love cradled in her arms. Cecily's dress was drenched with the contents of a cup that fell from her limp hand. Her lungs wheezed in wet desperation.

"It was necessary, Kai. You know that." Maeve's hand stroked the girl's hair. "She was pregnant. She could never be what you need. You are meant for so much more than the likes of her." Maeve raised arresting, vibrant eyes so like her son's. "Your grand future is assured and only someone truly worthy can share it with you."

Cecily gasped, staring up, then her heart stopped and her body fell limp. Maeve gently lowered her to the ground and stood, reaching for her son now the light was no longer a barrier. But Kai rushed past her, falling to his knees and cradling the girl's head to his chest.

Tears streamed down his cheeks and he rocked back on his heels and sobbed into her hair. His beautiful Cecily had been so sweet, so trusting—his one bright, gentle port in a storm of manipulations and intrigue. His hand curved over her stomach. Their child was dead now.

"You have to understand." A note of desperation crept into Maeve's voice as she stared at him. He'd always been hers and she refused to share. He'd known this about her and taken the risk anyway, believing it would all work out. Cecily's death was his fault.

"It was necessary. She could never have survived in your world. No matter how horrible, I always do what's necessary for you." Maeve's voice was the closest to pleading he'd ever heard it.

Kai's sobs halted as he ruthlessly crammed them inside. He knew what was expected of him. But he'd never realized his risk in loving Cecily would be so great, the price so very high. Slowly, he lowered Cecily to the floor, gasping when her dead eyes met his. He rose and carefully stepped to his mother's side. He was taller, but she always towered above him.

"It was necessary." She pursed her lips and raised her chin stubbornly.

"I know." His lips barely brushed her cheek, but he obediently kissed her. His eyes didn't meet hers. His tone and expression were carefully veiled. "Thank you, Mother."

DREUX FELT THE snap between his hands. The injured man slid down and Dreux tossed him aside, standing tall, waiting, prepared.

He would earn his spurs today. A hard-earned level of respect he'd waited his whole life for. Something he'd dreamed of with awe once, long ago, in a forgotten time. But now it was survival. He fought every waking moment to reach that level of freedom.

His final combatant stepped forward. The man was as hard and cold as Dreux felt inside. Today's battles weren't to the death—nothing so easy. Facing his opponent, Dreux knew both of them might well be bloody and near collapse before this battle ended.

They raised their arms, fists ready. It was barehanded combat, but that was never a safe thing. Not here.

DESPERATELY, KALYSS SEARCHED for the right memory through all the horrible images in their minds. The level of skill she forced from her gift was dizzying, nearly overwhelming. Something had to give before the pain and despair of both their pasts drowned her. She'd thought she'd known Dreux earlier when she'd read his memories. Now she realized she'd only skimmed the surface.

Kai had finally quit fighting and now lay limp, helpless, in Dreux's grasp. She sped up, fast-forwarding through their lives, searching for what she needed. How she could do this, she still didn't understand, but the knowledge to do it was there. Like a dormant command buried in her mind, her gift had sprung to life. Now she feared she couldn't turn it off.

Suddenly the images paused and—*yes,* there it was.

DREUX FACED HIS father's wife, hating her. Maeve had sent him to that place, made him what he was. It would serve her right if the monster she'd created were responsible for her death. If the grief she'd caused so many others were visited on her.

She screamed at him, the wind playing with the evil red of her hair until it flew like the writhing, furious snakes on Medusa's head. Her green eyes slanted wickedly, hatred a living beast inside her. Her full lips spouted words as poisonous as her hair.

His hands curled tightly into fists. She was a small woman for all her rage made her so large. It would be so easy to press his thumbs over her throat and watch her striking eyes bulge. When she gasped her last, he could snap her neck with only a slight movement, just to hear the satisfying crack.

Dreux opened his fists, clenched them, then breathed in the cold air. He loosened his fists, rolled the tension from his shoulders. She had murdered his parents then continued her whoring way through Normandy in fine style. No matter how many people he killed, he'd never be as evil as she, but he wouldn't be the one to kill her.

He refused to allow her spirit, above all others, to haunt his dreams. To darken his soul more than it was, with her hatred. Dreux turned and walked away from her.

She screamed at him, but he refused to hear her.

Kai jerked, his head tilted back and he screamed. "Lies!" With the finesse of a tsunami, he freed his memory in a destructive wave that nearly broke all the connections in Kalyss's mind.

Kai raced toward his mother's body lying still on the ground. Her hair fanned around her head like a beacon in the twilight. Maeve's guard, a ferocious berserker known as The Terror, knelt beside her, tears coating his beard. He wasn't the brightest of knights, but he fought like a bull, mindless and destructive in the heat of battle. His knuckles were scraped from his attempted defense of his lady.

Kai fell to his knees beside his mother, afraid to move her. Her lips were stained with her own blood. Her arms and fingers broken in so many places, it was amazing her skin could hold her together. Her face was swollen and bruised, her eye socket shattered, her jaw broken.

"Who?" Kai could barely speak in the face of such devastation. He'd never seen a woman suffer so very much and that the woman was his mother crushed him.

She moved her jaw, painfully struggling to form an intelligible sound. Her eyes were wide, tears trailing down her face. Finally, she gasped, "Dreux."

As if she'd lived only to tell him, and was now at rest, Maeve's eyes emptied and she slumped against him. Now that it couldn't hurt her, Kai pulled her close and kissed her broken cheek. "Thank you, Mother."

Kai struggled wildly again, his legs kicking out and his hands grabbing at her. Kalyss's hand dropped from his cheek and she grabbed for balance. The emerald cabochon at his throat burned in her hand and before she could gasp, they were thrust into another memory, someone else's memory.

Maeve faced Dreux's back, one hand clenched around her emerald, drawing on its power. How dare he walk away from her? She'd already suffered such treatment from one tall, broad-shouldered man. She wouldn't suffer it from his bastard. Not without recompense.

"I curse you, lowly by-blow. I curse you a thousand years, a thousand lives and more. May those you love turn from you and die, trapping you alone and cold, as I am. Unable to walk away from your pain." He never even paused, simply mounted his horse and rode away, oblivious to her words. But her curse held. She felt it in the heat of the emerald at her throat. She knew her powers. Even God couldn't take them from her.

She held out her hand and commanded the knight beside her. "Come to me, my terror."

He did, her berserk knight. Gervaise was always obedient, always faithful. It was time to release him, to allow his destructive nature free reign. He towered over her, holding obediently still, as she did what she'd never dared before. Not without a dozen chains to hold him down. She slapped him. Her rings cut stripes in his cheeks.

"No, lady," he begged.

"Yes, my beast," she crooned. "Do this last thing for me, then you are free. Free to find more of your amusements."

This is why she'd captured him, tortured and trained him. This was the plan—for him to release her from this life, to kill her. This time. As soon as all who witnessed her "death", when all the humans who knew her died, she could return.

With no one left who could recognize her, she could be someone new—anyone she wanted—a goddess again, maybe.

But before she went, she'd take one last ounce of vengeance. Her beast would trail Dreux's steps, wreaking havoc, as long as both men lived. She slapped him again and laughed when his eyes widened, reddened, and he snarled.

The image halted abruptly and a shriek split their minds, filling their thoughts with one last vivid, shocking image. A long-lashed, feminine eye snapped open, green and venomous, full of hatred and vengeance.

Then, an explosion of energy from the emerald rocked them, breaking Dreux's hold and throwing them aside until they lay like scattered refuse.

SILAS SUCKED IN a hissing breath of shock. Green and black energies, visible only in his realm, swirled inside the light barrier, pressing against it and seeking escape. When they couldn't, they converged on the three people within.

Alex threw himself against the barrier, panicked, but if the barrier still held, then all three hearts still beat, though none of them moved. Except Kalyss. Her body shook and convulsed until Silas was afraid she'd choke on her tongue, if not bite it completely off.

"I didn't think she'd awaken so soon," Draven breathed. "Certainly not before the curse was broken."

"It's broken, but trapped inside the barrier with them." Silas's gaze roamed from person to person, energy to energy, trying to read the signs. Kalyss's vision had revealed the truth, cracked the lies that trapped them in their cycles and rid them of the curse, but a few clear choices needed to be made or they'd never escape the barrier and the energies within.

Either way, once this trial was finished, Maeve was awake. From this second forward, the whole world was in danger. If the four lived, breaking the curse was worth it.

DREUX OPENED HIS eyes to the silence. The clearing was hushed, waiting. The sun rose higher and dawn's rays crept over them. He sat up.

Kai lay to his right, unmoving. His chest barely rose with breath. Movement caught his attention. Alex pounded on the barrier, his mouth opened as if to yell. But Dreux couldn't hear him. He shook his head and a distant ringing told him it would be a bit before his ears recovered. But Alex was frantic. Suddenly filled with dread, Dreux turned to his left.

Kalyss convulsed violently. She'd demanded much of her gift today and now she paid the price. Dreux grabbed his sword and dragged his stunned body to her side. Pulling her into his lap, he pushed the hilt of his sword between her teeth. He'd protect her from some damage, at least. The rest he was useless to prevent.

This precious woman had sacrificed herself for him yet again. He glanced briefly at Kai's immobile body. She'd wanted to save them all, but didn't she realize? Without her, there was no point to living.

A familiar hardening gripped him, a signal of his change to stone, but he willed it away. He had control now. He wouldn't leave her—even if she left him.

Dreux buried his face in her hair.

TRAPPED INSIDE THEIR mental connection, Kalyss faced Kai. He wouldn't win this time. She fell into her defensive stance, ready to take each of his movements and use them against him. If there were a weapon in here—Dreux's sword appeared in her hand.

"Cool." She smiled. Now if only she knew how to use it. Nothing happened. She shrugged. There were other ways to fight.

But Kai stood still, his sword pointed down. All around them, like a wall of TVs, her nine past deaths played out. Nine times she'd tried to fight him, to evade him. In the end, she'd always run. And, in the end, he'd always caught her.

This time she faced him, sword held high in a batter's stance and waited for the attack. Except, it didn't come. She frowned. He wouldn't throw her off that easy.

Kai grinned sadly. "Not this time, princess." He dropped his sword and knelt at her feet. "My life for yours."

"What are you talking about?" She scowled.

"The game is over and you've won." He sobered, his eyes serious with determined intent. "I am sorrier than I can ever say."

She tightened her fingers around the hilt, ready to strike first. He stayed still, waiting, accepting that it was her turn to kill him. To end it as they'd waited to do for so long. But she remembered the little boy manipulated by his mother. The young man nearly crushed by her.

Kalyss shook her head. He was dangerous, deadly, she reminded herself. But she wouldn't kill him. Even if he seemed to want her to. She dropped the sword to the ground.

His sad grin came back. "That's not the way it works, princess. My life for yours."

She shook her head. "I won't kill you."

"Then I will."

"No—" She shook her head wildly.

"Don't worry. It won't be the first time. Just the last." He took his sword in hand and placed the hilt on the ground. It was five feet long and he could do no damage to himself while kneeling, so he stood.

Kalyss grabbed his arm, shaking her head. "You can't do this."

"The barrier won't drop until a heart stops." Kai caressed her cheek. "No hearts have stopped. He's waiting for you."

"No." She frantically searched his face. How could she plead for the life of the man who'd taken hers? But she was alive and well and it made sense in her heart. "No one dies."

He'd given her a kiss promising death at the start of all this. But she'd forgiven him, for herself, and now—for him. She rose to her toes, her hands on the side of his face, and gave him a kiss promising peace.

When she pulled away, he smiled. Then he shoved her to the ground, angled his sword over his heart, and fell forward. She was free.

"HIS HEART HAS stopped beating." Alex strode toward Dreux, grim of mouth and tone.

Dreux closed his eyes a moment. When he opened them, Alex knelt in front of him, his hands braced over Kalyss. They began to glow with a blue light that grew steadily longer and wider until it enveloped her entire body.

Kalyss stopped convulsing and Alex's eyes rolled to white with small lines of electric blue zigzagging through them. The sword slipped from her mouth and Dreux laid it to the side. The grass burn on her cheek was the first physical mark to go. It appeared briefly on Alex's cheek before disappearing. The same with the knife cut from earlier, it transferred to Alex's throat, then sealed closed and was gone. Dreux looked along her entire body and watched as the cuff and tree scrapes faded from her wrists and arms.

When she was whole again, Alex leaned back and took a deep breath. Then, he knelt beside Kai's prone body.

"Can you heal the dead?"

"No." Alex examined Kai. "But maybe if he's only missed a few heartbeats, I can start it again." He turned serious eyes to Dreux. "Either way, I have to try."

It was Alex's nature to heal, Dreux could understand that. He pulled Kalyss higher on his chest, her head under his cheek. But Kai had gone to horrible lengths in his unquenchable thirst for vengeance. He'd repeatedly killed Kalyss and Geoffrey, then tormented a helpless Dreux with their deaths. He'd tortured Geoffrey and Alex all that day. Would saving him bring any good? Would he see the truth in the last vision of Maeve's death or would he consider it trickery and lies? Would he be healed only to renew his quest? There was no telling which way he'd go.

Dreux stared at his brother's profile. Maeve had marked him hers from his days in her womb. Kai bore her red hair, her green eyes, and a masculine version of her fine features. As she'd marked his body, throughout his childhood and adulthood, her cruel manipulations had warped his mind. Apparently, she'd continued even from the grave.

Dreux eyed the emerald at Kai's throat. The last vision had come from its forest green depths. For hundreds of years he'd watched it poison the sunlight when Kai entered the tower room. Now, he realized it had poisoned more than sunlight. It had tainted everything for over nine hundred years. Dreux yanked it from Kai's throat, breaking the chain.

Maybe all of them deserved another chance.

Dreux nodded to Alex. "Please do."

* * *

KALYSS BLINKED OPEN her eyes. Dreux's hand tangled in her hair and his arms were wrapped around her again—exactly what she'd prayed for since she'd seen him disappear over the edge of the waterfall. She snuggled her face closer to his neck and wrapped her arms tight around him. She'd never let him go so easily again.

His deep voice purred roughly against her ear. "I love you. Thank you for returning to me."

She inhaled his scent and held him tighter. "I love you, too. Thank you." Her voice cracked and tears pricked her eyes. "I was so afraid I'd lost you for good."

His hold nearly crushed her. "Never. You'll never lose me."

She pulled away far enough to stare into his eyes. One hand cradled his jaw. "And you haven't lost me."

He brought her fingers from his jaw to his lips and kissed them. Stretching them, he placed her hand over his heart. She closed her eyes as he lowered his head, then his lips settled gently over hers in a kiss she'd never thought to feel again.

A shifting sounded to their side and Kalyss pulled back, reluctantly turning her eyes away from Dreux to see Alex leaning over Kai. His eyes rolled, turning white the way she'd seen them do when he'd found her in the hospital four years ago.

It should probably bother her to see her best friend work so hard to heal the man who'd tortured him, imprisoned Dreux, and killed her so many times, but it wasn't in her to want Kai dead. Not now. Not after seeing all his mother had done. Kai was a sad, tragic victim, as much as she had ever been. Even were he to heal physically after this, how would he move on from the things he'd done in Maeve's name?

Perhaps he'd wondered the same thing before sacrificing himself for Kalyss. In which case, letting him die might be the kindest thing they could do for him. But she'd been there before, so immersed in blackness she couldn't see a way out, a way to ever enjoy life again. Dreux's arms tightened around her, reminding her of all the good reasons she'd had to keep living after her tragedy. If Kai made it through, perhaps there was a reason for him to survive as well.

Alex sat back, his arms shaking from the strain he'd been under. It was Alex's personality to heal and to put all he had into it. When he turned tired hazel eyes her way, Kalyss smiled gently in thanks. Alex grinned and said, "Sorry to interrupt the grand reunion, but if he's to live, he needs more help than I can give him."

Kalyss tried to rise, but Dreux's arms tightened briefly before reluctantly letting her go. Running her hands over Dreux's hair, unwilling to completely break contact herself, she looked at the still man lying on the ground. She'd feared him too deeply for that to have seeped away so quickly, but after what his sacrifice—what the truth—revealed, how could she continue to believe he'd hurt her? He needed help. "He sacrificed himself for me. So the barrier would fall. He's not all bad inside."

Dreux rose beside her, his hand caressing briefly down her back. Bending to her ear, he whispered, "Thank you for that."

Kalyss hugged him. "Let's get Kai more help, then."

Dreux lifted Kai's shoulders and Alex lifted his feet. Kalyss ran ahead and opened the back door to Geoffrey's SUV. They slid Kai inside. Then, just to be safe, she raised his hands above his head and pulled the cuffs from her back pocket. She secured his hands to the door and handed Alex the key. Looking at the guys, she shrugged.

"It'll at least give you notice before he's free."

Alex nodded. "If he wakes up."

Dreux handed Alex the keys to Geoffrey's SUV. "We'll follow behind you."

Alex shook his head. "Only into town. If he hasn't awakened by then, he won't." Alex eyed them both seriously. "Go find Geoffrey."

Dreux nodded and stepped back as Alex opened the driver's door and climbed in. The engine roared to life and slowly pulled away.

DREUX AND KALYSS got in Kai's vehicle and pulled out behind Alex. Dreux kept a close eye for movement from Kai. He'd honk to warn Alex if he saw anything.

Kalyss plucked a piece of paper from the dash and read it

as she buckled. Then snorted. "On the way here, Kai told me Geoffrey was down the block and around the corner. Not five miles away from the dojo."

Dreux shook his head. "He has our father's sense of humor."

THE PEARL ANGEL lay upon the roof of the SUV, one long hand reaching through the roof and through Kai's chest, manipulating the heart within. Apparently today was not the day Kai was meant to die.

Which was good. He'd lived long enough to be forgiven by both Kalyss and Dreux. Who'd both worked together to discover the truth. The curse was well and truly broken now.

Silas held one hand toward Draven. Draven held a palm over it and they left. One last thing. Geoffrey needed them.

Chapter 26

G eoffrey heard the raindrops first, then the wind and the gentle sway of trees. His gut still burned, like it would if he'd lived but—not if he'd died and come back. So, he was still waiting to die. A burst of brilliant white light appeared at the end of the alley, nearly blinding him. Geoffrey squinted as two figures walked from the center of it toward him. Each figure became more distinct with every step.

A man with long black hair and white toga-like robes stood in front of him, his hands clasped together, his arms bare. A gold belt adorned his waist, a small sword clasped to it. A larger sword crossed his back. And large, white, feathery wings flowed down his back.

"Surely I'm not so bad the archangel himself needs to send me to hell."

The angel smiled. "No. There will be no death here. There is still use for you."

The angel's companion was smaller, darker. A long black cloak swept the ground with each black booted step. Hands gloved in black leather were clasped in front of the cowled figure. For a moment, Geoffrey was distracted by the war of smoke and light between the two. Pirate ships of black smoke fired small black cannonballs at golden ships. The gold ships fired back with volleys of pure light. There in the alley, light and shadow mixed and swirled until he was dizzy from it. Finally he shook his head to clear away the fog.

Geoffrey eyed the two in front of him dispassionately. "Why the confusion? Betrayers go to hell."

The angel allowed a small grin to cross his face before his hand struck into Geoffrey's exposed gut. White heat flared so bright it woke him to the pain that had finally begun to disappear. Now, the intensity exploded through him. He cried out from the worst agony he'd ever felt, even after Kai had played with him, until the effects slowly began to dissipate.

Geoffrey hung before them, fully healed, though his body still trembled.

"The curse has ended. You are freed from its grip. But your friends have awakened a greater menace." The angel's brown eyes bore into his, impressing him with their conviction.

Geoffrey could barely breathe. "What greater menace? Who are you?"

"These are questions for another day, Geoffrey." The cloaked one spoke with a low, raspy voice. "For now, you must rest."

"But—"

The man's hand pressed against Geoffrey's forehead, shaking up the mind within until it buzzed with activity. "Your questions will be answered soon enough."

In a blink, they were gone. Geoffrey closed his eyes trying to understand why he felt clear headed and confused, all at once. Then fatigue clawed at him. His head dropped down and his body hung limp, oblivious to the passage of time.

SILAS STEPPED BACK from Geoffrey's limp form. He and Draven were on their own side of the realm barrier once again. No human could see them, but when he looked to his left, he saw they were being watched. Side by side, the Obsidian Angel and the Pearl Angel stood.

Silas looked at Draven, then at the Angels. Had he messed up somewhere? Over-stepped his bounds? Broken a law? His throat closed at the thought, but he raised his chin. Geoffrey deserved to be saved from an eternity in hell. He'd worked long and hard for that redemption. If saving him cost Silas, then he'd willingly pay the price. Any price.

"I asked if I could return when the curse was broken." As soon as he said it, Silas realized his mistake. He hadn't been specific enough. "But not if we could heal him."

The Obsidian Angel stared at him with bright, damning eyes.

What should he do? Grovel? Plead for forgiveness? He'd interfered and broken one of the most sacred laws his people were held to. Silas swallowed, bracing himself in front of Draven. It had been his mistake. His misunderstanding. No one else should have to pay for that.

Silas faced the Angels, prepared for his punishment. To his surprise, though, Draven's leather-clad hand slid into his and the cloaked figure moved forward to stand beside him. Shoulder to shoulder, they faced the Angels.

The Pearl Angel smiled. "Continue."

WHEN GEOFFREY OPENED his eyes again, the sun was brighter and higher in the sky. Suddenly his heart thumped hard against his chest and he saw the sight he'd prayed for and dreaded every day for the last nine-hundred-and-twenty-nine years.

Dreux exited Kai's vehicle, pulling a pair of black sunglasses from his face. Geoffrey stared at his mentor's eyes, brown instead of the grey they'd been for so long. Dreux's face was no longer twisted in the tragic expression that had haunted his dreams every night. His skin was tan and healthy and he wore the clothes Geoffrey had bought for him. In his right hand was Kai's knife, but that was okay. Geoffrey could die at peace now, if this last punishment was why he'd been saved.

Behind Dreux, Kalyss exited the passenger door, alive, vibrant, and smiling. For a moment, Geoffrey saw them both together, fitting each other perfectly. Dreux looked so strong and tall beside his tiny but resilient soul mate. They looked happy, in love. Yes, this was exactly what he'd fought for.

Dreux clenched the knife in his hand, taking in the damaged man hanging before him. Geoffrey was covered in blood, some dried, some fresh. Geoffrey had protected him from the damage he suffered for Dreux's sake. Far more than Dreux had suspected. It would have been yet another spur to the insane fury Dreux had suffered, knowing he was incapable of doing anything to prevent Kai's destruction.

Dreux strode toward Geoffrey, the knife still clenched in his hand. Geoffrey raised his gaze to Dreux's, his jaw firmed. Dreux halted directly in front of Geoffrey and eyed the man who'd betrayed him, then worked through incredible odds, with such stunning loyalty, in order to atone.

Geoffrey had come a long way from the novice knight who'd once served under him. And even though he hung bound and covered in blood, there seemed to be no weakness in him. No flinching from the death Dreux had owed him centuries ago. No fear. No hesitation. Just acceptance.

This was the man who'd then spent a millennia trying to atone for the grief he'd caused. The man who'd aided Kalyss, time and again, training her and guarding her. Trying to give her the desires of her heart and burying her when they failed. Dreux had seen him, when Geoffrey had stolen to the tower room late at night, safe until Kalyss was reborn and Kai tightened his guard. Kneeling at Dreux's feet, Geoffrey had grieved for her loss, before he'd lost the ability to grieve.

This was the man who'd spent a century educating a statue. Who'd drawn Dreux away from his insanity, changing his monotonous torment into an existence with purpose. Geoffrey had prepared him for this century, for this Kalyss. He'd been subordinate to Dreux once, so long ago. Now he was an equal. His debt fully repaid. Geoffrey was forgiven.

Dreux raised the knife in his hand and grinned. "Time to go home."

Geoffrey's brows twisted in confusion as Dreux raised the knife and cut his ropes, as if he couldn't believe it was finally all over. Geoffrey fell forward and Dreux caught him, bracing him.

Kalyss rushed forward to help carry him to the car. Her beautiful eyes sparkled as she turned to Geoffrey and smiled. "I think this is the least I can do for you."

Chapter 27

"I can't believe you're talking about Christmas, already." Alex threw tomatoes on his mile-high fajitas and tried to fold the tortilla around them. "It's not even Halloween yet."

Kalyss grinned, pulling four glasses from the cabinet and grabbing her tea pitcher. "I've had enough of monsters and death. I'm ready to celebrate family." Kalyss looked at all three men in her apartment. For someone who was sick of men, she was now surrounded by testosterone. But they were the closest thing to a family she'd ever had. "I have a lot to be thankful for."

Alex followed her gaze and grinned. Dreux and Geoffrey haggled over the digital cable remote, searching for something they hadn't already seen. "Yeah, I guess you do: newly awakened husband, new thousand-year-old—" Alex looked at her. "—what would you call Geoffrey?"

Kalyss laughed and shook her head. "New family."

Alex puffed out his chest mockingly. "Those damn kids. I guess I better do something before they break the remote."

Kalyss chuckled, watching as Alex sauntered over to Dreux and Geoffrey, laid a hand on a shoulder of each, and said, "Do you two need a time-out?"

Dreux scowled. "I've had enough 'time out'. It's my turn to pick the movie."

Geoffrey put his hands up and backed away. "I just wanted to make sure you knew how to use it."

"I sure hope so. You're the one who taught me," Dreux said. Geoffrey started to turn away, but Dreux stopped him and looked pointedly into his eyes. "Thank you."

Geoffrey's mouth relaxed, probably the closest he ever came to a smile. He nodded. "You're welcome."

Kalyss smiled, enjoying the moment, happy to witness it. But Alex apparently couldn't bear the tension. He had to make a joke.

"About time Dead Guy gave you the remote."

Kalyss shook her head, hoping Geoffrey could handle Alex's oddball humor.

"Quit calling me that," Geoffrey demanded.

"You're just mad because I called you a vampire," Alex goaded.

"You're just mad because I made you a druggie," Geoffrey returned before walking away.

"Hey, man, that concussion was not fun." Alex felt the clear spot over his eye. "Besides, what if I'd scarred?"

"It would have been an improvement," Geoffrey stated in a low but clear tone.

Kalyss laughed. Geoffrey could definitely hold his own. Alex gave Geoffrey's back a look, then showed Dreux her stash of DVDs. Kalyss grabbed Geoffrey's plate. When he reached the kitchen, she handed it and a piece of paper to him.

"I wrote the curse down, like you asked. I'm not sure what you can do with it now that the curse is broken, though."

Geoffrey tucked the paper into his shirt pocket. "I'm not sure, yet, either."

Kalyss shook her head and topped off the tea glasses. "Personally, I'm having a hard time accepting that she did what she did. Even with all the weird things we can do. I don't know what that makes her or us. All I do know is I'm tired of keeping one eye on the past. I'm ready to move forward."

Kalyss admired Dreux a moment, before turning back to

Geoffrey, who was fixing his plate. He apparently felt her gaze and looked up. "Good. You should. You've earned it."

Kalyss blinked at hearing those words from him. Geoffrey was so tall and strong, determined and relentless—and so alone. All the things he'd done had been for the love between two people—for her and Dreux. He'd done nothing for himself.

Kalyss touched his hand and smiled at his closed expression. "Couldn't have done it without you."

He blinked and nodded slightly, acknowledging her words, but uncomfortable with the attention. He'd already said he didn't deserve thanks for finally paying his debt.

Kalyss moved away, giving him space.

Geoffrey, who was fixing his plate, apparently felt her gaze and looked up. "Good you should you've earned it."

Dreux and Alex finished up and they all took their plates to the living area. The men sat on the couch and Kalyss chose to sit on her Pilates ball, using the coffee table as a dining table. Her apartment just wasn't big enough for a lot of furniture. The two-seater bar and large couch had always been enough for her and Alex. She'd have to redecorate now. Oh darn. A shopping spree. Whatever was a girl to do?

Dreux had decided that after a day like theirs, a comedy would be best. So he'd ignored the digital cable and pulled out her DVDs. They relaxed, ate fajitas, drank tea, and laughed at the lighthearted comedy they'd settled on.

When the movie was over, Kalyss washed dishes while Dreux put the food away. Alex leaned against the bar, watching them. Geoffrey sat on the stool next to him.

"So, I was wondering . . ." Alex trailed off as everyone turned to look at him. He gave a slight grin. "Sorry. I still have questions."

"Then ask them so I can go to bed and wake up and never think or dream about it again." Kalyss organized the dishes in the washer, trying not to be too loud.

"Well," Alex looked at Geoffrey. "Geoffrey originally helped Kai because he thought Dreux had killed Maeve and those other women."

"But he didn't kill them," Kalyss asserted.

"Right." Alex nodded, then held up his hands in puzzlement. "But who did?"

Dreux handed Kalyss a bag of lettuce, then scooped the onions and peppers into a bowl. "According to the last vision Kalyss showed us, Maeve's bodyguard was trained by her to kill her and the others and make me look guilty."

"Well, that's motherly," Alex said sarcastically.

"Exactly." Dreux nodded. "But she was very convincing. I think her emerald helped with that."

"Where is it? I haven't seen it since you took it from Kai's neck."

"Safely hidden, until Kai chooses to destroy it." Dreux snapped a lid on the bowl and handed it to Kalyss.

"You think he will?" Alex grabbed a paper towel and wiped out the cast-iron fajita pans.

"I think it's his mother's and his decision. But if he decides to free himself from her, he may need the symbolism of destroying it himself."

"What if he just goes wacky and vengeful again?"

Kalyss looked up from the fridge. "After sacrificing himself to free me from our mental link, I really don't think he will."

"You think he'll be a good guy?" Geoffrey asked, his expression closed, his thoughts hidden.

"I don't know about that, but he needs to be given that chance, doesn't he?" Dreux wiped down the counter and hung the rag in the sink. "If he ever wakes up from the coma he's in."

After finding Geoffrey, the three of them had joined Alex and Kai at the hospital. Kai was now in ICU in a coma. He had no marks on his body to explain it, so the doctors were going crazy trying to diagnose him. Dreux could only tell them he thought Kai had been shocked by an electrical current during the storm. Alex had found him lying on the ground and rushed him to the hospital. As next of kin, Kai was Dreux's responsibility and he took it seriously, paying for the medical care and signing all the papers, after Kalyss helped him learn his signature.

"If that's all, I'm ready to get some sleep." Kalyss started the dishwasher and tossed the kitchen towel on the counter.

"It's all I can think of for now." Alex smiled and gave her ponytail a tug before he reached into a cabinet.

Kalyss smiled and took Dreux's hand, leading him to the stairs to her bedroom loft. On the stairs, she watched Alex wave a bag of microwaveable popcorn at Geoffrey.

"I'm kinda revved. My headache is gone, my belly is full, and my bladder is empty. You wanna—" Alex raised his brow comically. "—hang?"

Geoffrey glowered. "I'd really rather not."

"Aw, come on," Alex cajoled. "We could pull out Michael, Jason, Freddie, and a stopwatch. Bet you could take 'em."

Kalyss chuckled at Alex's waggling eyebrows and the look on Geoffrey's face.

Looking severely put upon, Geoffrey stated unequivocally, "I will not kill myself for your entertainment."

Alex put the bag in the microwave and pushed a few buttons. "Why not?"

Geoffrey refilled his tea and headed to the couch. "You have a few homicidal tendencies and a love of blood I should know about?"

Alex grabbed a big bowl and stood by the microwave. "Why? You'd let me do it?"

Geoffrey smiled with frightening menace. "I'd let you try."

Dreux's shoulders shook with laughter and his hands clenched around hers. Kalyss shook her head, laughing, as she and Dreux took the last step into her room and closed her door on Alex's last words.

"*Maaan.* Where's a scientific psychopath when you need one?"

Kalyss put the towel from her earlier shower in a basket and straightened the bed, giving Dreux a few minutes in the bathroom. When he came out, she went in, trying to avoid that awkward moment where she realized there was another person in her life and they would be intimate in everything they did from now on.

It was surprising when there wasn't an awkward moment. It was either because she didn't look at him or because they were both acting good and proper due to the newness of their relationship. No doubt that wouldn't last, though. In no time, they'd be arguing over who takes out the garbage and does the dishes.

In the end, no amount of talking to herself, analyzing herself, or trying to predict the future could put it off any longer. Kalyss was ready for bed and it was time she went there. She froze outside the bathroom door and stared at the bed, her heart pounding.

Dreux leaned against the headboard, one leg outstretched on her bed and one bent, his bare foot flat against her dark blue comforter. His shirt was off and only a pair of sweats from Geoffrey's bottomless bag of tricks hid his body from her gaze.

She had examined him head to toe earlier that day, but this felt different. This wasn't a fling in the middle of danger, a thousand years of yearning boiling over or even a wedding night where everything was assured but how much the actual act would hurt. This was different from all of that.

It was Commitment. He didn't say the word, but it was in his eyes. From this moment forward, there would be no doubt. Either she promised forever or he would leave. No curse bound them. There would be no more chances. He could leave here and get hit by a bus and she'd always wonder *what if he'd stayed?*

The longer she stood there, the more her knees shook. But he gave no sign of impatience. No sighs, no irritated glances. It was her choice and he'd sit there until she made it. No forcing her. No pushing her. He was everything Sam hadn't been. Everything she wanted and needed.

What cut her heart the most, though, was remembering that moment before they'd reached the waterfall. That moment when he'd touched her lips with such yearning, but hadn't taken what he wanted. Instead, he'd told her he loved her and walked away.

"I made a promise to myself tonight, when I watched you fighting Kai."

He raised a brow in silent query.

She tilted her head to the side, studying him in all his masculine grace. "I promised that the next time I crawled into bed, it would be straight into your arms."

Without hesitation, he opened his arms wide. Two steps to the bed and two knee-walks on it, she fell against him and he hugged her tight. Kalyss buried her face in his shoulder and squeezed him, holding in her breath and her sudden tears.

Relief and fear mixed and swirled, cramping her stomach until she gasped and couldn't hold it in. Not the sexiest moment of her life, but she couldn't help it. She sobbed and he held her through it. Her body shook and trembled and his large chest cushioned her. Kalyss began running her hands over his skin, so warm and vibrant. So full of life.

She'd come so close to losing him, and not just because of Kai. Because of her fears and past traumas and her anger over them, she'd tried to push Dreux out of her life. Like being alone was so much better than this, lying on Dreux with his warmth surrounding her. Kai's words from his attack in the dojo drifted hauntingly through her mind.

Look at you, fighting so hard. Do you remember yet, what you're fighting for? Have you dreamt of him, when you're lying in your bed alone and lonely? What do you miss most? His embrace? His kiss?

She remembered now. And Dreux was worth the fight, no matter how long it had taken to win. But now it was time to quit fighting, quit yearning and dreaming, and allow herself to love the man she'd spent lifetimes trying to reach. And to accept his love in return.

Sniffing, she pulled back enough to wipe an eye. Dreux helped her wipe tears from the other, then their lips met, tasted, and clung. Hot and salty, wet and needy, they touched and caressed. Warm hands slid along hot flesh, shifting clothes and freeing skin as they went. She rejoiced in his strength, his need, his desire for her and returned all the same back to him, so he could revel in her need and desire for him.

Over nine hundred years of desperation fused them together, but when he slid over her, between her legs and inside her, filling and stretching what had been empty and barren for so long, it was as if they'd never been apart.

Kalyss pulled back from his kiss, her thighs cradling Dreux and trapping him at the same time. Her hands framed his face and she stared straight into the melting chocolate of his eyes, her words no less exhilarating, no less terrifying then the first time she'd uttered them, especially since fear of losing him was no longer a major concern driving her. "I love you."

He brushed a strand of hair from her face and smiled a tenderly wicked smile. "About time. How long did you think I could wait for you?"

EPILOGUE

The tunnel was black, so dark not even a torch could light it. The weight of the world rested in this spot and it left an atmosphere of oppression and doom. As if no being, no matter how strong, could lift more than a finger in the thick space. It sucked and clawed, ripping away any air that could fuel a person's lungs until they lay gasping beneath the horrible pressure. No one ventured here without a very good reason.

Thick boulders blocked twisted paths to caverns that lay even deeper into the tunnels. Small, tight caverns that were more like mausoleum plots, where the really old ones rested. Or the foolish ones were trapped, punished into insanity. Silence reigned here, in the Tunnels of the Forgotten Ones. Not even the guards whispered.

Until, behind one thick rock, Maeve's furious, shrieking voice could be heard. "Vengeance! I will have my vengeance!"

Silas shivered and felt Draven, beside him in the small space, do the same. Keeping his voice almost silent, he whispered, "Our time is limited. She will discover our interference."

By the light of his glow, he watched Draven's shoulders go

back, the figure standing tall and firm. "Then let her. I refuse to spend the time I have left cowering."

He had an idea, but he asked anyway. "What do you propose?"

Draven smiled beneath the cloak. "We continue."

Love is magic

Upcoming Paranormal Romances
FROM TOR

Solar Heat

Susan Kearney

978-0-7653-5844-8 • 0-7653-5844-1

FEBRUARY 2008

Timeless Moon

C. T. Adams and Cathy Clamp

978-0-7653-5665-9 • 0-7653-5665-1

MARCH 2008

Hellbent & Heartfirst

Kassandra Sims

978-0-7653-5801-1 • 0-7653-5801-8

APRIL 2008

Hungers of the Heart

Jenna Black

978-0-7653-5718-2 • 0-7653-5718-6

MAY 2008

www.tor-forge.com

TOR ROMANCE

Believe that love is magic

Please join us at the website below for more information about this author and other great romance selections, and to sign up for our monthly newsletter!